# four to **midnight**

**also by scott flander**

*Sons of the City*

# four to midnight

## scott flander

William Morrow *An Imprint of* HarperCollins*Publishers*

FOUR TO MIDNIGHT. Copyright © 2003 by Scott Flander. All rights reserved. Printed in the United States of America. No part of this book may be used or reproduced in any manner whatsoever without written permission except in the case of brief quotations embodied in critical articles and reviews. For information address HarperCollins Publishers Inc., 10 East 53rd Street, New York, NY 10022.

HarperCollins books may be purchased for educational, business, or sales promotional use. For information please write: Special Markets Department, HarperCollins Publishers Inc., 10 East 53rd Street, New York, NY 10022.

FIRST EDITION

Designed by Chris Welch

Printed on acid-free paper

Library of Congress Cataloging-in-Publication Data

Flander, Scott.
    Four to midnight : a novel / Scott Flander.—1st ed.
      p. cm.
    ISBN 0-06-018898-7
    1. Police—Pennsylvania—Philadelphia—Fiction. 2. Philadelphia (Pa.)—Fiction.
 I. Title.

PS3556.L346F685 2003
813'.54—dc21

2003043015

03 04 05 06 07  RRD  10 9 8 7 6 5 4 3 2 1

*for karen, with love*

# acknowledgments

My thanks to current and former Philadelphia cops Joe Escher, Mike Lynsky, Tom Nestel, John La Con, Michael Kopecki, Chas Yeiter, Joe Sorrentino, and Matt Farley.

I'm also grateful to my two terrific editors at William Morrow, Claire Wachtel and Jennifer Pooley. Their work on the manuscript was superb.

Marc Kristal, a great writer and a true friend, provided his usual wise advice. Thanks also to Vince Kasper for his sharp eyes, and to S.J.B. for his insight.

I consider myself lucky to have an agent like Barbara Lowenstein, who has always steered me right. And friends like Deen Kogan and the late Paige Rose, who supported me from the beginning. Paige is missed by us all.

Many thanks, of course, to my parents, Judy and Murray Flander, for everything.

My wife, Karen, deserves the most credit for this book. Her sure sense of language and story, of what works and what doesn't, guided me throughout. Had she chosen a career as an editor rather than as an engineer, she would have been one of the best.

**very cop who's been on the job for a while can tell** you about *the call*.

That one call over Police Radio, that if he had to do it all over again, there's no way in the world he'd answer it. Maybe he'd pretend his radio was turned off, or its battery was dead. As a last resort, he might try to leave work early—Hey, Sarge, I don't feel so good, I've been throwing up, I really think I should go home right away.

It might be an innocent-sounding call, part of the daily routine. Or one that hints of danger, the dispatcher's voice suddenly tense, just slightly higher pitched. A call out of nowhere, out of the air, a voice that breaks the silence as the patrol car cruises through the familiar streets. The cop doesn't know it yet, has no way of knowing, but it's the call. And once he answers it, it changes his life forever.

For me, it came late one night, near the end of my shift. I was already making plans, thinking about seeing Michelle and having that first cold beer.

*"Twenty-C-Charlie, we have a request for a supervisor."*

No big deal, I thought. It just meant one of my cops needed me, probably for something minor, maybe even idiotic. Uh, Sarge, we just broke up a fight between like eight dogs—do we got to do paperwork on it?

This time, it was Mutt and Roy who wanted me. Mutt had

radioed in, asking for a supervisor at 43rd and Market. The dispatcher, knowing I was the only 20th District sergeant on the street that night, relayed the request to me.

I headed down Market toward 43rd, past the darkened, run-down stores, the Chinese take-outs, the grim bars we were always going into to break up fights. The bars always seemed to have two or three black guys standing out front, hands in their pockets, doing nothing. I never understood that. Why would you want to be outside the bar, rather than inside?

There was no one at 43rd and Market, the intersection was clear. But then I saw, halfway down 43rd, Mutt and Roy's patrol car, overhead lights flashing, pulled up behind another vehicle. It looked like a routine car-stop.

I knew this block of 43rd pretty well, it was a real dead zone. On one side was a long stretch of empty lots, with an abandoned rowhouse here and there, like some homeless guy with just a couple of teeth left. On the other side of the street was a fenced-in, ramshackle used-car lot with bright plastic triangle-flags strung from pole to pole. As if in this neighborhood, all you needed was a little optimism.

I stopped my car behind Mutt and Roy's. Through the hazy darkness I could see them standing with a man next to his car, a black man in a suit and tie. I got out, and walked up to them, and saw that the man had a bald, round head and a graying beard. And that he was covered with blood.

It was everywhere, over his tailored brown suit, his white shirt, soaking the handkerchief that he was holding to his face.

He seemed filled with relief when he saw me, saw my stripes.

"Thank God someone's here," he said. He looked dazed, not quite sure where he was. He was leaning against his car for support.

Mutt and Roy glanced at me with worried looks.

"What's going on?" I asked them.

Mutt shook his head. "You tell us, Sarge."

"Get them away from me," the man said.

"Who?" I asked.

He seemed baffled at the question. "Who?" he repeated. His eyes flicked from Mutt to Roy, then back, as if he were expecting a punch at any moment.

He coughed and winced, grabbing his left side. Something was wrong with his ribs.

Mutt turned to me, half in panic. "We didn't touch him, Sarge. We found him like this."

The man seemed familiar, I had the feeling I knew who he was. But he still had the handkerchief to his face, and the street was full of shadows.

He looked at me and said in a calm voice, "They think they can get away with this."

He took the handkerchief away, and I could see bloody cuts on top of his smooth head, over his eyes, on his swollen lip.

And in the dim light, I recognized him.

I clicked the shoulder mike for my radio, and tilted my head down to talk.

*"This is Twenty-C-Charlie, we need Rescue at this location."*

"Councilman," I said, trying to keep my voice steady, "what happened here?"

Mutt and Roy jerked their heads at me, then back at the black man in the suit and tie.

"Oh, shit," said Roy. "This is Sonny Knight."

The man glanced at Roy, then turned to me. "Sergeant, get them away from me. Please."

I motioned for Mutt and Roy to step back.

"Sarge," said Mutt, "I hope you don't think . . ."

"Just move back," I said, motioning again with my hand.

They obeyed.

"Sir," I said. "Tell me what happened."

He wiped his face again. The bleeding had mostly stopped, but a few cuts were still leaking.

"Those two attacked me," he said, pointing at Mutt and Roy. "I thought they were going to kill me."

"Huh?" said Mutt. "What're you talking about?"

Knight kept his eyes on me. "I want them placed under arrest. Right now."

He rose to his full height. More confidcnt, now that I was there.

I tried to think clearly. Mutt and Roy couldn't have just beaten the shit out of Councilman Sonny Knight. They couldn't have.

Take it slowly, I told myself. One step at a time.

"Tell me what happened," I said again.

Knight looked at me, I could see he was thinking, deciding on the words he was going to use. I didn't want to hear them. I didn't want to hear what he was about to say. Not if it was about Mutt and Roy. They were good cops, both of them.

But this was Sonny Knight. The most powerful black man in Philadelphia. The one who decided which other blacks got to be congressmen, state senators, even police commissioners. Such as the man who was now my boss. Supposedly they were best friends.

"I was driving down the street here, I saw lights flashing in my rearview mirror. A police car. My first thought was, Did I run the light? I didn't think I did. But of course I pulled over."

His voice was growing stronger, more self-assured.

"They walked up to my car, side by side. I said, 'Hello, Officers, is there a problem?' I was very polite. I respect the job that police officers do for this city, I always have." Knight paused, to make sure I understood this.

"Then one of them said, 'Step out of the car.' I asked why, and the other one said, 'Hey, a black man driving an expensive car like this, maybe it's stolen.'"

"No way," said Roy, sputtering. "This isn't . . . I don't believe this."

He and Mutt were staring at Knight, their mouths half open. I looked at them, and I could feel my heart pounding. What had they done?

"I didn't get out of my car," Knight said. "Why should I? I didn't like that kind of accusation."

Anger was creeping into his face, for the first time. Telling his story was clearing away the confusion, making room for the anger.

He wiped some more blood away and gave a bitter smile.

"They got me out anyway. They yanked opened the door and just grabbed me and pulled me right out of the car. The next thing I know, I'm getting punched, hit, then I'm on the ground. They're kicking me, in the ribs, in the head. Yelling things like 'We're gonna teach you to respect the police.' "

"It's bullshit," said Mutt. "Everything he's saying is total bullshit."

"Guys," I said. "Just hold on for a second."

"I've lived in this city my whole life," said Knight. "For something like this to happen . . ."

He stared off into the night, as if he still could not imagine it.

Knight was a broad-shouldered man, but his shoulders looked tired, like he was used to carrying some kind of heavy load. It wasn't just his injuries. I had seen black leaders with that weight before, church leaders, community leaders.

"Thank God you showed up," he said. "That was lucky."

"Sir, these officers called for me."

He seemed puzzled by this. "They called for you? Well, it doesn't matter. You can be the one to arrest them."

He took a couple of steps toward Mutt and Roy. What was he going to do, try to lock them up himself? But he stopped short and focused on Mutt's silver nameplate.

"Officer . . . Hope," he said, like he was announcing the name at a banquet. "And Officer . . ." He turned to Roy. "Knopfler."

He looked up at Roy. "Half the people in the Police Department have that name."

Which was almost true. Everywhere you went, there was a Knopfler, and they were all related—brothers, cousins, uncles, sisters. There were so many of them, they practically could have had their own district.

Knight looked back at me. Still waiting.

Ever since I'd pulled up, I had been aware of dogs barking. But the sound seemed louder now, and I realized the dogs were right next to us. I looked over at the used-car lot. Behind the ten-foot chain-link fence, two smallish German shepherds were jumping up on the hoods of cars and barking, then jumping back down again. Taking turns, first one, then the other, barking, barking, barking.

"Shut up!" I yelled at them, but that only made them louder and even more frantic.

I was trying not to feel the same way. I looked back at Knight. He stood waiting. As if he expected me to slap the cuffs on Mutt and Roy and march them off.

"Sir," I said, "I can't arrest these officers. There has to be an investigation."

"You don't believe them, do you?"

He shook his head, like I was a waiter who somehow couldn't get the food order right.

"I've given you the information you need," he said.

"Mr. Knight, first of all, it's not up to me. And second, to be honest with you, at this point I don't know what to believe."

He nodded, as if this was what he had expected all along.

"The thin blue line, right?" he said. Now it was my nameplate he was looking at. "All right, Sergeant North. If that's the way it's going to be."

The way *what* was going to be?

I didn't get a chance to ask him—he stepped back over to his car, reached in, and retrieved a cell phone from the dashboard. Who was he going to call, his friend the commissioner? He started to push some buttons on his phone, but then saw us watching and walked a little way up the street, out of earshot. Still wiping his head and face with the bloody handkerchief.

This was not good. I got back on the radio and tried to raise the lieutenant. He wasn't answering, which didn't surprise me. Lately about this time of night, it had been tough to reach him. We had all heard the rumors, about a girlfriend who lived in the district. Possibly a Penn grad student. Whatever. All I knew was that I was on my own.

Mutt and Roy came over to me.

"This whole thing is fucked up," Mutt said.

"You got to believe us, Sarge," said Roy. "We found him like that. We didn't even know it was Sonny Knight."

"If he's calling the commissioner," I said, "and I think there's a very good chance he is, then this place is about to become a fucking zoo. I need to know exactly what happened here, right now."

The dogs had been quiet for a while, watching the street scene. I thought they might start up again when we walked over, but they didn't, they just looked at us, like they were interested in what we were going to say.

"We wouldn't do nothing like this, Sarge," said Mutt. "C'mon, you know us."

Mutt was a big, barrel-chested guy who just seemed to fill whatever space he was in. With his crew cut and huge forearms, some people found him intimidating. To me, though, he was just a friendly corner-boy from Frankford.

Sergeants were supposed to maintain a professional distance from their cops. But a lot of them, like me, had friends on the squad, guys they went out drinking with after work, or over to their houses for barbecues. The core group that worked hard and watched out for each other. We all hung together. Mutt and Roy were part of that. I liked them both. They were good, solid, aggressive cops. Like Mutt said, I did know them.

"I need to know what happened," I said again.

"Nothing happened," said Mutt. "Nothing at all."

"Fine," I said. "Then start from the beginning of nothing happening."

"Okay," he said, "we're driving around the east end, you know, checking the corners. We turn down here from Market, see this silver BMW in the middle of the street. We get closer, there's a black male lying by the side of the car."

"On the ground?" I asked.

"No, kind of propped up against the back tire. With his eyes closed."

"What, was he unconscious?" I asked.

Mutt shrugged. "Who knows, maybe he was sleeping. We came

up to him, we saw all the blood, we said, 'Hey, pal, you all right?'
He jumped up and started acting strange."

"What do you mean, strange?"

"Like he was afraid of us, or something. It was weird. Like I said,
we had no idea that was Sonny Knight."

Even without all the blood, that wouldn't have been surprising.
Knight's council district was in Germantown, on the other side of
the city. As far as I knew, he was never down here in West Philadelphia, not at community meetings or events or anything else.

"It's not like I never tuned nobody up before," said Mutt. "You
know, when they deserved it. But not this time. We did not lay a
finger on that man."

I looked at Roy, wondering whether I could see in his pale blue
eyes whether this was the truth.

If Mutt sort of spread himself over the world, Roy was just the
opposite: compact, self-contained, intense. Like Mutt, he was in his
twenties, but he looked a lot younger, you almost expected him to
have freckles. I'd never met anyone who was so excited about being
a cop. He loved coming in to work, whether it was the day shift or
four to midnight. He couldn't wait to get out on the street. He'd be
standing there at roll call, next to Mutt, and you could see him
looking out the window, dying to get going.

"Think about it," Roy said. "If we really beat him up, would we
call for a supervisor?"

That was a good point. And there was something else bothering
me. Knight had said Mutt and Roy approached the car side by side.
But I had seen them make car-stops, and they always did it the right
way—one guy goes along the driver's side, his partner goes along
the passenger side. That way he can look in the window and see if
the driver is reaching for a weapon. It's the only safe way to do it.

What I needed was evidence. It would have been nice to have a
witness. But there was no one else around, not even the usual kid
on a bike or slobbery alcoholic wandering the streets. And the
houses, if you could still call them that, were all boarded up. I
didn't even have the hope of finding some crackhead to talk to.

There weren't going to be any witnesses, I knew it then. In fact, this was probably the one block in the neighborhood where there would almost never be witnesses. The perfect place to make a car-stop, if what you were planning on doing, you didn't want anybody to see.

I glanced down at Mutt's and Roy's hands. Even in the shadowy light, I could see that their knuckles weren't raw, the way they would have been if they had been whaling on somebody's face. Their blue police shirts were neat, not in disarray. No spatters of blood. Their faces didn't look sweaty or flushed.

And yet City Councilman Sonny Knight was standing there, beat to shit. And he had clearly identified Mutt and Roy as his assailants.

Sonny Knight, who was as pro-cop as anyone on the City Council. We all knew he had gotten us more funding, new radios, the latest generation of vests. Which we were wearing right now.

"Why would he lie?" I asked Mutt and Roy.

They both shrugged.

"Maybe it was one of those gay things," said Mutt. "You know, maybe he picked up a male prostitute or something, and didn't pay."

"Yeah, but then why would he blame you guys?" I asked. "Why wouldn't he just say somebody tried to rob him or carjack him and he resisted? That'd be a lot simpler."

They shrugged again.

Knight had finished his phone call, but now he was pushing buttons again and talking to someone else. Who was it this time, the mayor? The president?

The dogs were still watching us. Above them, along the top of the fence, were strands of rusted and sagging barbed wire, interwoven with strings of some of the red and blue and yellow triangle flags. But the way the flags flapped in the darkness, sending shadows dancing at our feet, they looked like they had been snared in some kind of trap and were flailing around, trying to escape.

I looked back at the dogs. Hell, they saw what happened, maybe I should ask them.

*What did you see?*

*Bark, bark.*

*Really? You willing to testify to that?*

With some juries in Philadelphia, that might be enough to reach a verdict.

Knight was slowly heading back toward us, still on the phone. "Are you leaving now?" he said. "Good. I need you here, Carl."

Mutt turned to me. "Carl?"

I shrugged. Knight was talking in a low voice, and we strained to make out his words.

"I haven't talked to her yet. I don't want her to worry. Yes, I'm sure I'm okay."

We missed the next sentence or two, but then heard Knight say, "No, that's not a good idea. The media does not need to be here."

Knight glanced up and we looked away, pretending we couldn't hear.

"No, you don't need to call Channel Seven. Carl. Are you listening to me, Carl?"

Mutt let out a breath. "We're screwed."

"Yeah," I said. "We probably are."

## two

I heard a siren in the distance. **Must be Rescue, I** thought. Knight was walking over to us, his cell phone in his hand at his side.

"You still haven't arrested these two men."

"Sir, I told you, it's not up to me."

"It's all right, I've taken care of it."

Knight's battered face seemed filled with resolve. I had no doubt he would do everything in his considerable power to put Mutt and Roy in a jail cell. And he was obviously someone who was used to getting what he wanted.

Knight looked at Mutt and Roy. "Did you really think you could get away with this?"

"But we didn't do nothin'," said Roy.

"Right. Of course you didn't."

"Guys," I said to Mutt and Roy. "Why don't you wait over by your car."

My cell phone was clipped to my gun belt, and I pulled it off. Knight watched me, curious who I was going to call. Well, if he thought I was going to protect my cops, he was right. At least until I knew just what the hell had happened here.

I turned and headed up the street toward Market, the opposite direction Knight had gone for his own phone calls. I pulled out my wallet and looked over my phone list, hoping I still had a home number for Vince McAvoy.

Vince was one of the officers of the Fraternal Order of Police, our union. The FOP provided lawyers for cops who got into trouble, and I had a feeling Mutt and Roy were going to need one before they went home tonight—if they went home at all.

I checked my watch, it was 10:50 P.M. I hoped it wasn't too late to call.

"Hey, Vince, this is Eddie North," I said when he answered the phone. "I wake you up?"

"Nah, just watchin' TV."

I explained the situation, including Knight's cell-phone calls.

"Uh-oh," he said.

"Exactly," I said. "Any chance of my guys getting lawyers to-night?"

"No, it's too late, Eddie. Sorry. But first thing tomorrow, I'll take care of it myself."

"Thanks."

"In the meantime, tell them not to talk to anyone. No statements at all. Not to Internal Affairs, not to anybody, okay?"

"Sure."

"Things can get twisted, Eddie, I've seen it happen. Tell them to keep their mouths shut. Tight as a fuckin' drum."

I hung up and headed back toward Knight. A boxy red Fire Department ambulance, lights flashing, was coming down the one-way street the wrong way.

Knight waved me over. "What's this?"

"They'll take you to the hospital," I said.

"I don't need to go to the hospital."

"Sir, I think you might."

The ambulance was stopping toe-to-toe with Knight's BMW.

"You want me out of here," he said.

"I want you to get some medical help."

"No, you want me out of here. So there's no crime scene."

He said this very calm and matter-of-fact.

"But what I don't know yet," he said, "is whether you're doing this because you're a cop, and we all know cops stick together, or because you're part of what's going on."

"What do you mean, what's going on?"

He didn't answer.

Two paramedics in dark blue Fire Department shirts and pants were coming up, one with a blue canvas medical bag.

"It's Sonny Knight," I told them as they passed by me. "The city councilman."

They both nodded, like they got politicians all the time. Maybe they did. One of the paramedics, a short, stocky guy with a mustache, set the blue bag on the pavement and opened it up.

The other one pulled a penlight from his shirt and shined it into the cuts over Knight's eyes. Knight started to resist, but then gave in.

He coughed and grabbed his side.

The paramedic gently felt his ribs. "You get robbed or something?"

"No, I didn't get robbed," said Knight. "This was done by those two police officers over there."

He pointed to Mutt and Roy, who were talking quietly by their car. The paramedics glanced over at them, but stayed silent. Obviously they didn't want to get involved.

In another minute or two, they had finished their examination.

"Sir," said the one with the penlight, "you're gonna need some stitches and maybe a chest X-ray. We're gonna have to run you over to HUP, okay?"

That was the Hospital of the University of Pennsylvania.

"No, not okay," said Knight. "I'm going to wait."

Wait for who? The commissioner himself?

"Sir," the paramedic said, "you really should go."

"You can treat me here. Now what?" Knight was looking past me, up the street. A shiny, metallic-purple tow truck was pulling up. The driver probably saw the ambulance and police cars and figured it might be a wreck. Tow truck guys are always looking for a little extra business.

"So that's who you called," said Knight.

"Excuse me?"

"First the ambulance, to remove me from the scene. Now this tow truck, to remove my car. It'll be like nothing ever happened here."

"I didn't call for that truck."

"Of course you didn't. You know, Sergeant, I find it strange that there are no detectives here, no investigators, no crime-scene people. No one but that tow truck driver. Who's probably a friend of yours, right?"

I turned back toward the truck as the driver was climbing out, and got a look at his face. I couldn't believe it, it was Dominic Russo.

Oh, shit, I said to myself. Or at least I thought it was to myself. Knight gave me a sharp glance, as if I had spoken aloud.

I hurried over to the truck, hoping to intercept the driver before he could say anything. But he jumped out of the cab and hit the pavement with both feet, saying, "Yo, Sarge, how ya doin'?"

I cringed and glanced back at Knight. He was staring. I kept walking until I was close enough to the driver so Knight couldn't hear and said, "Listen, Dominic, you got to get out of here, right now."

Knight had left the paramedics and was walking toward us.

"What's going on?" Knight called out.

What was I going to tell him? That Dominic Russo used to drive a police tow truck, but got arrested a month ago for stealing stuff out of cars that got towed? And that now he was out on bail, driving a private truck?

And that Gee whiz, Mr. Councilman, I had no idea he was going to show up here?

I didn't know whether Dominic recognized Sonny Knight, but he seemed to instantly grasp the situation, and he hopped back in his truck.

"Hold it," Knight called.

But Dominic put the truck in reverse and started backing up.

Knight drew even with me, and together we watched Dominic back the truck all the way up to Market, then turn and roar away.

When the truck had disappeared, Knight looked at me. He seemed calm, even dignified.

"If you want to throw your fortune in with your two friends," he said, "that's fine with me."

**A few minutes** later, as Knight sat on the back step of the ambulance, getting the final touches from the paramedics, a uniformed captain pulled up in a marked car. Knight's cavalry was starting to arrive.

Though when I saw who it was, I almost laughed. I didn't think Del Falk was exactly who Knight had in mind. Del spotted me as he got out of his car, and smiled.

"Hey, pal, how you doin'?" he asked.

We shook hands. Del had been my sergeant in the 17th in South Philly years ago. We went way back.

"What you got here?" he asked. "Supposedly something happened to Sonny Knight?"

The rear of the ambulance faced away from us, so Knight was out of view.

"He was beaten pretty badly," I said. "He's over there with Rescue."

"Hmm," Del said, pursing his lips and nodding in approval. "Well deserved."

Del was a burly guy with thick, graying hair wetted and combed straight back, thick eyebrows, and a monstrous gray mustache that made him look angry all the time. Which he probably was.

"Del, he's claiming two of my cops did the beating. They said they didn't touch him."

"Really? Well, he's an asshole, so I'm sure he had it coming."

"Yeah, but they said he was lying on the street all bloody when they rolled up."

Del thought about that, then shrugged.

"Either way, I don't care. If Sonny Knight got the balls beat off him, then I have to believe he deserved it."

Del was starting to make me a little nervous. On the one hand, I was glad he was here, glad for his familiar face. On the other, what was he going to do, make this situation even worse?

I knew that Del Falk hated Sonny Knight, just hated him. A couple of years ago, Del had been the captain of the 14th District, up in Germantown. Sonny Knight's district. Knight was always calling Del, asking for officers to watch this person's store or that person's house. That's what all council members did, apparently they felt it was their God-given right to send us anywhere they wanted. Del got tired of it, and for an entire week turned Knight down, saying he was too short-staffed. One morning, Del found himself assigned to Night Command, the department's shithouse for captains. He had been there ever since, with little hope of parole.

"Those the two cops?" Del asked.

"Yeah. Alan Hope and Roy Knopfler."

Del nodded and pulled a pack of cigarettes from his shirt pocket, and lit one up. His mustache was so thick, you could barely see the filter.

"Who sent Night Command here?" I asked.

"You don't want to know."

"The commissioner?"

"Calling from home. And it ain't just going to be me. Internal Affairs is coming. So is West Detectives. Probably an inspector or two. Should be a fun party."

Great, I thought.

"Well," he said, "I guess it's time to have a chat with Councilman Asshole."

Just great.

We walked around to the back of the ambulance. Knight was still sitting on the back step. One of the paramedics was applying temporary cloth stitches to the cuts over his eyes. A roll of wide gauze had been wound around his head and wrapped on top, so that it looked like he was wearing a white skullcap.

Knight stood as Del approached, and immediately recognized him, I could tell by his expression. And he glared at me, like it was my fault for bringing this particular captain here.

"Jesus," said Del, staring at Knight's face. "No offense, Councilman, but you look like hell."

Knight stiffened. "Is anyone else coming?" he asked in an even voice.

"Quite a lot of people, I would imagine."

"When?"

"Oh, I don't know. Soon."

"Soon."

He seemed to wait for Del to elaborate, but Del just took a contemplative drag on his cigarette. I could see Knight's jaw muscles tightening.

Del tossed the cigarette away. "You want to tell me what happened, Councilman?"

"No."

Del shrugged. Mutt and Roy had come over and were listening. Del turned and said to them, "Some guys from West will be here any minute. They're going to want you to go back with them and give statements."

"No statements," I told them. "You're not going to be able to get lawyers tonight, so don't say anything."

This was such routine advice that I didn't realize how stupid it was for me to say it in front of Knight.

He looked at me in astonishment, then abruptly turned to Del.

"You want to know what happened, Captain? Ask Sergeant North why he just called in a tow truck to try to get rid of my car."

"A tow truck," said Del, turning to me, impressed.

"That's right. And he and the driver looked like they were the best of friends."

I thought I caught Del give me a slight smile.

"And when he realized I was onto him," said Knight, "when he realized I knew what he was doing, he got that truck out of here, fast."

A dark green Mercedes SUV drove past, then pulled over about a hundred feet in front of the ambulance. Knight left us without a word and headed toward it. The door opened, and a young black guy emerged. He was wearing a dark knit shirt and slacks.

"Perfect," said Del. "Now we got the son."

"He was talking to a Carl on the phone," I said.

"That's him. Carl Knight. And he is not a friend of the police."

We watched as Knight and his son met by the open door of the SUV. Carl Knight seemed filled with panic by the sight of the bandages, and he reached for his father's arm, as if he were afraid he would collapse at any moment.

Carl was in his mid-twenties, but he looked like a college student—serious, but at the same time kind of preppy, breezy, untroubled by responsibility.

"What do you mean," said Mutt, "not a friend of the police?"

"That's David Danforth's number-one supporter," said Del. "He's the leader of that group of morons."

"Oh, man," said Roy.

David Danforth was a black Penn professor, about to go on trial for killing a cop. And he had a whole "Free Danforth" movement behind him, Hollywood celebrities, politicians, various radical groups.

We could see that Sonny Knight was describing to his son what had happened to him. Every few moments, he'd point in our direction and his son would glare over at us.

"Sarge," said Roy, a new kind of alarm in his voice. "Look at this."

Roy was off to one side of the ambulance, looking back up the street toward Market. We all walked around to see.

A white Channel 7 van was coming toward us. It pulled up behind Del's car, as if it were just another police vehicle.

"What do we do?" said Roy.

"Get out of sight," I said. "Fade into the woodwork or some-thing."

Del and I looked back toward the TV van. The reporter and his cameraman had the side door open and were taking out equipment.

I glanced at Knight and his son. And realized that from where they were standing, they couldn't see the TV van. Which meant the reporter and his cameraman couldn't see them, either.

There was still a chance.

"Where you going?" said Del.

I walked quickly toward the van, past the ambulance, past Sonny Knight's car, past the police cars. The reporter saw me coming and turned to meet me.

"Sergeant," he said, "is Sonny Knight here?"

It was Tim Timberlane, from Channel 7. Terrific, I thought—the biggest jerkoff TV reporter in the city.

"I'm sorry," I said, "you're going to have to get back up to Mar-ket. The street's closed off."

"Can you just tell us what's going on?" he asked. "We heard that Sonny Knight was beaten up. By police officers."

Timberlane had the TV smile, the suit, the haircut, the whole works. I tried to sound as nonchalant as possible.

"We just had a minor incident here. There's nothing going on."

"Was the councilman hurt? Is he here?"

"He's fine," I said. "He doesn't want to talk to the media."

The cameraman, in a yellow T-shirt and blue jeans, had grabbed his camera and was joining us.

"You can't be on this street," I said. "I need you to get back in your truck, right now."

"If it was a minor incident," said Timberlane, "why would you close the street off?"

This was why I hated reporters.

"I'll tell you what," I said, "you take your van back up to the intersection, I'll have someone come over and talk to you. As soon as possible."

I could see that Timberlane wanted to argue, but wasn't sure whether that would hurt his chances. I held my breath. C'mon, I thought. Turn around and walk back to your truck. Just turn around.

But Timberlane was looking past me.

"There he is!" he said.

I turned to see. At that moment, Knight and his son, still talking, stepped into view. No, I said to myself. No.

"Jesus," said Timberlane, "Joel, look at those bandages."

Joel was hoisting the camera to his shoulder.

"Councilman!" Timberlane called.

Knight glanced up.

"He doesn't want to talk to the media," I said. "I told you to move. Do it. Now."

"Councilman!" Timberlane called again. "Can we talk to you?"

Knight seemed about to turn around and get back out of sight, but he hesitated.

"Sir, can you tell us what happened?"

Knight stood looking, deciding. His son was at his side, but silent. Waiting, like us.

"Can you tell us what happened?"

He won't do it, I thought. He's not going to do it.

And then Knight lifted his arm in the air and motioned for them. He was waving them over.

I should have stayed right where I was, I shouldn't have moved. But as Timberlane and Joel, camera at his side now, hurried toward Knight, I stayed with them. I had to see what was going to happen.

When we reached Knight, Joel lifted the camera back to his shoulder and flipped on its light. I took a quick step to get safely off to the side.

"Councilman," said Timberlane, "we heard you were beaten by police officers. Is that true?"

"That's right," said Knight. "Two police officers." He looked around, trying to find Mutt and Roy. I scanned the street myself, praying they were gone. They had disappeared.

"They dragged me from my car," Knight said. "They knocked me to the ground, kicked me."

Someone was pulling at my upper arm. It was Del. "Eddie," he whispered, "don't stay here."

"Why would they do that?" Timberlane asked. "Did they know who you were?"

"No, otherwise it never would have happened. They thought I was just another black man. At first they wouldn't let me see their faces, but then they gave up the charade. They didn't care."

Knight was playing to the camera now. Treating it like a friend.

"I saw them," he said. "I saw the face of police brutality."

"How badly are you hurt?" Timberlane asked.

"Would you like to see?"

Knight started unwrapping the bandage from his head, unwinding the gauze, showing the bloody pads underneath. I saw it and still could not believe it.

"Eddie," Del whispered.

Del knew what was coming. But I just stood there, transfixed.

"Now they're trying to cover it up. But I'm not going to let that happen. I want the two police officers arrested and charged. And there's someone else I want charged."

I was finally ready to go—but it was too late. Knight turned to me and pointed a finger.

"This sergeant here, who has been trying to cover it all up. This sergeant, who's guilty of obstruction of justice."

Knight looked at my nameplate again. "North is his name. Sergeant North."

The camera and its blinding light were on me now, catching me full in the face. I had to say something, I couldn't walk away. I knew: I'd say there'd be a full and fair investigation.

Somehow, though, I couldn't get the words out. I just stood there, paralyzed by the camera and its blinding light. Del was gone.

The dogs were barking, barking like crazy now. That's all I could hear. Why can't they shut up, I thought. Why can't they just shut the hell up?

# three

 **got the first phone call the next morning just after six.**

*Hello?*

*Eddie, honey, what did you do?*

*Uhh . . . Mom?*

*You're on CNN, did you know that?*

*Uhh . . .*

My mother was one of those people who got up in the morning much earlier than they had to—something I could never understand—and immediately switched on the TV. She was sort of the family alarm system. If something important was happening in the world, she found out first and phoned the rest of us. Though I don't think she ever expected to wake up and see her son's face all over the television screen.

I got her off the phone, staggered into the living room, and found my remote. I discovered I wasn't just on CNN, but all the network morning shows. Tim Timberlane's tape of a Philadelphia city councilman showing off his bloody wounds and blaming the cops had made national news. Close-up of Sonny Knight, unwrapping his head. Close-up of me, standing next to him, staring at the camera, not saying a word.

To my amazement, I didn't look quite as stupid as I expected. I had a concerned expression—complete with furrowed brow—as if I were listening to the councilman with sympathy and worry, ready to make some kind of statement on his behalf. Except that the newscasters were saying I was "allegedly" involved in a cover-up, using the word like I had already been charged. They didn't have any details about what had happened, but they didn't need any. The bloody image of Sonny Knight was enough.

I switched from channel to channel. There was Sonny Knight, there was me. At first I somehow imagined that I came across as the rugged type—with my thick brown hair, square jaw, and lean face, I kind of looked like one of those guys who leads "adventure vacations" out in Colorado. But then I realized it was just the beard stubble. I hadn't shaved in a couple of days, and I was getting a little scraggly. Usually no one cared, but here I was on national television, The Cop Who Doesn't Shave. I could picture people at home, looking at my face, saying to each other, Yeah, he does look kind of shady, doesn't he?

I called Mutt and then Roy to see how they were doing, I figured they'd be up, too. They were both as freaked out as I was.

"I knew it would be big," said Mutt, "but not this big."

"And it's just going to get bigger."

"Are you going to call Roy?" Mutt asked.

"He's next."

"Good. I got to tell you, he's pretty upset over what this is going to do to his family."

I called Roy, and asked him how he was doing.

"Fine, other than the fact that every Knopfler on the police force is now totally disgraced."

I could hear the TV blaring and kids squealing. Roy and Tina had three girls, including the baby. Cute kids.

"They're all going to love me," he said. "Hey, Roy, thanks for dragging the Knopfler name through the mud."

I tried to reassure him, but he shook it off. "Forget it. I might as well kill myself right now."

We talked for a few more minutes, but I didn't think I was much help.

All morning, my phone didn't stop ringing. Friends, relatives, everyone who knew me. They all wanted to be the first to let me know I was on TV. I even got a call from my next-door neighbor, the guy whose rowhouse adjoined mine. What, he couldn't wait until he saw me on my porch?

Everyone seemed disappointed to find out I was already watching TV. But that didn't stop them from pumping me for information. What really happened? they asked. Did those two cops really beat up Sonny Knight?

No one came right out and asked me whether I tried to cover it up. Instead, they said things like, So, what do you think about what they're saying about you?

I also got a lot of calls from cop friends, and they didn't beat around the bush. Most assumed, as Del Falk had, that my guys had beaten up Sonny Knight, probably for a good reason. And that I was a hero for protecting them.

A little after eight, Michelle showed up at my door. "You all right?" she asked, putting her arms around me.

"Yeah, sure," I said, "just been sitting here watching TV."

We glanced at the television. CNN had somehow forgotten me for the moment, and was doing a report on shopping for computers.

"I've been watching, too—well, watching and trying to reach you. Your phone's been busy nonstop, I couldn't even get through on your cell."

"I turned it off."

"I guess everybody's been calling?"

"Everybody."

"Have you eaten?" she asked me. "You want me to make you some breakfast?"

I turned down the TV, and Michelle made us fried eggs and bacon and coffee. She liked coming over and cooking me meals. For some reason, she found my place very relaxing.

I lived in Northeast Philadelphia, in the Oxford Circle rowhouse that Patricia and I had bought the year before we got divorced. It was an older house, and things were beginning to fall apart. I caulked a few windows after rainwater got in, but so much needed to be done that I had a hard time getting started on any of it.

At least I kept the inside looking reasonably nice. Of course, most of my guests were guys over for beer and spaghetti and football, and they wouldn't have noticed if the whole place was flooded. Michelle would have, though. Whenever she'd come over, she'd do the dishes or straighten up the living room.

We'd been seeing each other for about a year. She was a cop, too, a sergeant in the 9th. She was also the daughter of the former police commissioner, and for a while, we were a hot gossip item in the department. Now no one paid us much attention. We were just boyfriend-girlfriend. But every time I saw her I still got the same little thrill. Her blue eyes and soft, narrow face always mesmerized me. She had luxurious, shoulder-length brown hair and she looked great in tight jeans, like she was wearing now, and that always mesmerized me, too.

As we ate, I described what had happened the night before. She asked a few questions here and there, but mostly just listened, absorbing it all. Every minute or two, the phone would ring, but I let my machine take it.

And I told her how—after Sonny Knight's little impromptu press briefing—Mutt, Roy, and I had all gone over to West Detectives and given statements. Despite McAvoy's instructions, Mutt and Roy had insisted on talking. If they didn't, they said, they'd look guilty as hell. Their willingness to talk impressed me, it gave me more confidence that they had nothing to hide.

Naturally, once they gave statements, I had to as well. I sat down with a detective, a guy I knew pretty well, and simply told him what happened. Including the phone call to McAvoy.

"It had nothing to do with that tow truck arriving," I said.

I had no idea whether he believed me, but it didn't really matter. He was just there to type what I said into the computer, to get my version of events. It wasn't any kind of interrogation, with tough questions. About the only thing he asked me was: "What happened next?"

I left out the part about exactly who the tow truck driver was. That was one can of worms I definitely did not want opened.

Michelle took her plate to the sink, rinsed off the egg yolk, and turned to me.

"I think Mutt and Roy are telling the truth," she said.

"Why do you say that?"

"Think about it," she said. "If they did hit him, wouldn't it make more sense to admit it?"

"And just say he resisted arrest."

"Sure. At least then they'd have a decent defense. But this story about them just finding him on the ground, who's going to believe that? They should know that. They're not dumb guys, right?"

"No, but . . ."

"Eddie, look at the TV."

Mayor Shoemaker and Police Commissioner Ellsworth were speaking to the cameras, at a microphone-infested lectern in City Hall. I walked over and turned up the volume.

"There will be a full and fair investigation," the commissioner was saying.

"That's right," said the mayor. "Full and fair."

They were stealing my lines.

Michelle was standing next to the couch, sipping coffee.

"Look at them," she said. "Tweedledum and Tweedledee."

They weren't exactly identical—the mayor was white and the police commissioner was black—but they did wear remarkably similar expressions of outrage.

"We *will* get to the bottom of this," said the commissioner, pointing his finger. Like a politician, which was all Ellsworth really was. Not like the days before he had become commissioner, when he was respected throughout the department for his utter lack of bullshit.

Shoemaker was speaking again. "We will prosecute any crime to the full extent of the law."

"He sounds like one of those anti-shoplifting signs," said Michelle.

It always amazed me how shiny Shoemaker's balding head was—the TV lights just bounced right off it, blinding everyone in sight. He was short but seemed to be all muscle, the papers were always running pictures of him lifting weights in the gym.

"You know," said Michelle, "this is just going to add fuel to the fire for the Danforth people. They're going to say it's the perfect example of how we treat blacks."

"Just what we need."

I had no doubt Michelle was right. She had a particular interest in the Danforth case—she was a close friend of the cop's widow, and had been serving as the family's spokesman.

I sat on the couch and watched the rest of the press conference. Blah, blah, blah, keep the people happy. Finally it was over, and Michelle came over and sat beside me.

"Are you going to get a lawyer?" she asked.

"I don't need a lawyer."

"Get a lawyer."

I laughed. "Will you visit me in jail?"

She thought it over.

"Sure, at least for the first year," she said. "But then the visits will become less and less frequent, and I'll probably end up getting a new boyfriend . . ."

"Yeah, and I'll get out of prison early and beat him up."

"Oh, would you? That'd be exciting."

I laughed. "That turns you on, doesn't it?"

She put her coffee mug down on the table, and gave me a sly smile. "Yeah, it does, actually."

"Hmmm," I said. "Tell me more."

"Eddie," she said, scooting closer to me, "first of all, you're not going to jail, all right? And even if you did, I'd wait for you . . ."

"Forever?"

She considered. "Eighteen months. Twenty, tops."

"And this is what's called trying to cheer me up?"

Michelle put her arms around me and leaned forward so that her lips almost met mine. "Tell me again," she said softly, "how you're going to beat up my new boyfriend."

**That afternoon, there** was a full-blown three-ring media circus at 20th District headquarters. Color-splashed TV trucks were all over the street in the bright sunlight, each with a thick telescoping antenna extended high into the air, topped by a small satellite dish. It looked like a fleet of souped-up plumber's vans trying to pick up signals from outer space.

The 20th was a brown-brick, two-story building nestled, if you could call it that, in a working-class black neighborhood of aging rowhouses and tree-lined streets. It was rowhouse–rowhouse–police station–rowhouse. If we didn't quite blend in with our surroundings—our small parking lot was crammed with police cars—at least we liked to think that we didn't overwhelm the neighborhood. But with TV trucks halfway around the building, and camera crews and news photographers choking the sidewalks, we now looked like the unwanted neighbor that brings in trouble.

There were special parking spaces for sergeants, but the hell if I was going to announce myself that way. The TV crews were practically blocking the lot's main entrance, trying to interview every cop who drove in or out. I ended up parking a block away and walking through the lot from the far end, heading for the side door that said "Police Only." I was wearing jeans and a black polo shirt, and a baseball cap and sunglasses. That was about as much of a disguise as I could manage. I couldn't believe I was actually having to sneak into work, past people who didn't belong there.

I was halfway through the lot when I spotted Tim Timberlane on the sidewalk, talking with some other reporters. He was holding court, looking smug as ever, the reporters were all around him, hanging on his every word. He was probably recounting his moment of glory last night.

*Draw closer, and I'll tell you the story of how I got the tape that was shown across America.*

Fuck him, I thought. He glanced in my direction, as if I had said it out loud, then motioned to his cameraman—it was Joel again. Together, they headed toward the police entrance to intercept me.

But they were moving slowly, almost leisurely. It took me a moment to realize that Timberlane didn't want the other reporters to know he had found the prey. He wasn't even looking at me now, he was hurrying but not hurrying, his face a forced mask of calm.

I wanted to make a dash for the entrance, to get there before he did, but that would have given the game away. So we ended up in this little dance, a slow-motion race in which we were pitted against each other and yet in a strange collusion to keep the other reporters from noticing.

It didn't work. I heard someone yell, "There's North!" and suddenly six camera crews were squawking toward me like ducks going after a chunk of bread in the water. I was twenty feet from the door.

Timberlane, realizing his act was useless now, broke into a jog, and Joel, following, swung the camera onto his shoulder. They were going to beat me to the door.

Then I realized: How could this be worse than what they already had? My face was already all over television. Screw it. I started to walk even slower, and imagined myself yawning—a trick that I sometimes used when I wanted to appear more relaxed than I really was.

"Sergeant North! Sergeant North!" the reporters were yelling.

But then Timberlane was in front of the door, blocking my way, holding his microphone up as if I were actually going to talk to him, and Joel was at his side, aiming the camera at me like a bazooka. There was a two-foot gap between them, and I barreled through before they could seal me off. I pulled open one of the two blue metal doors and made it inside to safety. In my whole career, I'd never been so happy walking into a police station.

My first stop was the captain's office, also known as the bridge of the Starship *Enterprise*. It was commanded by Oliver Kirk, the red-haired *Star Trek* nut, who became a *Star Trek* nut only after he was promoted to captain and everyone joked about his name. Now, his entire office was filled with *Star Trek* paraphernalia, and just about every time I went in there he showed me some new addition.

His secretary, Dee-Dee, smiled when she saw me, but it was a nervous smile, not the kind I was used to getting from her. It was like I was bringing trouble wherever I went. Which maybe I was.

"I'll let him know you're here," she said, and poked her head into his office. "It's Sergeant North."

She turned and waved me in. Kirk was with Bowman, the lieutenant, and our new sergeant, George Laguerre, who had just transferred from the 16th District.

"Hey, Eddie, c'mon in," said Kirk.

The lieutenant and George were on their way out. They nodded to me as we passed, their faces serious. I had to laugh—George was taking his time leaving, he was fascinated by Kirk's little *Star Trek* shrine: the oil paintings of the original *Enterprise* crew (done by Kirk himself), the display case of phasers and other devices, the model spaceships hanging from the ceiling with fishing line. I knew George was thinking, What the hell kind of captain is this? It was a question we all asked from time to time.

Kirk motioned for me to close the door behind George and the lieutenant. I liked Kirk. To some people, he came across as well-meaning but ineffectual. Sort of a friendly bumbler. Maybe there was some truth to that, but he cared about his cops, which was more than you could say about a lot of bosses.

"You doing okay, Eddie?"

Kirk already knew the situation. He had been called in last night, and we'd had a long talk out on the street. He said he believed I was telling the truth, which I appreciated. As for Mutt and Roy, well, he said, he was going to withhold judgment until he had more information.

In his office now, he was friendly and relaxed, like it was any other day. He pointed to one of the chairs.

"Have a seat, take a load off."

I slipped into the chair. "Has Internal Affairs showed up yet?" I asked.

"Oh, yeah," said Kirk. "Most definitely. They're all over the place. Talking to people who were here last night, people who weren't here, people who were on the moon at the time, you tell me."

"What do you think they think?"

"What do I think they think? I think they think all three of you guys are guilty as hell."

I leaned back in my chair. "Great. Just great. I assume we're off the street, right?"

Kirk shook his head. "If you are, nobody's told me."

"You haven't heard from any of the bosses?"

"Oh, I've heard from them. But none of them said anything about taking you off the street. Who knows, maybe somebody's watching out for you. You got friends in high places, Eddie?"

"You're it."

Kirk laughed.

"Do you want to stay inside anyway, for a couple of days?" he asked. "Just to get out of the limelight?"

"Not me, I'm fine. Though I don't know about Mutt and Roy."

"Why don't you ask them," he said. "There's always plenty of paperwork."

"That's a generous offer, Captain," I said. "Thanks."


**I found Mutt** and Roy in the basement locker room, in front of Roy's open locker. Roy was sitting on a bench, slowly buttoning his blue police shirt over his white T-shirt. Mutt was talking to him in a low voice, it sounded like he was trying to cheer him up. Other than those two, the place was deserted.

Our locker room was pretty plain. Low cement ceiling, rows of six-foot-high lockers, long wooden benches bolted to the linoleum floor. No windows, no TV, no exercise equipment, like some districts had, no nothing. Along one wall, dusty cardboard boxes of old patrol logs and incident reports were not so much stacked as randomly thrown on top of one another, like someone's giant messy desk. This was our filing system.

They were glad to see me, they wanted to know if I had heard anything new. I told them about the captain's offer.

"Naw," said Mutt, "it would just make us look worse. Like we're hiding."

Roy nodded in agreement, but he seemed stuck to that bench, like the last thing in the world he wanted to do was leave this locker room.

"All right," I said. "Let me know if you change your mind. I'll see you up at roll call."

"Gee, I can hardly wait," said Roy. "Having everyone up there think we're fuckin' racists."

"No one's going to think that," I said.

"Some will."

"What do you care?" said Mutt. "We didn't do nothin'."

But Mutt knew, as I did, that Roy cared a lot. He loved being a part of the squad. He fed off the camaraderie. Most guys stuck to their own groups of friends in the squad, but to Roy, everyone was a friend. There'd be some lazy-ass cop who barely worked, a bump on a log, you'd see Roy in the roll-call room joking with him, asking if he wanted a Coke from the machine.

"You want to skip roll call today?" I asked.

Roy stood and tucked in his shirt.

"Let's just get this over with."

At 4 p.m., I led roll call in the dingy, green-tiled courtroom that was also used for on-site arraignments. George and I stood at the front of the room, facing the twenty-two cops who were lined up in three rows. Mutt and Roy were in their usual spots in the middle row. Roy was trying to put up a good front.

There was an empty pizza box up on the judge's desk, I tossed it into a nearby wastebasket. We were very informal in the 20th. Everyone kept glancing over at Mutt and Roy. I knew they were all dying to talk to them, to hear what they had to say.

Just as I was about to go over the day's announcements, a guy in a suit stepped in through the side door, and then stood there, watching us. Had to be one of the assholes from Internal Affairs. What did he want—to see what I was going to tell my cops? Whether I was going to tell them to lie on their reports?

George saw my anger and glared at the guy.

"You don't need to be in here," George snarled at him. "Why don't you leave, now?"

The guy narrowed his eyes at George, but turned and walked out. I gave George a nod of gratitude. My kind of sergeant.

After roll call, the squad stuck around to talk to me and the other guys. What happened last night? they all wanted to know. What really happened?

There was no hostility, no accusing looks. Roy was relieved, almost joyful. Not everyone had remained in the roll-call room—a couple of the black cops had already left for the street. But there was no way of knowing what that meant.

We told our stories, plain and simple. It didn't take long.

"And now," I said, "we're all famous. By the way, I'll be signing autographs over in the corner when we're done here."

"Hey, Sarge," said Marisol, "you know you got a fan outside?"

"Yeah," said Yvonne, "that blonde TV reporter, Samantha Sutherland. I think she likes you."

The rest of the squad cracked up. I just shook my head.

Marisol, a Latino with dark curly hair and funky red glasses, and Yvonne, who was black, had been partners for three years. They were great on the street together, they were smart, fearless. I could always count on them to do things the right way, whether it was dealing with a violent mental patient or searching through an alley for a man with a gun. I could also count on them to rag on me, whenever they saw an opportunity like this one.

"Seriously," said Marisol. "She was asking, did I know whether you were single, did you have a girlfriend, whatever."

"She said you had a nice smile," said Yvonne.

I laughed. "You two are so full of shit."

"Yo, Sarge," said Buster, "Samantha Sutherland. Did you see how short her skirt was out there? Hey, I'd go for it. She's hot."

Buster was a big, muscular guy, almost as big as Mutt, and his police shirts always fit him tight. He had wire-rim glasses and a lopsided grin, which he was flashing at me now.

I turned to him. "Shouldn't you be on the street right now?"

"She said when this is over," said Yvonne, "maybe you two could get together. She wanted us to put in a good word for her."

"I'm sure she did."

"You think we're kidding?" said Marisol. "She gave me her card to give to you. See?"

She handed it to me. It was Samantha Sutherland's card, all right, with the Channel 15 logo. Handwritten in pen on the back were the words "Call me if you'd like to go out."

Everyone gathered around to read it and laugh, and then guys started clapping me on the shoulder, taking out their cell phones and offering them to me.

I told them all to get the hell out on the street, but they just ignored me. I didn't mind. I knew this was their way of showing me, and Mutt and Roy, too, how they felt.

Finally we all headed for the door. Marisol and Yvonne took me aside. "You going out on the street now?" Marisol asked.

"Yeah," I said. "If I can get past the cameras."

She smiled. "We got it covered, Sarge."


**A few minutes** later, Yvonne, Marisol, Buster, and five or six other cops marched out the building's front entrance and announced that they were issuing a statement. Reporters, photographers, camera crews, radio people had been scattered all over the place; now they rushed to form a semicircle around the cops. Yvonne and Marisol were in the forefront, they were clearly the ones who would be speaking. Cameras moved closer. Microphones and tape recorders were shoved in their faces. A hush fell.

Marisol seemed about to say something, but then suddenly looked around and shook her head. "No, this isn't good," she said. "We're blocking the entrance."

She and Yvonne turned to their left and marched fifteen feet down the sidewalk, with the media keeping pace. They were all moving away from the parking lot, in the opposite direction. Which was good, because while all this was going on, Mutt, Roy, and I were standing by the side doors that led to the Yard and our patrol cars.

When Marisol and Yvonne finally settled on a new location, everyone resumed the pose.

"We all ready?" Marisol asked. A hush fell again.

Marisol waved a typewritten page in the air for everyone to see. "I'd like to read a statement," she said.

Buster, standing just behind her, clicked his radio three times. The signal. We headed out the side doors, unseen.

Marisol held the page in front of her.

"We, the police officers standing here, issue the following statement: We have no comment. We have nothing to say. Thank you very much."

There was stunned silence from the reporters. The only sound, Buster said later, was that of our police cars squealing out of the parking lot.

# four

**I**t probably wasn't the smartest thing in the world to do, but that afternoon I decided to take a ride past 43rd and Market. Not that I expected to find anything. The crime-scene guys had already gone over every inch, and they were a lot better at it than I was. But I figured that if I saw the street during daylight, saw it fresh, I might be able to understand what had really happened.

I knew, though, that there was another reason I went there. I was drawn to 43rd and Market the way cops are always drawn back to major crime scenes where they played a role. You want to see it, to remember, to make it real in your head. When you get there, of course, it's just an empty street, it looks the way it always did. For a moment, you wonder whether you imagined it all. So you search for something, anything, that proves it wasn't a dream: A smear of dried blood on the pavement. A remnant of crime-scene tape, still wrapped around a pole. A wadded-up rubber glove, discarded by a paramedic. Then you can say, Yeah, it did happen. I was here.

When I reached 43rd and Market that afternoon, I found a different kind of evidence. Three camera crews were filming the spot where Knight claimed he had been beaten. Of course there wasn't much to see—just a couple of parked cars that hadn't been there the night before.

I was on Market, about to turn down 43rd, when I saw the cameras. Fortunately, they didn't notice me, and I took off. It would have made great TV—The Crooked Cop Returns to the Scene of the Crime. Is he here to cover up even more evidence?

I decided to head for the area around 60th Street, where I'd be safe from the cameras. It was one of the poorest neighborhoods in the district. Abandoned houses, trash-strewn lots, drug dealers on almost every corner. The moment I arrived, I started to relax. This was home to me, familiar territory.

Cops have mixed feelings about bad neighborhoods. On the one hand, you see all the crime, all the violence that people do to one another, and you feel sorry for the innocent ones who have to suffer, particularly the children. You say to yourself, it's terrible that people have to live like this.

But on the other hand—and it's a very big hand—this is where the action is. This is where you're going to chase after stolen cars, and run through back alleys after purse snatchers, and face down bad guys with guns. It's where your adrenaline gets pumping, electrifying your body down to the fingertips. It's where you get your best war stories. It's where you feel most like a real cop. Not that you want bad things to happen—you just want to be there when they do.

But if I had come to this neighborhood today to escape, I had come to the wrong place. I got a lot of smirks and wagging fingers from the young guys who were clustered on the corners, drinking forty-ounce bottles of beer from paper bags. I doubted whether many of them had actually seen me on TV—they were probably sleeping all morning—but it didn't matter. By now, the story of Sonny Knight had whipped through the city, with my name attached. And all these guys knew me, like they knew all the cops who worked this part of the district.

We knew them, too. We knew which ones were the dealers, the dice shooters, the thieves, the crazies, the lowlifes, the anything-for-a-buck hustlers. You lock them up a few times, get in conversations with them, and when they get out of jail a few days later—nobody stays in jail—you see them on the street and maybe they'll nod to you. Next time you lock them up, you call them by their first names. It's like people you see in your office every day—they're part of the workplace. Hi, how ya doin'. How 'bout them Eagles?

Some of the cops, particularly the ones who are always making pinches, are given nicknames. Like Blondie or Fat Boy—something about a cop's appearance that everyone on the street can immediately identify. Or the name could be based on the way a cop acts. Like Badass—always said sarcastically—for a cop who likes to throw his weight around.

My own nickname in that neighborhood was Ladies' Man. That was because for two weeks one spring, we had a slew of Penn students doing ride-alongs in the district. Although the male students rode with regular cops, the bosses decreed—probably wisely—that female students should ride only with supervisors. Which meant that every night, a different young woman was sitting in the front seat of my car. The dealers and other street guys were impressed as hell. They'd never seen a cop do so well with the women.

Now I discovered that I was even more of a celebrity in the neighborhood. And I didn't realize how many friends I had on the street.

"Hey, Ladies' Man!" guys called out, toasting me with their paper-bagged forties. "Can I get your autograph?"

No one mentioned Sonny Knight. It was like the actual incident was irrelevant—what counted was that they could have fun giving me shit.

At one corner, I stopped at a light and looked over to see Rasheed Jackson staring back at me with an impish grin. Rasheed had done prison time, which meant he was a big man on his corner. And he was about twenty-three, which made him one of the old heads on the street. He was wearing the Philly drug-dealer uniform—black leather jacket, jeans, light brown Timberland boots.

"Yo, Ladies' Man!" he called to me. "I'm gonna help you out."

"Yeah, Rasheed? What are you gonna do?"

"If you go to prison, and I'm there too—you know, you and me are prison-mates—I'll protect you. I'll watch your back. You want, I'll even show you all the ropes."

All his pals were laughing, they thought this was hilarious.

This is great, I thought. Here I am getting my balls busted by a lowlife drug dealer. Boy, was I glad I decided to take a ride through *this* neighborhood.

**It was after** ten when I found myself back at 43rd and Market. By then it was dark, and the TV crews were long gone. I half expected that at least one reporter or photographer—even someone from a newspaper—would stick around, maybe hide in a car. That's what I would have done. You wait long enough, the cops are going to come back. Then you have your story, or your picture, or whatever else you want. It's not rocket science.

But there were no reporters, not even any cars around for people to hide in. I turned down 43rd and came to a stop in the same place that I had the night before. I didn't know why, it just seemed natural. Okay, this is my parking spot. It's in the middle of the street, but it's my parking spot.

I got out and stood by my car, feeling the light wind on my face, watching the shadows do their nightly dance on the street.

Everything was exactly the same. Somehow, it was almost as if it was going to happen again: Sonny Knight would come by in his car, and so would Mutt and Roy, but this time I would be here, I would be able to watch it unfold.

I shook my head. Maybe I was getting hypnotized by the shadows. What was I doing here? If a TV truck came by now, I'd be screwed.

Had Mutt and Roy been by tonight? Probably, at least just for a look. I heard a yip, and glanced over at the used-car lot. There were the dogs, noses to the fence, side by side, watching me silently. My witnesses.

"How you guys doing?" I called.

At the sound of my voice they snapped to the alert. Terrific, I thought—now I'm going to get them barking again. But they didn't seem interested in making a lot of noise tonight. Maybe they had been barking nonstop since last night and were finally tired. Dogs have to get tired.

*You want to keep barking?*

*No, do you?*

*No, I don't even remember why we were barking in the first place.*

*Me neither.*

I walked toward the dogs, I figured what the hell.

"Hey, guys," I said when I reached the fence. They both immediately relaxed, and stuck their noses through the chain-link, like they wanted me to pet them. I laughed. This place doesn't even have decent guard dogs.

"What'd you guys see last night?" I asked them.

They just looked at me, like I was supposed to come up with the answer myself. And what was the answer? Either Mutt and Roy beat up Sonny Knight, or they didn't. And if they didn't, why would a city councilman try to jam up two innocent cops?

I had been gazing through the fence at the office of the car lot, gazing—without realizing it—at something on its low roof. I focused on it now, I recognized its shape. It was a security camera, pointed right at the front gate and at the street beyond. Was it working? It had to be working. Because if it was, it would have caught everything.

This was it—the chance to see into the past, to peel back the truth. I wanted to get the tape right then, I wanted to scale the fence and brave the barbed wire and the dogs and break into the office. I was like a desperate drug addict. I had to have that tape.

I pulled myself away from the fence, forced myself toward my car. Do it by the book, I thought. You got to do it by the book.

. . .

**I found Larry** Timmons upstairs in West Detectives' "breakfast nook," the paint-peeled corner where they kept the coffee machine. Timmons was a lieutenant, he was the one running the investigation for West.

"That used-car lot on Forty-third," I said. "You know they got a security camera on the roof?"

I tried to sound nonchalant, like I was just passing along a tip that he could use or not use, it was all the same to me.

Timmons was a wiry black guy who had been around forever. A good, methodical detective. He always wore a black sports jacket, white shirt, and thin tie. Very retro, very sixties, but it worked for him.

He kept his eyes on the stream of black glop he was pouring into a "World's Best Daddy" mug.

"No film in it," he said.

"Don't tell me that."

"We checked it today," he said. "There's no film in it. That thing probably hasn't been used in ten years."

I stood there looking at him, feeling like an idiot. Not for coming to him about the camera, but for believing, like a child, it could be that easy.

I glanced at the radio handset on my gun belt. I had turned the volume down, almost all the way, so I could talk to Timmons, but now something was coming over the air, something important. My ear was picking up the faint sounds of panic. I turned the dial up.

"*Someone just tried to kill me!*" a cop was yelling. "*Tried to shoot me in my car!*"

I turned and ran back toward the stairs, detectives were jumping out of my way. It was Buster, I knew his voice.

"*Unit, what's your location?*" the dispatcher asked, trying to stay calm. "*We need a location.*"

I pounded down the stairs. The cops on the first floor were rushing out the door, into the Yard, and then I was out the door, too.

"*Forty-sixth and Market!*" Buster yelled. "*I need an assist!*"

Forty-sixth and Market. Three blocks from where I had just been.

. . .

**Street cops don't** like to talk about it, but deep down, it's something they all fear: that one night, while they're sitting alone in their patrol car, someone's going to come up and pull out a gun, and bang, it'll all be over. Maybe it's someone who's crazy and didn't take his medication that day. Maybe it's someone who just doesn't like cops.

It's not like when you're making a car-stop or chasing someone down an alley. There, you know the danger. But sitting in your patrol car, you're an easy target. If someone wants to take you out, there's not much you can do about it. Though you can't worry about it, either. If you did, you'd never be able to go out on the street, you'd spend the whole night hiding inside district headquarters. So you put it out of your mind. Until something happens like what happened to Buster.

He had been called to 46th Street to check out a report of an accident. When he pulled up, no one was around. We got that all the time—there'd be a fender bender, and the two parties would settle it among themselves and take off. It didn't matter, though, Buster still had to fill out an incident report. In the old days, you could just call Radio and tell them it was unfounded. Not anymore. Now, the bosses wanted reports on everything, no matter how minor. Which meant that cops were spending half their time doing paperwork. People are driving down the street, they see a police car pulled over to the side, they get a little nervous, they think, That cop's watching me, he's waiting to see whether I'm going to run this light. Probably not. Probably he's just catching up on his damn paperwork.

So there was Buster, filling out his report, with the car's inside light on so he could see what he was doing. He told us later he had his window rolled down, and he thought he heard a noise, like the jangling of keys. But it was dark out, and the inside light made it hard to see much on the street, and he wasn't the type to worry about it anyway. A moment later, he realized someone was standing outside his car. He glanced up, saw a man in a black ski mask. Then the barrel of a pistol, coming in through the open window, pointed right at his face.

At that point, you don't have time to plan a course of action. This is not something they teach at the academy. Instinctively, Buster reached up with his left hand, grabbed the gun barrel, and pushed it away from his head. There was an explosion of sound and flame, deafening, blinding, and the passenger window shattered out onto the street. Buster realized the bullet had passed about three inches in front of his nose.

Now Buster and the man in the black ski mask are wrestling with the gun, the barrel of the gun is tracing a wild arc through the inside of the car. Buster can see the man's finger on the trigger, the trigger is right there, he's got a close-up view. He isn't wondering who the man is or why he wants to kill him. All he's thinking is, If I lose this battle, I'm dead.

There's another explosion, and this time the bullet goes through the car roof. Buster has strong arms, but the man in the ski mask is standing and has the leverage, and he's steering the barrel back toward Buster's head.

Then Buster does something brilliant, though he does it before he's even had a chance to consider the idea. He drops his right hand for a moment, pulls up the door handle, and then throws all his weight against the door. He pushes the door open, against the man, surprising him, throwing him off balance. Buster watches as the gun barrel rushes back out the window. The man falls onto the street, but he's still got the gun. And now he raises it, aiming it at Buster's head.

Buster leans toward the passenger side, trying to make himself less of a target, and he jams the gearshift into drive and floors the gas pedal. His car screeches away from the curb, lurching as it picks up speed, flapping the open door. He gets on the radio and calls for help, still half ducking down, expecting a shot to come through the back window.

Fifty feet down the block, Buster glances over his shoulder and sees the man in the ski mask on his feet again, running away.

Buster makes a U-turn and charges back down the block, one hand steering, the other unsnapping his holster. He's closing in, but the man darts to his right, up onto to the sidewalk, toward a house. The man's running inside, Buster can see it's an abandoned house, the door is gone, the windows are boarded up. The man is probably racing through the house, heading for the back door. Buster considers pulling his car around the block into the alley. But that would take too long, the man would be gone. So he jumps out of the car, Glock in hand, and charges toward the abandoned house. It's dangerous, he knows that, the man could be waiting for him inside. But Buster doesn't slow down, not for a moment, he's thinking, The fuck if I'm going to let this motherfucker get away.

In a moment, Buster is up the steps and bursting through the doorway, into the darkness, smashing into old furniture, boxes, pieces of wood, but not slowing, not even for a moment, trying to stay in the straight line he knows will lead him to the kitchen and the back door. Then he's in the kitchen, the back door is wide open, a light from the alley is showing the way. Buster reaches the threshold and sees at the last moment that the back steps are gone, he almost falls, but catches himself, and jumps the three feet into the weeds. Then through the yard and into the alley. It's empty.

Buster looks around. Half the houses on the block are abandoned, the man could have gone into any one of them. Buster feels sick, he knows the chase is over. The man could be heading in almost any direction, leapfrogging from house to house, from street to street, disappearing into the realm of infinite possibility.

**We spent the** next few hours searching as many abandoned houses as we could. Though the odds were against it, there was always the chance the shooter was hiding nearby. Normally, you get SWAT to go through houses like that—they've got the armor, the weaponry, the training. But that would have taken all night.

So it was just us cops, stumbling through the treacherous, trash-filled rooms, our flashlight beams cutting through the pitch-black darkness, but making us perfect targets. You do something like this, you just have to hope that if you actually find the guy and corner him, he doesn't decide to open fire and take out as many cops as he can. But you can't not go in the house. Somebody's got to do it, you're there, it's your job. So you pick your way through, from one dark room to the next. All your senses are heightened—sight, sound, smell. Even the darkness is vivid. And if the house is clear, you move on to the next one and start all over again.

We didn't find the shooter. We combed through every alley for blocks, looked under every car. There were countless passageways between houses, choked with weeds and rubbish, and we went through every one of them. We checked the rooftops, too, with police helicopters that crisscrossed the night sky with their powerful searchlights, like an upside-down movie premiere. None of it did any good.

We didn't have much of a description of the guy to start with. Black jeans, black T-shirt, which were pretty common in that neighborhood. Medium height and build. We knew he was black—Buster had seen his hands and arms—but everyone in the neighborhood was black. Not that any of it mattered. He was gone.

Just before midnight, a chief inspector gave the order to resume patrol. George and I were standing on the street where the drama began, watching the crime-scene guys go through Buster's car, and comparing notes on how much of the neighborhood we'd covered. The chief, spotting two sergeants together, walked in our direction.

Or rather, waddled. His name was John Clopper, and he had to be one of the fattest cops in the department. His white police shirt bulged in every direction, and he had a monstrous potbelly that began under his shirt and continued outward and downward under his belt.

"Here comes the fat man," I said to George. "A walking advertisement for the Philly cheesesteak."

"Well, you know what they say about him," said George. "Clopper doesn't have command presence, he just has presence."

Clopper finally lumbered up to us and paused to catch his breath.

"I'm resuming the assist," Clopper said. "Have your squads report off."

I glanced at my watch and gave George a look. He was giving me the same look back. It was nearly midnight, the end of the shift, and Clopper was trying to get everyone back to district headquarters before overtime kicked in.

"Chief," I said, "I know the commissioner wants to cut down on OT . . ."

"This isn't about OT," Clopper bellowed, glaring at me. "That's bullshit." He gave me a hard look, but then jerked his head back in surprise.

"I know you," he said. "You're Eddie North." He half smiled. "You're the one covering up for his men."

"I'm not covering up for anybody."

"Yeah, yeah, sure. If it were up to me, you'd be off the street in a heartbeat. In fact, you'd probably be locked up."

"For what?"

Clopper stared at me, incredulous. "For what? Look around you. Why do think we're all here? Your men beat the living shit out of Sonny Knight, and now some asshole who's pissed off about it is going around shooting at cops." Clopper was puffing, his face was getting red. "You protect your men, you think you're a big hero. But you know what? It's going to get a cop killed."

I just stood there thinking, What the hell?

"That cop who just got shot at is in your squad, isn't he?" Clopper asked. Before I could respond, he said, "Which means you almost got one of your own men killed tonight. Big hero."

George took a step toward Clopper, putting himself partly between the two of us.

"You don't know the facts," he told Clopper evenly. "How can you make an accusation like that?"

Clopper's bulk, and anger, shifted toward George.

"Who the fuck are you?" he asked.

George didn't flinch a bit. He faced Clopper squarely, his back straight, like a soldier. He'd told me he had been an MP in the Army, and he looked it then, confident, absolutely resolute.

Clopper was staring at George's silver nameplate.

"It's Laguerre," said George. "Twentieth District. You want to transfer me, go right ahead."

"Fuck transferring you. You fuck with me, I'll take you to the fuckin' Front."

The Front was what we called our disciplinary board.

"For what?" George asked. "For reminding a chief inspector to consider a man innocent until he's proven guilty? What are they going to give me for that, three days without pay?"

I wondered whether George had talked to his Army superiors that way. I couldn't imagine it.

Clopper was silent, I could tell he was considering his options. If this conversation was repeated in front of the commissioner, he wouldn't come out smelling like a rose, and he knew it. Clopper glared at George, then at me, then back at George, but it was all an act now, the fire was gone.

"Tell your squads to report off," he said, and wheeled his massive frame around, like a tractor-trailer making a wide turn.

George must have had the same image. As we watched Clopper depart, he said, "If you can't see my mirrors, I can't see you."

I laughed. "Thanks," I said. "I owe you one."

George was still looking at Clopper. "What an asshole."

"Yeah," I said, "but a powerful asshole. I don't want you to get jammed up on my behalf."

"Fuck him," said George. "What's he going to do to me?"

"Bosses can be very creative. Especially when it comes to screwing people."

George nodded. "Yeah. As we all learn sooner or later."

"Actually," I said, "I owe you more than one. You been doing this all day. Maybe I should put you on my payroll."

George thought it over. "What kind of pay we looking at?"

"Beers after work. It's all I can afford."

"What kind of beers?"

"Are we negotiating?" I asked.

"Maybe."

"Okay, I can start you out at Coors Light. If things work out, I may be able to bump you up to Rolling Rock."

George shook his head. "Sorry. I couldn't start out with anything less than Rolling Rock."

"You're tough," I said. "But all right, Rolling Rock it is."

We shook hands to seal the deal.

"Some of us are taking Buster over to Fibber's after work," I said, "if you'd like to pick up your first paycheck."

"I'll be there."

Clopper was probably right about one thing—the attack on Buster was no doubt in retaliation for what had happened to Sonny Knight. What else could it be—people didn't usually go around trying to assassinate cops.

But why Buster? Maybe the man in the ski mask was hoping that by some chance he'd nail one of the cops who had beaten Knight. Mutt's and Roy's photos still hadn't been released, so the guy would just be guessing. But then again, maybe he didn't care who he got. Whatever cop happened to respond to the "accident" was the target. Maybe the guy figured one dead cop was as good as the next.

**Michelle's squad worked** the same hours as mine did, and when I told her we were all going over to Fibber's, she said she'd come along. She caught up with me at the 20th as I was about to head downstairs to the locker room to change.

"How's Buster?" she asked. Michelle was already in her civilian clothes—jeans and a sleeveless green blouse.

"He's fine," I said. "We're going to go out and get him nice and drunk."

"I was thinking about it on the way over," she said. "You know, this might have something to do with Danforth."

"Michelle, you think *everything* has to do with Danforth."

This was not a smart thing to say. It was true, but not smart.

"I also think you're a total jerk," she said. "Have fun at Fibber's." She spun around and headed toward the door.

I had to chase after her and convince her I was just kidding. It wasn't the first time we'd had this kind of conversation. Michelle ate, slept, and drank the Danforth case, sometimes it was all she thought about.

Let's go see a movie, I'd say.

No, I need to visit Marnie, she'd say. Marnie was the widow of Bobby Boland, the cop who was killed.

Let's go down to the shore for the weekend, I'd say.

No, I need to get ready for the trial, she'd say.

Once, I made the mistake of suggesting she might be getting a little obsessed with the case. She didn't speak to me for two days.

This time, though, I was able to do some quick damage control.

"So why do you think there's a connection with Danforth?" I asked her.

We were standing by the side doors to the Yard, and had to step out of the way so the cops coming in and out could get by. Fortunately for everyone, the TV crews were no longer hanging around—it was late, and all the reporters were gone.

"The Danforth people have got this website," Michelle said. "You know, with all the so-called facts about Danforth."

"All the lies."

"Yeah. People write essays, or whatever, on the site. And one guy, Tariq, I assume he's a guy, he thinks the Danforth people aren't going far enough. He almost comes right out and tells people to go around killing cops."

"You kidding me?"

"No, you should see it. He says stuff like 'Talk accomplishes nothing. The only way to teach the police a lesson is with violence.'"

"I wonder if that's our guy."

"If not him," said Michelle, "then maybe somebody who's read-ing this stuff. You know, someone thinking, Yeah, that's a good idea, I think I'll go out and shoot a cop."

"It could still be a coincidence," I said.

"Yeah, maybe. But you know who's the leader of the Danforth movement?"

"I heard it's Carl Knight."

"You got it. And I don't think he's exactly happy with the cops right now."

"So what are you saying? You think Carl Knight is the one writ-ing this crap?"

Michelle shook her head. "No. It doesn't quite fit, I don't think Carl is the type to actually advocate violence."

"Then what? The shooter might have been trying to get revenge on his behalf?"

"That's what I'm thinking."

"Interesting," I said. "It's worth looking into."

Michelle considered me. "You really believe that?"

"Sure."

"No, you don't. You think I'm obsessed."

"No, in fact I think you should tell Homicide."

"I'm going to. I have an appointment with them tomorrow morning."

"Good."

"And you're not just saying that?"

"Hey, just because you're obsessed doesn't mean you're not right."

She tried to stomp on my foot. But she was smiling.

# five

**I**f it hadn't been Sonny Knight, if the man in the silver BMW had turned out to be just an ordinary citizen on his way through West Philadelphia, the world wouldn't have known or cared. But that wasn't of much consolation to Mutt, Roy, and me. We were taking heat from all sides.

The politicians, the newspapers, the black clergy, the white clergy, the green clergy, they were all calling for our heads. That Thursday, three days after Sonny Knight was beaten, the *Philadelphia Post* ran an editorial with the headline "CHARGE THEM!"

I was sorry I didn't have a subscription to the paper so I could have canceled it.

That afternoon, the police commissioner held a press conference to give his response. We weren't there, on account of having to fight crime and everything, so we had to watch it on the six o'clock news. Us and a dozen or so other cops, crammed into the operations room at the 20th.

The room was already crowded with the battered gray metal desks where the inside cops did their paperwork. If you were to take a modern, state-of-the-art police station, plush, sleek, shiny, and then replace every single item with an older, outdated, beat-up version, you'd have our operations room. Along the upper third of an entire wall was a list of phone numbers, hand-painted, black on white, on sheets of plywood. Bomb Squad, Sex Crimes, Civil

Affairs, all up there in huge, clumsily written lettering, like something out of a World War II movie. We had rotary phones. We had ancient green filing cabinets that took two people to pry open. We had computers that were older than a lot of cops. What could we do? We got used to it. It was home.

So there we all were, staring up at the old TV set bolted to the wall near the ceiling. First up on the news was an NAACP press conference from that afternoon. Nothing noteworthy, if you didn't count the NAACP president pounding his podium with his fist and demanding that Mutt, Roy, and I be thrown in jail.

He was sorry that someone had tried to kill a police officer, he said, but maybe it wouldn't have happened if those cops weren't still on the street. Where, he added, they might be brutalizing other innocent black people, maybe at this very moment.

"If three black cops had beaten a white city councilman bloody, they would have been arrested then and there," he said. "Make no mistake about that."

I couldn't believe it. Now they had all three of us doing the beating.

"Looks like you've just been upgraded, Sarge," said Marisol. Laughter around the room.

What seemed to really go up this guy's ass was that it was a black police commissioner who was protecting these cops.

"It's offensive," said the obviously offended NAACP president. "Elijah Ellsworth should know better."

The scene then shifted to the parking lot of Police Headquarters downtown. Ellsworth was speaking into an overgrown jungle of padded microphones and minicassette recorders, all with hands and forearms attached.

He looked pained, uncomfortable, like he wanted to be anywhere else but where he was. I could picture a couple of the deputy commissioners pleading with him. Commissioner, you have to make a response. You can't ignore this.

The TV showed Ellsworth's face as someone asked, "Why haven't the officers been charged?"

"We're still investigating," he said. "I'm not going to cut short an investigation because of editorials and press conferences."

"Will they be charged?" one of the reporters asked.

"That'll be the DA's decision."

The reporter tried to ask another question, but he was overridden by a shrill female voice.

"Why are the officers still on the street while you're investigating? Why haven't they been given desk duty?"

We all listened closely to this one. We were dying to know.

"We don't pull officers from the street on the basis of allegations from citizens, unless there's other evidence," said Ellsworth. "And at this point there's no other evidence—just the statement by Councilman Knight."

"Isn't that enough?" the woman asked.

"No," said Ellsworth. "It's not. Look, I'm not going to make an exception because Councilman Knight is a public figure."

"And a friend," another reporter was heard saying, but the segment ended abruptly, without showing Ellsworth's response to that. The anchorman came on and moved to other news.

Someone turned down the TV, and the operations room was quiet for a moment.

"What's the catch?" Buster finally asked.

He was right. There had to be a catch.

**It took another** day before the first of the media, in this case the *Post*, was able to get photos of Mutt and Roy. The paper made up for this uncharacteristic delay by putting the pictures right on the front page, in color, and blown up so large you could have recognized Mutt's and Roy's faces a half mile away.

They got Roy with an ambush in front of his house. He was on his way to work, it was about 3:30 P.M. Roy had kissed Tina and the girls good-bye at the door, and stepped out to head for his car.

Two people emerged from a white Chevy Cavalier across the

street, a young blond guy and a young woman with a camera, a frizzy-haired redhead.

"What was I going to do, run away from them?" Roy asked Mutt and me.

The three of us were standing in the 7-Eleven near Penn, sipping cups of coffee, looking at the stack of *Post*s on the floor from a safe distance.

"Yeah, that would of made a good shot," said Roy. "Me runnin'."

"What'd you do?" I asked.

"I kept walking toward my car, like a normal American citizen. The blond guy, he comes up and says, 'Officer Knopfler, can we talk to you?' I just ignored him, but the whole time, this girl photographer's taking my picture. Click-click-click-click-click. I look back at the house, and there's Tina and the girls watching all this."

"Fuckin' newspaper," Mutt said.

"And I'm walking along," said Roy, "trying to look normal, not like I'm pissed off."

I laughed. "Well, you sure did a shitty job."

The photo in the paper showed Roy glowering at the camera, his face tight.

"That's where she wouldn't get out of my way," said Roy. "And of course that's the one picture they use."

"Of course," I said. "They have to make you look like a criminal."

"This is real bad," said Roy, growing quiet. "Everyone in my family is already humiliated. Now they got to deal with this."

He looked at the pile of newspapers. "I'm sure my entire family would like to see me just disappear."

"No way," said Mutt. "They been supporting you, right?"

"Oh, yeah, sure. But it's got to be affecting them, how could it not? And now they got to come into work and have this newspaper laying around. With a Knopfler right on the fuckin' front page."

"Yeah," said Mutt, "and an ugly one, too."

"What about you?" I said to Mutt. "At least you're smiling in yours."

We took another look at the newspapers on the floor. Mutt's photo was a little out of focus, you could tell it was from some kind of family photo taken outdoors.

"How'd they get that?" I asked.

"I have been trying to figure it out," said Mutt. "I think it came from Joe Kasper. My good neighbor Joe."

Mutt walked over to the stack of papers, picked one off the top, and showed it to us.

"See this red thing here?" he asked, pointing to a blurry splotch on the photo's upper-right-hand corner. "I think that's the picnic table umbrella from their back porch. They had a barbecue over at their place last spring, and Joe's wife was taking pictures. I think this is one of the pictures, you know, with all the other people cut out."

"And they gave it to the newspaper?" I asked.

"You need to see the story," said Mutt.

He handed me the paper. Mutt's neighbors had been interviewed, and most of what they said was pretty complimentary. Mutt was a great guy who would do anything for you. He'd shovel snow off people's walks, carry in old folks' groceries from the car, take neighborhood kids to the McDonald's.

But then came the comments from the neighbor who "asked not to be identified."

*"Sometimes he can be a hothead," the neighbor said. "If you double-park and block his car in, he'll yell at you."*

"That's Joe Kasper," said Mutt. "We used to get along fine. I always liked the guy, I really did. Then he got a new car, and he starts double-parking it in front of his house. To keep an eye on it. I complained about it to him one time. One time. So now I'm a hothead in the paper."

"Want me to slash his tires?" I asked Mutt.

Mutt laughed. "Would you? Tell you one thing, I'm never reading that fuckin' rag again."

"Yes, you will," said Roy. "For the sports."

"I don't have to read that paper."

Roy looked at me. "Yes, he does. He has to read both papers. Every day, every sports story, every word."

This was no doubt true. Mutt was not a sports fanatic, he was whatever came after that. He never minded when we were on day-work—though it was often boring—because it meant he could go see the Flyers or Sixers at night. He used his vacation time to take off Sundays in the fall, so he could go to Eagles games.

A lot of guys listened to music on the radio when they cruised in their patrol car. Mutt would have it tuned to the sports-talk shows. Before he got a cell phone, he'd have to stop at a pay phone to call up WIP and argue about the latest Phillies trade. Now he'd be driving, one hand on the wheel, the other holding the cell phone to his ear, he'd be almost yelling into the phone, his voice would be echoing from the car's AM radio on a seven-second delay, and meanwhile the police radio would be squawking away full blast. Sometimes it drove Roy crazy, but he put up with it, because they were partners and friends, and that's what you did.

Mutt grabbed the paper back from me and took another look at the front page.

"You know what the worst thing is? Now everyone knows what we look like. Including the asshole that went after Buster."

"Great," said Roy. "So now what? We're fuckin' targets?"


**I got a** call from Radio telling me to report back to the district. When I arrived, I was told that someone was in the roll-call room, waiting to talk to me.

It turned out to be the jerk from Internal Affairs who George had chased away from roll call.

"Lieutenant Gene Desmond," he said, extending his hand.

This presented something of a dilemma. I didn't particularly feel like shaking his hand, but I had to wonder. If I don't, is he enough of an asshole to go after me twice as hard? I ended up shaking his hand, but feeling bad about it.

We sat down at the table used by defense attorneys during the arraignments. The room was empty, if you didn't count the Coke machine and snack machine side by side against the back wall, both huge, lit-up, our twin money-grubbing sentinels.

Desmond told me he had read the statement I gave to West Detectives, and had a few more questions. Did I mind answering?

"Depends on the question," I said. "But let me ask you something first. Do you think I'm guilty of a cover-up?"

"Not yet," he said. "I don't have enough information to decide whether you're guilty. Do I think it looks bad? Yeah. That's why I'm sitting here talking to you."

At least he was honest. And he actually had a friendly face. It was a little pudgy, probably from too many hoagies and too little exercise. Sandy hair, sandy mustache, blue eyes that seemed to be without malice.

And yet it was his job to put cops in jail. This nice-guy routine probably got him a lot of good confessions.

Desmond asked me about my call to McAvoy, then about the tow truck.

"That truck driver who showed up," he asked, "did you know who he was?"

Why was he asking? Because he knew it was Dominic?

From that first night, I had assumed that as long as no one knew the identity of the driver, I'd be all right. I also assumed that if Dominic's name ever got out, that'd be it for me. No one would ever believe it was a coincidence.

And so how to answer his question? Say yes, you risk getting condemned by the truth. Say no, you risk getting caught in a lie.

I saw a patch of light in the middle.

"Hell, I didn't even know what company he worked for."

Which was true. The towing company's name was no doubt on the side of Dominic's truck, but I hadn't paid it any attention.

"The reason I ask," said Desmond, "is that Mr. Knight told us the driver called you 'Sarge.' Like he might have known you."

I pointed to the stripes on my arm. "These are kind of a dead giveaway, don't you think?"

Desmond asked a few more minor questions, then got up to leave. I hadn't lied to him, technically. But I didn't know whether he saw through my little tricks. If he had, then now he had more reason than ever to think I was guilty.

**Ten seconds after** Desmond left the roll-call room, Yvonne and Marisol walked in.

"We heard you were in here, Sarge," said Marisol. "Can we talk to you for a minute?"

"Have a seat in my office," I said, and motioned to them to sit at the desk.

"Me and Marisol wanted to talk to you about something," said Yvonne. "We didn't know whether we should, but . . ."

She looked to Marisol, who nodded for her to go ahead.

"Some of the black cops are pretty upset."

"About what?"

"About Mutt," said Yvonne.

I waited.

"He's got a reputation."

"What kind of reputation?"

"You know. Maybe being a little too aggressive sometimes, on the street. Especially when it comes to black people."

"So what are you saying? You guys think Mutt and Roy beat up Sonny Knight?"

They both shook their heads.

"Me, I don't think they did," said Yvonne. "And if they did do it, they probably had a good excuse. Councilman or no councilman."

"That's exactly how I feel," said Marisol. "I mean, me and Yvonne, we know Mutt. But there's some guys out there . . ."

"Black guys," said Yvonne.

"And some Latinos," said Marisol. "They're saying, Look at

what Mutt did, and look at what happened to Buster because of it. He's putting us all in danger."

"It's out there, bubbling up," said Yvonne. "We just don't want you to get hit on the blind side."

"Yeah, you watch out for us," said Marisol. "So we figured, we should watch out for you."

"Thanks," I said. "I appreciate that."

They left the roll-call room, and I sat in the old swivel chair behind the judge's raised desk. Was I wrong about Mutt and Roy? Was I just believing what I wanted to believe?

There was a night about three months ago, maybe four. We had a report of a fight outside a bar on Locust, and when I pulled up, Mutt was already there. He had two black guys out on the street, they were flailing at each other with drunken arms. Mutt shoved them apart, and one of them, a real skinny guy, took a swing at Mutt and missed by a mile.

The guy was so drunk, so off balance, he had no chance of hitting Mutt and wouldn't have hurt him if he had. But Mutt took a step forward and, with a quick movement of his fist, knocked the guy to the street. I was getting out of my car, I saw all this happen, and by the time I reached Mutt, he was pounding the guy, with both fists.

He stopped when I told him to, but he wasn't happy about it.

"I'm just trying to teach him a little lesson," he said. "You don't hit cops."

We watched as the skinny drunk popped to his feet. He didn't even look hurt. His mouth was bleeding, but he was smiling, happy as hell I was there and now things were all right.

I didn't say anything to Mutt right there, not in front of the crowd that was gathering outside the bar. But I knew that if I hadn't shown up when I did, there would have been nothing left of that guy. He would have just been a spot on the pavement.

. . .

**That Sunday my** squad was off. George had invited me to his neighborhood block party, and I figured I'd stop by for a while with Michelle.

When we got there, a little after three, the block party was in full swing. A hired DJ had set up his equipment and huge speakers in the middle of the closed-off street, and pounding pop music filled the air. Screaming kids were running back and forth across the street, and clusters of adults stood in their driveways or sat curbside on lawn chairs, eating hot dogs and macaroni salad from paper plates.

George lived in Rhawnhurst, a working-class neighborhood in Northeast Philly with cops and firefighters on every street. All the houses on George's block were twins, basically two rowhouses stuck together, with small yards on either side. You don't get as much privacy or land as you would with a separate house, but if you're living on a cop's salary, it's a good compromise.

Just about everyone had barbecues and private parties going on in their backyards and screened-in back porches, but they'd bring their food and their plastic cups of beer out front for the common neighborhood party. We found George hovering over his barbecue grill in the back, dodging the smoke and testing the hamburgers to see whether they were done. He was wearing a Hawaiian shirt and a blue plastic lei around his neck.

"Hey, Eddie," he said with a smile. "Glad you could make it."

I introduced him to Michelle, and he called over his wife, whose name was Nora, and everyone shook hands. Nora was dark-haired, trim, almost as tall as George, her long legs sharply outlined by her stonewashed blue jeans. Nora was pretty, especially when she smiled at us, but her face lacked any softness. Instead, she wore the hard, frank look you often see in women from Philly's working-class neighborhoods. Her voice was slightly husky, a sexy smoker's rasp, and I pegged her accent as being lower Northeast Philadelphia, possibly Frankford or Port Richmond.

George left Nora to keep an eye on the burgers, and led Michelle and me around the side of his house, where a keg of Coors Light was nestled in a blue plastic tub of ice underneath a tree. We each filled a red plastic cup with beer, then headed out front and across the street.

"There's some people I want you two to meet," George said.

We walked up to three guys who were standing on the sidewalk under a tree, drinking beer and talking. George introduced us; the three were cops, they all lived on the block. One was a beefy lieutenant in Narcotics. I had met him once before, but we really didn't remember each other.

Like George, all three were wearing Hawaiian shirts and had brightly colored plastic leis around their necks.

"What's all this *Five-O* stuff?" I asked.

George laughed. "Every year the block has a different theme for the party. This year it's Hawaiian. What can I say? Hey, as long as they got beer in Hawaii, it's fine with me."

All three cops immediately wanted to talk about Sonny Knight.

"What I don't understand," said the lieutenant, blustering at me, "is why your guys said they just found Knight there. You know, just lying on the street. I mean, c'mon, who's going to believe that? Why not just say Knight went crazy, he resisted arrest. Which is probably what happened."

"Really?" I said. "How do you know that? Were you there? I must have missed you."

George lifted his hand. "Whoa, whoa. C'mon, Fred, Eddie's been getting enough shit from the media and everyone else. This is his day off, he's here to have a good time, okay?"

Fred nodded, and then looked at me, a little abashed. "Sorry, pal."

"Fred was just telling us a story," said one of the other cops, a young guy named Don who worked down in the 4th. "Something about Police Jeopardy?"

"Oh, yeah," said Fred, happy to turn the conversation in a different direction.

"We had this knucklehead in a jail cell, we thought we might be able to charge him for drugs, but we couldn't, so we had to let him go. But, you know, we wanted to have a little fun. So me and a couple of guys go into the cell room and say to this asshole, 'We're going to play Police Jeopardy. If you can answer just one question, we'll let you go.' We gave him a choice of categories: history, geography, or science.

" 'I want sports,' the guy says. So I tell him, sorry, that's not one of the categories. So then he says, 'Okay, geology.' Like that's his area of expertise. I had to tell him, it's geography, not geology. Did he want that?

"He says yeah. So I say, 'Okay, what's the capital of Pennsylvania?'

"He's thinking about it, he's thinking real hard. This is a tough one. Finally he says, 'Could you repeat the question?'

" 'Yeah. What's the capital of Pennsylvania?'

"He thinks some more, then suddenly a lightbulb goes off in his head. He jumps up on the bed and yells out, 'P!'

"Which, of course, was right. So we had to let him go."

We all cracked up. Cop humor at its best.

Later, George and I sat on lawn chairs in front of his house and drank beer and talked quietly. Michelle was in the back; it turned out she had gone to high school with one of Nora's friends at the party, and the two were catching up.

Someone had brought out a portable basketball net and backboard and set it up on the street, and we watched a group of boys take turns trying to make a basket. Two of them were George's sons, J.T. and Charlie, they were about eight and ten. Often when they were about to shoot, they glanced over at George to make sure he was looking.

At one point he called them over and introduced them to me, and they were polite, but I could see they were waiting for their father to release them, so they could go back to their game.

"This is Sergeant North," said George. "He works with me."

The older boy, Charlie, nodded hello and then looked at me curiously.

"Are you the one on TV?" he asked.

"Yep," I said. "I'm the one."

"Sorry," George said to me, embarrassed. "Boys, go back out there now."

Charlie gave me another look, but they turned and took off.

"I'm really sorry," said George. "You shouldn't be getting it from my kids."

"It's okay." We watched Charlie grab the basketball and make a nice free throw.

"Two fine-looking boys," I said.

He smiled and nodded, pleased. We talked for a while about guys we knew in common, and the latest rumors about which captain or inspector might get transferred where.

The DJ started playing the Village People's "YMCA," and the street in front of us quickly filled with kids and young mothers, dancing and raising their arms to spell out the letters.

"I've been wanting to ask you something, Eddie," said George.

"Shoot."

He took a sip of beer. "You ever take stuff home?"

"What do you mean?" I asked, though I had a feeling I knew.

"You know, collect souvenirs from work?"

"Naw," I said, watching the boys aim at the basket. "I don't do that."

George paused a moment, then asked, "You ever done it?"

"Naw," I said again. "I've never been into that kind of thing."

George nodded, considering my answer. There was a shout from the makeshift basketball court, a boy was clutching onto the ball, and Charlie, a foot taller, was trying to violently wrest it away.

"Charlie!" George called. "Come over here."

He let go of the ball and jogged over to us. "It's my turn," he said, out of breath. "He won't give it to me."

"Charlie, that boy's smaller than you, you can't push him around like that."

"But, Dad . . ."

"He's just a little kid—you could hurt him. You be the grown-up one, okay?"

Charlie nodded. When he was gone, George asked, "You got any kids?"

I shook my head. "No, I was married once, but didn't have kids."

George talked about his boys for a while, and I wondered whether he was going to get back to the previous conversation. But he never did. Apparently he had found out what he wanted to know.

# six

t noon on Tuesday, there was a huge rally on the
Penn campus for David Danforth, the black professor
charged with killing a cop. I had known about the rally for several
days. What I hadn't known was that I'd be attending it, with
Michelle. As a member of the crowd.

She broke the news to me that morning, over the phone.

"You have to go with me," she said.

"I do?"

"You have to see what these Danforth people are like."

"I know what they're like. They're idiots."

"I want you to go with me anyway."

"Is this your idea of a date?"

"Very funny. No, I've had it with this department, Eddie. I've
talked to everybody—Homicide, Internal Affairs, West Detectives. I
told them all what's on the Danforth website, that it might be connected to what happened to Buster. But no one takes it seriously."

Michelle had shown me the Danforth site on her computer at
her apartment the last time I had spent the night. The site's home
page had a slick graphic with the slogan "Justice For Danforth.org,"
and underneath was a photo of Danforth giving a speech somewhere.

On the left side of the page was a list of the site's contents, stuff
like "Celebrity Supporters" and "News Articles."

If you clicked the one that said "Community Voices," there was a list of comments that people had sent in. Several of them were from "Tariq." Michelle called up a few.

One began: *When will the Police learn their lesson? First they beat up a Councilman and then someone tries to teach them a lesson, and do they do anything? No. They still need to be punished, and whoever does it will be a hero.*

Michelle had printed out the messages and shown them to detectives, but still no one was interested.

"They all say, 'People are always putting outrageous stuff on the Internet—it doesn't mean anything.' One lieutenant in Homicide that I had an 'overheated imagination.' "

"Nice."

"He said it was admirable that I was supporting Bobby Boland's family, but I shouldn't let my emotions get in the way."

"What an asshole."

"He said they weren't going to start accusing the councilman's son of going around trying to get revenge for his father."

"Wait, did you actually accuse Carl Knight?"

"No, not at all. I said it could be any Danforth supporter. But he wasn't listening, his eyes were glazing over. They're all like that, Eddie, every one of them."

"Don't they know who you are?"

"Yeah, in fact, I think that's the only reason they talk to me, because my father was the commissioner. But it's sort of like, thanks for the tip, little girl. Now, go back home."

Michelle was thirty-two—four years younger than me. Hardly a little girl.

"I need your help, Eddie. Come to this rally with me, see what these people are like up close. Maybe you can convince someone to pay attention to this."

"Oh, yeah," I said. "I'm really in good standing with the Police Department right now. *I'm* the guy who's going to give you credibility."

She was quiet for a moment, then said, "It's important to me, Eddie. I need you."

So now what could I say? Nothing, which was why, three hours later, I found myself on the Penn campus, standing with Michelle in the middle of a crowd of rabid cop-haters.

We were in our street clothes, and I was wearing my usual lame disguise of baseball cap and sunglasses. It was loads of fun. On our left was a white guy in blond dreadlocks—a concept I never understood—holding a handmade sign that said "Police are the Real Killers!" On our right were two bare-chested guys wearing plastic pig masks with little blue cop hats. Wasn't that something from the sixties?

Behind us, a young woman was yakking on her cell phone.

"You've got to get everyone in the dorm to come," she was saying. "They say if we get enough people here, the police won't try to storm us, or whatever it is they do. Is that what it's called, storming? You know, when they go through a crowd of protesters, beating people with their clubs?"

I wanted to turn around to her and say, *No, we call that aerobic exercise.*

At least it was a beautiful day, with a cloudless, deep-blue sky, the kind of day that may be common in places like California, but is so rare on the East Coast that when it happens people come out of their houses blinking in the bright sunshine, saying, What's wrong—why isn't the sky gray?

The rally was in an open area of grass and crisscrossed sidewalks, hemmed in by a ring of imposing old reddish-brown buildings, very Ivy-League-campus-like. Some of the buildings were actually covered with ivy, which made you wonder whether they did that on purpose, for the effect.

Not that I had anything against Penn. If I had kids and an extra forty thousand dollars a year to throw around, it's probably where I would have sent them. I just wouldn't have wanted them to associate with the other students.

Penn students weren't like real people. They had an amazing sense of entitlement, as if the world owed them everything. And they didn't seem to have much use for us cops.

You'd be walking near the campus, in uniform, and a group of students would pass by, and you'd smile and say hello, and they'd just ignore you. Like you were just another blue-collar worker to them, someone to clean the pool or take away the trash.

But of course the moment they ran into trouble—the moment they needed you—then they paid attention. Please, Officer, my apartment got broken into, please, you've got to help me. And of course you do, because that's your job. You didn't ask to be assigned to the police district that had the Penn campus, but that was your tough luck—every district has at least one undesirable neighborhood.

A stage had been set up in front of the undergraduate library, and for the past twenty minutes it had been occupied by a band playing crap music.

Finally the rally started. Carl Knight was introduced, and walked up to the microphone to wild cheers, like he was some kind of rock star. He was wearing an orange T-shirt that said "Justice for Danforth."

"I'm sure you've all heard by now what happened to my father last week," Carl told the crowd. "One thing's for sure: it would not have happened, it could not have happened, if Professor Danforth's proposals had been adopted in Philadelphia."

He waited for the crowd to yell its approval, which it did.

"As I'm sure many of you know, Professor Danforth believes that in our society, the main goal of the police is to protect the rich. And, of course, to keep the poor in their place.

"You can see it everywhere, especially right here in Philly: the police are an occupying army in the poor neighborhoods, and they're border guards in the rich neighborhoods."

I looked around as the crowd cheered again. Half of them kids from rich neighborhoods.

"Now, some people believe the solution is to have the police watched over by citizen review boards," said Carl. "But Professor Danforth goes beyond that. He proposes a radical idea—that in poor neighborhoods, regular police should be replaced with a police force from the community."

"Yeah, that's really going to work," I said.

Michelle poked me in the ribs with her elbow. "Shhh."

"They alone patrol the streets," said Carl. "They alone make an arrest *if and when* a crime occurs. They alone decide whether there is enough real evidence to prosecute."

"This is all very interesting," I told Michelle. "And I must admit, I find Professor Danforth's theories quite scintillating. Can we go now?"

"Shhh."

"You can see why this is such a dangerous idea to the powers that be," said Carl, "and why they want to lock Professor Danforth away in prison. Because if you have community police, then you don't have the racist police keeping the poor in their place. You don't have police harassing young African-American and Latino men for simply walking down the street."

Loud cheers.

"And," he said, anger coming into his voice, "you don't have racist police beating up black men who happen to be driving through West Philadelphia in their cars."

Carl was looking right at me. What could I do, I just looked back. He obviously recognized me. I waited for him to announce my presence to the crowd. *There he is,* I expected him to say. *There's one of the racist cops right now.*

"If it's any consolation," Michelle said, keeping her eyes on Carl, "he knows I'm here, too. He knows who I am."

"Good," I said, "then we'll shoot our way out of here together."

But Carl didn't give us up, at least not then. Instead, he introduced the rally's star attraction—Glenn Rippen, Hollywood actor. Actually, Hollywood has-been.

Rippen was one of dozens of celebrities who had been recruited to support Danforth. It was sickening. These celebrities knew nothing about the case, other than what they had gotten from the Danforth people. Which was, basically, that a heroic Penn professor, who had acted in self-defense, was being railroaded on murder charges solely because of his fight against police brutality.

It was nice and simple, easy to understand. And how could a Hollywood type fail to support such a noble cause?

Rippen, with his TV anchorman's haircut and toothpaste-ad smile, waved at the crowd. Many applauded politely, as if they weren't quite sure who he was.

That wasn't surprising. Rippen's sole claim to fame was that, a few years back, he had costarred in a dumb detective show supposedly set in Philadelphia. It was one of those shows where every scene, every line is totally predictable.

Rippen was the young cop, learning the ropes, getting too caught up in the lives of the people he was supposed to help. His partner was the gruff but lovable veteran, dispensing insults and advice in the same breath.

They talked to each other in what was supposed to be hilarious cop banter, which usually went like this:

Older cop: "I'm hungry, let's stop for doughnuts."

Younger cop: "If you eat any more doughnuts, we're going to have to get new shocks for the car."

Ha, ha, ha, ha.

Their captain was always complaining about getting "heat from downtown," and always threatening to pull Rippen and his partner off the case. He never did, though, and each week the two heroes solved the crime and marched the bad guys off to jail.

There were some shots of Philly neighborhoods, though most of the filming actually took place in Los Angeles. Which would explain why the Philadelphia sky was blue all the time.

Now I had to listen to Rippen give a speech about how David Danforth was the victim of injustice.

"He's obviously an expert on Philly cops," I said. "After all, he did play one on TV."

Michelle rolled her eyes.

Fortunately, Rippen didn't know enough about the case to talk very long, and with another wave at the crowd, he gave the microphone to the next speaker.

For the next half hour, there was a mind-numbing succession of speeches from other Danforth supporters—fellow Penn professors, students, leaders of various fringe groups. Michelle wouldn't let me leave.

"I want you to see," she said.

"I'm seeing, I'm seeing. I just want a beer."

Finally Carl took the microphone back, and said he wanted to present the "facts" of the Danforth case.

"Oh, yeah," said Michelle, "I'm sure he's got the facts."

"Shhh," I said, and poked my elbow in her direction.

"What you won't read in the newspapers," said Carl, "is that the police officer who was killed thought of himself as a real cowboy. You know, one of those cops that tries to be a tough guy."

Which was not even close to the truth. Bobby Boland wasn't in my squad, but our schedules overlapped enough that I got to know him. He was definitely not a cowboy. In March, when this happened, he had been on the job for about four years, all in the 20th. That was a long time for a combat district, but he never got hard and cynical the way a lot of cops do. Just the opposite—he had a kind of gentleness about him.

"I'm going to tell you how it all started," said Carl, quieting his voice, drawing in the crowd. "It's late at night. This cowboy cop is riding in his police car through the streets, on the lookout for young black men to harass. Suddenly he finds what he's looking for. A young black man named Devon Horn, who is minding his own business, just walking home."

Devon Horn was not minding his own business. He had just robbed a corner store at gunpoint, about eight blocks away. The owner had called 911 with a description: black male, late teens or early twenties, blue sweater with yellow stripes, blue jeans, black sneakers. About fifteen minutes later, Bobby spotted Devon Horn at 57th and Hazel. Everything matched, including the sweater: it was dark blue and had a bright yellow stripe circling the chest.

Actually, Devon Horn saw Bobby first. A woman who had been walking her dog later told us that the man in the blue sweater ducked into an alley as the police car was cruising by. But Bobby must have caught a glimpse of Horn, because he stepped on the gas, drove up onto the sidewalk at the alley, jumped out of his car, and pursued him into the darkness.

At that point, Bobby should have got on his handheld radio and called for backup. We don't know why he didn't. Maybe he was running too hard, and was afraid that if he slowed down, he'd lose the suspect. Maybe he did try to call but was in a dead spot, where he couldn't send or receive transmissions. There's a few of those in the district, and it can be pretty scary when you find yourself in one.

We do know that the radio itself was working properly. Twice that night, Bobby called for help, and both times, his voice came over the air with chilling clarity.

"When Devon Horn saw the cop," said Carl, "he started running. Why? Because he recognized the cop, he knew that this particular cop was a world of trouble. And, of course, the cop chased after Devon Horn. Why? Because in this city, if you run from the cops, they assume you must be guilty of something. Anything. They'll even shoot you if you don't stop running. They don't even have to know why you're running. It happens all the time."

I glanced over at Michelle. She was starting to get tense.

"You want to go?" I asked.

She shook her head no as Carl continued.

"This cop gets out of his car and chases Devon Horn through an alley. He's got his gun out. He fires at him, once, twice, three times. Then after he fires, he yells, 'Halt!' *After* he fires."

"Bullshit!" I said, loud enough to draw a few looks.

Bobby never fired his gun that night. When it was recovered at his side, no rounds had been discharged.

If Carl heard me, he chose not to respond.

"Devon Horn is now running for his life," he said. "He has to get away from this killer cop. But where does he go? He tries to get to a place of safety. His house. It's not far. He runs up to the house, to the door. But he doesn't have his keys. He's pounding on the door. 'Let me in! Let me in!' The cop catches up to him, the cop says to him, 'I got you now. I'm gonna blow you away, motherfucker.'"

This, as Michelle and I knew, was more bullshit. It was ten o'clock at night, but there were still a few people on the street, there were witnesses. They saw Horn emerge from an alley and run around a corner onto Larchwood Street, where he lived. They saw him run up onto the porch of his rowhouse and start pounding on the front door. Bobby was far behind, still in the alley. Horn may have believed that if he was able to get into his house quickly, he would be okay. But no one was home. And so Horn was still pounding when Bobby came out of the alley and cornered him on his porch. Neighbors heard the noise and came to their windows, cracked open their front doors. Witnesses said Bobby had his gun out. They heard him order Horn to put his hands on the door. The part about Bobby saying he was going to blow Horn away came from Horn himself, later. No witness heard that.

"So now what does Devon Horn do?" Carl asked. "There's nowhere to run. He's yelling, 'Don't shoot me! Don't shoot me! I don't have a gun.'"

Bobby apparently believed the suspect still had the gun used in the robbery. Horn now had his hands on the door, and Bobby quickly patted him down. There was no gun. We found it later, in the alley. The fingerprints on it were Horn's.

Bobby got on his radio, for the first time, and called for backup.

"I got the guy from the store robbery," he told the dispatcher. "Apprehension made." He was still so out of breath he could barely talk.

What happened next happened fast, and every witness seemed to give a different account. Bobby had his handcuffs out, and he holstered his gun and started to cuff Horn's left wrist. But then Horn spun back around and bulldozed into Bobby, knocking him off the porch, down the steps, and onto the ground.

"Devon Horn feared for his life," Carl told the crowd. "And so, out of self-preservation, he did the only thing he could do, he started to fight. To fight for his life."

It was at that moment that Professor David Danforth, Devon Horn's next-door neighbor, came out onto his porch. He was wearing dark slacks and a gray knit shirt, and he had a .38-caliber pistol tucked in his waistband.

We don't know whether Bobby saw Danforth's gun, at least at first. He was probably too busy wrestling with Horn. The suspect was younger than Bobby, and maybe stronger, but Bobby had more experience in situations like this, and he flipped Horn facedown onto the ground and then straddled his back. Witnesses said Bobby was looking around, probably for his handcuffs. They had been knocked a few feet away. Danforth was on his steps now. "What are you doing to that boy?" he bellowed.

"Now," said Carl, "you have to picture in your mind. Professor Danforth is a very respectable member of the community. He's a college professor. He's in his house, and he hears all this commotion outside. He looks out his window—there's a cop out there, abusing his neighbor. Right outside his door.

"Professor Danforth wants to stop it. But he knows that if he goes out there, he's likely to get abused himself. So he takes along some personal protection. If you were in that situation, I'm sure you would, too."

"Yeah," I said, loud enough for my voice to carry to the stage, "everybody's got a thirty-eight sitting around their house."

Students nearby turned in the direction of my voice. Carl's eyes rested on me a moment.

"Professor Danforth goes outside with his personal protection," he told the crowd. "Which, yes, is a gun. Which he bought to protect his family. He politely—politely—asks the cop, 'What's going on?' As he has every right to do. It's in front of his house, after all. The cop doesn't answer. So Professor Danforth asks again. The cop still doesn't answer."

By now, Bobby must have seen the gun. And Danforth was far from polite. All the witnesses said he came down the steps from his porch and demanded that Bobby—who was still on the ground on top of Horn—let his captive go.

"I will not allow this!" Danforth yelled. "Not in my neighborhood, not in front of my house!"

Bobby had two threats now, one not yet under control, the other unknown but clearly dangerous. He had called for help, but he knew that until it arrived, he would have to face the threats alone.

"The cop tells Professor Danforth to go back into his house," said Carl. "But of course he's not going to that. Not until the cop tells him what's going on. But the cop doesn't do that."

Somehow Bobby managed to get to the cuffs, and he wrestled them onto Horn's wrists. Horn was on his stomach, cuffed in the back, and Bobby could finally get to his feet and deal with Danforth.

"Get back onto your porch and into your house," Bobby ordered. "This has nothing to do with you."

"No, you're wrong," Danforth yelled. "This has everything to do with me. I will not allow police officers to brutalize young black men right before my eyes. Do you hear me? I will not allow it!"

Bobby didn't know what Danforth was prepared to do—how could he have? He faced Danforth and put his hand on his gun.

"Turn around and put your hands on your head," he ordered.

Other cops might have handled the situation in another way. I probably would have pulled my gun out and stuck it in Danforth's face. But that wasn't what Bobby did. He simply put his hand on his gun. A warning.

"That's when the cop goes for his gun," said Carl. "He's going to shoot down Professor Danforth in cold blood."

With his free hand, Bobby called for help for the last time. "Get me an assist," he told Radio. "Fifty-three-fifty-two Larchwood. I got a man with a gun here."

Cars were already speeding toward him, the closest was probably not more than a block away. Witnesses said they heard the sirens. Bobby must have, too.

One of the odd things about that night was that none of the witnesses—and there had to be at least a dozen by then—none of them said they saw Danforth pull his gun. It was in his waistband one moment, the next, in his hand, pointed at Bobby Boland.

"Are you going to shoot me, is that it?" Danforth screamed at Bobby. "Are you going to shoot me?"

"No," said Bobby, and he quickly lifted his hand off his gun.

And Danforth fired.

Maybe Bobby's move startled him. Maybe it wouldn't have made any difference.

"Professor Danforth shoots the cop, yes, but in self-defense. Luckily, he hit the cop first. Professor Danforth was faster on the draw. In the Wild West, that wasn't a crime, that was survival."

Bobby was wearing a bulletproof vest under his police shirt. The bullet hit the vest on the right side of the chest, knocking him back onto the ground. According to the Medical Examiner's report, the impact broke a rib and bruised his right lung, but didn't penetrate his skin. Bobby was lying on the ground now, gasping for breath, writhing in pain. He looked up and saw Danforth's gun, still pointed at him. Bobby struggled to get his own gun out. Danforth fired again.

This time, the bullet went through Bobby's left eye and into his brain, killing him instantly.

"It was pure self-defense," said Carl. "Professor Danforth was protecting his home, his family, his neighbors—and himself—from a cowboy cop with a gun."

"Fucking asshole," I said, though low enough so only Michelle could hear. "I'll show him a cowboy cop with a gun."

"As you all know," said Carl, "Devon Horn is now in prison. And Professor Danforth could be sent there for the rest of his life."

Carl had finished his little fairy tale and was wrapping up the rally.

"Don't forget, the trial starts next Monday," he told the crowd. "We're going to need you at the Criminal Justice Center, across from City Hall, we're going to be having rallies every day."

I glanced at Michelle. She was still tense, but not as upset as I might have thought.

"You're handling this pretty well," I said.

"Well, after you've heard it about twenty times, the shock kind of wears off. He's leaving the stage, c'mon, I want to talk to him."

She took off through the crowd, and I had to move fast to keep up with her. We got to the side of the stage just as Carl was coming down the steps.

"Hello, Michelle," he said, grim-faced. Then, looking at me, "What's he doing here?"

"The sergeant's a friend of mine," said Michelle. "He's never seen your dog-and-pony show before."

Carl pointed at me. "You're going to go to jail, you know that."

"So I've heard."

Carl studied me, like a soldier looking at his prisoner of war. So here's what the enemy looks like. He's not so tough, after all.

"Carl, who's Tariq?" Michelle asked.

He turned to her in surprise. "Tariq?"

"The person who's been writing all this 'Let's kill cops' stuff on your website. Who is he?"

Carl gave a little laugh. "People can write whatever they want."

"I know that. But who is he?"

"Why would you care?"

"Why? I'm sure you heard that someone tried to kill a cop in West Philly last week."

"Yeah?"

"It might have been this Tariq person. Or possibly one of your followers, who might have taken Tariq just a little too seriously."

"Yeah, right, it was a Danforth supporter, of course it would have to be one of us." He shook his head. "This is so typical of the way you people think."

"So who's Tariq, Carl?"

"I don't know, Michelle. And even if I did, I wouldn't tell you."

"Why? Because you agree with his views?"

"I didn't say that."

"It doesn't bother you that you might know who the person is? That he might have even been here today?"

Carl waved his hand at Michelle, like he wanted her to just disappear.

"I cannot believe I'm standing here listening to this," he said. He started to walk away, but then stopped short and pointed at me again.

"You're going to jail," he said.

We watched him walk around the rear of the stage, where some of the other Danforth people had gathered.

"He could help us if he wanted to," said Michelle.

"It's not going to happen."

"Yeah. And who else are we going to ask? I don't exactly know any of Carl's associates."

"I do," I said.

She looked at me. "Really?"

"His cousin, Victor Knight."

"And how do you know *him*?"

"Let's just say he provides me with information from time to time."

"He's a *snitch*?"

I glanced around, making sure no one could hear, and then said softly, "One of the best."

### seven

**ictor Knight knew everybody. At least everybody** with a criminal record. He lived up in the 16th, our neighboring police district to the north. Unlike some guys, whose sphere of influence was limited to their own neighborhoods, Victor had connections throughout West Philadelphia, including the 20th. This made him very valuable as a snitch.

He had been a fairly high-level drug dealer at one time, but had been convicted and put on probation so often that prosecutors were actually on the verge of being able to send him to prison. That would count as a minor miracle in Philly, where the jails were so overcrowded you practically had to kill someone to be guaranteed a cell.

As a result of this pressure, Victor had curtailed his drug dealing, or so he said. He seemed to be too plugged in to be out of it altogether. And he had adopted a very effective survival technique: he'd formed a secret alliance with the police. He would provide me, and, I assumed, at least one or two other cops, with information about various drug operations, and in exchange, we wouldn't look too hard at what he was doing. It was a common deal with the devil— you let one guy go to get a wider catch. Usually the people he ratted out were his and his pals' rivals, but that was okay. As long as he didn't throw it in our faces by being too obvious about his own activity.

Victor ran a small auto-repair shop in the 16th. He once told me that his uncle, the councilman, had bought the place and put him in charge, to help keep him out of trouble. That's how I knew about the family connection. Knight was a common name in West Philly, and most people didn't know they were related.

I told Michelle that talking to Victor might be a long shot. I'd never heard him mention his cousin Carl, so I had no idea how close they were. Didn't matter, she said. It was worth a shot. And so the next afternoon before work, I drove her to Victor's garage, on 42nd Street near Parrish.

Although we wore our street clothes, we still stood out, two white people in a poor black neighborhood. I knew Victor wouldn't mind, though. If anyone noticed, they'd probably just think we were there to buy drugs.

We certainly wouldn't be there to get our car fixed. This was not the kind of garage you found in other neighborhoods. Everything was off the books—cash only. You didn't pay much for parts, but then again you didn't ask where they came from. You could also take your car there night or day—the place was open twenty-four hours. Victor lived upstairs, and there was a bell that you could ring in the middle of the night, and he'd come down and make emergency repairs.

It didn't even look like a regular garage. It was once a normal two-story rowhouse, but the entire first floor had been opened up to create the single garage bay, so that you got your car worked on in someone's former living room. The rest of the block was still completely residential, and there were rowhouses on both sides of the garage. The garage door was open, but Victor was nowhere around.

Michelle couldn't believe it. "He just leaves the place unattended in the middle of the day?"

"Yeah, sometimes," I said. "But I don't think he's ever gone for very long."

When we returned to the garage a half hour later, Victor was inside, working on a beat-up old Lincoln, doing something under the dashboard. He didn't seem overly happy to see me.

"What the fuck happened to my uncle? Why'd your boys fuck him up like that?"

"They didn't do nothin' to him, pal."

He almost laughed. "Yeah, I heard that before. 'He was beat up when we found him.' How come us black people are *always* beat up when the cops find us?"

"I give up, Victor, how come?"

Victor was in his mid-twenties, like Carl, but they didn't look at all alike. Victor was leaner, his face was harder, his eyes watchful, alert. But in a way he was also more relaxed, more laid-back. Victor was of the street, where people don't have much left to lose, and the prevailing philosophy is that whatever's going to happen is going to happen anyway.

"I seen you on TV," he said. "You're getting to be famous. You got that whole cover-up thing goin' on."

"Whatever you heard is bullshit."

This time he did laugh. "Yeah, that's what they all say. Heard that before. Who's this?"

Since we had arrived, Victor had barely taken his eyes off Michelle. She was wearing tight faded jeans, with the cuffs over her brown cowboy boots, and a white blouse. Her soft brown hair, usually up under her police hat, was down around her shoulders.

"This is Michelle," I said. "She's a friend."

Victor gave me an astonished laugh.

"A friend? She's a cop, you don't think I can tell that?"

He started to act insulted, but lost interest and turned back to Michelle.

"But you are a pretty cop, no doubt about that."

"Thanks, I guess," said Michelle.

"Speaking of which," he said to me, "I got a waterbed upstairs now. The ladies love it. Gets me lots of pussy."

"I'll bet it does."

"Some of it's customer pussy. Bitch can't pay, she got to fuck."

I knew he was saying all this as much for Michelle's benefit as mine, he wanted to see how she was going to react. But Michelle was just casually surveying the garage, unaffected. She had been a cop on the streets for seven years, there wasn't much she hadn't heard before.

Victor saw her looking around, and said, "Careful where you step. Don't want to get grease on them nice clothes."

Which basically meant she couldn't move an inch. The whole place was in disarray, full of tools and discarded engine parts, and strangely out-of-place items like old TVs and VCRs.

There was a workbench scattered with tools, but it was also crowded with light sockets and doorknobs and empty flowerpots, as if people traded stuff they found on the street for car repairs. Against the side wall was a grease-smeared refrigerator. Once, when I asked Victor about it, he opened it for me. It was full of mysterious tools, like valve-spring compressors, top to bottom. Next to it was an old safe that looked like it was from the 1920s. Also a tool chest.

We talked for a little longer, then Victor said, "Y'all are going to let me know when we're done with the chitchat, right? 'Cause, you know, I got stuff to do around here."

"Like get the place condemned?" I asked.

"Hey, don't fuckin' knock it, it serves the purpose."

Which we both knew was providing a front for his other activities.

"Tell you why we came by," I said. "There's something we want you to do. And it will earn you a very big deposit in the favor bank."

"How big?"

"You might be able to name your own price."

"Damn, what you want me to do, beat up some black people for you?"

"You're really hilarious, Victor, has anyone ever told you that?"

"All the time. The ladies love it." He smiled at Michelle, but she just rolled her eyes.

"You heard about that cop getting shot at in his car the other day," I said.

"Yeah?"

I gestured to Michelle to have her explain. She told Victor about the possible Danforth connection, particularly Tariq, and how Carl was unwilling to cooperate.

"I don't know nothin' about that Danforth thing," said Victor. "That's Carl's deal, that ain't mine."

"But you know he's been involved in it," I said.

Victor gave a sarcastic laugh. "He thinks he's helping the 'black community.' That's his thing these days. Except that the boy's never been on the fuckin' street. None of them people have."

"They've got some radical ideas."

"Radical? They wouldn't even know what the fuck radical is. That's college bullshit, that's play stuff. Don't mean nothin' on the street."

I let his words settle toward the ground, then said, "We'd like you to check around. See if Carl knows anything about Tariq. See if anybody does."

Victor looked at me. "What the fuck? You want me to rat out my cousin? What you take me for?"

"I'm not asking you to rat out anybody," I said. "We're just trying to find out who this Tariq is."

"Well, I ain't the one to help you. I really don't have nothing to do with Carl no more."

"You enemies or something?" I asked.

"Fuck, we used to hang out, we came up together, in Germantown. But then he got into all this college bullshit, and now the boy's too fucking good to talk to me. His father's not like that. But Carl is. So fuck him."

"You ever play Monopoly?" I asked.

"When I was a kid."

"You remember the Get-out-of-jail-free card?"

"Yeah?"

"You want one?"

This stopped Victor, as I knew it would. Another arrest would likely mean prison. If I could get him off the hook . . .

"You can't fuckin' do that."

"Wanna bet?"

Victor thought about it for a moment. "No way I can do nothin'
for you this time. But you come back with that card next time, you
and me can make a deal."

"There may not be a next time," I said. "This is it."

"Then there ain't nothing I can do. Like I said, me and Carl don't
talk."

"Can't you give him a call, patch things up?"

Victor shrugged. "Maybe. But it don't matter. He's family, and I
ain't gonna rat out my family."

He said this as if he didn't really expect me to understand. As if
we were from such separate worlds that we could talk the same
language but never really communicate, or know each other.
Maybe he was right.

But then he had a smile again, to show there were no hard feelings.

"You hang on to that card," he said to me.

He turned to Michelle. "And you, pretty lady, you can come back
any time you want. 'Specially if you wear them cowboy boots."


**That night, the** squad got together at Fibber McGee's Grille, for
the first time since we took Buster there after he almost got shot. It
was a block from Penn, and was mostly a hangout for students. But
we went there anyway—it was one of the few decent bars in the
district.

Two things attracted us to Fibber's in particular. First, it had a
huge rectangular bar, with stools all around, and plenty of space on
one side where a large group of guys could stand around and shoot
the shit. Second, the place was populated by large flocks of female
students, who often wore very revealing attire, such as tight
stretchy tops, which led us to give Fibber's its nickname, which
was The Nipple Farm.

It was great, particularly after a long night of slogging around with society's festering lowlife. We'd get off work at midnight and head over, still trying to shake off the stink of the streets, and when we walked in the door of Fibber's, there was all this sweet-smelling sexy freshness. That and a cold beer was like diving into a pool on a sweltering summer afternoon.

Not that any of us had a chance with these girls, not even the younger cops who were the same age. Almost none of the cops had any college, they were just $32,000-a-year stiffs who'd max out at $42,000 in ten years. What would these girls want with any of us?

We were content to just enjoy the view. It gave us something to look at while we had to listen to Ralph or somebody tell, for the hundredth time, how he single-handedly disarmed a man with a gun. Yeah, Ralph, that's real interesting. Hey, Charlie, take a look at that rack. *Damn.*

That night, there were about fifteen or twenty of us from the district at the bar. Buster, Yvonne and Marisol, Tony D, Paulie, our usual crowd. It was Marisol's birthday, so it was kind of a celebration. As if we needed an excuse to go out drinking. Mutt was there, but not Roy. He had called in sick that afternoon.

After a half hour or so, Billy and Hap, two plainclothes burglary guys from the 16th, walked in the door. I waved them over to join us, and got them both beers.

"We just came in for a quick one," said Billy.

"Too bad," I said. "Now you got to stay all night."

Michelle arrived a little later. She sometimes filled in at the 20th, and she knew most of the people in my squad. They were all happy to see her, particularly Marisol and Yvonne, who gave her hugs.

"Didn't think you'd ever come back and see us," Marisol said. "Now that you're in *Hollywood.*"

That's what we all called the 9th District, across the river. It covered the western half of Center City, Philadelphia's downtown. Slick blue-glass skyscrapers, valet-parking restaurants, multimillion-dollar brownstones where the city's movers and shakers got the

*New York Times* delivered every morning. Not exactly like the 20th, where a mover and shaker was more likely to be a strung-out heroin addict desperately trying to find his next hit.

"Yes, yes," Michelle said, primly lifting her nose into the air. "I have generously decided to bestow my presence on you little people here."

Most of us had changed into street clothes, but some guys hadn't brought theirs into work, so they made do the best they could. White T-shirts—the ones they had worn under their police shirts—and their dark blue uniform pants. And, of course, their shiny black cop shoes. Maybe not exactly a turn-on for the Penn girls, but who gave a shit about them and their tits anyway, right?

Probably the majority of us were carrying our guns, under our untucked polo shirts or in ankle holsters. Just a cop habit. You stagger out of the bar at two o'clock in the morning, someone might come out of the shadows. Or someone might even try to rob the bar. Though to be honest, Fibber McGee's probably wasn't the most likely target. Usually, the bars that got hit were in working-class neighborhoods, and every once in a while a group of off-duty cops would be inside, sipping their beers. Not a good career move for the robbers. They would come in with sawed-off shotguns, planning to take everyone's wallet and whatever was in the cash register, and suddenly two dozen Glocks would be pointed in their faces. Someone would call 911—eventually. And then it would be for an ambulance, to take the robbers to the hospital.

Tonight, our get-together at Fibber's was a little more subdued than usual. Maybe a lot more. There had been a story in the *Post* that morning on Mutt, Roy, and me, and everyone was doing their best not to talk about it. That made things a little uncomfortable. Some of the guys kept glancing over at me and Mutt, particularly Mutt, but no one wanted to broach the subject.

The story was written by a reporter named Ben Bacon. I hadn't met him, but I'd heard all about him. Apparently his job on the paper was to trash cops, because he did it all the time. Whenever there was a negative story about the Police Department, or about some cop getting into trouble, his name was on it. Anything to sell newspapers. Here's how his story began:

> During the past five years, nine prior physical-abuse complaints have been filed against Alan Hope, one of the two Philadelphia police officers being investigated for the beating of Councilman Sonny Knight, according to police sources.
>
> Eight of those complaints were dismissed by Internal Affairs as "unsustained," and the ninth resulted in a one-week suspension, the sources said.
>
> There has also been one physical-abuse complaint against the sergeant under investigation in the case, Edward North. There have been no previous complaints against the second officer, Roy Knopfler.
>
> Although only one of the complaints against Hope was sustained, a high-ranking police official said nine complaints in five years is unusual, and Hope's supervisors should have been monitoring him more closely.
>
> "Nine's a lot," the police official said. "Usually where there's smoke, there's fire."

Actually, nine *was* a lot. I had no idea Mutt had that many complaints against him. There had been two since I'd been in the district, but both were total bullshit, like the one against me. Still, it did give me pause. I remembered again the skinny drunk Mutt had decked outside that bar on Locust—and that wasn't even one of the nine complaints.

The fact that most were dismissed didn't mean much, I knew that. Sometimes witnesses back out, sometimes the guys in Internal Affairs decide to believe a cop rather than some smartass street hustler who's probably just trying to get some money out of the city. You can never tell.

And now, at the bar, everyone was thinking about the story, and no one was bringing it up. Except Michelle, who asked me when I was getting a lawyer. It was about the tenth time she had asked.

Michelle and I had been sitting at the bar together, and when she got up to talk to a friend, Mutt came over and stood next to me. He ordered a bottle of Bud Light and got me another Rolling Rock.

"I'm getting worried about Roy," he said.

"What do you mean?"

"He's having trouble dealing with all this."

"I think we all are."

"Yeah, but Roy is . . . I don't know. It's like today. I talked to him—he's not sick, he just doesn't want to come in."

"He's got to come in."

"That's what I told him. But you know how when you talk to someone, and it's like they're not even listening? That's the way it is with Roy anymore."

I'd noticed the same thing. It was getting hard to talk to Roy.

"Tina is, like, going nuts," said Mutt. "She has no idea what to do."

Mutt took a long drink of beer, and sat the bottle down very gently, as if he were afraid he might just decide to smash it.

"Sonny Knight is fucking up Roy's life." Mutt shook his head. "Of course, he's fucking up my life, too, but Roy's got a family. He's got a real life to get fucked up, as opposed to mine. And you know what I want to know? Why is Sonny Knight doing this? You fuckin' tell me why."

"Mutt, I don't know."

I could see Mutt trying to calm himself down. It was hard for him. He took another sip of beer, a normal one this time.

It didn't surprise me that Mutt would be so concerned about Roy. When I'd put them together as partners two years before, they'd hit it off right away. Sometimes you never know with cops, what's going to make them click as a team. But Mutt and Roy did, probably because if they'd met under other circumstances, they no doubt would have become friends anyway.

"So, Sarge," he said, "think you might want to go over to Roy's with me? I was thinking maybe we could both talk to him, you know, away from work."

"Sure," I said. "If you think it might help."

"Yeah, I'm hoping."

Buster was coming over, carrying a gym bag.

"Hey, Mutt," he said. "Got something for you."

He put the bag down on the bar, unzipped it, and pulled out his scarred wooden nightstick.

"Here," said Buster, chomping on his gum, "take this for a second."

"Why?"

"Just take it."

Mutt shrugged and took the nightstick. Buster reached in the bag again and took out his point-and-shoot camera. This was Buster's new thing, taking pictures of the squad. Usually documenting the more humorous moments.

Mutt saw the camera and quickly put the stick on the bar next to his beer.

"You're not getting my picture with this."

"C'mon, Mutt," said Buster. "It'll be great."

"No way."

"Just one shot."

"Forget it."

Yvonne and Marisol were standing nearby, they saw this.

"Yeah, c'mon, Mutt," said Yvonne. "For posterity."

Paulie started egging Mutt on, too, and pretty soon everyone was yelling at him to just pick up the friggin' nightstick.

Mutt was getting red, but he was smiling. He knew what it meant—the squad wasn't taking the *Post* story that seriously, they weren't holding it against him. You don't bust somebody's balls unless you like them.

I looked around to see if anyone else was watching. But the music was loud, and the Penn students weren't paying us any attention.

Finally, Mutt picked the stick back up off the bar.

"Nightstick for sale, cheap," Buster said as the flash went off. "Only been used nine times."

We all laughed.

"How much you want for it?" Paulie called out.

But not everyone was joining in on the fun. Darryl Shay and his wagon partner, Ricky Veree, both black guys, had been quietly drinking their beers and watching the scene with unsmiling faces.

Now, Darryl walked over, ripped the nightstick out of Mutt's hand, and threw it to the floor.

The bar went silent.

"This is all a big joke to you, isn't it?" he said to Mutt.

"C'mon, Darryl," said Buster. "We're just having fun."

Darryl kept his eyes on Mutt. "I'll bet every one of those complaints, the guy was black, right?"

Mutt stared back, not saying anything.

"Right?" said Darryl. "They were all black, right?"

"Not all of them," Mutt said calmly. "One was your mother."

Darryl's fist was a blur, but Mutt was ready for him, he was swinging, too, and somehow they were able to hit each other in the face at the same moment. I'd never seen that happen before. The mutual impact knocked them both back, two or three feet apart, enough space for me and Buster and a couple of other guys to rush in, like Moses into the Red Sea. But we weren't Moses, and the waves rushed back in toward us, Mutt and Darryl slamming together again, and now Darryl laid a perfect right on Mutt's jaw, and Mutt went down.

We all got between them now, six or seven guys surrounding Darryl, pushing him away, another six or seven getting Mutt off the floor, moving him in the opposite direction.

There wasn't going to be any more drinking that night. It was time to go home.

# eight

In the back of my mind, I probably knew it was inevitable that Internal Affairs would find out about Dominic Russo. And later that week, the inevitable pulled up like a grime-covered, exhaust-belching city bus. It had finally reached my stop, and its door folded open for me to enter.

I was cruising in my patrol car in the east end of the district, along the Schuylkill River, looking at the Center City skyline. The Promised Land. Hollywood. Michelle was there, I wondered what kind of day she was having.

Just on our side of the river was the Schuylkill Expressway, a sad-sack of an interstate that cut through the middle of the city. Apparently it was built before they invented cars, because it was impossibly narrow and didn't have real entrance ramps. To merge with the traffic, you had to go from zero to sixty in two seconds, which was fine for all the cars that were outfitted with rocket engines. Everyone else just stepped on the gas and prayed.

If the highway wasn't designed for cars, it certainly wasn't designed for trucks—but they careened around the sharp curves anyway, frequently jackknifing and disgorging their loads out across the pavement. One day it might be cartons of ice cream, the next, live turkeys. You never knew what to expect.

Naturally, the highway offered rich hunting grounds for the tow truck drivers who prowled the city in search of crashes. You'd often see them near highway entrances, listening to their police scanners, waiting to swoop in. And when they got to a scene, they could be a real pain in the ass. We'd be trying to sort out an accident, and three or four tow trucks would arrive at the same time. The drivers would get into fights—sometimes with their fists—over who'd get to tow away the wrecked cars.

It wasn't uncommon for a tow truck to get to a scene even before an ambulance arrived.

*Hi, ma'am, sorry your arm's hanging off, is it okay if I tow your car to Joe's Body Shop? He'll get those dents out, give you a good deal. Can you just sign here? Maybe with your other hand?*

As I stopped for a light near the expressway's Walnut Street on-ramp, I glanced to my left and saw Dominic sitting in his parked tow truck, reading a newspaper. He looked up and saw me, and when the light turned green, he pulled out and followed me through the intersection. I knew he wanted to talk, and he was leaving it up to me to find a good place.

We were near the city's main post office, a massive, pre–World War II public works building that overlooked the Schuylkill River. I circled around behind it, then took a road that led under the Walnut Street bridge and to the lower level of the post office loading docks. We were under an elevated street, almost entirely hidden from public view. A dozen Postal Service tractor-trailers were backed into the docks, but it was quiet, there was no one around.

Dominic and I pulled over and got out.

"What's up?" I asked him.

"I was just trying to figure out how to reach you," he said.

"We're going to have to make this quick."

"Eddie, the garage I work out of? Two guys from Internal Affairs came by this morning, they wanted to talk to me."

"About what?"

"About you. About that night. I've been reading about it in the paper, what a load of bullshit. What they're accusing you of. Right?"

"What did they want to know?" I asked.

"Why did I show up there, who called me, that kind of thing. They asked, 'Did Eddie North call you? Did the FOP call you?'"

"Did you say you knew me?" I asked. I held my breath, praying he'd say no.

"Yeah, why not?"

"These guys from Internal Affairs," I said. "You remember their names?"

"There was a lieutenant, I think he said Desmond."

"You did tell them you were just passing by, didn't you?"

"Yeah, of course. But they said they didn't believe it. Somebody must of called me. 'Who was it, you better tell us or you're getting locked up.' I said nobody called me. It was like pissing into the wind."

"Talking to Internal Affairs can be like that. How'd they know it was your truck?"

"They said the councilman saw part of the name on the side. Eddie, I don't even know what they think I did."

"It's not you they're after," I said. "It's me. They think I called you to get that car out of there. You know, to clean up the scene."

"To cover up for your cops."

"Right."

"Shit. That means I'm involved, right?"

"As long as you tell the truth, you'll be fine."

He looked at me, worried. "Do you really believe that?"


**Late that afternoon,** I got a page I didn't recognize. When I called back on my cell, I reached a secretary at the FOP. Vince McAvoy wanted to talk to me, she said. Was there any way I could stop in this afternoon? I said sure, I could come by now.

I got George to cover for me and headed into Center City. I had no idea what McAvoy wanted, but at least it would give me an opportunity to talk about finally getting a lawyer. After that little conversation with Dominic, I figured it was just about time.

I had spoken with McAvoy only once since Sonny Knight was beaten, the day after. We'd talked about Knight's accusation, and he told me not to worry about it. He tried to be reassuring.

The Fraternal Order of Police's headquarters was on Spring Garden Street, on the northern edge of Center City. Upstairs was a large hall, for awards ceremonies and retirement parties and beef-and-beers. In the basement was a bar and lounge. On Friday nights, the dance floor would be crowded with cops and female cop-groupies—a strange breed of often overweight women we called badge-bangers—all doing the Electric Slide.

The offices for the FOP were on the ground floor, and I asked at the lobby desk for Vince McAvoy. He was on the phone, the receptionist said, could I wait?

Off the lobby was the Cop Shop, where you could buy all kinds of police-related paraphernalia—baseball caps, sweatshirts, jackets, mugs, all with the Philadelphia Police Department logo, gold charms that said "Cop's Girlfriend," even ceramic figurines that showed cops in action. There was a T-shirt that said "Justice for Bobby Boland," and another that showed a dog taking a shit on a copy of the *Philadelphia Post*.

I needed some new black leather gloves, so I picked up a pair. A secretary came in and said, "Sergeant North? Mr. McAvoy can see you now."

Vince McAvoy was one of the tallest cops I knew, and yet he had an impossibly tiny office, almost a broom closet, with plaques and certificates on the walls. When I walked in, he was behind his desk, crammed behind it, like a basketball player stuffed into a VW Bug.

He motioned for me to close the door, and the moment I did, he rose from his chair.

"What are you trying to pull?" he yelled.

"What? What do you mean?"

"What the fuck do you think I mean? Why didn't you tell me that tow truck driver was Dominic Russo?"

"To protect you, Vince. I figured the less you knew, the better—for you."

"Well, you figured wrong, pal. You want to get rid of Sonny Knight's car, fine, I don't fucking care what you do. You want to go to jail, fine. But what I want to know is, why did you have to get me jammed up doing it?"

"Wait a second, Vince. It wasn't like that."

"The fuck it wasn't. Some lieutenant from Internal Affairs came by here this afternoon, you know that? He thinks *I* called Russo. At your request."

"That's bullshit."

"Of course it's bullshit. But Eddie, why don't you go tell him who you *did* call to get Russo there. And get me off the fuckin' hook."

"I didn't call anybody, Vince. Russo was just passing by."

"Dominic fucking *Russo*? Just *happened* to be passing by?"

"That's right."

McAvoy pointed his finger at me, accusing. "Well, fuck you, too. You know, right after you called me that night, I left my house, I went over to my girlfriend's. And you know what they think now? They think the real reason I left was so that I could call Russo from a pay phone. So that there wouldn't be any record of it."

"All right, maybe I should have told you about Dominic."

"You're damn fucking right you should have. They're threatening me with obstruction of justice. At the very least I could lose my pension."

"I didn't mean for this to happen, Vince."

"Then tell them who you called."

"I didn't call anybody."

"I don't believe it."

"You want me to show you my cell phone bill? It'll show one call—made to you."

"Maybe you used another phone."

"You know what, Vince, you're worse than those assholes at IAD. Here you are, you're with the union, and you believe them, not me. You won't even give a cop the benefit of the doubt."

He shook his head at me, his face turning red, his mouth hanging open in a sarcastic sneer. "Dominic fucking *Russo*?"

"That's right, Vince. Sometimes things just happen."

"Yeah, well, you know what? I'm through with you. Get out of my office."

He didn't have to ask twice. I turned and yanked open the door and stormed out past the secretaries. It was only when I had climbed back into my car, seething, that I realized I had left the paper bag with my new gloves on his desk. And that I had never had a chance to ask him about a lawyer. Well, I thought, too late for either of those things now.

**Philadelphia has only** about three stars in the sky at night, four at the most. And that fourth one usually turns out to be a plane. You look up, and you say, Wow, you can see the stars tonight, look at that one, it's twinkling. No, wait, it's flashing. And it's moving. Damn, it's just another plane. You go out into the country, you look up, you see hundreds of stars, thousands of them, layer upon layer. You get the feeling most of those stars don't even exist in Philadelphia, as if the city lights have literally obliterated them, permanently erased them from the sky.

It's different with the moon. We get the same moon the country does, bright orange near the horizon, or gleaming white high over-head. And you can actually see the Man in the Moon. His features are just as sharp as they would be if you were out in a field, stand-ing next to a cow. Of course, half the time you think the moon is actually a streetlight, and when you realize your mistake, you're startled. What the heck is that? Oh, yeah, the moon. It's like some-thing that we probably shouldn't have, because of all the city lights, but for some reason we do. A little bit of nature creeps in, if you can call the moon nature.

That night there was a brilliant moon, not quite full, but still bright enough to wipe out all three of our stars. And it was actually casting its own shadows, which in the city is a very hard thing to do, considering the competition. Usually there's a moon but no moonlight, no soft, milky glow on anything. But on this night, there was.

I was sleepwalking through my shift, thinking not about the streets, but about Dominic Russo and Vince McAvoy and what I assumed was an impending visit from Gene Desmond. Unless I got indicted first. I hoped to hell they wouldn't lock me up in front of all my cops.

I had to talk to Michelle. She'd be clearheaded, she'd be able to put it in perspective. I imagined holding her tight, talking but then putting the talk aside. I really just wanted to be with her.

Not far from Penn, on a block of upscale, cooler-than-you stores, two patrol cars were parked along the curb. As I got closer, I could see George and two other cops standing on the brick sidewalk. They were peering through the plate-glass windows of a leather jacket store that was closed for the night. I hadn't heard any calls on Police Radio for a burglary alarm at the store, but maybe they had passed by and seen something suspicious.

The two cops were Lewis Portland and Sam Robbins, guys who had both worked with George up in the neighboring 16th District. After he came to the 20th, he somehow got them over here as well. I couldn't blame George, you're a new sergeant, you want people you can trust, people you can depend on.

Though once I got to know Lewis and Sam a little, I was kind of surprised that George would bring along those two. Neither seemed to be very aggressive or hardworking or even very smart. Sam reminded me of a high school jock, the loud, beer-drinking type. I immediately pegged Lewis as one of those go-along, get-along guys, someone who's always trying to become part of the group, always seeking approval from others. He seemed to look up to George the way George's son Charlie did, with the same hopeful, imploring eyes.

I was a block past the store, drifting back into my thoughts, when a call came over Radio—report of a rape in progress. It was halfway across the district, and I flipped on my lights and siren and took off. By the time I got there, a dozen other cops were on the scene. It turned out to be a domestic disturbance, not a rape. The woman who called 911 admitted she was just trying to get cops to lock up her boyfriend.

I saw George, Sam, and Lewis there, and meant to ask them about the leather store. But by the time the job was over, they were gone.

An hour later, I found myself cruising by the store again. Somehow, I knew that George, Sam, and Lewis would be there, and they were. George and Lewis were out front, Sam was walking around the side, all of them bathed in that milky moonlight. I didn't have to stop and ask what was going on; I knew. Through the windows, you could see hundreds of expensive leather jackets, on display, on racks. Inviting. Tempting.

George turned and saw me, his eyes met mine. He knew that I knew. And now that I had seen them, this place was out of the question, they'd have to find another opportunity. But there was no anger in George's face, or worry, or even any disappointment. It was just something that had happened.

I nodded to him and drove on, thinking, I've got enough problems. I don't want any part of this.

## nine

ometimes when cops get jammed up, they find out right away how much trouble they're really in. They get a letter from the commissioner saying he's suspending them for thirty days with the "intent to dismiss." Then they stop by their lawyer's office, and he sits them down in a nice leather chair and says, Hey, I got you a great deal from the DA—you'll only have to spend 18 months in prison!

In most cases, though, you're never really sure where things stand. You know you're being investigated, but you don't know how much information Internal Affairs has, or what they're going to do with it. It's not like they invite you to their weekly planning sessions.

And so you wake up every morning wondering whether you're going to stay a cop, or even whether you're going to stay free. You try not to worry, you put it aside so you can make it through the day. When people talk to you, you seem fine, you seem normal. They're surprised you're handling it so well. But it's with you all the time, it's always right there below the surface. It never goes away.

After that day with Dominic and McAvoy, I kept waiting for the other shoe to drop. Now that Gene Desmond knew about Dominic, why hadn't he confronted me? Why hadn't he asked why I lied to him?

I knew someone in Internal Affairs, Chris Zook, my old wagon partner in the 17th down in South Philly, where we both started out. Many times, I thought about calling him, asking what was happening with the investigation. But it would be risky, for both him and me, and we weren't so close anymore.

It was a shame. You form a tight bond with someone, you expect it to last. When we worked the wagon, our job was to transport prisoners from one place to another. A cop makes a pinch, he calls for a wagon, you show up. Even if the cop has already searched the guy, you have to search him all over again, in case he missed something. You don't want to open up those back doors and have the guy coming at you with a knife or a gun. I'd seen it happen. It was dangerous work, and Chris and I put our lives in each other's hands a dozen times a day.

Chris and I shared a lot of beers after work, talked a lot about what we wanted to do with our lives. We kept in touch with each other even after we got transferred to other districts, but eventually something happened that split us apart. After I got divorced from Patricia and started dating, Chris fixed me up with his sister. She and I went out a few times, but it didn't work out, at least from my point of view. She wanted to keep seeing me. I promised to call, but never did.

Chris got in touch with me. How come you haven't called my sister, he asked, she's waiting by the phone. I said I would. But I never did. When I saw him in court a couple of months after that, and said hello, he said hello back, but he seemed distant and cold.

But he was my only contact in Internal Affairs. If I was going to find out anything, it had to be from him. I had to give it a shot. One afternoon as I was getting ready for work, I called IAD and asked for him. I was put on hold for a few seconds, then heard his voice.

"Zook."

"Hey, Chris, this is Eddie North. How you doin'?"

There was silence. Then, in a low voice. "You shouldn't be calling here."

"I know. I don't want to get you jammed up."

"Well, you could."

"I was hoping you might be able to help me out a little."

More silence. At least he wasn't hanging up.

"Just so you'll know, Chris. I didn't try to cover up anything. And I don't think my guys did what they're accused of doing."

I was getting tired of having to tell the same thing to everybody these days. Like someone with a cast on his leg, who has to tell the story of what happened, over and over.

"I don't know how I can help you," said Chris. "I'm not involved in that investigation."

"But you have to be hearing about it. I mean, has Desmond talked about turning my case over to the DA?"

"I couldn't say. I haven't been involved in any of those discussions."

His tone was very formal. Maybe someone was nearby. Maybe no one was nearby, and this was just the way he was going to be.

"How about my two guys? Have they found any evidence against them? At all?"

"Like I said, I haven't been involved. Sorry."

I could tell he wanted to get me off the phone. He hadn't hung up, for old times' sake, but that was the most he could give me.

"Can you at least tell me whether you guys are looking into what else might have happened that night? You know, how else Sonny Knight might have got beaten?"

More silence. I thought he was going to hang up. But then he said, almost whispering, "You really think we're going to start douching out all of Sonny Knight's friends? Tell us, is the councilman a crackhead, is he a fag? Can you imagine? Black people in this town would go fuckin' apeshit."

"So if someone else beat up Sonny Knight, you really don't care."

"That's right. We're just looking at your two cops. And if there's no evidence against them, fine, they're off the hook, case closed."

"Chris, you know that's not true. The DA can still take it to court, to see whose story the jury will believe, the cops or Sonny Knight. And they might believe Knight."

"There's nothing we can do about that."

"The fuck there isn't. You can try to find out what really happened that night."

"I gotta go."

The conversation was over. At least I found out something.

"All right, Chris," I said. "Thanks."

"For what? I didn't tell you nothin'."

**That night, some** lowlife predator knocked a woman down in the main concourse of 30th Street Station, grabbed her purse, and ran from the building. The woman had just stepped off a Metroliner from New York, and apparently she was used to this kind of treatment, because she jumped up and dashed after the guy, out the door, followed by a pack of Amtrak cops.

We later concluded that the lowlife was also an idiot, because he ran out the wrong side of the building. The train station sat on the West Philadelphia side of the Schuylkill River, its main entrance facing the river and Center City. Had he run out the back way, he might have been able to escape into the hustle-bustle of West Philadelphia. Instead, he ran through the doors on the river side, scampered across the street, and immediately found his way blocked by the embankment of the Schuylkill.

At that point, he probably should have given up. But he decided he was going to run across the Market Street bridge into Center City. Who knows what he planned to do there? Open an online brokerage account at Charles Schwab? Dine at one of the outdoor cafés? He made it halfway across the bridge and then, only inches ahead of his pursuers, leapt over the parapet and into the river.

It wasn't a tall bridge—the roadway was only about fifty feet above the river. People had survived the jump before. But the lowlife predator, and the purse, vanished beneath the surface of the water.

A half hour later, I was standing on the bridge, looking down at the two police rescue boats that were scanning the dark river with their searchlights. Behind me, the bridge was ablaze with the flashing red lights of fire engines, ambulances, police cars—as if the fate of the world depended on saving this guy if we could.

"Hey, pal," came a voice from my left. It was Del Falk. I hadn't seen him since that fun night at 43rd and Market.

"Any sign of our jumper?" he asked, glancing down at the river.

"Not yet."

"Yeah, well, I'm not surprised. Ten to one he didn't know how to swim."

He lit a cigarette, neatly avoiding setting fire to his mustache.

*"When am I going to get my purse?"*

Falk and I turned to look. It was the New York woman, the purse snatchee, hands on narrow hips, arguing with Lou Schiavone, one of the detectives from West. She had shoulder-length black hair, black T-shirt, black jeans, black shoes.

"I assume," said Falk, "that her purse is black."

"Oh, but of course," I said.

"Sergeant North?" Another voice. I turned and saw a tall, lanky blond guy, blue dress shirt, khaki pants, brown dress shoes. A forty-year-old preppy.

"I'm Ben Bacon," he said. "With the *Post*."

"Yeah?" I asked, staring at him hard. So this was what he looked like.

"I heard this on the scanner and came over, hoping you might be here. I'd like to talk to you."

"I don't have any comment."

"It's about Dominic Russo."

"No comment."

"I just wanted to get your side of the story." Sincere, concerned. The conscientious reporter.

"Sorry."

"I'm writing a story, it's going to be in the paper tomorrow."

"Yeah?"

"About how Internal Affairs believes you may have conspired with the FOP and Dominic Russo to get Sonny Knight's car towed. From the scene, where he got beat up."

I wanted to ask him how he knew this, but I didn't bother. Whatever asshole leaked it probably just assumed we were guilty, and was pissed that we were making the department look bad.

"I want to give you the chance to tell your side," said Bacon, blond head slightly tilted, to show he was relaxed. Hoping to get me relaxed.

"Sorry," I said.

"You don't have anything to say at all?"

I thought about it. "I will say it's not true. And anybody who knows me would know that."

I glanced at Falk. He was looking at me like, why are you even talking to this guy?

Bacon spent the next five minutes trying to get me to say something else, he just wouldn't give up. I managed to stay polite, and he finally left.

Falk gave me a look. "You said you weren't going to comment, and then you commented."

"What I said is not going to hurt me."

"He's a reporter. He's going to misquote you. He'll put it in a way that will make you look bad."

"Yeah, Del, probably."

Falk was a pessimistic son of a bitch, but I was glad he was there. Many times when he was my sergeant, we'd hang out at scenes long after everyone else was gone and just bullshit. He was someone I could talk to. I decided to tell him about my conversation that morning with Chris Zook, though I didn't mention Chris by name.

"No one's looking at Sonny Knight," I told Falk. "No one."

He thought about that for a while as he watched the white rescue boats below.

"Then why don't *you* do it?" he finally asked.

"Do what?"

"Why was Sonny Knight in West Philadelphia?"

"Who knows?" I said. "He hasn't said anything about that."

"Maybe not publicly," said Falk. "But I'll bet he gave some kind of story to the detectives. It's in his statement."

"Except, Del, that I don't happen to have access to the case file."

Normally, I would have just gone upstairs to West Detectives and looked at the file myself. I was up there all the time, it wouldn't have been a big deal. But since I happened to be one of the people under investigation, I wasn't allowed to see the file. And I had no doubt that if I started poking around in the filing cabinets, some detective would come over and say, What are you doin' up here, pal?

"Well, maybe," said Falk, "you should find someone who does have access. If I wanted to check out what happened with Sonny Knight, that's where I'd start. With what he said in his statement to West."

*"Can you look over there? I don't think you looked over there."*

It was the New York woman, calling down to the boats. Lou, the detective, looked pained. He tried to gently escort her away from the railing.

"I'll tell you, Eddie, if you can dig up anything, that'll be good. That'll be real good. But just don't get your hopes up too high."

"Why do you say that?"

"Because it probably doesn't matter what you do. The bosses will probably fuck you over, one way or the other. It's something they're very good at."

"No, Del, you were right to begin with. All I'm doing now is sitting around with my thumb up my ass, not getting anywhere. Waiting for something to happen."

"Well, be prepared to wait a long time, pal. 'Cause nobody cares. And nobody will care."

"Yeah, and that's all the more reason for me to do something."

Falk moved his big mustache back and forth, the way he did when he was contemplating some deep matter. "On second thought, Eddie, it might be better just to get a lawyer and let him take over."

"Del, two minutes ago, you told me I should be more active in this."

"Well, yeah. I know I did. But if the Philadelphia Police Department is out to get you, they'll definitely get you. And there's nothing you can do about it."

"So, Del, what you're saying is, you *don't* think I should try to find out whatever I can about Sonny Knight. I shouldn't even try."

He moved his mustache around again, thinking it over, then he pointed his finger at me with the answer.

"No, you definitely should. But it won't do any good."

I laughed and shook my head. "My momma always told me, never ask advice from a cynical man."

There was a shout from one of the rescue boats. Everyone looked over the railing—the firefighters, the cops, the paramedics, the New York woman, still arguing with poor Lou. Had the guy's body finally floated to the surface?

Something was being lifted out of the water with a hooked pole. Even in the darkness, we could see it was a purse, shiny bright yellow.

"No way," the New York woman called down to the boat. "That's not mine." She glanced around, embarrassed, and then said to Lou, "I don't even own a yellow purse. I *wouldn't* own one."

He just stared at her. She turned her attention back to the river, and then called down to the boats again, pointing to one of the bridge supports.

*"How about over there? I see something in the water."*

"Know what I think?" Falk asked me.

"Yeah?"

"I think the wrong damn person went into that river."

**I did know** someone who had access to the file at West Detectives, and he was right on the bridge. And he owed me.

After the purse snatcher's body was finally fished out of the river that night—minus the New York woman's black purse—I had a little chat with Lou Schiavone. Can you get me that case file, I asked. Lou seemed almost overjoyed at my request. This was his chance to repay the favor I had done for him, to make things even. Cops do each other favors all the time, but this one was a little more significant than most.

One Saturday evening about six months before, Lou came into work straight from a wedding reception. He had been drinking heavily all afternoon, and was absolutely, totally shit-faced. Lou told me later he was planning to just sleep it off in some quiet corner, but a job came in right away and the supervisor sent him out on the street. Lou was halfway to his destination in his unmarked detective's car when he blew a stop sign and broadsided a cab.

No one was hurt, but it was a fucking mess. As the sergeant on the scene, I had to help sort it out. The cab's passenger, a middle-aged black woman who was being carted back from the supermarket with three bags of groceries, started complaining about a sore neck—particularly after she realized that it was a police car that had hit her. This was, after all, Philadelphia, where someone who didn't make money off an accident wasn't trying.

When I got there, Lou was still sitting in his smashed-up car. He had a dazed look, and at first I thought he was injured. But then I saw his bloodshot eyes and caught a whiff of stale beer, and I pretty much figured out what had happened.

I called for Mutt and Roy, and told them to drive Lou home.

"Get him out of here," I said. "Now."

A few minutes later, a cop from the Accident Investigation Division arrived.

Where's the detective, he asked me.

Lou was pretty shaken up, I said. He's gone home.

The cop nodded. He understood. He knew I was doing Lou Schiavone a favor.

Lou knew it, too. Had he stayed at the scene, he would have been charged with DUI while on the job, an infraction the department tended to take very seriously. He probably would have been fired, and would have been left to face the inevitable lawsuits on his own.

None of that happened. Lou was merely suspended for three days for a "preventable accident." The cab company and grocery lady did sue, but the city threw a few thousand dollars their way, and that was the end of that. No muss, no fuss.

"You ever need anything," Lou said to me at the time, "you got it."

Now, Lou was happy to see me. Sure, he said. I'll get that file for you.

## ten

**e were off the next day, and early that after-**noon, Mutt and I drove over to Roy's house in Mayfair. This was one of my favorite neighborhoods in Philly—here the rowhouses actually had lawns out front where parents could put small, inflatable swimming pools in the summertime. It was a good neighborhood for kids.

I picked Mutt up at his place in Frankford, and together we headed up to Mayfair. Roy had been managing to get himself into work the last couple of days, but just barely. Mutt had called me that morning, and said he was going to Roy's, did I want to join him. Then he called Roy, who said don't bother coming over, but Tina got on the phone and asked us to come.

"Tina's great," Mutt said as we drove to Roy's.

I'd been to the house once before, and I'd met Tina a few other times, at beef-and-beers, Christmas parties, backyard barbecues. Roy had told me they'd met in high school as freshmen, and never dated anyone else. Tina looked young for her age, too, and when you saw them together, you could picture them as gawky kids, holding hands in the hall. Tina had soft black hair and a round, soft face; she had probably been the quiet type in high school. Not shy, but just not mouthy like some of the girls she hung out with. Her father was a police captain, and she was a real daddy's girl, even now. I could just imagine Roy spotting her a few desks away in ninth-grade homeroom the first day of school, this cute, black-haired girl in a fuzzy white sweater, or whatever she was wearing. Tina had a warm, totally open smile, Roy probably had to see it only once to get hooked.

In the car on the way to Roy's, Mutt told me that Tina was the one who had introduced him to Barb, the girl he had almost married. Tina and Barb were close friends, and after Mutt and Roy became partners, Tina hooked Barb and Mutt up. Mutt was crazy about her. They got engaged, he was excited about buying a house, raising a family. The way Mutt described it, I could tell he wanted what Roy had.

A month before their wedding, though, Mutt found out Barb was running around on him. That was it, it was over.

"Tina was so mad about what Barb did to me, she broke off their friendship," said Mutt. "She sided with me over her best friend. I don't know no one else who would do something like that."

I knew that since Mutt and Barb had broken up, he'd never had a steady girlfriend. He'd bring some girl to one of our barbecues, introduce her around, and when we asked about her a couple of weeks later, he'd shrug and say it didn't work out. Sometimes, on nights the Flyers were out of town, he and Buster would hit the clubs on Delaware Avenue, but I had a feeling he didn't enjoy it much.

It turned out Roy wasn't home.

"He had to go to the hardware store," Tina said as she let us in. She was holding the baby, Caroline. "I'm really sorry about this. He knew you were coming. But he just took off."

Tina turned and led us through the living room toward the kitchen. Emily, who was six, and Julia, the four-year-old, were on the couch, under a blanket, watching cartoons.

"It's Uncle Mutt!" shouted Julia, and she jumped off the couch for a hug.

Emily stayed put but gave Mutt an electric smile that reminded me of her mother, and said, "Hi, Uncle Mutt."

I'd met the girls the last time I was here, but I could tell they didn't remember me. They were both polite, and at their mother's prompting, said, "Hello, Mr. North."

The living room was a Barbieland obstacle course. Barbie dolls were everywhere, scattered across the floor in various stages of undress. There was a Barbie horse, a purple Barbie minivan, even a two-story Barbie house with a Barbie waving from the balcony. It was like Roy's family were just tenants here, and the dolls were the ones that really owned the place.

When we reached the kitchen, Tina asked us if we wanted a beer. Sure, we said. She was still holding the baby, so Mutt opened the refrigerator and got out two bottles of Killian's. The top half of the refrigerator door was covered with color snapshots of the girls—in the backyard, at school, on vacation. The bottom was reserved for crayon drawings, palm prints, and various other works of art, each signed by Emily or Julia in huge scrawl.

Tina put the baby in a high chair at the table. "I'm glad you guys came," she said.

She was wearing red plaid shorts and a green T-shirt with flowers that said "Mount Pocono," and her soft hair was pulled back in a ponytail. She was twenty-five and she looked fifteen.

"Being a cop is everything to Roy," she said. "I don't think people realize that. Maybe it shouldn't be, but it is."

She gave the baby a small plastic bottle of milk that had been on the table, then looked at me.

"I need you to answer something," she said. "I ask Roy, he doesn't know. I ask Mutt, he doesn't know."

"I'll try," I said.

"Why is that man doing this?"

"Sonny Knight?"

"What is he hoping to gain?"

I hesitated, and she said, "I'm asking a serious question. I need to know. What is he looking to do?"

As if the answer was all she needed to get Roy back to normal.

"Tina, I wish knew. I really do."

She nodded, disappointed. Emily appeared in the doorway. "Have you washed my dress?"

"Yes, honey, it's all nice and clean."

Tina looked at us. "She's got a big birthday party this afternoon. In fact, I got to start getting her ready. You guys want to wait downstairs for Roy?"

Mutt and I took our beers and headed down the steps into the wood-paneled basement. There was a plush brown sofa facing the big-screen TV, and Mutt walked over and plopped down. I took the matching stuffed chair.

One of the walls was covered with framed photos. I recognized some of the people, cops in Roy's family. One large photo was of Tina and the three girls, with a soft blue background. I'd seen the smaller version that Roy always carried in his uniform shirt pocket. He'd take it out and show it at the drop of a hat, like some soldier in a war movie.

Mutt and I were quiet for a while, taking sips of beer, looking at the wall of photos.

"Eddie."

"Yeah."

"How come you never asked me about that story in the paper?"

"About all those complaints?"

"Yeah. I figured you were going to ask."

I shrugged. "I don't know."

"You didn't want to know the answer?"

"Yeah, maybe."

"You could of asked. They're all bullshit." I could hear the hurt in his voice.

"Every one of them?"

"Every one."

"Mutt," I said, "I'm putting everything on the line for you guys."

"I know that. Me and Roy both know that. You don't got to worry."

"I hope not."

"You don't."

We heard footsteps in the kitchen above, then saw Roy coming down the steps.

"Hey, guys," he said. "Oh, you already got beers. Good."

He was carrying a small paper bag, and he put it down in front of a ripped-out corner of the basement, where he had been doing some kind of plumbing work. We got up and shook his hand, asked him how things were going.

Roy was one of those guys who was always working on his place, always making renovations. New windows in the front bedroom, new tub in the bathroom, adding a deck out back, expanding the deck, installing a small pond with Japanese goldfish, installing a fountain in the pond. It never ended. I was surprised he didn't build carnival rides for the fish. There was a house down at the shore, in North Wildwood, that had been in the Knopfler family for years, and Roy worked on that, too. He even worked on other people's houses, for free. He didn't care about the money, as long as they covered the cost of materials.

"I thought you were finished down here," Mutt said, looking at the exposed pipes.

I would have thought so, too. The time I'd been here before, Roy showed off the new tile floor, the new pressed-tin ceiling, the indirect lighting, the cabinets, the entertainment center. I figured he'd covered every square inch of the basement.

"I'm puttin' in a bar. This is where the sink's going to go."

"What do you need a sink for?" I asked. "All you drink is beer."

"Gotta have a sink," said Mutt. "What else are we going to piss in?"

Roy looked at me and shrugged. "Sad, but true."

"So how you doing?" I asked him.

"I'm okay. You should ask Mutt." He raised his eyebrows. "Did you tell him about your car?"

Mutt laughed, embarrassed. "Had a little accident coming home the other night."

"He hit two parked cars," Roy said.

"Hey, they jumped out at me. Honest, Officer."

We all sat down and talked for a while. And Roy did seem okay, almost. He seemed willing to talk about anything, except Sonny Knight, and the investigation, and why he didn't want to come into work anymore.

**If a captain** calls you into his office and sits you down, one of the things you really don't want to hear him say is, "So, do you have a lawyer yet?"

Which is what Kirk said after he called me into his office that afternoon and sat me down.

I asked him why he was asking. He looked at me for a moment, puzzled. "Don't you read the newspapers?"

"Not if I can help it."

"So you didn't see today's paper?"

"No."

"And no one's talked to you about it? Said anything?"

"No, but if you want to be the one to tell me, Captain, go right ahead."

"Eddie, you got to get a lawyer. I talked to Mutt and Roy, they've already got them, the FOP hooked them up. You got to get one, too."

"Fine. I will. Now tell me why."

Kirk hesitated. He was a good guy, but he just had a hard time breaking bad news to people. "So you didn't hear about Tommy Nolan's speech."

Tommy Nolan was the DA.

"No, Captain, but if you've got some change, I'll go out and buy a paper, because it looks like that's the fastest way I'm going to find out."

"All right, I'll just tell you. Nolan gave a speech last night, at some kind of dinner. He wants to charge all three of you guys, right now."

"What do you mean, right now?"

"He says he's ready to take the case to trial."

I felt like I was in an elevator that just dropped three floors.

"Has he got some kind of evidence?" I asked. "Against Mutt and Roy?"

"He says he doesn't care—Sonny Knight's word is good enough for him. He wants to let the jury decide."

"Has the commissioner said anything about this?"

"Not as far as I know," said Kirk. "But it's got to put more pressure on him. That's why I'm saying, you really should get a lawyer right away."

This was why I liked Kirk. His guys get jammed up, and the first thing he thinks about is whether they have legal protection. Not too many captains are like that.

I told him about what had happened with McAvoy, and how I didn't think the police union would be willing to pay for me to get a lawyer.

"They have to," Kirk said. "It's in the contract."

"Yeah, but even if they think I screwed them over? I'm sure they can find some way to get out of it."

Kirk shook his head. "Not as long as you're paying your union dues."

I spent the next hour on the phone with the FOP, bouncing from one person to another. They all knew who I was, and nobody wanted to have anything to do with me.

At one point, even McAvoy came on the line.

"What do you fuckin' want now?" he asked.

"Just what I'm entitled to, Vince."

"Which is nothin'." He put me back on hold. Finally, some assistant to the FOP president got on the phone, and told me that the union would pay.

"But only for the first ten thousand dollars," he said. "After that, you're on your own."

"Fine."

"Look, pal, that's all we have to pay. That's what the contract says." Like I was arguing with him.

"Fine."

"Don't expect any special treatment. Don't even bother asking."

"I didn't ask."

"Well, don't."

**There were some** things, though, I didn't need a lawyer for. At six o'clock that night, I pulled my patrol car into the empty parking lot of a middle school on Locust. Lou Schiavone was waiting for me in his unmarked brown Plymouth, and I pulled up to him driver's-side-to-driver's-side, the way cops always do.

"The name is Bond," I said. "James Bond."

Lou smiled and handed me a large brown envelope. The case folder.

"You know, this isn't everything," he said.

"What do you mean?"

"Internal Affairs has its own file. And since they're doing the main investigation, I'm sure they've got all this and a lot more."

I looked at the folder. It did seem kind of thin. "What's in here?"

Lou shrugged. "I didn't look, but probably not much more than the incident report and the statements the detectives took the first night."

That was okay. As long as it had Sonny Knight's statement.

"Thanks, Lou. Back here tomorrow, same time?"

He nodded and headed out of the parking lot. I looked at the outside of the envelope. It was a typical case folder, with forms printed on the front and back for the detective to fill out. Case number, name of the investigator, type of crime. I had seen plenty of these. Except that on this particular case folder, in the section for "Name of Subject or Defendant," someone had written:

*Sgt. Edward North*
*P/O Alan Hope*
*P/O Roy Knopfler*

You see that and your life changes, right there. You realize you're no longer one of us—you're one of them.

When I got home that night, I went into the kitchen, got a bottle of Rolling Rock from the refrigerator, and sat down at the table with the file.

Lou was right. There wasn't much in it—a copy of the initial police report and typed summaries of the interviews. But when I skimmed through Sonny Knight's, one sentence got my attention.

*Complainant states that he left his residence in Germantown approx. 10:45 P.M. en route to visit his son Carl Knight, 6721 Kingsessing.*

Except that that Kingsessing Avenue was down in Southwest Philly. Which was nowhere near 43rd and Market. You're coming from Germantown, you get off the expressway at University Avenue or Passyunk, not Market. That wouldn't make any sense.

Apparently the detective who interviewed Knight didn't ask him to explain that. Because the narrative went right into how the councilman was pulled over by two cops and dragged from his car. I read through the rest of the statement, but found nothing new.

I drank my beer and thought about it some more. What if Sonny Knight wasn't coming from his home in Germantown? What if he was coming from somewhere in West Philly?

And then I realized: he was probably at Victor's garage, in the 16th District. Maybe more than probably—that was exactly the route you'd take from the garage. South on 42nd to Powelton Avenue, where it dead-ends, then over to 43rd and south again. At that point, you'd still be in the 16th District. But once you crossed Market Street—the dividing line between the two districts—you'd be in the 20th. Where Sonny Knight said he was beaten.

Sonny Knight had been at his nephew's garage, I was sure of it. And he had taken the trouble to lie about it on a police report.

## eleven

hen I walked into work the next afternoon, the case folder was tucked in the bottom of my black gym bag. I said hello to a couple of people, including Jeff Bouvier, a young black detective who was Mutt's old partner.

"Sarge," he said. "Got a second?"

Jeff was a good guy, and very smart. We had given him the nickname "Commissioner," because we figured that would eventually be his job title.

"Timmons is looking for you," Jeff said. "And he's not happy."

"Why? What's going on?"

"You haven't heard? The file on Sonny Knight is missing."

"Yeah?"

"Yeah. And Timmons thinks you took it."

Jeff saw something over my shoulder, and vanished. I turned. It was Timmons, coming toward me, and he was staring at my gym bag like he had X-ray vision.

"If you know where that file is," he said, "I would strongly suggest you tell me, right now."

His eyes were drilling into me.

"What file?"

"You know what file, I saw you talking to Bouvier. Who, by the way, is now in a shitload of trouble. Was he the one who got it for you?"

"Lieutenant, I don't know what you're talking about. Jeff came up to me, he said you were looking for me. He didn't say anything about any file. So I'll ask you again: What file?"

"If I find you have it, North, you're going to the Front. And if someone got it for you, they're going, too."

I squinted at Timmons, like I was wondering whether he had been drinking.

"I assume that at some point," I said, "you're going to tell me what it is you're accusing me of."

He took in a deep breath through his nose, then wheeled around and strode off.

This was a problem. Lou wouldn't be able to put the file back now, not without being seen. Everyone would be watching the filing cabinets, waiting for someone to try to sneak the folder back in.

Maybe I should just take it home and burn it, I thought. It wasn't like I'd be destroying anything permanently—it was all on the computer. But if the file never turned up, that would just keep me under suspicion indefinitely.

I headed down the stairs to the locker room. By the time I hit the last step, I had figured out what to do.

I walked over to my locker, took out an old pair of black leather gloves, and put them on. There was a T-shirt in my locker, on a hanger, and I took that out, too.

I sat on the bench and fished out the folder from my gym bag, and spent the next five minutes using the T-shirt to wipe down the folder, and every page inside. When I was done, I put away the gloves and T-shirt, picked up the folder, and headed upstairs to West Detectives.

Timmons was standing next to a desk, talking to a detective. He didn't notice me at first, though everyone else in the room did. They watched as I walked toward him, and then he saw me, too, and stopped talking.

I slapped the file down on the desk.

"Is this what you're looking for?" I asked. "The folder on Sonny Knight?"

He glanced at it in mild astonishment, but didn't pick it up.

"You were right," I said, louder now. "Someone did get it for me. Put it right on top of my locker."

I waited for that to sink in.

"Maybe," I continued, "it was a friend. Someone who thought he was trying to help me. Or maybe—just maybe—it was someone who was trying to get me jammed up. Now, Lieutenant, who do you think might have done that?"

Timmons glared at me, but I could see in his face, in his eyes, that doubt was starting to take shape. He wasn't so absolutely sure anymore.

"All I can say, Lieutenant, if it was you, fuck you. If it wasn't you, still fuck you for accusing me. You can take this fucking file and you can stick it up your fucking ass."

Timmons's jaw got slack, and so did everyone else's in the room. Guys were looking at me like I was out of my mind. Maybe I was, but at least the file was back where it belonged.

**Right after that,** I made two phone calls. Three, if you count calling directory assistance to get the number for Jimmy Musgrave. He was a lawyer. I was finally going to make Michelle happy.

I talked to Musgrave for about fifteen minutes, on my cell phone out in the Yard. He agreed to represent me. Come into my office tomorrow, he said. We'll talk about it.

My other call was to Gene Desmond. I needed to tell him what I'd found out about Sonny Knight.

He didn't seem the least surprised to hear from me, and I knew why. He no doubt figured that once he talked to Dominic and McAvoy, they'd get back to me about it right away. At that point, I'd realize the cover-up had been discovered. And I would have no choice but to come forward, to minimize the damage before it was too late.

Desmond told me he was glad I called. "You want to come up here?" he asked.

He meant to Northeast Philly, where Internal Affairs had its headquarters. What was he expecting, that I'd sit in one of his interrogation rooms and make a formal confession?

No, I said, not up there. I told him about a parking area off 32nd, next to a Penn athletic field, where we could meet.

We both showed up at the same time. For some reason, I thought the field would probably be empty. But the Penn girls' soccer team was having a practice, they were running around on the grass, yelling, cheering from the sidelines. Some coach was whistle-happy.

Desmond and I walked to the fence, but neither of us were interested in what was happening on the field.

"I got a question," I said. "Is Sonny Knight still claiming he drove directly from his home to Forty-third Street?"

Desmond seemed dumbfounded. Of all the scenarios of our conversation he had run through his head on the way over, this clearly was not one of them.

"Why do you care about that?" he asked.

"Because he wasn't coming from his home," I said.

"And how would you know that?"

"Are you aware," I asked, "that his nephew has a garage at Forty-second and Parrish?"

He was silent.

"And that if you were going from there to his son's house down in Southwest Philly, you'd probably go right by Forty-third and Market?"

I could tell Desmond was considering this, though his face gave up nothing.

"What's your point?" he asked.

"My point is that Sonny Knight lied."

"And what about you?"

"Why would he lie?"

"Why would *you*?"

"You're not going to check it out? You're just going to let it go?"

"Would you like to talk about Dominic Russo now?" he asked.

"Forget Russo for second," I said. "Me, Hope, Knopfler, we're all getting screwed. You got to check this out."

"What about Dominic Russo, Sergeant?"

"You got to give us a chance."

"What about Dominic Russo?"

**That night as** I was about to report off, Michelle called me.

"I'd like you to come over to my apartment after work, if you don't mind," she said.

"I never mind."

"I want to show you something."

"Really? Have you been shopping at Victoria's Secret again?"

"Not this time."

I always liked going to Michelle's apartment. She had a two-bedroom in a leafy garden-apartment complex near Rhawn and the Boulevard, about three miles from my house. There was nothing special about her building, it was pretty plain-Jane, but Michelle had made her space so relaxing and comfortable that I slept better there than in my own house. It was all cushions and soft colors and sunlight streaming through the windows in the morning. Even her Siamese cat was friendly to me, we got along fine.

When I showed up at her door, Michelle was wearing sweatpants and a T-shirt, and she was in her socks. She wrapped her arms around me, pulling me close to her, and we kissed deeply. My whole day, everything I had been through, disappeared into that kiss. I could feel her face getting warmer, flushed. Her breathing became more hurried, and mine did, too, and I wanted us to be kissing in bed now, our clothes torn away, holding each other even tighter, feeling each other's bodies.

"Let's go upstairs," I said.

"I don't have an upstairs."

"Let's go upstairs anyway."

"Later. There's something I want you to see."

She walked toward the bedrooms, but instead of going into the one on the left, where her bed lay in darkness, she led me into the one on the right, where she had her office. Her computer was on, she had obviously just been using it, and she sat down in front of it on her padded swivel chair.

"Pull up a seat," she said, pointing to a high-backed chair that looked like it had once been part of a dining room set.

Even Michelle's office was comfortable. It had bookshelves and brown mini-blinds, and a clean, uncluttered look that felt effortless. There were stacks of folders and papers on her desk, as well as on a polished-wood filing cabinet, but everything seemed organized, simple.

"By the way," I said, "I got a lawyer today."

Michelle turned her chair to me.

"Finally. So who is it?"

"Jimmy Musgrave."

"I've seen him in court before, he's good."

"That's why I got him. I've seen him, too—actually, I've been his victim. Three times, he's been the defense attorney on cases I had. And all three times, he got me on the witness stand, started asking me questions, I didn't know which fucking end was up. I went to his office this morning. He's a very sharp guy, very no-bullshit."

"And black. Smart move on your part."

"I didn't get him because he's black."

"Doesn't matter. If you go to trial, and he's sitting at the table next to you, it can't hurt with the jury."

"Michelle, I didn't pick him because he's black."

"It's still a smart move. Hey, you got a lawyer, I feel better about that. Because I sure don't feel good about this."

She turned back to her computer and tapped a couple of keys.

"Here's the latest posting from Tariq," she said.

We read it together:

*The police still do nothing about the brutality against Sonny Knight. They still must be taught a lesson. You can bet a police officer will be targeted very soon. It doesn't matter which one because they're all the same.*

"This is a direct threat," I said. "Can't we subpoena the website? Or whatever it is that you subpoena?"

"I've been looking into it," said Michelle. "It's very tough to do."

"Have you shown this message to Homicide?"

"That's my plan. Not that it'll make any difference."

"What about Carl Knight?" I asked. "He still won't cooperate?"

Michelle shook her head. "I see him every day at the trial. There's this barricaded-off area across the street where they have their protests. I've tried to talk with him. He's polite and everything, but he's not interested in helping."

I looked at the message again.

"I'm going to talk to the captain about this tomorrow morning," I said. "At the very least, we have to get this out at the roll calls. People need to be on their guard."

"I think so, too," said Michelle. "And that includes you."

"You're worried about me? Aw, gee whiz."

"Of course I'm worried about you."

I swiveled her chair back to face me and pulled the armrests, sliding her toward me, until our lips met.

She laughed. "You're a real smooth operator."

"Turn off the computer," I said.

She glanced at the screen. "It'll take too long. Let's just go upstairs."

She stood and took my hand, and this time she led me to the correct bedroom. I reached for the light switch, but she moved my hand away, and we took off each other's clothes by the soft glow, coming from across the hall, of the computer screen.

## twelve

**I**t was raining the next night when I started knocking on the doors of Victor's neighbors, around 42nd and Parrish. A hard, late-summer rain that turned my uniform shirt from light to dark blue, though I tried to move from porch to porch as quickly as I could.

Do you remember, I asked the neighbors, seeing Sonny Knight at his nephew's garage? That night he got beaten?

Gene Desmond obviously wasn't going to ask this question. Which meant I was the one who would have to do it.

But they all said no. One after another, they all shook their heads no, peering out in the darkness at me. Worn-out old black men in bifocals, high-school-age boys in sleeveless T-shirts, young mothers holding babies. Nothing. I was hoping no one would recognize me, but if anyone did, they didn't let on. Not that it made any difference. I would have had better luck going door-to-door trying to sell vacuum cleaners.

I wasn't supposed to be here, up in the 16th District. But I also shouldn't have been doing my own investigation, so what the hell.

Victor wasn't at his garage, otherwise I might have asked him, too. Though I had a feeling that if Sonny Knight was hiding something, Victor would be hiding it as well.

I got back in my car and was about to pull off when I saw a

teenage girl hurrying through the rain toward me. She had been at one of the first houses I had hit, and said she hadn't seen anything.

"My grandma wants to talk to you," the girl said.

Grandma was about forty-five, though her tired face and graying hair made her look older. You could tell she got up every morning and worked her life away. She invited me in, but I didn't want to drip water on her floor, so I stayed out on the porch.

"There was police cars," she said.

"What do you mean?"

"My granddaughter says you just came by asking about the garage across the street."

"That's right."

"About the night the councilman got all beat up."

"Whatever you can remember."

"There was two police cars there. Parked right in front of the garage."

She told me she had heard voices on the street—from her description, it was probably a police radio—and she had looked through her blinds.

"I didn't think anything of it, at the time," she said. "We got some problem neighbors on this block. So we do see police here, sad to say. Next day, when I saw TV, I said hmmm, maybe them police cars was there for Victor. Maybe they was giving him the news. I don't know, is that what you were asking about?"

"What time do you think you saw the cars?" I asked the woman.

"I couldn't even guess, couldn't even guess. Maybe ten o'clock."

"Definitely before eleven, do you think?"

She laughed. "Honey, I'm in bed by eleven, and I mean sound asleep."

Which meant that those police cars were in front of Victor's garage just around the time Sonny Knight was beaten. Possibly a few minutes before, or a few minutes after. But only a few minutes either way. It was too much of a coincidence.

The woman didn't see any actual cops—just their cars—and she didn't know whether they were there for Victor or for someone else on the block.

That was okay. I knew a way to find out.

When I got to the squat, grungy building that housed the 16th District's headquarters, I ran into Billy and Hap coming out. I hadn't seen them since that night at Fibber's, and we shot the shit for a couple of minutes.

I asked if the lieutenant or the sergeants were around.

"Naw," said Billy. "They're all on the street."

That was good, that's what I was hoping for. The fewer people asking me questions, the better.

I headed into the operations room. It was very quiet—the only people working that night were two female cops at their desks, doing paperwork, and the corporal, going through his stack of incident reports. What the hell was his name? I couldn't remember it.

He was a white-haired guy about a hundred years old, and like all corporals, worked steady inside. He drank his coffee from Styrofoam cups, which he'd always identify by writing his badge number on the side with a blue ballpoint pen. For some reason, he didn't have a regular mug.

"Hey, Corp," I said.

"Eddie North," he said. "Thought you'd forgotten all about us."

"Never," I said. I walked over to the bank of filing cabinets that held the daily logs.

"Mind if I snoop around?" I asked.

"Hell if I care, Eddie. Knock yourself out." He went back to his paperwork, like I wasn't even there.

Cops in every patrol car keep a running log of the jobs they get assigned, including the address and the time they arrive. At the end of the shift, the sheets are collected, bound together with a rubber band, and stuffed in a filing cabinet.

I pulled out the batch for the four-to-midnight shift the day Sonny Knight was beaten. There were fourteen sheets, each with about fifteen to twenty jobs. I scanned the addresses on each sheet, and found nothing even close to Victor's garage.

There was still another possibility. Those two patrol cars might have been on 42nd Street as part of another job. It was pretty common—you'd go to one place, start asking questions, and find out you had to check out someplace else. Usually when that happened, though, people would tell Police Radio where they were going.

Which meant there might have been something on Radio's tapes from that night. But there was a slight problem: the tapes were downtown, at Police Headquarters, under lock and key. I didn't have access to them, and I didn't know anybody who did. They might as well have been on Mars.

**That night, there** was a burglary at Inner Visions, a high-end electronics store near Penn. George got on the radio and said he was responding, and so did Sam and Lewis. Gee, I thought, I wonder why. I decided to swing by for a look.

It had finally stopped raining, but the streets were still quiet. I passed by the front of the store. No police cars were around—maybe they were in the alley. I pulled around behind, and two police cars were there, both with their trunks open. Generally, that's not a good sign.

I got out of my car and took a look. Each trunk was half full of unopened boxes—CD players, DVD players, portable HDTVs.

The back door to the shop was propped open with a board, and I could see into a dimly lit storage area. I stepped in, and someone came around a corner of shelves, arms piled high with boxes, and before I could jump out of the way, he smacked into me, knocking the boxes against my chest. I managed to keep my balance, but he went down on his ass, and the boxes flew in all directions and crashed to the floor. It was Lewis. He looked up at me like a dog that was caught digging in the trash under the sink.

George appeared, along with Sam. Why did none of this surprise me?

"Hey, Eddie," said George. "Sorry about this klutz here." He looked down at Lewis. "What the fuck you doing, running into the sergeant?"

"Sorry," Lewis said to me, getting to his feet. He bent back down to retrieve one of the spilled boxes, but George growled at him.

"Not those, you idiot, now they're smashed up. Get some fresh ones."

George turned to me with a smile. "It's open house, Eddie, if you want to grab something for yourself."

He was wearing his leather gloves. All three of them were wearing their gloves.

"Tell me," I said, "was there an actual, real burglary here?"

"Oh, yeah. And whoever did it got away with a shitload of merchandise."

"And you're just picking up the crumbs."

George laughed. "They're very nice crumbs, Eddie. Come here, I want to show you something."

I followed him out into the showroom. This was not a stereo store for the masses. Beautiful wood-paneled walls, DVD players on pedestals, listening rooms with plush chairs facing walls of speakers and big-screen TVs.

"It's all top-of-the-line surround-sound, home-theater shit," said George. "Look at this."

Mounted on one wall, like a painting, was a large, super-thin TV screen.

"Look at the price."

I checked the tag: $11,999.

"Wow, they give you a buck off," I said. "That's nice of them."

"The screen's plasma," said George.

"What do you mean, plasma?"

"Fuck if I know. That's what it says right here."

He called into the storeroom. "Sam."

Sam came out.

"You find any more of these yet?" George asked, pointing to the plasma screen.

Sam shook his head. "I think that's the only one."

"Then let's take this one."

I looked at him. "You're going to take that right off the wall?"

"For twelve fucking thousand dollars? Fuck yes, I'm going to take it off the wall."

Lewis came out of the storeroom, and I was struck by how nervous and edgy he seemed. He kept glancing at the front windows. Sam was excited, full of adrenaline, this was making him high. But Lewis looked like he wanted to be anywhere but here.

George was examining the plasma TV's wall mounting.

"Needs a Phillips," he said. "See if you guys can find one in the back."

I waited until they were gone.

"In here," I said to George, motioning to one of the listening rooms. I wanted to get away from the store's big front windows. Although the place wasn't kept brightly lit at night, someone walking by would be able to look right in and see us.

When we had stepped into the room, I said to George in a low voice, "Not for nothing, George, but what are you, a fucking idiot?"

"Hey, no big deal. The insurance company's going to pay for it."

"Look, you've been a really good guy to me since you came to the district. You've been a friend, and I appreciate it. But there's a lot of shit going on in this district right now, and I'm trying to climb out of it, and the very last thing I need is for you to do this."

"Aw, don't worry, Eddie, nothing's going to happen."

"Yeah? Internal Affairs is crawling all over this district. For all I know, they could be following me around, right now."

He shook his head. "They're not following you around."

"How do you know that? How do you know? With all the shit I got on my plate, you're doing this? I can't have it, pal. And you know what? I won't have it."

Sam and Lewis were coming back into the showroom with some screwdrivers.

"All right," George said to me. "If you insist, we'll leave."

Then he smiled. "Just as soon as we move that little twelve-thousand-dollar item out of here."

When I got back in my car I was so pissed off, I couldn't even start the engine. George was a fucking asshole. And he wasn't going to stop stealing, I knew that. He was going to hit another store, and another, and another. And what was I supposed to do? Snitch on him? Word gets out you're a rat, your career goes right in the fucking toilet. That's fucking suicide. Not to mention that Internal Affairs probably wouldn't believe I had nothing to do with him, that I was all innocent here.

So what was the answer? I had no idea. I didn't even know if there was an answer.

**Later, as the** squad was coming back to district headquarters to report off, Lewis took me aside.

"Sarge," he said, "can I talk to you out in the Yard?"

We walked together out to a far corner of the lot, and stopped in the semidarkness. Lewis's nervous eyes darted around the parked police cars.

"You're not going to say nothing to nobody, are you?" he asked me.

"Lewis, I don't know what I'm going to do."

He took a deep breath. I could see he was trying to give himself courage to continue.

"I just want you to understand," he said. "This stuff with George? I really don't want to be doing it."

He was serious.

"George is forcing you at gunpoint?" I asked.

"No . . ."

"Then what?"

He searched for the words. "I'm doing it for George. You know, you're supposed to do things for your sergeant, right?"

"Yeah, but I don't think this is one of those things, Lewis."

"Maybe I should tell you how I got into this."

"I'm not interested."

I could see him getting desperate. "I just hope you're not going to say anything to anybody."

"Because you don't want to get caught."

He nodded. "And because I'm just doing it for the sergeant."

Yeah, I thought, you probably are. He got you somehow, didn't he? Got you to go along on one of his souvenir hunts one time, and now you're in it for good, you can't get out.

"It's not my problem," I said. "It's your problem."

Out of the quiet night came a deep, thunderous boom.

"Gunshot," said Lewis.

"That was no gunshot," I said.

How far away? Five blocks? Ten? Impossible to tell. I ran toward my car, turning my radio up.

Before I was out of the lot, the dispatcher came over the air, her voice frantic. A police car, with an officer inside, was in flames.

## thirteen

y early afternoon the next day, probably everybody in the 20th had stopped by the burn unit at St.
Agnes in South Philly to see Paulie. He was in the ICU, and they
were allowing only members of the immediate family to see him, so
we all congregated in a large waiting room area by the elevators. It
was pretty comfortable—couches, big chairs with armrests, a television on full blast with the judge shows. Just like home.

Now and then a family member would come out and talk to us,
and let us know how happy Paulie was that we came by. Paulie was
all drugged up but awake, and he knew we were out here, the family said. When we asked them how he was doing, they just kind of
shrugged. He was going to need skin grafts, they said. He was going
to be in the hospital for a while.

Most of us brought some kind of gift for Paulie—flowers, fruit
baskets, magazines, books. A couple of the female officers brought
teddy bears, which I didn't quite understand. It was hard to picture
this tough old Italian cop lying in a hospital bed, all bandaged up,
holding a teddy bear.

Our squad didn't have to be at work until 4 P.M., so we were in
our street clothes. But a lot of on-duty cops from other squads, and
other districts, were stopping in. Paulie had been on the job for
something like twenty-six years, and he knew cops all over the
city. They all had their own stories about Paulie.

One guy would say, "Yeah, I worked with him in a wagon in the 39th. He drove like a fuckin' maniac, I remember one time he went around a corner on two wheels. I almost pissed my pants."

And we'd all say, "Yeah, that's Paulie."

Even cops who didn't know him showed up at St. Agnes. Paulie's son, Paul Jr., was a cop up in the 5th, and guys from his squad came to visit the father, out of respect.

All morning, the cops from the various other units were asking, What happened out there last night? Are they going to catch the asshole that did it?

We told them what we knew, which wasn't much. There was a 911 call for an illegal parker on a run-down block on Pine. That in itself was a joke. The block had half a dozen crack houses, and if someone was parked in front of a fire hydrant, that was the least of the neighbors' problems. But we had to respond to all 911 calls, no matter how minor, and Paulie was dispatched to check it out. The moment he pulled up at the address, someone threw a Molotov cocktail at his patrol car. It hit the trunk and exploded, blowing in the back window and setting the car on fire. Paulie was momentarily knocked unconscious by the blast, and would have certainly burned to death, but somehow he woke up, got the car door open, and crawled out.

The only witnesses—or at least the only ones we found—were a crack whore and a fifteen-year-old boy. They both saw a man running up behind the police car.

"He had a bottle," the kid told us. "With the top burning."

"What'd he do?" we asked.

The kid shrugged. "Threw it at the police car."

Like this was normal activity, something he saw every day.

The crack whore, wearing dirty jeans and a soiled red top, had been coming out of one of the abandoned houses when this happened.

"What'd the guy look like?" we asked.

"Jus' a normal guy," she said. "Ski mask."

"What?"

"He was wearin' one them ski-mask things."

We were all thinking, What would it take in this neighborhood to really get people's attention?

Now we were sitting in the hospital, with the empty feeling you get when some asshole who's hurt a cop is still on the street and there's nothing you can do about it.

Every now and then, Paulie's wife, Maryanne, would come out and talk to us. She was a fleshy, friendly woman with a sweet smile. And she looked like a nurse, which she was. She had worked for years at Methodist Hospital, just down the street, now she was a visiting home nurse. She said she knew some of the people who worked here in the burn unit, though, and they promised her they'd take real good care of Paulie.

I had met Maryanne once before, at a beef-and-beer at the FOP, and she recognized me right away.

"Paulie thinks very highly of you," she said. "I'm sure he's going to be glad you stopped by."

Their daughter was Denise. She was about twenty-three and so good-looking that guys were falling all over themselves to say hello to her. One of those Italian beauties, oval face, long eyelashes, long black hair, and she was wearing the tightest jeans in the world. It was tough—here she is, Paulie's daughter, he's lying in a room all burned up, you're trying to be respectful, and you have to force yourself not to stare at her butt whenever she walks away.

I half expected someone to propose marriage to her right on the spot. One young guy had some flowers for Paulie, but he was so flustered that he gave them to Denise, saying, "These are for you."

"What do you mean?" she asked, genuinely puzzled.

You could see the guy catch himself, he realized he was acting like an asshole.

"For the whole family. You know, to show we care."

"Oh. Okay, thanks."

New guys would come into the waiting room, they'd say, "How's Paulie doing?"

And someone would say, "He's okay. You got to see his daughter."

Not exactly the height of decorum.

Around noon, Tony D came in with a box of soft pretzels, still warm from the bakery, and a squeeze bottle of French's mustard, to give to Paulie.

"That's real smart, Tony," said Buster. "What are you gonna do, cram it in his IV?"

Maryanne said, Why don't you all eat the pretzels? So we did, and somehow, it was a real comfort. And we were lounging around on the sofas, chewing the doughy pretzels, when Commissioner Ellsworth stepped off the elevator. We all stood up, brushing the salt from our shirts, wiping the mustard from our upper lips. The commissioner just nodded to us and headed straight for the nurses' station. The last we saw of him, one of the nurses was leading him toward Paulie's room.

"That's funny," said Marisol. "I wouldn't have guessed that Eli was a member of Paulie's immediate family."

"Must be the black sheep," said Yvonne.

About ten minutes later, the commissioner came out and shook hands with everyone in the waiting room. I wasn't in uniform, and I wondered whether he'd recognize me.

"Hello, Sergeant," he said.

I wanted to pull him aside and say, We appreciate you supporting us, don't get us wrong. But why in the world are you doing this?

In the last week or so, Ellsworth had been coming under tremendous pressure to fire us. Newspaper editorials were suggesting that if the current police commissioner wasn't going to take action, maybe the mayor should find one who would.

I wondered whether Ellsworth had questions for me as well, like, Am I backing the wrong horse here?

But neither of us said anything. We just shook hands and nodded to each other, and then he moved on to the next cop.

When he got to Yvonne, she asked him whether there were any new leads.

No, he said, but Homicide was working on it as hard as they

could. They'd get the guy. And there was a $25,000 reward, he said. Maybe that would shake loose a witness or two.

I'd read about the reward in the *Post*. The paper itself had put in $5,000, as if it had suddenly decided to care about cops.

Not long after the commissioner left, Mutt showed up, carrying a Stephen King book for Paulie. Guys in the squad spotted him and their faces hardened. Everyone either avoided his glance or stared at him like, What are you doing here?

Mutt came over to me and asked how Paulie was doing, and I told him what I knew. He only half listened, he was searching the room for friendly faces. Other than Buster, and Yvonne and Marisol—who gave him small waves—I don't think he found any. He hadn't expected this, and I could see the hurt in his eyes. I knew he wanted to tell them all, Hey, what happened to Paulie wasn't my fault.

"Forget it," I said. "They're just upset."

"Yeah," he said. He handed me the book. "Would you give this to Paulie, tell him I stopped by?"

"They'll get over it," I said. But I didn't believe it, and neither did he.

Mutt got on an elevator and was gone.

I didn't blame Mutt. I blamed Sonny Knight. He was obviously lying about something. And now my cops were getting hurt.

**There was no** way I should have had any contact with Knight. I shouldn't have even considered it. I knew that. But when I heard that he was going to be at Penn that night, I decided to have a little chat with the councilman.

I didn't mention this to Michelle when we spoke over the phone that afternoon. She would have tried to talk me out of it. She probably would have even gone to Penn, to stop me in case I showed up. So I didn't tell her. I didn't tell anybody.

It was a forum on police brutality. Some kind of panel discussion, with the people on the panel being civil rights leaders and college-professor types, and a certain city councilman who just happened to be an alleged victim of police brutality himself. There was a mention of the forum in the *Post*, it was supposed to start at Houston Hall at 7 P.M.

I got there at six-thirty and waited under a tree for Knight to show up. I was in uniform now, and I was hoping no one would recognize me. I didn't have to worry—no one paid me the slightest attention. They no doubt thought I was just a Penn cop, keeping the campus safe. Two of the real Penn cops, both guys I knew, came over and said hello. I told them I was waiting for someone, and we chatted for a while before they moved on.

I was amazed at how many people were going into the building, they were just streaming up the steps like somebody inside was giving away free money. All to hear about police brutality. It's not how I would have spent a free evening.

At almost exactly seven, Sonny Knight came around the side of the building, heading for the main entrance. He was alone, which surprised me. I figured he'd have at least a couple of people with him, if for nothing else than to be witnesses the next time the cops beat him up.

I moved quickly to intercept him.

"Councilman," I said.

He saw me and hesitated, just for a moment, but kept going. I closed in.

"What were you doing at your nephew Victor's that night?" I called.

As if this were an established fact, rather than a guess on my part. I wanted to see whether he'd acknowledge it in any way. Whether he'd say anything at all that I could take back to Desmond.

Knight stopped and faced me.

"What did you say?" he asked.

He was wearing a dark blue suit, and looked pretty much the

same as the first time I had seen him, though without the blood. The same determined, angry look, the same weighted, heavy shoulders. As I came closer, I saw that the cuts on his face had mostly healed and were now just fading red marks.

"You were at Victor's garage the night you got beat up," I said. "How come you didn't mention that in your statement to the detectives?"

He stared at me for a few moments. Two young black men, who I'd noticed standing at the steps, were heading toward us. They had humorless faces, the hallmark of the Penn student. Knight was about to say something to me, but then saw the students approaching and held his tongue.

They introduced themselves to him, they seemed to be his welcoming committee at the forum. One of the students, severe behind his wire-rimmed glasses, recognized me instantly. His mouth dropped open. Satan in the flesh!

Knight seemed to forget about me then, he turned and resumed his journey to Houston Hall with the students in tow. But the one with the wire-rimmed glasses gave me a backward look, glaring. His eyes shooting out knives, swords, nuclear-tipped missiles.

**That night it** was quiet on the street, at least until Buster called in the car-stop over Radio. He had four black males, all in their teens, in a green Corolla, at 61st and Cedar. The dispatcher asked for someone to back him up, and Tony D said he'd handle it.

A couple of minutes later, Buster called Radio again. He was asking for me. There was something in his voice I couldn't quite place. Not a sense of unease, which you might expect in a potentially dangerous car-stop, but something else. I got on the air, and said I'd be there in two minutes.

Buster's car, overhead lights flashing, was parked behind the Corolla, and behind his was Tony D's. They had the four kids out of the car, hands on the trunk, one on each side, two in the back.

None of them could have been more than sixteen. Buster and Tony D were patting down their baggy pants, reaching into their enormous pockets.

And over on the sidewalk, eight feet away, was Carl Knight, filming it all with a camcorder.

"The officers are now searching the driver and the passengers," Carl said in an even voice. He seemed to be narrating his own movie.

Two young white guys were with him, one with a handheld police scanner. They had been monitoring our radio calls—that's how they knew to be here.

Buster and Tony D continued their work, pretending not to hear or see Carl. When I walked up, relief filled their faces, and Buster nodded toward the sidewalk.

"Figured you'd better see this, Sarge."

"Fucking assholes," Tony D said in a low voice. "Paulie's in the hospital, and they're doing this shit?"

"Is that North?" I heard Carl say. When I looked up, he had the camera on me. "Sergeant Edward North has just arrived."

What was I supposed to do, give a speech? I took Buster out of range, and asked him what the deal was with the car-stop.

"I was driving down the street behind the Corolla," he said. "I wasn't even paying attention to who was inside. But they must have seen me, because they threw something out the window."

Something they obviously didn't want to be caught with. A good enough reason for a car-stop in anybody's book.

"You find it?" I asked.

He shook his head sadly. "No, Tony D went back down the street to look. Couldn't find nothing. Then these three knuckleheads show up with their camera. And we called you."

"Why, so I could be the one on camera instead of you?"

"Hey, you got more experience."

"Thanks."

Over his shoulder, I saw Carl stepping off the sidewalk, moving toward the car with the camera.

"Have they told you why they stopped you?" Carl asked the kids.

"Get back on the sidewalk," said Tony D.

Carl ignored him. "They haven't told you, have they?"

The four kids exchanged glances and giggled a little, but they were more confused than anything else.

"On the sidewalk," said Tony D. "Now." He was totally unafraid of the camera.

I quickly maneuvered between Carl and Tony D, and Carl focused the camera on me. I knew he was waiting for me to say something, preferably something incriminating, but I just smiled pleasantly. He finally lowered the camera, for the first time.

His two young white cohorts moved closer, as if they were protecting him, but I had a feeling it was more the other way around. They seemed totally out of their element here, as if they had taken a wrong turn coming out of some suburban mall. I think even they knew they wouldn't last two seconds on a street like this if the police weren't around.

Like Carl, they were wearing white shorts and loose-fitting, colorful knit shirts, as if they imagined this were the uniform for coming out to film cops. Very fashionable, particularly for this neighborhood.

"What are you doing here, Carl?" I asked him.

Tony D looked at me. "You know this asshole?"

I held up my hand toward him. "I'll take care of this," I said.

Carl had the camera up again, training it on Tony. "This officer just called me an asshole," he narrated.

"Carl," I said. "Can you put the camera down for a second?"

I turned to Tony. "This is Sonny Knight's son."

Carl lowered the camera a little, so Tony could get a better look.

Tony raised his eyebrows. "What does that mean, everyone in the family is a cop hater?"

Up with the camera, which for all I knew hadn't stopped recording. I turned my back on it and gave Tony a would-you-get-the-hell-out-of-here look.

The kids were laughing, but I could see they had no idea what was going on. It all just bounced off their smooth, untroubled faces.

Tony walked away, and I turned back to Carl.

"What are you doing here?" I asked again.

He lowered the camera again. This time I saw the red "recording" light go off.

"We're monitoring the police. Making sure the young men of the African-American community are treated fairly."

"That's nice. I've got a cop in the hospital. How come you didn't make sure he was treated fairly?"

Carl tilted his head, puzzled. "By doing what?"

"We came to you asking about Tariq," I said. "You refused to help us. And now a cop's hurt."

"You can't put that on me."

"If you know who he is, Carl, then it's all on you."

"Well, I don't know who he is. And anyway, it's your job to find him, not mine."

He turned to the two young white guys with him.

"See," he said. "This is typical. The cops think they can have it both ways. They think they can treat the black community with disrespect, but when they need us, we're supposed to jump."

The two guys nodded knowingly, like it happened to them all the time, too.

"You know what?" I said. "You people make me sick."

"What people? Black people? That's what this is all about, isn't it?"

"No, not black people, Carl. *Danforth* people. All you Danforth idiots, running around claiming to speak for the black community. You wouldn't know the black community if it bit you in the ass."

He turned back to the white guys. "This is what I mean about respect."

"This isn't about respect, Carl," I said. "This is about cops getting hurt."

He gave a short laugh. "You have no idea what I'm talking about, do you?" he asked.

Carl was looking at me like Victor had, just taking it for granted that I couldn't possibly comprehend his world.

I glanced behind me, at our audience, the four kids, their hands still on the trunk. They were listening intently now.

"Get 'em out of here," I said to Buster.

He nodded and turned to them.

"Bye," he said.

They stared at him, not moving.

"Bye," Buster said again.

"We can go?" one asked.

"Bye."

They laughed and moved slowly to get back into the car, like they were tough guys. Like they'd put something over on us.

Carl filmed them leaving, keeping them in his camera sight until the Corolla was around the corner.

"Carl," I said.

Once more he lowered the camera.

"I've got a friend in the hospital with burns over half his body," I said. "If you can help us, then help us."

As soon as I said that, I regretted it. You don't show weakness to people like Carl. They just fold it over back on you, and use it like a vise to squeeze you tighter.

But he looked at me, not saying anything, and I thought I caught a flicker of something in his eyes. Maybe of sympathy, maybe of something else. I had no idea what.

It didn't matter, though. Because an hour later, just after 10 P.M., City Councilman Sonny Knight was found shot to death outside Houston Hall.

## fourteen

**t was one of those deals where everyone heard the** shot, but no one saw the shooting.

As Sonny Knight was walking back to his car, on a darkened, little-used walkway between two university buildings, someone intercepted him and shot him once through the heart.

The campus police department was instantly flooded with calls, from the nearby dorms, from the undergraduate library, open late, from half a dozen security guards manning the lobby desks at surrounding campus buildings.

There was a gunshot, callers said. Somewhere close.

Penn cops converged on the area and almost immediately found Sonny Knight, crumpled on the grass next to the walkway, the front of his white shirt dripping red. They called for an ambulance, and for us.

He was already dead. His pierced heart had given a spasm or two, gushing out the thick blood that stained his clothes, and then stopped. The city Fire Department paramedics arrived, realized he was dead, and then started to leave. One of the Penn cops who had been at the forum knew it was Sonny Knight.

Aren't you going to take him away, he asked.

The firefighters shook their heads. Take him where? A hospital ain't going to do much good at this point.

Expressing the gruesome truth: if you ever happen to get mur-

dered, your body's going to lie where it fell, out in the open, for
hours probably, until all the evidence on you and around you has
been catalogued. The best you can hope for is that bystanders, cran-
ing their necks in ghoulish curiosity, will be kept far enough back,
and that eventually, someone will think to at least cover your body
with a sheet of yellow plastic, perhaps leaving only your upturned
shoes on view.

I wasn't far away when I heard the call, and it didn't take me long
to get there. I didn't know who had been shot—only that there had
been a shooting, and it wasn't until I saw the body, saw the face,
that I realized it was Sonny Knight.

A cluster of Penn cops was gathered around him on the path.
They were just standing there, they didn't know what the hell to
do. A blond Penn sergeant came up to me, I could tell he was looking for direction.

"Any flash on the shooter?" I asked.

"No, we got no description at all. I got a couple of my people
looking for witnesses."

"Get *everyone* looking. We need some flash now."

He nodded. "Okay."

"And get all your guys out of here. They're going to fuck up the
crime scene."

Students, some with backpacks over their shoulders, some walking their bikes, were starting to gather. I heard someone mention
Sonny Knight. Word was spreading fast.

"We need to tape off this whole area between the buildings," I
said. "I don't want anybody coming down here."

He nodded again, but didn't move. I realized he was waiting for
any further instructions.

"That's it," I said. "Let's go."

I got on my cell phone and called Police Radio. This wasn't the
kind of thing I wanted to put out over the air. A lieutenant got on
the phone, he said "Shit" when I told him we had a homicide, and
"Holy shit" when I told him it was Sonny Knight.

It was his job to start making notifications, calling everybody in the department who needed to know.

"You might want to start with the commissioner," I said. "This guy was his pal."

"Yeah, that's a good idea. Wait, he's gonna want to know—this look like a robbery?"

And I said, Hell if I know.

When I hung up, though, the Penn sergeant and I talked it over. It could have easily been a robbery. Guy hides in the bushes, waits for someone to walk by, then comes out with a gun. Sonny Knight still had his wallet, but that didn't mean anything. It happens all the time—the robber demands money, the victim refuses or just doesn't move fast enough, the robber fires, or stabs or whatever, then realizes what he's done and runs off in a panic. In fact, usually when someone's killed in a robbery, nothing is taken. And then, of course, the TV news says the killing was "senseless," as if it would have been better somehow if the robber had at least picked the guy's pocket before he ran off.

It wasn't uncommon for people to get mugged near the campus, or even on it. After all, Penn was in West Philadelphia, not exactly a peaceful rural setting. For the crackheads and the would-be gangstas from the projects, Penn and the leafy neighborhoods around it were like a candy store with no one behind the counter. Just grab what you want.

But who knew, maybe it wasn't a robbery. Maybe somebody had been waiting in ambush for Sonny Knight, knowing he was at Houston Hall, knowing he'd take that deserted walkway back to his car. Though that possibility seemed a little far-fetched to me. Philadelphia was a tough town, but usually we didn't go around assassinating our politicians.

Over the next few minutes, various bosses arrived, including His Royal Fatness, Chief Inspector Clopper. The last time I saw him was the night Buster almost got shot. And now here he was again, trying to figure out how to get his landmass under the crime-scene tape.

I decided to be a nice guy. I walked over and lifted up the tape, high enough so he didn't have to bend over. Not that he could have if he wanted to.

"You again, huh?" he sneered.

"Officer," someone nearby said. It was the black student in wire-rimmed glasses who had been shooting me looks of hate in front of Houston Hall.

"I heard that's Councilman Knight," he said. "Is that true?"

"I can't comment," I said.

As Clopper and I walked away, toward Knight's body, the student muttered to our backs, "Another cover-up, right?" And then louder, just to make sure we heard: "Who did this? Alan Hope and Roy Knopfler?"

Clopper smiled. "Smart kid, huh?"

"He's an idiot."

"I don't know. Seems like Hope is the violent type, don't you think?"

"He wouldn't do something like this."

"And you're unbiased about it, right, Sergeant?"

He gave me a smirk. I almost said something, but I turned and walked away. The fuck if I was going to escort this asshole any further.

I got out my cell phone, and I called Mutt on his.

"Where are you?" I asked him. Roy was off sick again, so Mutt was working solo. Radio had assigned him to take a burglary report at 56th and Pine, and I couldn't remember whether he'd put himself back into service.

"I'm still at Five-six and Pine," Mutt said. "You got a founded shooting at Penn?"

"Yeah, very founded," I said. "In fact, it's Sonny Knight. And right now, he's very dead."

"No shit," said Mutt. "Well, good. I'm glad. That motherfucker was ruining our lives."

I pictured Mutt in some little gray-haired lady's living room, she's hearing this.

"I'll be right there," he said.

"No. You don't want to come over here."

"Why not? I'm almost done with the report."

"Don't. It would not be a good idea."

"What do you mean? What's the problem?"

"People in the crowd are starting to bring up your name. Also, there's this chief inspector . . . let me put it this way, you don't want to be here."

"Yes, I do."

"No, Mutt. Stay away."

He was pissed, he tried to argue, but I told him I had to get off the phone, and hung up.

I called Roy at home, or at least tried to. He wasn't there. I left a message saying to call me as soon as he could. I tried his cell phone, but got no answer. I left the same message.

The first guys from Homicide had arrived, and I could see them talking with Clopper. A couple of times, he looked over in my direction, and they did, too.

During the next half hour, more bosses showed up, then the commissioner, and finally the mayor. By the time he stepped out of his car, there was a forest of television cameras behind the yellow tape, and news helicopters were pounding overhead.

Kirk had come from home, and he and I were talking with a couple of other captains when the Penn cops found a witness, a female student. They led her under the tape, toward the tree where we all were standing. She was one of those big-boned girls, wide-open face, freckles, she looked like she wrestled cows on the farm she just came from. You saw girls like this at Penn State all the time, but not here. She must have taken the wrong bus from Cowlick, Pa.

"Tell them what you told us," one of the Penn cops said.

She was across the street and heard a shot. Cars were passing both ways, there was a lot of noise, she wasn't sure where it came from. And then, over near Houston Hall, she saw a police officer running.

"What do you mean, running?" Kirk asked.

"Down that way." She was pointing to a sidewalk that led from the passageway.

That couldn't be right.

"You mean away from here?" Kirk asked.

The girl seemed nervous, surrounded by all these solemn male faces. I couldn't tell whether she realized the significance of what she was saying. Other cops were gathering around now. They knew something was up.

"Try to remember," Kirk said. "Is it possible the officer was running toward Houston Hall, maybe responding to the shot?"

She tilted her head up, looking toward the sky, as if the answer was written there.

"No, I think he was running away from it."

"You think he was."

"I'm pretty sure. It happened so fast. I'm not positive, but I think so."

"And this was right after the shot."

"Yeah. Yes, sir."

There was dead silence. Kirk finally spoke again.

"Do you remember what he looked like? Was he black, was he white? Tall, short?"

She shook her head no. "I didn't get a good look. I just saw the blue uniform. I'm sorry."

Which meant there was no way of telling whether it was a Penn cop or a city cop—our uniforms looked the same—or even whether it was some security guard.

A whole crowd of cops was listening in now, inspectors, detectives, crime-scene guys. This was ridiculous, this was no way to question a witness.

And someone else was standing there listening, too. Carl Knight. He must have gotten a call. But they shouldn't have let him under the tape, you don't let relatives into a crime scene like this. And now he was hearing that a cop might have been involved in his father's killing. He saw me looking at him, and he just stared back.

. . .

**A few minutes** later, the two Homicide detectives I'd seen talking to Clopper came up to me.

"Sergeant, do you know where Officers Hope and Knopfler are?" one of them asked. He was a black guy, I'd met him before, his name was Cranston. Supposedly he knew his stuff.

"Why?"

"We'd like to talk to them."

"Why?"

"Because we'd like to talk with them."

"They had nothing to do with this."

"You going to tell us where they are?" said Cranston. "Or are we going to have to call Radio?"

"I don't know where they are. Hope's on the street, and Knopfler's out sick. And he's not home, at least he wasn't a half hour ago."

That was a stupid thing to say.

"You called him?" Cranston asked.

"Sure. To let him know what happened here."

"Why?"

"Why do you fucking think?"

"I don't know."

"Because I knew that before this night was out, someone like you was going to come by and ask where he was."

"Did you call Hope, too?"

This was getting screwed up, fast. And it was just the start. Cranston asked me to get on the radio and have Mutt meet me at district headquarters. I knew what was going on. They wanted to get to Mutt before he realized he was under investigation, to catch him off guard.

What was I going to do? If I refused, it would just make things look even worse for Mutt. It would look like I was covering up for him. Again.

"Okay," I said, "but not at the district. I don't want everyone there to see you question him, like a criminal."

They agreed to that. I didn't use the radio, though. Instead, I called Mutt on my cell phone, and told him to meet me at Conrad Park. This was as much of a code as I could manage. Because we never called it Conrad—to the cops of the 20th, it was always Dogshit Park. Mutt got the message.

"You bringing someone?" he asked.

"Yeah."

"Someone from Homicide?"

"Yeah." Smart boy.

"Thanks."

I knew Mutt understood why I had given him the heads-up. Not because I thought he needed it. That was really irrelevant. But because if I brought these detectives to him without warning, he'd know he could never trust me again.

The detectives followed me over to the park in their unmarked Crown Vic. Mutt was there when we arrived, parked at the corner under a streetlight. He gave me a questioning look, but all I could do was shrug.

They wanted to see Mutt's gun. He unsnapped his holster and without a word handed it over. Cranston pulled back the slide and sniffed the ejector port.

"When was the last time you fired this?" he asked Mutt.

"I don't know. March? The last time I had firearms training."

"That was five months ago," I said. "Does it smell like it's just been fired?"

"Can't always tell," said Cranston. He closed the gun back up. "I'm going to hang on to this."

"I don't get my gun back?" Mutt asked.

Cranston turned to me. "I understand you were talking to Sonny Knight this evening. Before he went into that meeting of his."

I could see him looking for my reaction.

"Just a friendly conversation," I said.

He nodded, and looked at Mutt and me. "You guys don't mind

leaving your cars here, do you? We're going to need both of you to come down to Homicide."

**Mutt told me** later that Cranston and his pals had spent most of their time trying to scare the crap out of him. They kept telling him, All we need is motive, means, and opportunity. We already have two of them—motive, that's obvious, means, hey, you had a gun. And you had the opportunity, too, didn't you? Yeah, a nice window of opportunity. That call to handle the burglary report, when did you get that? When did you arrive at the woman's house? And when did you leave, exactly?

Mutt ended up telling them he wouldn't answer any questions until he had an attorney. He hadn't planned to say that—on the way downtown in the Crown Vic, he assured me he wouldn't need one. But he was stunned by the ferocity of the questioning, and he changed his mind.

Other detectives were waiting for Roy when he got home, and they brought him downtown as well.

Where were you tonight, they asked. You were supposed to be sick, how come you weren't home? Roy asked for a lawyer, too.

I walked into Homicide absolutely unconcerned. But then Cranston, along with his lieutenant and another detective, led me into an interview room and asked me to sit down. On the wrong side of the table.

"You want to ask me some questions," I said to the lieutenant, "do it out in the main room. I'm not going to sit here where the suspects sit."

I'd seen Cranston's lieutenant at homicide scenes in the 20th. He had jet-black hair and a taut, pockmarked face that gave the impression he was a scarred combat veteran. It was a fearsome face that had no doubt intimidated a great many people in this room. But I wasn't going to be one of them. To me, he was just another cop. He got his paycheck the same day I did.

"There's really no place out there we can all sit," he said. "It's too crowded."

I was still standing. I wasn't going to sit in that chair.

"Would you like some coffee?" the other detective asked.

That was it, that was all it took.

"Fuck you," I said. "If I want some fucking coffee, I'll go down to the cafeteria and get it my own fucking self. I don't want to hear your make-the-suspect-comfortable-so-he'll-talk bullshit, you got that? I'm not interested in your fucking games."

"It's just coffee, Sergeant."

"Just coffee, fuck you. And fuck you for bringing me down here, you fucking assholes. If you think I had anything to do with Sonny Knight getting his ass shot, or that any of my guys did, then fuck you all."

I was out of control. Perhaps not the wisest approach to take in a situation like this. But all I could think of was that to the Philadelphia Police Department, my eighteen years as a cop was worth absolutely nothing. A career spent making sure things were done the right way, going the extra mile for crime victims, taking care of the men and women I worked with. Just trying to be a good cop, day in and day out. Even risking my life a few times. And now none of it mattered. None of it. I looked at those three detectives and thought, They don't give a shit. No one gives a shit.

"I want to talk to my lawyer," I said.

My cell phone rang. The lieutenant gave me a look, like, *You're not going to answer that, are you?* I gave him a look back, like, *Fuck you.*

It was Michelle. I'd tried to reach her while I was being taken to Homicide, but her cell phone was busy and I had to leave a message, just to let her know what was happening.

"Where are you?" she said. "Are you at Homicide?"

"Unfortunately."

"Oh, I'm really sorry, Eddie. It's a shame you have to go through this."

There was a knock on the door, and Cranston opened it. Gene Desmond walked in.

Michelle asked me whether I had called Musgrave.

"I'm just about to," I said. "Don't worry, I'll be all right."

Desmond said something to the lieutenant, and then the lieutenant nodded and left the room with Cranston and the other detective. Desmond and I were alone.

"Let me call you back," I told Michelle.

Desmond sat on the table and lit a cigarette, waiting for me to hang up. I pushed the button to end the call and looked at him.

"I just have one question," he said.

"What's that?"

"What'd you talk about with Sonny Knight?"

I didn't need a lawyer to tell the truth.

"I asked him what he was doing at his nephew's garage."

Desmond nodded, and looked at me in a way I hadn't seen before. Like he almost believed me.

## fifteen

e weren't arrested, but as far as the public was concerned, we might as well have been. The papers and TV reported that Mutt, Roy, and I were "being questioned," as if we were somehow still down at Police Headquarters, getting the third degree.

And of course, if we were being questioned, that meant we were suspects, right? The media certainly seemed to think so. They ran our pictures again, bigger than ever, with captions that said "Being questioned by police."

None of this was surprising. From the moment that Mutt and I got in the Crown Vic at Dogshit Park, I knew that someone would leak our names. How could it not happen? A high-profile case like this, the public demands action. The department can't say, We have no clue what's going on, we're just sitting around scratching our asses. They've got to show they're doing something, making progress. And so they toss the media a few morsels. In this case, us.

The whole process is like a meat grinder: If you happen to get too close, it'll take you right in and crush you to bits. Not because it's malicious, but because it's a meat grinder, that's what it does, it grinds meat. And it never questions the origins of its raw material.

Naturally, the city went nuts. Particularly after word got out— another leak—that a witness had spotted a police officer running from the murder scene. Which wasn't quite true. The witness had said she wasn't positive which way he was running. But that uncertainty never made it into the news stories. Nor did the possibility that the shooter wasn't one of our cops at all. Everyone simply assumed he was a member of Philly's Not-So-Finest. Most likely, Mutt, Roy, or me.

After all, the only witness to Sonny Knight's beating—Sonny Knight—was now dead. Which meant that the DA's office could no longer bring a case against Mutt and Roy. Various lawyers were quoted in the papers on this subject, and they all said the same thing: It didn't matter that the councilman had given a statement to investigators. Unless Sonny Knight had been cross-examined by defense attorneys—which, of course, hadn't happened yet—nothing he had said about the beating could be used in court.

Several of the lawyers made a point of saying I could still be charged with obstruction of justice. Sonny Knight's testimony wasn't needed for that. And Mutt and Roy could still be fired, and sued. But not put in jail. And that outraged the black community even more.

When the tests came back from Ballistics showing that none of us had fired our guns, I hoped it would take some of the pressure off. It had absolutely no effect.

Over the next few days, the streets were filled with so many antipolice demonstrations that sometimes even the protesters got confused. One morning, a group of demonstrators showed up outside the Danforth trial, carrying a huge sign that said GUILTY. They were referring to Mutt, Roy, and me, of course, but when the regular Danforth supporters saw the sign, they freaked out, worried the jurors might see it and get the wrong idea.

This led to shoving and fistfights, which the cops monitoring the demonstration politely ignored until contingents from both sides pleaded for their help.

The media invasion was just as bad. It was one thing when CNN ran a clip from a story in Philadelphia, it was another when they actually sent in their own reporters to cover it. After Sonny Knight was beaten, a handful of TV news trucks had parked in front of district headquarters for a day or two. Now they were camped out, up and down the street and around the block. You'd come into work and see reporters and cameramen lounging in beach chairs, reading newspapers, barbecuing on their grills.

When the neighbors complained about the noise, the congestion, the loss of parking spaces, the news crews would say, Hey, we're just doing our job.

**Roy dealt with** this by simply not coming into work, at all. We tried to get him to come back. Mutt went over to his house every day, but it was useless. I called a couple of times. Roy came to the phone, but didn't stay on long. Sorry, he said, there's stuff I got to do. And then he'd hang up.

Late one morning I stopped by, I called and said I'm on my way. When I got there, Roy was gone. I had a long conversation with Tina. She said that not only Mutt but half of Roy's family had been coming over, trying to talk him into going back to work. In fact, his two brothers had been by an hour before.

"I don't know whether you know them, Dave and Ronnie," said Tina. "They're both in the department."

"Yeah, I've met them," I said. "Good guys."

"They were just here, talking with Roy. They said the same thing his family's been saying since Day One—they're all behind him, one hundred percent."

"And it doesn't do any good."

"Well, he appreciates it, but he still doesn't want to go back to work."

"Did his brothers tell him he'll be fired?"

"Everybody tells him that. I've told him that. And you know what he says? 'Good. The sooner the better.' "

"He should at least get a doctor's note, Tina. You know, from a psychologist, saying he's under stress. That way he can stay out for a while."

"He knows that. He won't do it."

"He won't even get a note?"

"I don't think Roy wants to be a cop anymore. If you want my opinion."

"That's hard to believe."

"Yes, it is. And it's very sad, I'll tell you that. But it's like, whatever he had as a cop, is gone."

**There were more** website warnings from Tariq, rantings that sputtered with outrage and anger. In one message Michelle showed me, Tariq suggested that it was no longer appropriate to target random cops. Now, the ones responsible for Sonny Knight's death had to be held accountable. They were the ones who needed to pay.

After reading that, I pulled Mutt from the street. He wasn't happy about it, not at all. He didn't want to spend every night inside, shuffling paperwork at a desk. I didn't care. I wasn't going to take any chances.

Michelle didn't want me on the street, either. But I told her I needed to be there, to help protect my people. I think she understood that.

She still couldn't get Homicide to investigate Tariq's messages. The detectives assured her it was just some idiot with a computer. That's half the people on the Internet these days, they said. If they had to check out every outrageous thing on the Internet . . .

At least I read the messages at roll call, and asked the sergeants in the other squads to do the same. It didn't matter that the threats seemed to be directed against Mutt and Roy. Every cop was a potential target.

And we really didn't need Tariq's warnings to understand the danger. We all knew that whoever had attacked Buster and Paulie could strike again. And now, after what happened to Sonny Knight, probably would.

We took what precautions we could. Captain Kirk met with the lieutenants and sergeants, and we all agreed: no more footbeats for a while, except in crowded areas, during daylight hours. No solo cars—everyone had to have a partner. And all the cops in the district's specialty teams, like Narcotics, Auto Theft, and Burglary, were put on patrol, in uniform, to make sure we had plenty of people going in on every job.

Whenever we got a 911 call from a pay phone—which meant the caller was anonymous—we were extra careful, and sent more cars in than we usually would.

Each cop had his or her own coping strategy. Some kept their guns under their right leg as they drove on patrol. We all scrutinized people on the street much more carefully, wondering, Is that the guy who got Paulie? No, over there, maybe that's the one.

We didn't let anyone walk up to our cars anymore. Sometimes people will flag down cops as they drive by, or come out of their houses after they call 911. Now when people did that, we drove a little further down the street, so no one could get the drop on us, and when we climbed out of our cars, we had our hand on our gun. I did that one time to a guy who was just trying to call my attention to a fender bender down the block. He raised his hands, eyes wide, I could tell he was thinking, Ohmygod, this cop's going to shoot me because I'm black.

I think we all had the feeling, though, that no matter how careful we were, something was eventually going to happen. We weren't going to be able to stop it.

And then, in a little incident that didn't do much to calm our nerves, two cops got attacked by a crowd at Sonny Knight's funeral up in Germantown, far from the 20th.

Actually, it wasn't at the funeral itself, but on Germantown Avenue, along the route of the procession from the church to the cemetery. Cops had been detailed along the avenue to block off the major cross streets as the procession came by. At Germantown and Chelten, a wide, busy intersection, large crowds had gathered. It wasn't any kind of protest, just a spontaneous outpouring of emotion.

The procession was almost endless—the funeral was one of largest the city had seen in decades. Hundreds of mourners had crowded into the church, hundreds more had stood outside.

The route to the cemetery had been printed in the papers, and all along the way, people strained forward to get a glimpse of the hearse. Everyone knew Sonny Knight, one way or another, and they came to say good-bye.

At Germantown and Chelten, two officers from the 14th District were detailed to handle traffic. That was enough, if all you wanted to do was keep the intersection clear when the funeral procession came through. But when the crowd started growing, in anticipation of the procession, it might have made sense to get those guys a little help. We never got the whole story on why that didn't happen. Supposedly they did inform Radio that there was a crowd of several hundred people, but for some reason the bosses didn't get the message, or weren't bright enough to understand the implications.

As the hearse and the long line of headlighted cars drove by, the crowd was quiet, solemn, respectful. But when the procession had passed, many of those in the street stayed where they were. Their sadness had turned to anger, and when they looked for an outlet, they found it in the two 14th District cops.

First came insults, then bottles, then fists and feet. By the time help arrived, they were both bloody, noses broken, heads gashed open. It was only a miracle that no one had grabbed the cops' guns.

Naturally, everyone blamed the Police Department. If only it had taken proper action against Mutt, Roy, and me, none of this would have happened. No one could believe we still hadn't been fired, at the very least. Here you had three cops, who not only had beaten Sonny Knight, but now probably had killed him to eliminate the only witness, and they were still on the streets? How was it possible?

Everywhere Commissioner Ellsworth went, he was besieged by reporters. Why haven't they been fired? What are you waiting for? And when he answered that there still wasn't any evidence against us, it was as if he were speaking a foreign language, and no one understood his words.

The politicians, the press, the black community, appealed to the mayor. Order Commissioner Ellsworth to fire the three cops, they said. And if he doesn't, fire *him*.

A week after Sonny Knight was killed, the *Post* reported that Mayor Shoemaker was "strongly urging" Ellsworth to fire us. And still the commissioner refused.

What was his angle? Trying to figure that out became Philly's favorite pastime. Because he had to have an angle. Why else would a black commissioner stand by three white cops who may very well have killed his friend?

When people asked him why he was doing this, he'd say, Because it's the right thing, and they'd say, Yeah, yeah, sure, but why are you *really* doing it? In letters to the editor and on radio call-in shows, there were wild conspiracy theories. Mutt, Roy, or I must have caught the commissioner driving drunk one time. Or maybe we had something on a member of his family. We had to be blackmailing him with photos, tapes, secretly recorded phone conversations. No one could accept the commissioner at his word. Even I had a hard time accepting it. After all, the commissioner was as much of a politician as anyone else, and this was Philly. And the welcome signs on I-95 might have said Birthplace of Liberty, but they didn't say anything about Birthplace of Ethics.

**After a couple** of days, the TV crews at the district decided it wasn't enough to simply get video of cops driving in and out of a parking lot. They wanted to see me—in action. And so one afternoon, they tried following me in my patrol car. It wasn't just one news van, but a whole convoy of hairsprayed TV soldiers. I doubted they had it planned in advance. Probably one of them took off after me, and the others didn't want to get beat. Gee whiz, maybe we should follow him, too. TV people are very creative that way.

At first I simply tried to lose them. I'd run a few lights, make a few turns, and they'd disappear from my rearview mirror. Two minutes later, though, they'd be right behind me again. I couldn't figure it out until I saw a helicopter overhead. Of course. My car's number, 20-C, was written in huge black letters on the roof.

There was no way I could escape. I drove around for the next half hour, trying to come up with an idea. Then I heard Yvonne and Marisol call in a car-stop at 52nd Street, under the Market Street El. And I had an idea.

I flipped on my overhead lights and took off. The helicopter would follow my progress, I knew, but it would take time for the convoy to catch up. A couple of minutes later, when I pulled up behind Marisol and Yvonne's car, under the elevated train tracks, I could still hear the copter, but I couldn't see it. Which meant it couldn't see me.

Marisol and Yvonne had stopped a beat-up brown Caddy with an old black man behind the wheel. I waved them over to me.

"I need a favor," I said.

"You got it," said Marisol.

I told them about the TV news trucks. "Switch cars with me," I said. "Drive around, get 'em off my tail."

"Sure," said Yvonne. "But sooner or later, they'll see it's us in your car, and not you."

"Yeah," I said, "but they won't know which car I'm really in."

Marisol pushed up her red glasses and thought it over. "Maybe we could actually have some fun with this."

"What about our car-stop?" Yvonne asked. "He's got no license, no registration . . ."

"Today's his lucky day," I said.

My plan worked. When we pulled our cars out from under the El, the helicopter started shadowing Marisol and Yvonne. I had to drive around in a car that smelled of perfume, but I didn't mind. It was a nice smell, and the TV trucks were nowhere in sight.

Later, back at the district, Marisol and Yvonne said they couldn't remember when they'd had such a good time.

"It was great," said Marisol. "We let them follow us, we didn't try to run away. But we never let them catch up—whenever they got close, we'd speed up a little.

"Like a couple times at traffic lights," said Yvonne. "We'd be stopped, and one of the trucks would try to scoot up next to us. And Marisol would just step on the gas—*zoom*, we just shot through the light."

"Tell him about the car wash," said Marisol.

"You're gonna love this," said Yvonne. "You know that car wash on Walnut? We're driving by, the TV trucks are right behind us, and I say to Marisol, pull in. We drive around to the back, where you go into the car wash."

"Did they follow you?" I asked.

Yvonne shook her head. "With their satellite dishes? No way. So we go through, staying in the car. And when we come out, there's six TV cameras, all lined up next to each other."

"It was like an ambush," said Marisol. "It was like, now we got him."

"As we're driving out," said Yvonne, "we power down our windows and say, 'Hi, guys.' "

"They're looking at us," said Marisol, "then they're looking back at the car wash, then they're looking back at us again. Like, wait a second, what happened to that cop that was in the car? Like they're wondering, is he still in there someplace?"

Yvonne laughed. "We said, 'Bye, guys,' and just drove away. And that was it. They didn't follow us around anymore."

"You're the best," I said to them. "Not only did you get rid of the media for me, but you also cleaned my car. You're fine officers. Fine officers."

. . .

**Marisol and Yvonne** weren't alone in standing by me. In the days after Sonny Knight's murder, nearly every cop in the squad took me aside. We don't care what's in the newspapers and on TV, they said. We know you didn't have anything to do with that.

Mutt wasn't so lucky. No one believed he killed Sonny Knight. But in the vague, disjointed way that people think, they blamed him for bringing it all on. If he hadn't beaten up Sonny Knight in the first place—which most cops in the squad eventually concluded that he did—then Buster would never have been attacked, Paulie would never have been hurt, and whoever did kill Sonny Knight somehow wouldn't have been pushed into the act. There was no logic to this progression, it was all emotion. The squad was angry, fearful, confused, and they took it out on Mutt.

Had Roy been there, he would have been spared from this. The consensus was that he had simply gone along with Mutt out of loyalty, which in itself was not a bad thing. But in their eyes, that just made Mutt more culpable.

Few cops would have anything to do with Mutt now. Guys would stand apart from him at roll call. If he came into a room, they'd stop talking. About the only people who talked to him were Buster, Yvonne, and Marisol, they all stayed loyal, and George and his guys, Sam and Lewis. They didn't seem to care.

It takes a lot for cops to cast adrift a fellow officer. They don't do it lightly. But Mutt's violent tendencies, they felt, had put the squad in danger. And so most of the squad had decided, in an unspoken pact, that he was no longer one of them.

He claimed it didn't bother him. What the fuck do I care, he'd say. That was his new motto, What the fuck do I care. But something inside him was hardening. I could see it more each day. Particularly in his choice of new friends.

One night, Mimi's Lounge on Larchwood Street was robbed by a guy who was so stupid, or desperate, that he decided to hit a place where he was a regular customer. Mimi's was a broken-down bar in a broken-down black neighborhood. Other than the dimly lit "Mimi's Lounge" sign that hung over the sidewalk at the corner entrance, the place didn't seem interested in attracting customers. There was just a dirty gray steel door and walls of dirty gray brick. No colorful neon signs advertising beer, no credit card decals on the door. If you didn't already know what was inside, you didn't belong there anyway.

We got called to Mimi's all the time—usually for fights, sometimes for a stabbing or a shooting. And often for the noise out front, particularly late at night. People would step outside, beers in hand, to chat and smoke, to argue and yell at each other. The neighbors, their alarm clocks set for 5 A.M. so they could get up for work, would lie in their beds, unable to sleep. Finally, they'd grab the bedside phone and punch in 911, and we'd show up to provide some temporary relief.

Occasionally, the place got robbed, and on this night the bandit was Otis, a forty-five-year-old man who lived on the next block. None of the customers at the bar even knew Otis owned a gun, but there he was, pointing it at Freddie the bartender, demanding money.

Freddie made his own threat back. Put the gun away and go home, Otis, or you'll be banned from the bar forever. This apparently put the fear of God into Otis, because he put the gun back in his waistband and headed for the door.

In the meantime, though, a nervous customer had got on the pay phone in the back and called 911. The cops arrived just as Otis was leaving, and they grabbed his gun and put him in handcuffs.

When I swung by a few minutes later, Freddie and about a dozen of his customers were standing on the sidewalk, waiting for the cops inside to finish their paperwork and let the bar reopen. I was surprised Freddie had been asked to wait outside with everyone else—usually the bartender doesn't have to leave.

"Can I go back in, Sergeant?" he asked me.

I told him I'd check and pulled open the steel door. I walked in just in time to see George, behind the bar, pouring himself a shot of Dewar's. Sam and Lewis each were sipping bottles of beer, and Mutt, standing closest to the door, was draining a glass of what might have been whiskey. Not your typical bar scene—four uniformed cops, helping themselves to the beverages.

"What the fuck," I said.

George ignored me. He topped off the shot glass, then drained it with a long gulp.

I couldn't tell what Mutt was thinking. He seemed to be a little embarrassed, but not enough to put the drink down.

"Hey, Sarge," he said quietly.

"Get the fuck out of here," I said to him. "Now."

He put his glass on a nearby table and obeyed without a word. I waited until the door closed behind him, then walked over to George.

"I don't care what you do with your own fucking cops," I said, "but stay away from mine. Mutt's got enough fucking problems."

George poured himself another shot.

"I didn't make him take that drink," he said. "He's a big boy. He can make his own decisions."

## sixteen

ow'd you like to go to France?" I asked Michelle as we lay in bed one morning.

She turned toward me, leaning on an elbow. "Oh, I'd love to see Paris."

"I was thinking kind of more out in the country," I said. "You know, some old farmhouse or something, in a village where no one speaks any English."

"In other words, as far away from Philadelphia as possible."

"Exactly. I was talking to my lawyer yesterday . . ."

"Musgrave?"

"He told me that if I get convicted, I could be looking at some real jail time."

"He really believes that?"

"Yep. So maybe I should start thinking about that farmhouse. Get out while the getting's good."

"Very funny."

"Hey, it makes sense. It's not like they find you guilty, and then the judge says, 'Okay, just in case you want to skip town before I sentence you, I'll give you a couple days to plan your getaway.' You kind of get put in handcuffs, and that's pretty much it for the next ten years."

"You are joking, right?"

I let out a breath. "Yeah, I guess I am. I mean, what am I going to do in France, milk goats or something? Though I'm not thrilled about the alternative. You know, this morning I woke up, and I was watching you sleep . . ."

"I hope I wasn't drooling."

"Not too much. I mean, the pillow wasn't totally soaking wet."

"Oh, thanks."

"And I was thinking what would happen if I actually did go to prison. You know, really thinking about it, which I hadn't done before. I realized, I could probably handle it if I had to. But I would miss you. That's the only reason I'd go to France, or wherever. So we could still be together."

Michelle smiled. "That's sweet, Eddie."

"It's true."

Michelle's smooth face, her neck, her breasts, half covered by the sheets, just seemed to drink in the morning light, to make it softer.

"You know what Musgrave told me?" I asked. "The only reason I might go to jail is because Sonny Knight's dead. If he were still alive and I got convicted of covering up the beating, I'd probably just get probation."

"But not now," Michelle said.

I shook my head. "Not now."

I recounted our conversation, how Musgrave had said that in a high-profile case like this, the judge would be under a lot of pressure to come down hard.

"How hard?" Michelle asked.

"He said possibly two years. Maybe even three."

"Three? He said that?"

"Because it was Sonny Knight, and because Sonny Knight's dead."

I told Michelle that Musgrave had asked me a lot of questions. Including, was there anything at all that might cast doubt on Sonny Knight's version of events?

As a matter of fact, I said, there was. And I told him about Victor's garage.

"Did you mention this to the detectives?" Musgrave asked me.

"Yeah," I said. "They're not interested."

Musgrave thought about it, then said, "We have to try to pursue it. Even if we have to do it on our own."

Michelle shook her head when she heard this. "Easy for him to say."

She asked me about Mutt and Roy, and I told her that neither of them had been handling things very well. Mutt drinking at that bar was not a good sign.

"I'm worried about him," I said. "That's something he never would have done before."

"Drinking on duty, or hanging out with George and his guys?"

"Both. And that's the thing—him coming under George's influence. I don't like that at all."

"Mutt's just a kid," said Michelle.

"In many ways."

I told her I was worried about Roy as well, how he had stopped coming into work.

"Is he close to getting fired?"

"I don't know. So far Kirk's cutting him a break."

"Yeah, but how long is that going to last?"

"Not forever."

We talked about Mutt and Roy for a while longer, then Michelle said, "Eddie, how are *you* doing?"

"Me? I'm all right."

"You know, I think it's great that you're concerned about your men, I know that's important. But you have to make sure you also take care of yourself."

"C'mon, you're not really worried about me, are you?"

She gave me a pissed look. "Of course not. Someone out there might be trying to kill you, and now you might go to jail? Why should I be worried?"

"I'll be okay," I said.

"You know, Eddie, maybe you're right. Maybe we should go to France."

"If we do, would you wear one of those little French maid's outfits?"

Michelle's face relaxed, and she smiled. "What would you do if I did?"

"I'd chase you around the farmhouse, get you in a corner, lift up your skirt . . ."

"And then what?"

I reached under the covers and slid my hand between her legs.

"Then I'd say, Why don't you dust that table over there, and bend over while you're doing it?"

"And then what?"

"And then I'd pull down your panties . . ."

"What if I wasn't wearing any?"

"Then I would just pull down my pants."

"And then what?"

"Let me show you," I said. I turned Michelle over so that she faced away from me, and then I moved next to her, and then I showed her.

**Later that morning,** I stopped by the police and fire credit union at Grant and Academy. As I came out the door, Tina was pulling into a parking space in their Plymouth Voyager minivan. The three girls were in the back, lined up in their car seats.

Tina got out, saw me and smiled a hello, and I walked up to her.

"Hi, Tina," I said. "How's Roy doing?"

Her face darkened. "You didn't hear? He's at the shore."

"What's he doing there?"

"He's at the house. By himself. He's been there for five days."

"Five? Oh, man. That must be tough on you guys."

"I'm more concerned about him. I went down there two nights ago, he says he's fine, he just wants to be alone. Well, maybe he wants to be alone, but he's not fine."

She turned to check on the girls. Emily and Julia were watching us through the closed window.

"Has Mutt been down?"

"A couple times. And Roy's father went, too. Didn't make any difference—Roy wants to stay down there. And what can we do, we can't force him to come back."

"Sounds like he's hiding."

"That's exactly what he's doing. He's just trying to get as far away from all this as possible."

I thought about it. "I'm off today," I said. "Maybe I'll take a ride down there."

"Really?" she said. "That's so nice of you." She seemed to be suddenly full of hope. "Who knows, maybe you can say something to him we haven't thought of."

As soon as she said that, I wondered whether it was a mistake to say I'd go. What could I say to Roy that she hadn't already said? Or that his father or Mutt hadn't already said? I didn't want to set her up for another disappointment.

But it was too late. Tina was getting a pen and little notepad from her purse and writing down the address and phone number.

She smiled again. "He's lucky to have a sergeant like you."

**The Knopfler family's** shore house in North Wildwood was four blocks from the beach, not far from the house where my own family spent two weeks every summer when I was a kid. It was only about an hour and a half from Philly, not a bad drive unless you were coming back on a Sunday night, when the Parkway was an endless stream of brake lights, and you were tired and irritable and itchy with sand and suntan lotion, and all you wanted was to get back home.

I made pretty good time getting down there, crossing the causeway from the mainland a little after noon. It was a perfect beach day—glistening sunshine, pure blue sky, nice little breeze keeping the air from getting too hot. I thought about going straight to Roy's, but decided to stop and take at look at the ocean first. Hell, I realized, I hadn't been to the shore all summer, for the first time since I could remember. Usually I went down at least two or three times and stayed with cop friends who were renting a house. We'd spend the day on the beach, then have a barbecue in the backyard. Then we'd spend all night getting shitfaced in bars that fortunately were close enough to crawl home from, and we'd show up at work the next day lobster-red and still badly hung over.

I drove down a street that dead-ended into the beach, parked next to a fire hydrant, and took the wooded walkway over the low dunes. Me and about two thousand other people. It was the height of the beach rush hour, when families have finally gotten their acts together and tromp to the beach loaded down with cribs and chairs and big umbrellas and Igloo coolers. Once they were on the beach, they fanned out, searching for new homesteads on the sand.

I was wearing shorts and a T-shirt, so I didn't feel too out of place, and I pulled off my white sneakers and socks and headed toward the ocean. Crowds of kids were splashing in the water, though only in front of the high, white-painted lifeguard stands. You stray too far to the left or right, try to have a little fun, you get whistled back.

Meanwhile, the adults were power-walking along the water's edge, or standing in the surf arguing into cell phones. Working as hard as they possibly could to enjoy themselves, trying to make up for all those summer days they never quite took advantage of, though they had promised themselves, as always, that this year would be different.

I reached the water and let the cool waves wash over my feet. Girls in bikinis were strolling by, they all had spectacular tans, their great achievement of the summer. Of course, by late August everybody's dark, at least those who adhere to the Jersey shore sun ritual. From morning until early afternoon, they face the water. But as it gets later in the day, and the sun moves to the right—toward the south—they get up and move their chairs with it. By the end of the day the ocean is on everyone's left, forgotten, irrelevant. A hundred thousand beach chairs, all facing nowhere.

I walked into the water up to my knees, letting the small swells wet the bottom of my shorts. The ocean glittered in the sun, it was almost blinding. For a moment, I forgot where I was.

And then I remembered and thought, What am I going to say to Roy? I had listened to music on the way down, letting my mind drift. I should have thought out what I was going to tell him.

Who knows, maybe he should just leave the Police Department, if he's not going to enjoy it anymore. Maybe he should stay at the shore, have Tina and the kids come down. They could all spend the rest of the summer on the beach. Roy could even get a job down here, maybe at one of the casinos.

Yeah, right, I thought, that's smart. Tell Roy not to come home. Tina would love that. Gee, thanks, Sergeant.

I wished I was better at giving advice. I wanted to just stand there in the water, not come out. I could understand why Roy was hiding. Maybe I wanted to do it, too.

**Like a lot** of houses at the shore, the Knopflers' didn't have a front lawn, just a plateful of white gravel that never needed watering. It had that windswept shore feel—faded pastel-green clapboard, kids' bicycles leaning against each other, against a wall, barren cement front porch, rusted wind chimes hanging from a hook.

This was going to be a surprise visit. I hadn't called Roy first—why give him a chance to tell me not to come?

I knocked on the door. No answer. I knocked again. Still nothing. My first thought was that maybe he was at the beach. Then I had a flash of worry. I hope he's okay, I hope nothing's happened.

I could hear movement inside the house, then the door opened. Roy took a hit of the bright sunlight and recoiled, squinting, blinking, like he hadn't seen the sun in months.

"Sarge," he said. "What're you doin' here?"

He was wearing old shorts and a dirty T-shirt. His hair was uncombed, his face unshaven, he had dark circles around his eyes. The whole works.

"C'mon in," he said.

The place was gloomy as hell—the neighboring houses were so close, almost no sunlight got in, and Roy hadn't bothered to turn on any lights. He also hadn't opened any of the windows, and the house was hot, stuffy, smelling of garbage and mildew. Clothes and towels were hanging on chairs or were bunched up on the floor. The coffee table was stacked with grimy pizza boxes, and every available flat space was covered with beer cans and dirty plates.

"What is this, a fuckin' crack house?" I asked.

That got a smile from him. "Sorry. If I would've known you were coming, I would have straightened up a little." He looked around, trying to figure out where to start.

"You don't have to clean up," I said. "I'm just busting your balls."

"I probably should, sooner or later. Want a beer?"

I said sure, and he went into the kitchen and came back with two bottles.

"Sit down," he said, pointing to an upholstered rocking chair, but it was covered with dirty clothes. He gave me one of the beers, and with his free hand cleared off the chair, tossing all the clothes into a pile on the floor.

"Gotta do laundry," he said.

He sat on the couch and I sat in the chair and we drank our beers. The heat and smell were stifling.

"Can I open a window?" I asked.

"I'll get it," he said, and opened one behind me. Thankfully, there was a slight breeze.

"Roy," I said, "what the hell you been doing down here?"

"I don't know. Thinking."

"Do you leave the house at all?"

"Yeah, sure. I do a lot of walking and swimming. At night."

"What do you mean, at night?"

"You know, when no one's around. I'll go down to the beach, maybe at one or two in the morning, and just walk along the water for miles."

"You swim at night, too?"

"That's the only time to do it. You go out past the breakers, swim, just float around. You're out there in that darkness, by yourself, you're just totally alone. It's great. Though like three nights ago? I'm coming out of the water, there's this couple right in the surf, just humping away, just going at it. It was so dark, I didn't even see them until I was almost right on top of them. I fuckin' scared the living shit out of them. I'm coming out of the water, out of fuckin' nowhere, dripping wet, they were like, 'Yaaaah!' They thought I was the creature from the green fuckin' lagoon or something."

We laughed at that for a while.

Roy took a sip of beer, then said, "You think I should come back to work, right?"

"I don't know, Roy. Whatever you want to do."

"Everybody wants me to. I've been getting a regular parade of visitors down here."

"People care about you."

"I know that. I feel bad, leaving Tina up there with the kids."

I didn't say anything.

"What difference would it make, going back?" he said. "We're just going to get fired. What would be the point, so I can get on the fuckin' news again? Hey, been there, done that, you know what I mean?"

I did know.

He smiled. "I'd much rather go swimming," he said. "It's like the only peace I get."

"Sounds good."

"It is good. You know, every night I've been going out further and further. Just to see how far I can go before I get tired. I know it sounds stupid, you know, like, what's his problem, but it just kind of draws me out there. And I think, what would happen if one day I just kept going?"

"What do you mean, just kept going?"

"I don't know. Just kept going."

"Roy, I hope you're not serious."

He shrugged. "I wouldn't do nothin' like that."

I didn't know whether to believe him.

"You know," I said, "being a cop isn't everything."

"It is if you're a Knopfler."

"So this is about pressure from your family?"

"No," he said quietly. "No, it's not."

I tried to think of something else to say, something that might help. I pictured him out there in that dark water. I just couldn't shake away the image.

"What about you?" he asked. "What would you do if you weren't a cop?"

"I don't know."

"Would you want to do anything else?"

"I don't know."

"You haven't thought about it? Probably, all three of us are going to get fired."

"It's possible."

"How do *you* deal with it, Eddie? Having everybody think you're a fuckin' criminal, everywhere you go?"

"I guess I don't think about it."

"Well, it's affecting you, whether you know it or not. I guarantee it."

"Maybe."

"And how are you ever going to get another job? Everybody knows your fuckin' name. Where you going to move to, Altoona?"

"Hey, pal, give me a break. I'm supposed to be the one cheering *you* up."

"Then you see where I'm coming from."

"Yeah, I do."

"So you see how it might be kinda nice, swimming out in the water at night, not having nobody bother you?"

"Is that an invitation?"

"Fuck no. Get your own fuckin' beach."

We laughed and had another beer, and then I realized it was probably time for me to go. As I got up, I felt I had to say something before I left. Make one last effort.

"Roy, all the things you're worried about will happen whether you come back or not. The only thing that's going to be different is what happens to other people when you're not there."

He didn't say anything to that, he got up and shook my hand, and said thanks for coming. I left him there and headed back up the Parkway.

But as I drove, my throat got dry. Maybe I didn't say the right things. Maybe I didn't try hard enough.

## seventeen

**ith all this going on, the last thing I needed was** to have to worry about George Laguerre. My life would have been a lot easier if he would have just transferred the hell back to the 16th—or anyplace else. I wanted nothing to do with him.

And so when I saw his empty patrol car outside one of the Osage Plaza high-rises the next afternoon, I said to myself, Don't ask any questions. Just let it go.

Osage Plaza was a public housing project in West Philly, and it was patrolled by the Housing Authority police. Which meant that unless we were chasing somebody, or there was some kind of major drama, like a shooting, there'd be no reason for any of us to be there. I figured George was probably up in one of the buildings, getting into something he shouldn't. Which would be typical.

It amazed me that he would even go near the place. They were getting ready to tear down all four of the high-rises, and residents were being relocated. Not a big deal, except that the empty apartments were being taken over by squatters and drug dealers and five-dollar-a-blowjob crack whores. Osage Plaza had never been a nice place, but now it was becoming a trashed-out mini-city of filth and criminality. Even the housing police didn't want to go into the buildings anymore.

If that's what George wants, I thought, fine. I'm just going to keep driving.

And then I heard two gunshots, echoing from the upper floors of the closest building. Maybe kids having target practice?

Then two more shots, sharper, a different caliber. Then more shots, one after the other, back and forth. This wasn't target practice, this was a gunfight.

And George was up there, somewhere. I clicked my radio.

"Twenty-Andy," I said, trying to keep my voice calm.

George didn't respond.

"Twenty-Andy," I repeated.

Still nothing. I jumped out of my car and looked up, scanning the building. Twenty stories of brick and faded blue sheet metal. Balconies all covered with chain-link fencing, prison-style, so nothing could be thrown overboard. But there was no movement anywhere, nothing to tell me where the shooting was coming from, or what was going on.

Then George's voice came over the radio, gunshots thundering in the background: *"This is twenty-Andy, get me an assist, Osage Plaza, Building B. I'm under fire. Ninth floor, I'm on the ninth floor."*

I clicked my shoulder mike. "Radio, this is twenty-Charlie. I'm on location, I'm going in."

*"Use caution,"* the dispatcher said.

Yeah, no shit.

I sprinted toward the main entrance, pulling my gun from its holster, thinking, George, you motherfucker, what are you getting me into?

There was a guard booth in the tiny lobby, with an actual guard inside, but he was worthless, an unarmed rent-a-cop whose job was to stay alive for eight hours. He looked at me like, What do you expect me to do?

I considered taking an elevator up to the tenth floor, then coming down one flight. That way when I got to the ninth, I wouldn't be tired or out of breath. But five or six women, with kids in tow, were already waiting for an elevator to show up, and who knew how long they had been there? Maybe forever. A good elevator at a public housing project in Philly was one that when the doors opened, you didn't step into empty space.

I ran to the right, through an open door into a fire tower, and up the trash-covered concrete steps. After the first floor, one side of the tower was exposed to the open air, and fenced in, like the balconies. I had to be careful going up—one of the shooters could be coming down, they could be right on top of me before I knew it. I took the steps as fast as I could, but paused and did a sneak-and-peek at every turn, holding my gun out with both hands.

It wasn't like I was alone. I had to dodge people who were standing on the landings, or sitting on the steps or old dinette chairs amid the empty crack vials, drinking beer. The fact that there was a shootout going on a few floors above made absolutely no impression on anyone, they didn't even seem to notice. Here I was, coming through with a big gun in my hand, yelling at people to get out of my way, they barely moved. Gunfire, cops, so what? No more of a nuisance around here than someone's loud stereo.

By the fifth floor I was breathing hard, I wasn't used to this. It's one thing to walk up a few flights of stairs, it's another to do it at a run, weighed down with a gunbelt and a vest that's heavy and fits so tight you can't even take a deep breath. All the way up, I kept asking myself, How come this couldn't have been on the first floor? Why is it never on the first floor?

But I kept moving. When I finally reached the landing on eight, I could hear the gun battle on the floor above me, the shots echoing like crazy in the halls, into the stairwells.

One more floor. I took it quickly, up to the ninth, and reached for the handle of the red metal fire door. I was exhausted, soaked with sweat, gasping for breath. The gunshots were deafening now.

I pulled the door open slowly. There was a three-foot space between the door and the hallway, kind of a tiny vestibule, and I stepped into it. I could tell that whatever was happening was down the hallway, to my left, and I did a quick peek around the corner.

About halfway down the hall was another fire-tower vestibule, but this one came in from the opposite direction mine did. Two young black guys were in the vestibule, my angle didn't give me a full view, but I could see them peeking around their own corner, firing shots further down the hallway. What was down there? I tried to see. A huge pile of mattresses, rugs, furniture, all kinds of trash. There was some kind of movement behind the pile, and then the flash from a gun muzzle. It had to be George. He was pinned down.

I had been in these buildings before. Osage Plaza wasn't like a regular apartment building, but public housing projects never are. The hallways had low ceilings and were narrow, claustrophobic, more on a child's scale than an adult's. The walls were pale yellow cinder block, covered with graffiti and grimy from the dirty hands of a million kids. The apartment doors never had any numbers, they were all unfinished-wood replacements of the originals. Some people simply wrote their names on the walls with a Magic Marker: Tone & Lakeisha, Trey, Ra-Shel. Everything had a cheap feel, cheap and inconsequential, like the place had cost five whole dollars to build.

I stood up and backed away, trying to figure out my next move. I had the advantage—they didn't know I was there. I could probably take out at least one of them. It was quiet for a moment, and I quickly switched off my radio so it wouldn't give me away. I could hear my labored breathing, feel the blood pounding in my head.

Should I open fire, or give them a chance to surrender? My instinct said, just go ahead and shoot. Once you give away your position, you become a target. But I knew I might be able to do this without killing anybody. Once they saw me, they'd know they were outflanked, that they couldn't win. And they wouldn't know how many cops I had with me, or how many others were on the way.

I hadn't heard any more firing. Were those guys even still there? I took three deep breaths to control my breathing, then swung my gun around the corner, holding it with both hands. There they were, talking to each other, probably trying to figure out what to do. I had a clear shot at one, the other was half hidden. I took aim and was astonished to see the front sight of my gun bobbing and weaving. I knew it was the adrenaline and physical exertion. I took another deep breath, and the sight gradually steadied.

But I had to decide, now. Fire, or give them a chance?

"Police!" I yelled. "Drop the gun!"

The guy in plain view looked around, up, down, he had no fucking idea where my voice was coming from. But the other one knew, and in an instant he had his gun around the corner and he looked me right in the eyes and fired. The wall exploded to my right and I fired back, a reflex, before I realized what I was doing. I didn't know where my bullet went, but I knew it wasn't even close.

I pulled back behind the wall. Fuck. You blew it. Now what are you going to do? Take another shot, quick. Kneel down so you're lower than he's expecting. And this time fucking aim.

I got down on one knee, tilted out from the corner and started to squeeze the trigger, looking down my sight. But they were gone, there was just the sound of the fire door slamming shut.

They were getting away.

I took off down the hallway toward the vestibule, full of fury. I'd chase them all the way down to the first floor and out the building if I had to.

George had emerged from the pile of trash, he was pounding toward me. There was someone behind him, another cop. It was Mutt, what the fuck was he doing here?

George beat me to the vestibule, I thought he was going to lead the way, but instead he turned and faced me, blocking my path.

"Let 'em go," he said.

I heard him, but what he said didn't register, and I tried to push him aside. He pushed back, staying between me and the door.

"Let 'em go," he said again.

I was still pushing at him, I couldn't believe this. "Move, move! They're fuckin' getting away!"

George was fighting me now. He had holstered his gun and was pushing me back with both hands, like his life depended on me not going down those steps. I finally just stopped and looked at him, then Mutt. This was too bizarre for words.

I knew that other cops would be converging on the building, rushing up both fire towers. I turned my radio back on and clicked the shoulder mike.

"Twenty-C-Charlie to Radio. Two black males are coming down the north fire tower from nine. They're armed with guns, they're the shooters. Anyone coming up is going to run right into them."

That is, if they were still in the fire tower. More than likely, they had already left the stairwell, and were on some other floor, hiding in one of the apartments.

George and Mutt were just standing there, looking at me.

"Laguerre," I said, "you want to tell me what the fuck is going on?"

George turned to Mutt. "Get out of here, right now. Go down the other fire tower, the one Eddie came up."

"Wait a second, Mutt," I said, stopping him. "I want to know what you're doing here."

Mutt glanced at George, then back at me, uncertain.

"Mutt," I said, my voice even. "Who were those fucking guys?"

George grabbed Mutt's arm. "You got to get off this floor, now. You don't want to be seen here."

"Mutt," I said. "Talk to me."

"Go," said George. "Hurry. They'll be here any second."

Mutt kept looking back and forth between me and George, torn. He slowly put his gun back in his holster. He was buying time, thinking.

I could see his face harden as he made up his mind. "Sorry, Eddie," he said, and took off in a jog down the hallway.

I started to go after him, but then stopped. Fuck it. When I looked back at George, he was heading down the hall in the opposite direction. Where was *he* going?

I walked quickly to catch up with him. "I want answers, George," I called to him. "Now."

There was open apartment door on the left, I hadn't seen it before. George stepped in to close the door, and I got there just in time to catch a glimpse inside.

There were two overturned metal boxes on the living room floor, and money, piles of bills, were spilling out of both. Money was scattered all over the place.

George pulled the door shut and turned back to me, and I understood.

"This is a stash house, isn't it?" I asked.

He didn't answer.

"I think that's exactly what it is," I said. "I think you brought Mutt here so you could rip off some fucking drug dealers when they weren't around. Except they came back, right? While you were in there."

George waited for me to finish.

"How much did they have in there?" I asked. "Fifty thousand?

George shrugged. "We didn't have time to count it."

"Right. And they come back, and they're not going to let that fucking money go without a fight, and now there's a fucking shootout."

"Eddie, it's all over, and no one got hurt, right?"

"You motherfucker, I came up here to save your fucking ass."

"And I thank you for that."

"Fuck you, I don't want your fucking thanks. And you're getting Mutt involved in this shit? What the fuck are you doing?"

"Mutt wasn't here," George said calmly. "Unless you want to say he was. And I didn't see you fire your gun."

I stared at George. The sly motherfucker was offering me a deal. Keep quiet, Mutt would stay out of trouble. And if no one knew I had fired my gun, I wouldn't be taken off the street, the usual procedure while this whole thing was investigated.

The fire doors from the two stairwells slammed open at the same time. Cops were rushing in, surrounding us. A Housing

Authority lieutenant saw George and me. What happened? he asked.

George looked at me, and when I didn't say anything, he quickly told his story. He was driving down the street next to the projects and saw two guys on the sidewalk. He realized right away that they matched the descriptions of the two guys from that liquor store robbery on Carpenter Street a couple of days ago. He called for backup on his radio, but it didn't seem to be working, so he tried to make the arrests himself. He ended up chasing them into this building and up the stairs, up here to the ninth floor. They had guns and opened fire, and he dove behind that pile of trash over there.

When George finished, he looked at me, waiting to see whether I would dispute any of his story. Knowing that I wouldn't.

**Later, when I** came back down the stairs and walked out of the building, Mutt was waiting for me.

"Sarge," he said. "Can I talk to you?"

"No," I said.

"*No?*"

"No." I walked quickly toward my car, but he fell in beside me.

"Listen, I'm sorry you got involved."

In other words, not sorry for what he was doing up there, just sorry it didn't work out the way he thought it would.

"We watched those guys leave," said Mutt. "George said they weren't supposed to come back."

I just ignored him.

"Sarge, I know you could have been killed . . ."

I gave him a look and walked a little faster. He kept pace with me.

"I know you stuck by me this whole time."

I gave him another look.

We were almost at my car. I could tell Mutt was thinking as fast as he could, trying to figure out what else he could say to me. I opened my car door and got in.

"Eddie," he said.

I waited. He either wouldn't or couldn't speak, and I closed the car door and started the engine and pulled away.

If George had been alone up on the ninth floor right then, I would have walked all the way back up the stairs and smashed his head against that grimy yellow cinder-block wall. He knew that Mutt was confused and vulnerable, and he was taking advantage of it, using him.

How could I keep closing my eyes to what George was doing? He was going too far, getting Mutt involved.

Maybe I should go to Internal Affairs, I thought. Tell them all about Sergeant George Laguerre. But that would have meant getting Mutt jammed up, too. And I couldn't do that, not now, not with what he was going through. Mutt was like a child, he didn't know what the hell he was doing.

Unlike George, who knew exactly what he was doing.

## eighteen

**oy was right about at least one thing. The pres-**sure was beginning to affect me, whether or not I realized it.

I'd be addressing my cops at roll call, and wonder, Is this the last time I'm going to do this? Is this the last time I'm going to be standing in front of my cops?

Or when I'd go to the coffeemaker in the operations room and pour myself a cup of glop. And wonder, What kind of glop do they give you in prison?

Not that I had these thoughts all the time. But when they did come, it'd be without warning, and that in itself was a little unnerving. It made me question just how well I was dealing with it all.

I started having trouble getting enough sleep, particularly after working nights. You don't go right to sleep anyway, not after eight hours on the streets, you're usually too keyed up. So I'd either go out drinking with guys from the squad, or go home and have a couple of beers and watch TV. A couple of times, I called Roy, and we talked for a while. I usually didn't get to sleep until around two or three. If Michelle came over, we might stay up all night.

Then the phone would ring at eight o'clock in the morning, when I was still half asleep. And my heart would start pounding. It's too early for someone to call, I'd think. It has to be something important.

Every single time that happened, my first thought was, It's the lawyer. He's going to tell me, Get ready. Today's the day. The indictment's coming down.

It wouldn't be the lawyer, though. It would usually be some cop I knew, passing along this or that rumor about the investigation, or just wanting to talk about it. I should have just hung up, but I didn't, I stayed on the phone, and the longer I talked about my situation, the more upset I got, the more the adrenaline started flowing. By the time the conversation was over, there was no way I could get back to sleep.

All of this would have been easier to take if only I'd been able to fight back. I wanted, more than anything, to prove that Mutt and Roy and I were innocent, that we had been unfairly accused. Assuming that Mutt and Roy *were* innocent. When I saw Mutt at Osage Plaza, I had to wonder: What else is he not telling me?

Though I still felt sure that Sonny Knight had lied about that night. He had been at Victor's garage. And if two police cars had been there as well, then it was all tied together, somehow.

What I really wanted was that tape of the 16th District's radio transmissions. But I still couldn't figure out how to get a copy. I called a few close friends, people I could trust. Do you know anybody in Radio, I asked them, anybody who can help me get that tape?

No, they all said. They didn't have that kind of connection.

I even hung out at the FOP's basement lounge one Friday night, knowing I'd see Holly. She was one of the dispatchers for the 20th, she knew all the cops, and we'd always got along. But she couldn't help me, she said. She wouldn't know how to do it without getting caught.

And so I pretty much gave up on that angle. At least until the night I ran into Del Falk again on the street in West Philly, and he asked how things were going. When I told him I had hit a dead end with the tape, he said, "I can get it for you. How come you didn't come to me?"

He said this while we were standing on 58th Street, watching the guys from the crime-scene unit work around the body of a sixteen-year-old drug dealer.

"I can't ask you to do that," I told Del.

"You don't have to. I just offered."

"I don't want you getting jammed up."

"What are they going to do," he asked, "put me in Night Command?"

Del said he was friends with the night captain in the Radio Room. They often went over to Chinatown together on their dinner breaks.

"This won't be a problem," Del said. "Leave it to me."

So I did. And Del did get me the tape, just like he promised. But he also got caught.

It was a simple plan, and it almost worked. In one part of the Radio Room were the 911 call-takers, who dealt with the public, working the phones. They typed the information on their computer screens—like "Man with a gun, corner of 24th and Lehigh"—and sent it over to the dispatchers on the other side of the room.

The dispatchers had their own computer screens, showing the jobs coming in, and the status of all the patrol cars in the districts they handled. They could tell at a glance whether a car was assigned to a particular job, for example, and whether it was on location yet.

Years ago, all the activity on Police Radio—the back-and-forth between the dispatchers and the cops on the street—was recorded on huge reel-to-reel tapes. Now everything was stored digitally. It all went straight into the computers.

It was easy enough to listen to a few minutes of radio activity. Supervisors in the Radio Room did it all the time, usually in response to complaints. Like the one I once made against a dispatcher—Holly's predecessor.

What pissed me off about this dispatcher was that she treated the street cops like her personal servants. She expected them to bow down to her on the air. And if they didn't, she'd get nasty.

"You don't tell me you're taking a lunch break," she'd say to a cop. "You *ask* me. I might have something else for you to do first."

Guys wanted to drive downtown and wring her skinny little chicken neck.

One night she sent Buster and Tony D to handle a domestic disturbance. I recognized the address, and I remembered that the last time we got called there, the husband pulled a knife on the cops and had to be subdued.

"Radio," I said, "send another unit over there. We've had trouble in the past."

"Twenty-fifteen is two-man," the dispatcher sneered back. "That's enough."

"That's not enough," I said. "He had a knife last time. Send another unit."

She refused, the husband pulled a knife again, and Buster and Tony D both came close to getting slashed. When it was all over, I drove back to the district and called the Radio Room.

"Get me the captain on duty," I said.

When the captain picked up the phone, I lit into him. One of your fucking people almost got my cops hurt, I yelled. And I want to know, right now, what the fuck you're going to do about it.

The captain said he'd call me back. And he did, about a half hour later. He told me he had got on the computer and played back the radio transmissions, and then had called in the dispatcher and had her listen to them, too.

That was the last time she was ever on Police Radio. I'd heard they assigned her to other duties. Cleaning the bathrooms, I hoped.

But while a supervisor had access to the computer, they didn't exactly allow cops—especially cops like me—to come in off the street and play back whatever they wanted, like it was the public library.

Occasionally, they made tapes off the computer, usually when the commissioner or some other top boss wanted a copy. But to get a tape, you needed to make a written request. And it had to be approved by the commissioner himself.

When I mentioned this to Del, as we stood there on 58th Street, he assured me it wouldn't be required in our particular case.

"We don't need no stinkin' written request," he said.

A few days later, he got back to me and said it was all set. Just pull into the lot at Police Headquarters tonight about ten, he said. I'll bring the tape out to you.

I got there five minutes early and parked my Blazer in one of the detectives' empty spaces. Headquarters was a four-story, poured-concrete figure eight, its two circular sections connected like Siamese twins. Its offices were pie shaped, or in some other way deformed, so that the whole place had an other-dimensional feel. This no doubt accounted for many of the policies and directives that had emanated from the building over the years.

It felt strange sitting there in that parking lot. Here I was, a cop at Police Headquarters, and yet I was worried about someone seeing me. Getting caught by the cops.

Del emerged from the building a little after ten, saw my Blazer, and walked over.

"Here you go, pal," he said, handing me an unmarked cassette tape in a clear plastic case. "Remember me in your will."

And that should have been it, except for what happened when Del went back inside.

"I figured I'd stop back by Radio on my way up, just to say thanks again to Danny," Del told me later that night. Danny was the captain who had made the tape.

"I walked in the room, and there was the fucking inspector, talking to Danny. And neither of them looked very happy."

The inspector was in charge of the Radio Room, which meant he was Danny's boss. Supposedly he never came in at night.

"Can you believe it?" Del asked me. "The one fucking time he comes in. Danny's over at the operations desk, and when he comes back, he sees the inspector standing over the computer we were using to make the tape. It turned out Danny had forgot to clear the screen."

"Danny was hemming and hawing," Del said. "The inspector was saying, 'I don't remember approving this request.' Danny saw me coming in, it was like, you better get the fuck out of here. But I wasn't going to just let him hang there. I wasn't going to do that. So I told the inspector, the captain did it for me."

Del said he made up some bullshit story about how a lieutenant in the 16th was supposedly seen drinking in bars while on the job, and he wanted to listen to the tapes to see whether the guy was answering his calls.

Why didn't you make a written request? the inspector asked. Del explained that he didn't want to hurt the lieutenant's reputation if the drinking thing wasn't true.

"The inspector listens to all this," Del said. "And he's convinced. He's nodding, his head's bobbing up and down. I'm thinking, I've pulled the wool right over his fuckin' eyes. Then he says to me, 'Captain, I can't blame you a bit for wanting to handle it the way you did.' And he turns to Danny and says, 'Danny, that was nice of you to want to help him out.' I knew there was a 'but' coming, and I was right. He says to Danny, 'But you know that's a violation of policy, and the policy's there for a reason. It's not up to you, Danny, to decide who gets tapes and who doesn't. And I can't have someone working for me who isn't going to follow the rules. So, what's going to happen is this: You're out of here. You're going to join your friend here in Night Command.' And then he turns to me and says, 'And you, Captain, I wouldn't count on getting out of there any time soon. Like, any time during the rest of your career. By the way, where's the tape?' "

Del told him it was down in his office.

"Go get it," the inspector said.

Del went down one floor, to his office, and called the inspector on the phone.

"We got a drama going on in South Philly," Del told him. "My boss wants me out there right away. I'll get the tape to you when I get back. Sorry."

He hung up before the inspector could argue.

Of course, there was no drama in South Philly, but Del left the building anyway, heading for the 20th. He showed up there not long after I got back. I was in my Blazer, parked in the Yard, getting ready to listen to the tape, when Del knocked on the passenger window.

"I need it back," he said. I unlocked the door, and he climbed in and explained what had happened. When I heard the story, I felt sick. I hit the eject button on the tape player.

Del pushed the tape back in. "Let's at least listen to it first," he said. "We've come this far."

We heard a couple of routine calls, then:

*"Sixteen-Andy."*

That was George's voice. I remembered that he had been filling in at the 16th the night the councilman was beaten. It was common for sergeants to be sent over to another district when someone was out sick, and since George had recently come from the 16th, they were always sending him back over there.

*"Sixteen-Andy,"* the dispatcher echoed back.

*"Let me get a meet with Sixteen-fourteen, Forty-second and Parrish."*

Victor's garage.

*"Sixteen-fourteen, you copy that?"* the dispatcher asked.

*"Sixteen-fourteen, yeah, we got it, thanks."*

Del looked at me. "Who's sixteen-fourteen?"

"Who knows?" I said. But I was thinking, George is at that garage for some reason. And it wouldn't surprise me a bit if he was calling for his two pals, Sam and Lewis. They were still in the 16th at the time—George got them transferred to the 20th, but not until a week later.

"When we're done here," I told Del, "I'm going to head over to the 16th. I want to take a look at that assignment sheet."

We listened to the rest of the tape, but there was nothing else of interest. I rewound it and handed it to Del.

"I'm sorry," I said. "I can't believe I fucked up two people's careers in one night."

"You didn't fuck up my career, Eddie, I did that a long time ago."

"What about the captain?"

"He's a golden boy, he won't be in Night Command for long. And anyway, that's for me to feel guilty about, not you."

"If I hadn't asked you . . ."

"You didn't ask me."

"I just hope this isn't all for nothing," I said.

"Hey," said Del, "when you're doing battle with the bosses, it's never for nothing. Not in this department."

I laughed. "They don't make 'em like you anymore."

"Good thing," he said. "There's not enough desks in Night Command."

I drove back over to the 16th, said hello to the white-haired corporal whose name I still couldn't remember, and got his okay to go back into the filing cabinets. I found the assignment sheet from that night. I was right: 16-14 car was Robbins and Portland. Sam and Lewis.

Then they were all there that night—George, Sam and Lewis, and Sonny Knight. And something definitely happened.

# nineteen

o Michelle, the Danforth trial had been forefront in her life. To the rest of us, it was part of the ever present background. We all followed the case on TV and in the papers. We argued about how good a job the lawyers were doing, we railed against the judge whenever he excluded evidence for the prosecution.

And one thing we all knew: if Danforth got convicted, there was likely to be trouble on the streets.

That Friday, the case finally went to the jury. The Police Department was put on alert. Emergency Response Groups—officers in wagons—were stationed near traditional trouble spots throughout the city. Contingency plans for each district were drawn up.

We didn't even get a break for the weekend—the judge ordered that deliberations continue through Saturday and Sunday. It was busy for us both days, there was plenty of the usual crime.

Including one incident, on Sunday, that escalated the growing war between me and George Laguerre.

A little after noon, there was a rape in Westmount, the Italian section of the 20th District. Or rather, an attempted rape. Not only did the guy fail, he ended up in the hospital.

He was some creepy guy from the neighborhood. He broke into a woman's house, chased her upstairs, and tried to rape her in the front bedroom. She was able to get to a window and yell for help, and though he pulled her away a couple of times, she kept getting to the window and screaming, and eventually neighbors heard her and stormed into the house. They grabbed the guy and dragged him onto the street, where they proceeded to beat the living shit out of him. When we arrived, a beefy young guy with no shirt was banging the would-be rapist's head on the sidewalk, like he was playing a tune. One thing about Italian neighborhoods in Philly, they take care of their own.

Somehow the guy survived, and Rescue took him off to the hospital. I had to send a couple of cops over there for a security detail. I spotted Sam and Lewis, standing around smoking cigarettes with a couple of the woman's rescuers, and told them to head over to the hospital.

They weren't thrilled about going. A hospital detail meant they'd be tied up for the rest of the shift. If something good happened, they'd miss out on the action.

Lewis didn't argue, though. I think he was afraid to confront me. Sam had no such fear.

"Can't you get someone else?" he asked.

"Nope."

"Why? Why does it have to be us?"

" 'Cause I'm the sergeant, and I'm telling you to."

Sam was unhappy as hell that his pal George wasn't there to get them off the hook. But George was stuck back at the district doing paperwork, on desk duty while the shootout at Osage Plaza was being investigated. Sometimes they can keep you off the street for weeks, but since no one got hurt, it probably wouldn't take them long to clear the job. Too bad. I kind of liked not having George around.

About an hour after we all left the woman's house, we had a pursuit, a good one. Yvonne and Marisol stopped two kids in a new Mercedes in West Philly. As they were walking up to the car, the kid behind the wheel stepped on the gas and spun off, almost hitting a boy on a bike. Yvonne and Marisol jumped back in their car and took off after the Mercedes, just as Radio was getting back to them with information on the license plate. The car had been stolen, a fact that Yvonne and Marisol had pretty much already figured out.

A pursuit is just about the most exciting thing a cop can do without shooting off his gun. You're rocketing through narrow city streets trying not to kill anybody or yourself in a crash, and your blood is turning to pure adrenaline. Naturally, everyone wants to join the fun. Sometimes guys from other districts, even guys halfway across the city, will try to get in on a good pursuit before it's over.

Yvonne and Marisol chased the Mercedes down Spruce Street and onto the Schuylkill Expressway. For a cop, a pursuit that jumps to a highway is like hitting the lottery. Now we're *really* going to go fast! Police Radio couldn't keep up with all the cars calling in to say they were joining the pursuit. And somehow, I wasn't surprised when Sam and Lewis told Radio they were going in on it, too.

They'd never made it to the hospital. As soon as they had left the rape scene, Sam had called George on his cell phone to bitch and moan. George told them not to worry about the hospital detail, he'd give it to someone else.

I learned all this from Sam and Lewis themselves, down by the stadium complex, where the two kids had crashed the Mercedes and bailed out, and led us on a three-block foot pursuit before they were finally caught.

"Sergeant Laguerre said we didn't have to go to the hospital," said Sam. Like an eighth-grade kid talking to a substitute teacher.

"Is that what he told you?" I asked. "In that case, I think I'll have a little chat with him. In the meantime, you two are at the hospital. Bye."

"But the sergeant said . . ."

"You really want to argue with me about this? Really? After going around me like you did? You really want to fuck with me now?"

They turned and walked to their car, grumbling something I couldn't hear, and drove off.

. . .

**It was a** long way back to the district, but the ride didn't do anything to calm me down. By the time I pulled up at headquarters, I couldn't even see straight. I walked into the operations room and up to the desk where George was studying the assignment sheet.

"Who the fuck do you think you are to countermand my orders?" I yelled. "Don't ever do that the fuck again."

George stood up. "I'll do it any time I fucking want. You got a crap hospital detail, you give it to your people, not mine."

I could feel the five other people in the room—four female officers and Sammy, the corporal—all getting tense.

"Don't fuck with me, George."

"Or what? You're a short-timer, we all know that. They're probably warming up your jail cell right now."

He laughed. He thought that was very funny.

My punch caught him in the side of the jaw and sent him staggering backward, into the bank of portable radios nestled in their chargers. Four or five of them popped out and crashed to the floor. George was able to keep his balance, and he came around the desk at me, sending his right fist toward my face. I blocked it, but then he punched with his left, clipping my jaw, almost knocking me down.

Everyone in the room scattered. The women started flying out the door, leaving only Sammy to try to break up the fight, which was a mistake. He got between us at exactly the wrong moment and got nailed by us both. Even he fled after that.

George and I were about the same weight and same strength, and we started trading punches, we were just whaling away on each other. The operations room was not a large space, and it was like we were in a cage match, a fight to the death. We were slamming each other into computers, into the TV, the coffee machine, it was like we were in one of those cowboy movies, tearing the saloon apart.

There were windows along one side of the room, and cops were gathering to watch the show. We also had another audience—three skinny black kids in the glassed-in juvenile holding cell. The cell's windows looked right into the operations room—so we could keep an eye on the occupants—and the three kids were laughing and clapping. They were probably thinking, Damn, that looks like fun! Maybe we should become cops!

If this really had been a cowboy movie, George and I would have been smashing each other with chairs and whiskey bottles. We just used our fists. I had blood running from my eyes, my mouth, and so did George. We were just tearing each other apart.

Someone else was moving between us. It was Captain Kirk. He didn't even raise his hands to keep us apart.

"Touch me," he dared us. "Just one of you even accidentally touch me."

George and I froze.

"What the fuck are you two doing?" Kirk yelled.

"Nothing," I said, staring at George. "Let's take this out in the Yard."

"No one's going out in the Yard," said Kirk. "This stops right here."

George and I were standing there panting, bleeding, dying to throw more punches. I knew what was going to happen next. Kirk would take us into his office, one at a time, like a school vice principal. He'd yell at us, threaten us, tell us we better find another way to resolve our differences. Except that for George and me, there was no other way.

After I got cleaned up, and got the bleeding to stop, I went into Kirk's office for my little lecture. It was over quick—Kirk said he knew George was an asshole and had no doubt provoked the fight.

"Do me a favor," he said. "Just stay as far away from him as possible, okay?"

As I came out of the office, Sammy took me aside. "That lieutenant from Internal Affairs is here," he said. "He's looking for you."

My first thought was, Good, I'm glad. Maybe it's about time I told Gene Desmond about my pal George.

But then the same question came back—what about Mutt? What would happen to him? I needed time to think. I still hadn't calmed down from the fight. I needed to get some fresh air, to clear my head. I walked outside and toward my patrol car.

Someone must have seen me leave the building, and told Desmond, because he came through the side doors as I was pulling my car out.

"Sergeant," he called.

I pretended not to hear, and headed out onto the street.

Two blocks later, I realized he was following me. I was stopped at a light, and I saw his car coming up in the rearview mirror. He didn't have a chance to signal me, if that's what he was going to do, because the light changed. I took a left. He took a left. At the next corner, I took a right. He took a right.

I felt like an idiot. First I get followed a convoy of television vans, now by Internal Affairs—and this was far worse, because I couldn't run. You don't run from another cop.

So there I was, driving through the streets of West Philly on this beautiful Sunday afternoon, minding my own business, getting followed around by someone who wanted to put my ass in jail.

Cops will tell you that when they cruise the streets, not really heading anywhere, their paths are determined solely by chance. We know that there are no unseen forces in the universe telling us to turn here or turn there.

But it often feels as if there are. Particularly when we stumble onto something that we could have easily missed if we had just gone straight instead of taking a right, two blocks back. And when that happens, you get the unshakable feeling that it was somehow predetermined you would come down this particular street at this particular moment. As if God had been steering your car around, like a kid playing with a toy police car on his bedroom floor.

In this case, God must have been laughing, because he steered me, and Gene Desmond on my tail, right past Dominic and his tow truck. This was at the corner of 55th and Locust, right at Dogshit Park. Dominic was standing behind his truck, working the levers to jack up a car, chatting with a guy who looked like he might be the car's owner.

I stopped at the stop sign. Dominic saw me and called out, "Hey, Eddie."

I look in my rearview mirror, and I see Desmond staring at Dominic, then staring at me. And I'm thinking, Boy, I am sure glad I came by the park just when I did. Otherwise I might have missed the chance to have Gene Desmond see Dominic-fucking-Russo greet me like a long-lost friend. Thanks, God. You couldn't have had me take another right or a left, somewhere back there?

I did the only thing I could do, which was to keep driving. I pulled through the intersection and headed down Pine alongside the park. The place was jammed with people having picnics and barbecues, black families from the neighborhood taking advantage of the nice weather. Dogshit Park was like a huge bowl, with grass and trees gently sloping down toward the center on three of the four sides. Throughout the bowl were picnic tables, all of them filled with women and kids, and the men were at the nearby brick grills, cooking ribs and burgers. I could smell the smoke as it drifted up, it made me hungry.

A very idyllic scene, except for the super-loud rap music blasting from two of the cars parked by the tables. You weren't supposed to take your cars down there, but we really didn't enforce it when people had their picnics and needed to cart stuff in.

The two cars with the rap music were a couple of hundred yards apart, at different picnics, and they appeared to be competing with each other over who could destroy the most eardrums. The earth seemed to shake from the noise, you could practically see the air being pushed around by the violent sound waves. And it wasn't as if the music from the two cars went together. One was going BOOM DA BOOM, while the other went DA BOOM DA. I'd seen grand finales at fireworks displays that were quieter.

Rowhouses surrounded the park, and I had a feeling the neighbors weren't too thrilled by all this. Sure enough, before I was halfway down the block, a large black woman in a blue housedress came out onto the street and flagged me down. She was shaking her head in anger.

"About time you got here," she said, hands on her hips. "About time. We been calling nine-one-one for an hour."

"About the music?" I asked.

She stared at me, dumbstruck.

"About the music?" I repeated.

Finally, words came to her. "What do you think? *Of course* about the music!"

Other women were coming off their porches toward my car, like I was the ice cream man. I glanced in my rearview mirror—Gene Desmond had pulled up behind me. He saw me looking, and gave a short wave. He'd wait until I was done before getting out of his car.

Another woman said to me, "We can't get our babies to sleep with all this noise."

The one in the blue dress said, "You want to come inside my house to see? It's rattling every one of my windows."

"I don't need to," I said. "I'll take care of the music."

I got out of my car and walked back to Desmond. "What's up?" I asked.

"When you get done with this, I need to talk to you."

"About anything in particular?"

"I don't know. Should we go see your pal with the tow truck?"

"Wonderful," I said, and walked across the street to the park. Once on the grass, I was very careful where I stepped. Cops didn't call it Dogshit Park for nothing—we hated running in here at night after suspects. Fortunately, only part of the park was used as the neighborhood's canine crap field, the rest was kept relatively clear. But I had to walk through the danger zone to get to the picnic area. I'd always wondered: when people brought their dogs here every day, what did they think was going to happen to the shit? That it would magically disappear? That city workers would come by and clean it all up?

I got clear of no-man's-land, and walked past the first groups of picnickers. My first stop was a lime green RAV4, an SUV wanna-be that had its doors and back hatch open, the better to turn it into a giant speaker. It was sitting there in the grass, blasting away, at least thirty feet from the nearest picnic table. BOOM DA BOOM DA BOOM DA BOOM.

I walked over to the table. Two women, both holding babies, were talking away, seemingly oblivious to the music.

"Whose truck is that?" I asked.

"What?" they both asked at the same time, both cupping their ears.

"WHOSE TRUCK IS THAT?"

They pointed to two young guys at a brick barbecue. So I went over to them.

"Whose truck is that?" I asked.

"What?"

"TRUCK. WHOSE?"

One of the guys, in green shorts and a purple T-shirt, tapped his chest. I could see he was tensing up, expecting to get hassled.

"Why don't you just move the truck closer to the picnic table," I said. "So you don't need the music so loud?"

"What?"

"Just turn the music down."

"What?"

"TURN! THE MUSIC! DOWN!"

He heard me, and he didn't argue or put up a fight. He just walked over to the truck, reached inside, and shut the music off. My ears were ringing.

"You don't have to turn it off," I called to him. "Just down. The neighbors are complaining."

He shrugged. "It's all right."

You can tell when someone's had a lot of experience with the police—they often will immediately do what a cop says. They don't want any trouble. They don't want the cop to start checking whether there's a bench warrant out for their arrest. They don't want the cop to search them, because of what he might find in their pockets. Sure, it might make them feel better to talk back to the cops, especially in front of their friends, but in the end it won't be worth it. In the end, it'll bring nothing but grief.

The second offending car was a red Subaru Legacy, trunk open, on the other side of the bowl.

People stared after me as I walked amid the picnic tables and barbecue pits. I knew they were thinking, How come the cops always have to come in and spoil a good time?

And it did look like people were having fun. The tables were piled with casserole dishes and bags of potato chips and bowls of macaroni salad, and there were gallon jugs of water and big bottles of soda.

The Subaru's owner had filled his trunk with an enormous, state-of-the-art speaker system, guaranteed to be heard twenty miles away. It had to be worth thousands. I looked at that and thought, George and his boys would love it if there was a burglary at whatever store sold these.

Again, I had to ask around for the owner. But no one seemed to know who had the Subaru. Was it possible someone just parked the car, turned the music up full blast, and took off?

Eventually I did find the owner, he was three picnic tables away, sipping on a can of Olde English 800. He was in his early thirties, and had a shaved head and Fu Manchu mustache and beard. There was something about him, my sensors were picking up low-level danger emissions.

"Sir, we got neighbors complaining about the music," I told him. "I'm going to have to ask you to turn it down."

At first I thought he didn't hear me. He seemed to be listening, but there was no response. I glanced at the table. A couple of the guy's pals and three young women were in the middle of eating. They were all looking up at me.

"We're just having a nice little picnic, Sergeant," the Subaru owner said. "You got to have music at a picnic."

"You can have music," I said. "Just not so loud."

"We like it loud," he said.

And then you had people like him. Guys who wanted to argue with the cops, it didn't matter what about.

I noticed one of the women at the table reading my silver name-plate, then staring up at me.

"North," she said. "You're that cop, aren't you?"

I turned back to the Subaru owner. "Sir, you're going to have to turn down the music."

The guy looked at the woman, then back at me. "What cop?" he asked her.

"You know, that cop. North. See, it says it right on his shirt."

"What cop?" the guy asked again.

"That cop, that cop. You know."

Another woman, sitting next to her, pointed at me. "He *is* the one."

I kept my eyes on the Subaru owner. "If you don't turn the music down, I'm going to do it for you."

"Yeah," said the first woman. "It's that cop that killed Sonny Knight."

Everyone at the table was quietly staring at me now, some in openmouthed astonishment. In a way I was like a celebrity, though a horrible one. I probably should have just turned around and walked back up the hill. It's what any commander would have told me to do. Walk away, they'd say. Get one of your cops to deal with the loud music.

But there wasn't a chance in the world I was going to do that. I should humiliate myself? For who? For what?

The shaved-head Subaru owner was looking up at me with a half-smile. Like now there was no way he was going to touch that music.

"You want me to turn it down for you?" I asked him. "Fine."

I wheeled around and headed toward the Subaru. The guy popped up from the table, and so did everyone else, and they all followed me.

"Leave that car alone," they yelled. "Leave the car alone."

Naturally, this little procession caught the attention of the various people at the picnic tables we passed. Particularly since the same woman who recognized me was now shouting, "He killed Sonny Knight! He killed Sonny!"

Soon it was like I was the Pied Piper—everyone was joining my march to the Subaru. Except they were screaming names at me, like "Murderer!" and "Killer cop!"

I glanced around the park. Everywhere, people were abandoning their grills and picnic tables and streaming toward us. By the time I reached the car, I pretty much had the attention of all of Dogshit Park.

My plan was to pull the keys out of the ignition. But the Subaru owner anticipated that and had rushed to block me from opening the car door. He knew I wouldn't touch him, not with all those people around.

Though I did touch him. I elbowed him aside, reached in through the open window, turned off the ignition, and grabbed the keys.

The picnickers did not like this move. Their relaxed Sunday-afternoon faces were turning murderous. I was everything evil about white cops, and I was standing there, right in front of them. The enemy.

As if by agreement, they began hemming me in, forming a tight semicircle so that my back was to the car door. I had nowhere to go, unless I was going to push through and start knocking people down.

But then the crowd was parting from behind. It was Gene Desmond, coming through.

"You okay, Sergeant?" he asked me.

I didn't know which was worse, getting attacked by an angry mob or getting saved by an Internal Affairs cop.

"Yeah, everything's under control," I said, looking at the crowd.

They had their eyes on Desmond. His sudden arrival had thrown everyone off. He was wearing a blue sports jacket, tie, and slacks, but everyone knew he was a cop. People got silent, stepped back a little. Desmond was a reminder that no cop is really ever alone, at least not for long.

"Let's get out of here," he said.

. . .

**I had to** hand it to Desmond—he showed some class, not asking me about Dominic as we walked through the park. You don't argue in front of civilians. Not every cop knew that. But when we reached our cars, he turned to me, trying to restrain his anger.

"What was that thing with Dominic Russo back there? You told me you didn't even know who he was."

"I know a lot of guys who work for the Tow Squad, just from seeing them on the street."

Desmond shook his head. "I can't believe you're insulting me like this. Treating me like I'm an idiot."

"I don't think you're an idiot. But I do think you have a little trouble accepting the truth. You've been trying to nail me from Day One."

"Really? You know, if it wasn't for me, my captain would've already had you charged with impeding our investigation."

"How am I doing that?"

"To start with, you were up in the 16th District, asking questions about Sonny Knight."

"Only because you wouldn't do it."

"Well, you know what? One of the neighbors recognized you. They called the captain up there, what's her name, Raye? And she called my captain. And he thinks you're tainting possible witnesses."

"They're only witnesses if you guys actually talk to them."

"Secondly," said Desmond, "you were seen looking through the logs at the 16th's headquarters. Twice. Including last night."

"Well, pardon me for doing a little investigating."

"And then there's the matter of the tape."

"What tape?"

"The one that has the radio transmissions from the night Sonny Knight got beat up."

"I don't know anything about that."

"Well, my captain thinks you do. He thinks you had Del Falk get it for you. And I tend to agree."

"Del Falk? What's he got to do with it?"

There was no way I could admit that Del had the tape made for me. He would have been fired immediately, he would have lost his pension, everything. You don't violate police procedures on behalf of someone who's under investigation by Internal Affairs.

"And still," said Desmond, "I stopped my captain from locking you up. Because I thought you were onto something."

"You did?"

"I went out to that neighborhood and talked to the same woman you did. I also checked the logs at the 16th District, same as you. I even listened to the tape from that night. *Before* you did. A week before."

I stayed silent.

"I found out what you found out," said Desmond. "Which was that a few minutes before Sonny Knight was beaten, Sergeant George Laguerre and two 16th District officers—who are now assigned to Laguerre in the 20th—were outside Victor Knight's garage."

I still couldn't say anything, or Del Falk was screwed.

"You want to know why I came out here today?" Desmond asked. "To get your help. Though I'm now wondering whether I should have even bothered."

"What do you mean, help?"

"I need to know what Laguerre and those two cops were doing there."

"And you're asking me."

"You work with Laguerre. And those cops. You've been looking into what happened that night."

"Except I don't know anything about a tape."

Desmond let out a breath. "Fuck the tape, all right? I'm not trying to get Falk jammed up. I'm just trying to find out what Laguerre was doing at that garage. If you know something, now's the time to tell me."

This was my shot, I knew it. Desmond was pushing in the same direction I was, and he could go further, to places I couldn't. How long was he going to stay interested if I kept silent now?

I looked back at the bowl, the crowded picnic tables. Things were already back to normal. Maybe Mutt could still be kept out of it, I thought. Maybe.

I'd have to take that chance.

I turned back to Desmond. "I assume you know about Victor Knight. His criminal history."

"Yeah. Into drugs, big-time. Or used to be."

"Well, I can't say for sure what Laguerre was doing there, but I do know one thing: he's a dirty cop. So are Sam Robbins and Lewis Portland."

"We know that."

"You do?"

"Can't prove it yet, but, yeah. We've known about them."

"For how long?"

Desmond hesitated, deciding how much he wanted to tell me. His cell phone rang, and he pulled it off his belt and held it to his ear.

"Yeah," he said.

I watched as his face went white. He mumbled a thanks and hung up.

"Fucking son of a bitch," he said.

I waited.

"David Danforth just got acquitted."

## twenty

**M**ichelle was inconsolable. She had been in the courtroom with Marnie when the verdict was announced, and that night on my couch she told me how Danforth's supporters had erupted into cheers and applause.

"It was like they were at a football game and they got a big touchdown," she said. "It was like, We win! We win!"

In the courtroom, and afterwards, Michelle had stayed strong for Marnie, holding her hand, escorting her tight-lipped past the television cameras on the way out, driving her home, making her dinner. And it wasn't until Michelle was at my house, after I had gotten home from work, and it was nearly midnight and she walked in the door and fell into my arms, that she could at last cry. We sat on the couch, and I held her.

"It was horrible," she said. "Everyone's leaving the courtroom, and some jerk who was at the trial walks by us and laughs in our faces. I mean, it was an evil laugh. And Marnie had to see that."

Michelle and Marnie hadn't expected an acquittal. They hadn't even considered it to be a possibility. How could a jury let Danforth go? It couldn't happen. And yet it did.

"When the jury said 'not guilty,' neither of us could move," Michelle told me. "I was holding Marnie's hand, and we both just stiffened up, like we were paralyzed. We had to listen to the cheers and shouts, and the clapping. I can't describe it, Eddie. I almost threw up right there."

It had been a unanimous verdict by the jury of eight blacks and four whites. And jurors interviewed outside the courthouse all said the same thing: David Danforth had acted in self-defense. He was justified in his fear of Bobby Boland because he feared all police.

One juror was asked by a television reporter whether Sonny Knight's beating and later murder were factors in the verdict.

"Of course," said the juror, a stocky black woman with large, square glasses. "We all talked about it in the jury room. For us, that just brought home how violent the police can be. Particularly when black folks are involved."

Reporters also tried to get a comment from Marnie, but Michelle hurried her out of there and into a waiting car.

"Marnie said she didn't want the cameras to see her crying," Michelle said.

Michelle was crying as she sat there on the couch, telling me this, a full day's worth of tears finally allowed to come out. We sat there until two in the morning. Michelle was sad for Marnie, and I was sad for them both.

**There was a** lot of sadness throughout the Police Department, too, but even more anger. To us, the jury had sent the message that it was now okay to kill cops. And we couldn't let that go unchallenged. Within hours of the verdict, a protest march was being planned for the next day. Word of it spread fast, in the districts and the special units, and in phone calls, and e-mail, and computer messages between patrol cars. All the marchers would be off-duty and in street clothes. We didn't need our uniforms to make a point.

Everyone wanted to go. Cops took off work, called in sick, claimed their grandmothers had died, just so they could make it. And not only white cops—black cops, too, lots of them. If no one had to go into work that day, probably every cop in the city would have been there.

The plan for the march was simple, or should have been. Gather at the empty parking lot next to Hawthorne Field at noon. March to 20th District headquarters to show support for the cops there, then continue on to the spot where Bobby Boland was killed, and pause for a moment of silence. Then back to the parking lot. That was it.

And it might have worked out okay, except that Bobby had been killed in front of David Danforth's house. And when the cops marched by, there happened to be a "welcome home" rally for Danforth already in full swing.

My squad was working 8 A.M. to 4 P.M. that day, which meant we'd be handling the march. Kirk addressed us at roll call, went over the drill. I took him aside afterward and asked him whether I really needed to be there. I couldn't imagine it would help matters if people along the march route recognized me. Don't worry, he said, no one's going to pay you any attention.

The march got started more than an hour late, mostly because the cops arriving at Hawthorne Field all wanted to talk with each other, to visit. Hey, pal, haven't seen you in a while, where are you now, still in the 22nd? There were more than seven hundred marchers, and they probably would have all stood around and talked the entire afternoon if the organizers hadn't said, C'mon, guys, and herded everyone onto Baltimore Avenue.

Most of the cops were wearing sneakers and jeans, and at least two-thirds had on light blue T-shirts with a silk-screened photo of Bobby Boland on the front, along with his badge number. On the back were the words "We Remember Bobby." Before and during the trial, the T-shirts were a hot item at the districts. Now, as people gathered for the march, guys were walking through the parking lot with armloads of the shirts, selling them for five bucks apiece.

As I walked through the lot, Michelle found me and gave me a big kiss in front of everyone. She was wearing one of the T-shirts, which she'd had for a long time, and I think it had shrunk in the wash, because it fit her pretty tight, which attracted attention from some of the guys. A lot of the guys. I thought about buying her a new shirt, maybe an XXL, or an XXXL, but hers was one of the originals, and I knew she wasn't going to give it up.

The cops had wanted Marnie to lead the march, but she begged off, saying she was too exhausted. She had asked Michelle to take her place.

After some confusion—such as over which direction the march was going to go—things finally got moving. My job was to stay at the front of the march, on foot. Not with the marchers, but off to the side, keeping an eye out for any trouble. I had six cops with me, three on each side of the procession, front, middle, and back. We purposely kept the uniformed police presence almost invisible, so it wouldn't look like we were providing our own guys some kind of armed escort. Still, we had half a dozen Trojan horses—wagons filled with cops—shadowing the march on parallel streets, and three busloads of cops standing by at different locations.

With a couple of Traffic Division Jeeps leading the way, lights flashing, the march headed up Baltimore Avenue, along the silver trolley tracks. And it wasn't just a march of the cops, it was a march of the media, too.

Rolling along behind the Jeeps were three TV vans, each with a cameraman on the roof, for the high, long view of the march.

On the ground, reporters were everywhere, walking alongside the cops, asking questions and writing in their notebooks; newspaper photographers were running up ahead, then standing off to the side and going click-click-click as the river of marchers passed by; still more TV cameramen planted themselves in the middle of the street and faced backwards, and held their cameras near to the ground so they could get the cliché shot of moving legs and feet.

At 50th Street the march veered north, toward our district headquarters, through a working-class black neighborhood of shaded rowhouses and broken sidewalks.

It was a quiet march. No bullhorns, no chanted slogans. A few people carried hand-lettered signs that said things like "Justice for

Bobby" and "A Killer Got Away," but all in all, it was pretty low-key. The way everyone was talking with each other, joking, ambling along, it looked more like a 5K charity walk than a protest march.

There were very few spectators. A few women and kids on porches, the kids with fingers in their mouths, seeing but not understanding. Old guys, longtime neighbors, standing on the sidewalk, their afternoon chat temporarily interrupted. Young guys hanging in front of the Chinese take-outs, watching with amused smiles.

I stayed even with the front row of the marchers, which included Michelle, and now and then she caught my eye and smiled. Some reporter was walking next to Yvonne and Marisol, interviewing them, writing in his notebook as he kept pace. When the march reached Locust, it swung around the corner to the right and there we were, in front of the district. Everyone just kind of stopped haphazardly and milled around, not sure of what to do, like we were all waiting for someone to run in and get some cigarettes.

That's when we first got word that something was happening at David Danforth's house. A TV reporter, talking on his cell phone, walked over to me. He took the phone away from his ear and asked, "Sergeant, you know anything about a 'welcome home' rally for David Danforth?"

"No," I said. "Why, do you?"

"My station just got a call about it."

"It's news to me," I said. Kirk had come outside the building, and I walked over. Other reporters were coming up to us, asking the same thing.

Kirk got on the radio and told a sector car to swing by Danforth's house. A minute later the report came back: there were ten people in front of the house, with a banner that said "Welcome Home." Kirk told the officer to stay there, and to get back on the radio if anything changed.

The march organizers held a brief conference, and decided to go ahead as planned. Phil Ellena, a beanpole, Adam's-apple guy who was in charge of the march, climbed on the hood of an empty patrol car parked at the curb. He had a bullhorn, and he put it to his mouth.

"There's a small demonstration at David Danforth's house," he said. "It shouldn't interfere with us. We're still going there to have our moment of silence."

Everyone cheered. The TV reporters hurried to their vans and raced off.

Danforth's house was eight blocks from the district. We were halfway there when the cop at the scene gave a second report. The number of people at the house had grown to twenty-five, and more were arriving.

I passed this along to Phil and the other organizers, and they talked it over as they marched. I listened on the radio as one of the inspectors ordered the Trojan horses to unload on the next street over from Danforth's.

When we were getting close to the house—one block up, then around the corner—the cop called in again. Fifty people.

The march was halted. Phil climbed on the rear bumper of one of the police Jeeps to let everyone know what was happening.

Should we continue? he asked through the bullhorn.

Damn right, the marchers said.

So we're in agreement? Phil asked.

Damn right, the marchers said.

Everyone began moving again. As the march approached the final corner, I jogged up ahead to take a look. In the middle of the block, the street was filled with people. This was not good. I signaled for the two Jeeps to go straight, to peel away from the march. The last thing we needed were police vehicles trying to bulldoze their way through a crowd.

The cops rounded the corner, not hesitating. We could see the Danforth supporters turn to face us. My six cops were scattered along the march, and I was the only uniform in the front. I was the buffer.

Like many of the houses in this part of West Philly, the ones on

Danforth's street were all two-story twins, conjoined pairs separated from their neighbors by narrow passageways. They weren't anything like the ones on George's block—these were larger and much older. They had bay windows on the second floor, and front porches with roofs that ran the length of the two houses, though they were usually separated by a railing.

The twins were never identical. Half the porch of one might have a wooden railing, the other half, wrought iron. One house might have brown brick facing, the other might be painted gray. Some twins reminded me of those movies where two convicts escape from a chain gang, and though they hate each other, they're shackled together, and they have to learn to get along.

Danforth's half of the twin was considerably nicer than its partner—fresher paint, new aluminum siding—but both houses had grass out front, so that there was a nice little green lawn. The lawn where Bobby Boland had been shot to death. And it was in the process of being trampled by Danforth supporters when the cop march came down the block.

Some of the Danforth people started to move onto the sidewalk, but about half stood their ground. Daring the cops to keep coming. They were mostly young, and nearly all were wearing orange "Justice for Danforth" T-shirts.

Past them, at the other end of the block, I could see blue uniforms gathering, but making no move toward us. It was obvious the bosses had decided to lay back, at least for the moment, and see what unfolded.

The march was now maybe thirty yards from the Danforth people, and it wasn't slowing down. What are they going to do, I thought, just knock those people right over? The Danforth supporters looked like they were wondering the same thing—as the phalanx of cops bore down on them, they seemed less and less confident. Still, no one bolted. On the other side of the street were the TV camera crews and the newspaper photographers, all set to record the crash.

The gap narrowed to twenty yards, and then to ten. I glanced over at Michelle. Like the others, she was staring ahead, jaw tight.

And then the marchers simply washed over the Danforth people, not touching them, but weaving around them and between them, like they were inconsequential highway barrels. When the cops finally halted, the Danforth supporters were totally engulfed, in pockets of two or three, cut off from the others.

One young white kid was standing near me, alone, surrounded. Scraggly beard, hair dyed bright banana-yellow, tattoos all over his arms and legs, orange bike-messenger bag slung over his shoulder. Scared as hell and trying not to show it. He was totally out of his element, like someone who joins the National Guard to get computer training, then finds himself getting shot at in a desert somewhere. He took off, out of the sea of cops, heading for the safety of the sidewalk shore. The rest of the Danforth supporters were abandoning their posts as well, and soon the street was all cops, and the two sides were once again apart.

Still, the Danforth people didn't totally give up. On the lawn, several of them had been holding the banner that said "Welcome Home." They had been facing it toward Danforth's house, but now they turned it around so that it faced the cops.

The cops booed.

Someone on the lawn yelled out, "Justice for Danforth," and the cops booed again.

Phil Ellena, who stood a couple of clumps of cops away from us, raised his bullhorn again.

"Okay, people," he said. "As you know, we're here to honor the memory of Bobby Boland—"

He stopped short. Danforth had come out onto his front porch, followed by Carl Knight, and cheers went up from Danforth's supporters. Four or five TV camera crews quickly pushed their way up to him.

Danforth had a stately look about him. He stood very straight, like he had spent his life in the military, and when he stepped to the front wooden railing of the porch, his movements were surprisingly smooth and graceful. He had a rectangular, sharp-angled face that seemed stern and formal, and he wore a close-cropped beard with some flecks of gray.

He held out his hands, palms up, to the crowd.

"What is he, the Pope?" I asked Michelle.

"I thank my friends for coming out here today," Danforth said loudly. "And for all they did to support me and stand by me in my hour of need."

His friends cheered and clapped. The TV cameras in front of the porch seemed to be pointed up at him adoringly. Carl stood off to the side, making sure Danforth got the spotlight.

Danforth gestured at the mass of cops on the street. "But I don't welcome everyone here," he said. "I don't welcome those people, who would crush the spirit of the black community."

"Are you done yet?" a cop called out.

"No, I am not done," Danforth called back. And then, to his audience: "I will never be done. I will never stop speaking out against this city's racist police force. Look at those people—turn and look at them."

His supporters turned and looked at us.

"Just plain folks, right? Black and white, men and women, just plain folks out for an afternoon stroll. Don't be fooled. They're here to intimidate this neighborhood. They want us to be afraid. And don't be fooled by those black faces—they're even worse than the white ones, because there's nothing worse than your own people keeping you down."

When Michelle had cried in my arms the night before, I figured she was releasing all her pent-up emotion. But it turned out that she had a whole lot left. She pushed her way through Danforth's supporters on the sidewalk, just elbowed them aside, until she reached the patch of grass where Bobby Boland had fallen. She looked around for a particular spot, found it, and then shoved people away, so no one would stand on it. The Danforth people stepped back from her, onto each other's toes, like she was a crazy woman.

She was close to the porch now, right in front of the TV cameras. Danforth stopped his speech short and watched her.

"Ms. Ryder," he said, playing to the crowd. "Can we help you?"

The cameras swung toward her.

"We're going to have a moment of silence in the memory of Bobby Boland," she said, loud enough so even the cops on the fringes of the march could hear. "Remember him? The man you shot down in cold blood?"

The cameras swung back to him.

"According to the jury, I did the right thing," he said. "And as far as I'm concerned, the city's better off, because it has one less racist cop."

There was an angry roar from the cops, shouts of "Fuck you" and "Motherfucker" and "Asshole," and a momentary surge of light blue toward the porch.

"Why don't you shoot me?" Michelle yelled at him.

Danforth stared at her. Everyone was staring at her.

"Why don't you kill me, right here, where you killed Bobby Boland?"

I'd never seen Michelle this way. This couldn't have been just for the cameras.

"Go get a gun," she yelled at him. "Go get one, right now. I'm unarmed. You can shoot me down right now."

"Ms. Ryder, our courts have decided—"

"You want to kill cops, start with me. Put a bullet in my face. Just like you did with Bobby. Right in my face." She was pointing. "Right here, see? Get your gun and aim. You're good at killing cops, you can do it again. C'mon, get a gun."

Danforth shifted his weight from his right foot to his left. Some of the cameras were on him now, and he did not look comfortable.

Michelle turned to face the marchers in the street. "We're going to have our moment of silence now. If everyone—"

"Ms. Ryder, I need you to get off my property."

There was a collective gasp from the street, even from the side-walk and lawn around Michelle.

"I will not have the police on my property," said Danforth.

Another chorus of *Fuck you*'s.

"Professor," one of his supporters called out. "Let them have their moment of silence."

"I will not. Not as long as there is a single police officer on my property."

"Let them have their moment of silence," someone else called out.

Other voices assented.

"All right," said Danforth. "If that's what it takes to get these police officers, this force of racism, out of my neighborhood. But I will not watch."

He turned and walked back into his house. Michelle asked that everyone bow their heads for one minute in memory of Bobby Boland.

And then something amazing happened. Not only did the cops bow their heads, but many of the Danforth supporters did as well. The cops noticed that. And when the minute was over and Michelle said, "Thank you," the street remained silent. The cops in their T-shirts and the Danforth supporters in theirs were eyeing each other, but in a different way now. Something had changed.

It was as if each side had gotten a brief glimpse into the heart of the other, and had been astonished even to find one. Maybe it would be forgotten in a day, or even an hour. And maybe in a city like Philadelphia, a glimpse was all you could hope for. But for a moment, on that street, it was there.

## twenty-one

ne of the problems with silver linings is that you have to have a cloud first. Our cloud was Danforth's acquittal, and it was devastating. But we did have a hope that something good would come out of it.

Maybe now, we thought, the politicians and the press will leave us alone. Maybe now the guy trying to kill cops will abandon his mission.

And things did seem to quiet down. Except for the pay-phone calls.

In the days after Sonny Knight was killed, the 20th District had started getting a large number of unfounded assist-officer calls. They all came from pay phones. A cop's in trouble, the caller would say. He's getting beat up. He's getting shot at. Hurry.

So the dispatcher would get on the air and say, "*Assist officer, civilian by phone.*"

As opposed to "*police by radio,*" which was us calling for help.

In the past, the pay-phone callers were usually just kids, looking for the excitement of lights and sirens. But these new calls were all being made by adult males, possibly the same adult male.

He had us racing around the district. When you think a cop's in trouble, you go about eight times as fast as you would to any other emergency. It's dangerous, but you can't not go—it might be the one time a cop really does need help.

We assumed that this caller was somebody pissed off at what happened to Sonny Knight. And we had hoped that after Danforth's acquittal, he'd stop. He didn't. And so we all had to keep rushing in on the calls.

Even Mutt. I was still keeping him off the street, for his own safety, but when an assist came out, he wouldn't hesitate, he'd run out the door and jump in a car. Everyone else was running, too, so who was going to stop him?

Maybe I should have, but I didn't try. You can't keep a cop from going in on an assist. Besides, when Mutt got there, plenty of cops were always around.

But going in on those assists was tough on him. I didn't realize how tough until the night after the police protest march, when we got a call about a cop in trouble at 51st and Webster.

I was first on the scene, and saw right away that it was another false alarm. There was nothing going on anywhere near the intersection. I got on the radio.

"The assist's unfounded," I said. "Tell everyone to resume patrol."

When cops hear "resume patrol," they're supposed to turn off their lights and sirens and go back to whatever it was they were doing.

Philly cops do not do this. They keep going. It's habit, it's instinct, and besides, there's always a possibility that someone really is in trouble, somewhere nearby, and the first cops there just missed it.

They also go because it gives them a chance to stand around and shoot the shit. At some offices, coworkers gather around the water-cooler, or maybe the copying machine. What cops do is gather in the street after a job is over. It's often the only time they have to trade stories, or to catch up on the latest gossip.

So naturally, the intersection of 51st and Webster quickly filled with police cars. Cops were climbing out of their cars, talking with each other. All we needed was some beer, we could have had a party right there.

And then Mutt came through the intersection, and everyone stopped talking and stared.

*What are you doing here*, their eyes said. *You don't belong.*

This is bad, I thought. When you don't even want someone to respond to an assist, it's about as bad as it gets. Mutt looked stricken. He tried to hide it, but I could see it in his face. He turned his head away, and he drove on.

Mutt and I hadn't talked much since that day at Osage Plaza. He had tried a few times, after roll call or on the street, but I always said I was too busy, and left him standing there.

Now, seeing him get treated like this, I realized that I'd been freezing him out, like everyone else. Whatever he had done or not done, he needed help, he couldn't handle it on his own. I was his sergeant and his friend. I had to reach out. I took off after him.

When I was halfway down the block, a bronze Honda suddenly pulled out from a parking space, right in front of me. I slammed on my brakes and muttered a curse. The guy kept going, like nothing had happened, and when he got to the intersection, he ran the light, went right through it. I couldn't believe it. If I hadn't been trying to catch up with Mutt, I would have pulled the guy over and given him a blizzard of tickets.

I got behind Mutt on the next block and flashed my high beams. We both pulled over.

"You always get treated like that at assists?" I asked.

"Always."

"You don't have to go, you know."

"Yes, I do."

"Maybe you shouldn't, Mutt. Don't do this to yourself."

He looked at me. "You're sayin' I should just ignore the radio."

"It might make sense."

"No," he said. "I can't do that."

There was another assist the next night, and Mutt showed up again. So did the bronze Honda. I didn't notice it until I had told everyone to resume patrol, and we were all heading back to our cars. The Honda was pulling away from the curb, a half block up. I was sure it was the same car.

Either this is an amazing coincidence, I thought, or that's the asshole who's been making all these calls. He fucks with us, then shows up to watch.

I clicked my shoulder mike.

"This is twenty-C-Charlie, there's a bronze Honda heading west on Christian from 55th. Have it stopped for investigation."

With all the patrol cars on the street, it should have been easy to get him. But we were all blocking each other in, and by the time guys ran back to their cars and we were able to get out, the Honda was gone. We searched for him, up one street, down the next. He had vanished.

**As I was** getting ready for work the next afternoon, Roy called me at home.

"What happened with Mutt?" he asked.

"What do you mean?"

Roy was still at the shore, and had gotten a call from Mutt about 2 A.M. Mutt was pretty drunk and started rambling. At one point he said something about getting into a shootout at Osage Plaza the week before. Roy pressed him for details, but Mutt wouldn't say anything more. He tried to laugh it off, like it was all a joke.

It wasn't like Mutt, said Roy, to hold back, especially about something like a shooting. Which meant something was wrong.

"He said you were there," said Roy.

I wasn't sure how much to tell him. But then I figured, why not? Roy's his partner, he knows Mutt a lot better than I do. Maybe he has some ideas, because I sure don't.

And so I told Roy about Osage. And what had been happening to Mutt since, his increasing isolation from the squad.

"How come you didn't tell me this before?" Roy asked. I could tell he was pissed.

"You had enough problems."

"You should have told me. This is something I would want to know."

"You're right. I should have."

"Let me ask you something. Am I fired yet?"

"Not yet. Kirk's like your fuckin' guardian angel. But why do you care?"

He didn't answer, but I knew why. I knew he was going to come back.

That night, the bronze Honda made a third appearance. This time the assist call was for 65th and Chestnut. Buster and Tony D, in separate cars, got there before me, and reported into Radio that it looked unfounded.

I rolled in anyway to look for the bronze Honda, and there it was, not far from the intersection, lights out, parked at the curb. I came up behind it and pulled over. At first I thought the Honda was empty, but then I saw movement in the driver's seat. This was our guy. We had him.

The moment I put on my flashing overhead lights, the Honda shot away from the curb. I took off after it, I was right on its tail. As we roared through the intersection, passing the other patrol cars, I caught a glimpse of Buster's astonished face.

I got on the radio, and it was an instant pursuit—the Honda, followed by me, followed by Buster, followed by Tony D, all screeching through the streets of West Philadelphia. The Honda ran every light, every stop sign, he never even slowed.

I had called in the license tag to Radio. The dispatcher was coming back with the information.

"*Twenty-C-Charlie, that vehicle is reported stolen.*"

That didn't make any sense, you don't steal a car and then drive to where the cops are. Then what was he doing? I remembered what had happened to Buster and Paulie. What if this guy's our shooter? I wondered. What if he's calling in these assists to set another trap?

I got on the radio again.

"This is twenty-C-Charlie. Be advised this could be the doer in the assaults on police. Use caution, he may be armed."

More and more cars were joining the pursuit, and we almost caught the guy. We came very close. He had swung onto Baltimore Avenue and immediately got boxed in behind a stopped trolley that was picking up passengers. He couldn't go around—another trolley was coming from the opposite direction. The only thing he could have done was jump the curb, which was what he did. He popped up right on the sidewalk, went the length of the trolley, almost hitting half a dozen people, then bumped back down onto the street.

By the time we got around the trolley, the Honda had faded away. One of our police helicopters was in the air, on its way to help us. When the chopper arrived five minutes later, its crew spotted the Honda almost immediately. It was parked behind a nearby gas station, abandoned.

**Roy returned to** work the next night. Guys in the squad smiled and shook his hand and said, Glad to see you, pal. They might turn their backs on Mutt, but not on Roy. He was still one of them.

Roy had actually gotten a haircut for the occasion, and instead of looking beery and haggard, he seemed sharp, relaxed. It was an amazing transformation, and at first it puzzled me. Then I realized it was probably part of the Knopfler credo, drilled into him from birth: when you go in to work as a cop, you look like a cop. You look professional.

Mutt, meanwhile, was like a drowning man who had been pulled from the water. That afternoon at roll call, for once he didn't seem to mind the hostility from the squad. Standing next to Roy, he seemed absolutely exhilarated, his face almost pink with happiness.

And there was no question that hooking back up with Mutt had rejuvenated Roy as well. It was as if the last six weeks had all been just a dream, and there had never been a person named Sonny Knight.

I watched them, and thought, It's like they're saving each other, two guys drowning, pulling each other from the ocean. I felt like I had played a part in getting Roy back. It was the best thing I'd done in a long time.

Mutt came to me and asked whether they could start working the street again. It had been three weeks since Sonny Knight had been killed, he reminded me. Nothing had happened since then.

I knew that Mutt was dying to get out of district headquarters. Sitting at a desk eight hours a day, getting the cold shoulder from everyone around him. What kind of life was that for a cop, for anyone?

And so I relented. I told them I still wasn't going to let them answer radio calls—that's how Buster and Paulie had been trapped. But I could give them an assignment that would at least keep them out of danger.

We had been getting complaints about kids drag-racing on Mitchell Road, on the southern end of the district, and it was time to do another one of our crackdowns. I told Mutt and Roy they could have that detail for a few nights.

"So you want us to chase after these guys?" Mutt asked, smiling, as if I had just assigned them to spend the night in a strip club.

I shook my head. "I don't want you doing anything. Just being down there will be enough."

"Not even any car-stops?"

"No car-stops. You wouldn't be able to catch them anyway, with what you're driving."

"Wanna bet?"

"Mutt . . ."

"I'm just playing with you, Sarge. We'll be good, I promise."

.  .  .

**The call came** in a little after nine.

"*Assist officer, civilian by phone, 43rd and Locust, report of an officer down.*"

Within moments, every cop in the district was screaming toward there, no one hesitating because it might have been a bullshit call. You can't take that chance, you think, Maybe this one is real. Get there. Now.

Yvonne and Marisol were first on the scene, and Yvonne's voice came over the radio: "*Twenty-eleven on location. There's nothing out here.*"

Of course everyone continued in. And by the time I pulled up, six or seven patrol cars were on the scene, parked all over the street. Neighbors were coming out onto their porches, attracted by the growing sea of flashing blue and red lights, no doubt wondering what the hell was going on.

And what was going on? Nothing, just a bunch of cops getting out of their cars, not investigating anything, not hurrying anywhere, just lighting up cigarettes and chatting with each other. The neighbors must have been scratching their heads, wondering, Is this some kind of strange cop ritual we never heard about?

I was hoping Mutt and Roy wouldn't show up, but they did. Mutt was driving, and it looked like he was just going to pass through the intersection as usual. But Marisol and Yvonne called out Roy's name, they wanted to talk to him. Mutt pulled the car over.

Roy got out and came over to us, leaving Mutt in the car.

"Hey, Roy," said Marisol, sliding up to him, putting her arm through his, like he was going to escort her somewhere, "you're coming out with us tonight, aren't you?"

"Fibber's?"

"You think we found another place since you been gone?"

Yvonne slipped through Roy's other arm. "It's your first night back," she cooed. "You have to go out drinking. That's the law."

"Which means if you refuse," said Marisol, "we'll lock you up and take you anyway."

Roy smiled blissfully. I knew that here on the street, protected by the night, among his friends again, he felt he was home. I was glad for him, glad to see him happy.

But we all saw him glance over at the darkened patrol car, parked down the street, where Mutt sat behind the wheel. Roy didn't have to be told, the invitation was for him only.

"I gotta go," he said.

"Not yet," said Marisol, holding his arm tighter. "Stay with us."

"Maybe we should lock him up now," said Yvonne.

Buster had been standing with us, and he had disappeared, but now he was back, with his camera.

"Roy on his first day back," Buster announced, framing the shot. "And the two loose women he picked up at a local bar."

They all laughed, and the flash went off.

Roy stuck around for another minute or two, but then headed back to rejoin Mutt. We all knew Roy wasn't going to showing up at Fibber's. He wasn't going to abandon his partner.

One thing that had been worrying me—if this assist was called in by the same person, then the guy from the Honda might be around somewhere. He might be watching us.

I told everyone to search the area.

"Look for someone sitting in a car," I said. "Or anything unusual. But be careful."

Mutt and Roy were driving up the block, rounding the corner onto Spruce. They were the ones I was worried about most. I hadn't seen anyone follow them, that was good. Still, I didn't want to take any chances. I got on the radio.

"Twenty-fifteen," I said.

"*Twenty-fifteen*," Roy came back.

"You see any cars behind you?"

There was a pause.

"*Lots of them.*"

No wonder, Spruce was a busy street.

"Use caution," I said.

Maybe I was being paranoid, but I still felt uncomfortable. I headed for my car. I'd follow them down to Mitchell Road. I was going to watch their backs.

As I was about to pull off, Buster got my attention and walked over. Or rather, limped. He'd twisted his ankle running for his car to get here, now it was really starting to hurt. What should he do? While we were talking about it, Tony D came up. Tony, I said, run Buster over to HUP, would you?

I remembered Mutt and Roy. I got back on the radio, raised them again. They were on 62nd Street now, heading toward Mitchell.

"I'll meet you on Mitchell," I told them.

Roy started to respond, then said, "*Stand by, Sarge.*"

He never got back on the air. The dispatcher did, though, less than a minute later.

"*Twentieth District assist officer civilian-by-phone Six-two and Carpenter. We have multiple calls of police officers shot. Assist officer, Six-two and Carpenter, we may have officers shot. First-car-on-scene conditions to Radio.*"

I was already on my way there, already blasting through the West Philly night. Toward the end of the world.

## twenty-two

**police car stopped in the middle of the street.**
Its windshield, a thick spiderweb of cracks, with dark
holes clustered to the left and to the right, where the passenger and
the driver would be sitting. There is no movement, no sound, nothing but the faint smell of gunpowder hanging in the air.

I did not want to look inside the car. I ran toward it, praying they
would be alive, knowing that I would look, that I'd be ready for
whatever I saw, yet still not wanting to.

It didn't matter what I wanted. Other cars were closing in, I
could hear their sirens whipping the air, and I knew Rescue was
coming, too. But I was the first on the scene. The only one there for
them right now.

It was a residential neighborhood, and people were standing on
the sidewalk in twos and threes. Keeping their distance. Unwilling
to approach the car, to try to help.

They were in there, both of them. I pulled open the driver's-side
door, where Mutt was. And saw. They had fallen toward each other
and were slumped together, shoulder to shoulder, heads almost
touching. Blood was everywhere.

I heard a noise, a rasping. It was coming from Mutt. He was trying to breathe.

"Mutt," I said.

I put my arm around him and pulled him upright. He was looking at me, his eyes to mine, and his mouth was open, like a fish, trying to suck in air. He had been hit, but where? There was no blood coming from his head, no splotches of red on his blue shirt.

Roy was dead. I knew that. I didn't have to look at his face, torn and twisted. I wondered, for an instant, whether the life that had been in him was still in the car somewhere. Was it still here? Could we get it back to him, pump it back into him somehow? There had to be a way. Rescue was coming, maybe they would know.

I caught myself, and my legs went weak. You have to help Mutt, I thought. You can only help Mutt.

Other cops were with me now, and we gently pulled Mutt from the car and laid him on the ground. He was still gasping, still looking at me. I knelt down, and in the light, I could see two torn spots in his shirt. I ripped the shirt open, and there they were, the two smashed slugs, embedded in his vest.

This had happened to me once. You can't speak, you can't breathe, the pain is so intense you almost pass out. But all that goes away, and you live.

"You're okay," I said to him. "They didn't make it past the vest."

Mutt didn't seem surprised at this. I think he already knew, or guessed. But his eyes held mine. I saw now that they were full of fear.

I glanced at the car. "We don't know yet," I said to Mutt.

He didn't believe me. He tried to prop himself up on one elbow, so he could see into the car himself. I put my hand on his shoulder.

"Let's just wait for Rescue," I said.

**A wake. A** funeral service. A burial. All passing in a haze.

The single-file line of mourners going into the church, that first evening, was the longest I had ever seen. It extended out the doors of St. Sebastian's, down the steps and to the sidewalk that ran along Rising Sun Avenue. From there it continued down to the corner, and then around, an endless line of cops talking quietly or lost in thought as they moved along, a few steps at a time.

The line moved very slowly. So many family members inside to shake hands with, to offer a few words to, before you reached Roy's open casket. Not just Tina and the girls, and Roy's father and mother and his two brothers and his sister. But the whole clan, side by side, halfway up the aisle. If Roy had ever imagined that a single one of them would abandon him, he was wrong.

The city's cops didn't abandon him, either. It didn't matter whether they'd known Roy, they came anyway. Perhaps some were there partly out of respect to a Knopfler they did know, maybe someone in their squad. In the end, though, they all came for Roy, because he was one of them. And always had been.

Our squad got to the church before six, when the wake began, and we stayed until after it was over. His other family. We were all there, every one of us, even Darryl, all in our dark blue dress uniforms.

We did what we could. We handed out prayer cards, and made sure there was a pen with the sign-in book, and straightened the floral arrangements that stretched out on either side of the casket.

Michelle was with me the whole time. She wore a black dress, a sad one. Sometimes when I was talking with people, she would rest her hand on my shoulder or lightly touch my back to let me know she was there.

We spent a little time with Tina before people started filing in. She had left the baby with her mother, in one of the front pews, but Emily and Julia were at her side, in their church dresses, clinging to her.

I hugged Tina and introduced her to Michelle. Tina was clear-eyed, matter-of-fact, but I had the feeling she was just trying to get through this, doing what she had to do. Her soft dark hair fell onto the shoulders of her dress and curled in. She just seemed so young. I noticed that as we talked, she always kept her back to the casket.

I asked her how the girls were doing. Tina looked down at them and said she wasn't sure how much either of them understood. The girls didn't seem to want to look at the casket, either. Neither did I, really. But when I first got there, I went over.

There was Roy, his head on a satin pillow, his damaged face repaired. He was wearing his uniform, and in his breast pocket, partly sticking out, I recognized the photo of Tina and the kids. There were other things in the casket with him. A maroon basketball jersey from Cardinal Dougherty High School. A framed photo of his parents.

Wrapped in his fingers was a thin necklace, like the kind a high school girl might wear, and by his side were a couple of stuffed animals and a pink baby's toy.

How hard would it have been for me to have followed Mutt and Roy right away, so that the shooter would have seen two police cars, not one?

How hard would it have been for me to have just told Buster, Sorry, I got to go?

In the four days since Roy had been killed, Michelle had spent many hours trying to talk me out of seeing it this way. She tried to get me to understand that the only one who killed Roy was the man who fired the bullets. The man in the black ski mask who had pulled up in front of Mutt and Roy's car at a light, and jumped out, and started shooting.

He's the one, Michelle said. No one else.

In a pew a dozen rows back, Mutt sat alone, staring at the casket. I knew that he felt his own complicity.

He had recovered quickly, at least physically. He had a bruised chest, but nothing more serious, and they'd released him from the hospital the next day.

I'd been worried he might be blamed by every cop in Philly for what had happened to Roy, as he had been for everything else. But that turned out not to be the case. No one was willing to argue that Mutt—even if he had beaten up Sonny Knight—could be held accountable for this level of violence against cops. He had been shot, he had lost his partner, that's what mattered. And so the string that had connected him to all our troubles was snapped. The squad closed ranks and turned its anger outward toward the common enemy. Once more, it was us against them, not us against each other. No one in the squad made Mutt a hero, because no one believed he was. But they accepted him back in.

He sat in that pew, though, his eyes on the casket, as if no one else were there. I knew that he, too, was unable to forgive himself. Because he was the reason Roy had come back to work. Because, simply, he had survived, and Roy had not. It was as though our grief wasn't enough. There had to be endless guilt as well, for both of us.

**It was also** hard on Michelle.

A few nights after the funeral, she was waiting for me in the Yard as I left work.

"I want you to go home with me tonight," she said.

I got in my car and followed her to her apartment. When we walked in, she got me a beer and then led me to the spare bedroom.

"I emptied out this dresser for you," she said, opening the top drawer to show me. "I wasn't sure how much space you're going to need."

"Wait a minute, I'm not moving in here."

"Eddie, if this guy thought Mutt and Roy had something to do with Sonny Knight, then he probably thinks you did, too."

"He's not going to follow me all the way to my house."

"You don't know that."

"He could follow me to your house."

"Maybe, but at least I'll be here. I can drive behind you on the way to the district, and on the way back home, in case anything happens."

"You're joking."

"And I want you to get the captain to take you off the street. There's other sergeants."

"Michelle, I'm not going to ask to get taken off the street. And I don't need you to . . ."

I stopped short.

"Eddie, this is what you get when someone cares about you, okay?"

I had forgotten. It had been a long time.

"You're not alone anymore," she said.

She looked at me, trying to see whether I understood.

"I know," I said.

She smiled, almost shyly. "This is what you have to put up with, okay?"

I smiled back. "Okay." I took a step forward and drew her to me, and we kissed. I could feel her relax, and we kissed even more deeply.

I stayed the night, but I didn't move in with her. As much as I wanted to give her the comfort that she needed, to ease her fears, I didn't want to have to be protected by my girlfriend. It wasn't just how it would look to other people—though I had to admit to myself that was part of it—but how it would feel to me.

I tried to get Michelle to understand this. I told her I'd be careful.

For now, though, that was the most I could do.

**Since our epic** battle in the operations room, George and I had barely spoken. There was only the minimum necessary communication, to find out things like which cops were assigned to which cars. Even at Roy's funeral, we had stayed far apart.

When someone close to us dies, for a while we believe the loss will somehow change us and make us all better people. And then one day we wake up, and wonder how we could be so naive. For me, that awakening occurred a few days after Roy's funeral, when I was driving in to work and saw George in a white U-Haul van.

He was parallel-parking it about two blocks from headquarters and didn't notice me as I passed.

It was the size of a large passenger van, but without any side windows. It reminded me of our wagons, except that instead of saying "Dial 911" on the side, it had "Rent This Van for $19.95."

I drove on, thinking, Oh, so the trunk of a police car isn't big enough for you now, George? You actually need to bring in a van to cart away all the shit you're stealing?

And I had no doubt that's why George had rented it—if he was using the van for legitimate purposes, he wouldn't be parking it two blocks from the district. There were plenty of parking spaces much closer to the building.

I could feel myself getting more tense by the moment. We have a cop barely in the ground, and this motherfucker can't stop stealing for one minute? Fuck him, I'm going to stake out the van. I'm going to find out where he's going.

But it was busy that night, and I never got a chance. And then about eight o'clock, we got a report of a burglary at a fur-storage warehouse off of Market. As soon as I heard that one come over Radio, I knew. Furs, huh? Going big-time, are we now, George? No wonder you need a van. Asshole.

I got over there as fast as I could, I wanted to catch him in the act. But it turned out the burglary was long over. The 911 call hadn't come from a passerby, but from the owner himself, who had happened to stop by the warehouse that night. He'd discovered that someone had disabled the alarm system and then broken in through a side door by drilling out the lock.

The detectives who came out to investigate were very impressed.

"It was a shitty alarm system," the detective said. "Not really that difficult to knock out. But whoever did this knew what he was doing."

I thought about getting on the radio, saying I wanted any white U-Haul van stopped for investigation. But I knew that wouldn't have been a good idea. If a cop stopped a van and saw George was driving, they'd let him go without thinking about it. Or George might panic, and there might be a confrontation. I couldn't put a cop in that situation.

I went over my options, considered the possibilities. But I hadn't counted on the one that happened—that I would find the van first.

At the corner of 55th and Cedar was a tiny store, the kind that serves just the surrounding couple of blocks, a place where kids can trade their quarters for candy, and their parents can grab a pack of cigarettes.

And parked out front, next to the corner, was a white U-Haul van. I was coming from the opposite direction, and I could see someone sitting in the driver's seat.

"If this is George," I said aloud, "thank you, God."

I slowed down as I passed, to get a good look. And there was Mutt behind the wheel, looking back at me. I could not fucking believe it. I jerked my car to a stop and stared at him, too stunned to even think.

Finally, I threw open my door and strode toward him. I didn't know what expression I had on my face, but he saw it and got a look of panic. You *should* fucking panic, I thought.

I could see him bracing himself as I walked up.

"Get out," I said.

He just looked at me.

"Get the fuck out of this truck."

He opened the door, I grabbed his arm and pulled him down from the seat.

"What the fuck are you doing?" I was yelling now.

No answer.

"You get shot, your partner gets killed, and you're fucking doing this? What the fuck is wrong with you?"

No answer.

I stuck my head in the van and tried to look in the back. But there was a metal divider, I couldn't see what was inside. Mutt stood there, not saying anything. At least he wasn't trying to lie to me, giving me some bullshit story.

"Where is he?" I asked.

Mutt nodded toward the store. The door opened, and out came George, slapping the end of a pack of cigarettes against his palm. Mutt and I were on the other side of the van, and at first he didn't see me. But he saw my patrol car and stopped short, and glanced around.

I waited. He finally spotted me through the windows of the van, and came around the front, acting like we were all friends.

"Hey, Eddie, what's going on?"

"Laguerre," I said, "you are the worst fucking slime. This kid just got shot, for fuck's sake. You can't leave him the fuck alone?"

George looked at Mutt and shrugged, like he was saying to Mutt, What's up with this guy? Like they had some kind of special bond.

"What's in the van, George?" I asked.

"None of your concern."

"Fuck you. What's in the van?"

"You want to take a fuckin' look, go ahead."

I walked to the back and pulled open the rear doors. The van was empty.

George and Mutt had followed me. "Okay?" George asked. "Satisfied?"

"Let me ask you something, George. Suppose I were to get the crime lab out here. Suppose I asked them to search the back of this van for fibers. What do you think they might find?"

Something in George's face changed.

"Don't fuck with me, North."

I looked at him, then at Mutt, and thought, I brought them both here. I did this. All the opportunities I had to stop George. Knowing what he was doing. Knowing he was getting Mutt involved.

This is what happens when you close your eyes, I thought. This is what happens when you just hope things will go away.

"Get in my car, Mutt," I said.

Mutt didn't look to George, like he had at Osage Plaza. He headed across the street without a word, eyes down.

George kept silent, too. I could see him assessing the situation, thinking. And then he moved quickly, climbing into the van, pulling away from the curb. Getting out of there as fast as he could.

## twenty-three

**hat I wanted now was evidence. Something to** take to Desmond and say, Here's what you've been looking for on George Laguerre. Now lock him up.

My line about having the van checked for fibers was bullshit, I'd never be able to make that happen. George knew it, but he also knew I'd be waiting for him now, which meant he'd be extra careful. I'd made a mistake by showing him my hand without acting on it. That's the worst thing you can do with an adversary.

It was Michelle who suggested going to Victor Knight. If George had been at his garage, then Victor no doubt knew all about him. He might throw me something about George. Of course, I'd be asking him to rat out one sergeant to another, and who knew which way he'd go. It might simply be a matter of who had more over Victor's head, me or George.

And so around noon the next day, after making sure the 20th was reasonably quiet, I headed out of the district, up to Victor's garage.

He didn't seem to be around. The place was wide open—a car in the driveway with the hood up, another car inside the garage. I walked in, one eye on the puddles of oil and grease, and called Victor's name. No response. Maybe he was out again. On the other hand, maybe he was upstairs on that waterbed with one of his customers. I went halfway up the steps and listened. No moans, no sloshing.

"Yo, Victor," I called. Still nothing.

There was a door to a room in the back, I remembered Victor once telling me that was his office. I gave it a knock, then pushed the door open.

It was an office, all right, as filled with junk as the rest of the garage. There was another grease-smeared refrigerator—which I didn't want to open—a half-disassembled copying machine, and a brand-new toilet bowl sitting in the corner, surprisingly spotless.

On the desk was a computer, but it was so dirty, it looked like Victor primarily used it to wipe off his hands after he worked on a car. If IBM had seen that, the whole company would have shit in its pants. The desk itself was a mess, covered with piles of paper, all stained with grease fingerprints, as if Victor had been practicing for the next time he got arrested.

On the wall were some family photos in wooden frames, and a framed dollar. I had to remember to ask Victor whether that was the first one he ever earned for selling drugs.

There was still another room further back, and I figured what the hell, I'll take the whole tour. I pushed open the door but it was too dark to see anything, and I had to feel around for a while for the light switch.

And when I found it, and the room was bathed in light, my mouth opened in astonishment. There were the furs, piled high on two card tables, mounds of soft black and brown, soaking up the light. They were from the warehouse burglary, they had to be.

There were boxes stacked all over the place, unopened cartons of power tools, computer equipment, electronics. Some of the boxes I recognized from George's recent visit to Inner Visions.

All this time I'd thought that Victor was just into drugs. And here he was a fence. George's fence.

No wonder George was over here with Sam and Lewis that night—they were probably dropping off some fresh loot. But what would that have to do with Sonny Knight getting beat up in the 20th?

I heard a noise, people talking. I flipped off the light, stepped back into the office, and closed the door. I could see, through the office door, through the garage and onto the sidewalk out front, two drunks yelling at each other. After a minute or so, they moved on.

I glanced around the office again. Victor had said his uncle bought this place for him to run. Maybe Sonny Knight knew about the fencing operation. Maybe he was even in charge of it.

Next to the computer was a sheaf of rumpled papers, and something about the top one looked familiar. I picked it up. It was from the "Justice for Danforth" website. One of the postings from Tariq. I picked up the rest of the stack. They were all Tariq's postings. This was weird.

I dropped the papers back on the desk, thinking about it, and found myself looking at a photo of Sonny Knight on the wall. He was laughing. I glanced at the other pictures—a woman and three kids on a couch next to a Christmas tree, Victor arm in arm with some young lady, a faded photo, obviously taken years ago, of two boys in caped costumes, standing in front of a car. From their faces, I guessed that it was Victor and Carl when they were kids.

And that photo stopped me, because there was writing, in felt-tip pen, in the white border at the bottom. Under the boy who looked like Carl, it said "Superfly." Under the one who looked like Victor, it said "Tariq."

For a moment I stared at it, not even thinking, like this was some kind of hallucination, and that somehow my mind had lifted the name Tariq from the papers and placed it onto the photo.

But there was no question what it meant. Tariq was Victor's nickname, or had been when he was a kid. Victor was the one who had written all those threats.

I tried to picture it, I tried to picture Victor sitting at the computer writing that shit. How could he hate cops—he was a snitch for me for years, and it now turns out he's a fence for George. It was hard to believe. And what if he was the shooter?

I pulled the cell phone off my belt and called Michelle. I needed to tell her about this.

She answered, but there was yelling in the background.

"Hold on," she said, and then I heard her shout, "Everybody just shut up for a second!"

Then, to me again, "Sorry. I got called to a fight at Starbucks. I think some people here have had a little too much caffeine. What's up?"

I told her about the pile of Tariq postings and the photo. I grabbed the pile with my free hand.

"There's at least twenty of them here," I said.

More yelling in the background.

"I said to *shut up*!"

The phone went silent.

"You there?" I asked Michelle.

"And you're sure the picture is of Carl and Victor?" she asked.

"I can't be positive. But it sure as hell looks like them."

"What are you going to do?"

"I don't know yet."

"I'll be right there," said Michelle.

"You're working."

"I can get someone to cover."

"You're going to leave your district?"

"Are you in *your* district?"

She had a point. We agreed to meet down the block, at Reno Street. That's where I had parked my car—I never liked to advertise that I was visiting Victor.

As I put the cell phone back on my belt, I heard footsteps in the garage. I put my hand on my gun and waited. It was Carl. He started to come through the doorway, then froze when he saw me. I still had the pile of papers in my hand, and I tossed them onto the desk.

"What are you doing here?" he asked.

"Looking for your cousin."

"You just walked in here? You can't do that, police can't walk into someone's property like this."

"I'm on my way out."

"What do you want Victor for?"

Carl was trying to come across as a tough guy, but there was something in his voice. He really was interested in why I was here.

"Just wanted to talk to him," I said.

"About what? Why are you so interested in him?"

He glanced at the papers.

"What were you looking at there?"

"Nothing, I'm just nosy. Listen, I got to go."

But Carl had already stepped over to the desk, and he picked up one of the Tariq postings. He studied it, frowning, then picked up another, and another. Finally he grabbed the pile and looked through it.

His eyes darted to the wall and the photo of Superfly and Tariq. He knew I had seen it.

"So Victor's Tariq, so what?" he said. "It doesn't mean anything."

"You knew it all the time."

"What's the big deal? Yeah, maybe he wrote this stuff, but that doesn't mean he had anything to do with that cop getting killed."

"How would you know?"

"Because we're not killers in our family. We're not like the police."

"Carl, I'm sorry about your father. . . ."

"No, you're not."

"We don't have to argue. I'm leaving."

"Victor messes with people's minds. But he's not a killer."

"Fine."

"This is really all about me and him." He waved it away. "Never mind, forget it."

"Fine, Carl. Whatever. I'm leaving."

"I'm just telling you, you don't have to worry about him. That's why you're here, isn't it?"

No, Carl, I thought. That's why *you're* here.

"This is all nothing. It's just Victor's way of showing me up."

"What?"

"So I don't think I'm better than him, because I went to college."

"And that's why he wrote all that? C'mon, Carl."

"I've known Victor all my life. And I know he's just trying to prove to me that I don't understand the streets. Because on the streets, you answer violence with violence, right? But this is just Victor. It's just talk."

"And you're sure about that?" I said.

He hesitated for an instant, for half an instant, then shook it off.

"The cops are the killers. Not us. You know, I think you should leave now."

That was fine with me. I didn't want Victor surprising us here. I also didn't want him tipped off to how much I knew about him. But what could I do? Carl might keep his mouth shut, if he had his own suspicions, but I wasn't going to bet on it.

He escorted me out through the garage and onto the sidewalk.

"Don't come back," he said as we stepped into the sunlight.

"Carl, if your cousin did kill Roy Knopfler, wouldn't you want to know about it?"

"I'd rather know who killed my father."

"But what about who killed Roy Knopfler?"

He shrugged. "What is it to me?"

"I guess nothing." I turned and walked down the short block to Reno, then looked back. Carl was standing in front of the garage. Was he waiting for Victor?

I pulled my car out of sight, then walked back to the corner. I had no idea what I was going to do if Victor came back. Call in the troops? Under what pretext? I wasn't even supposed to be in this district.

Carl eventually did leave, though, and a minute or two later, Michelle drove up.

"I can't believe we found out who Tariq is!" she said. "This is great."

"I still don't get Victor," I said. "He's one of my best snitches."

"Hey, don't flatter yourself," said Michelle. "He uses cops to get what he wants."

"True."

"He's a scammer, he's a street hustler. He's a fence for George. It's all probably just a game to him. Think about it, if he hated cops, would he let you know?"

"No, you're right."

We talked about our next move.

"It's a shame we can't get back in there," Michelle said. "And get some of Victor's DNA out of that garage."

It was a good thought. The crime-scene guys had gotten plenty of DNA evidence from the stolen bronze Honda, including dried saliva on the butt of a cigarette that didn't belong to the car's owner. All we'd have to do is see whether it matched Victor's.

"Except," I said, "how are we going to get a search warrant for the garage?"

It wasn't an easy problem. Even if we were sure Victor Knight had written those things on the website, that wouldn't be enough to get a judge to approve a search warrant in a murder investigation. Free speech and all.

And while I did come across some stolen merchandise in the garage, I didn't exactly do it in a legal manner. You can't go onto someone's property without their permission and then say, Gee, look what I found. No judge will give you a search warrant on that. You need probable cause. Which I didn't have.

There was a shooting in Michelle's district, we listened to it on Police Radio.

"You probably should get back there," I said.

"It doesn't sound like a big deal," she said. "No one's dead."

"Yeah, but what if the bosses are going to show up?" I asked. "And start asking questions, like, where's 9-A?"

That was Michelle's car number.

"I think I should stay here," she said. "Until we figure out what to do."

I kept encouraging her to go, and she finally headed for her car.

"Call me if Victor comes back," she said.

"I will."

"And just be careful, all right?"

I said I would. But I wanted her out of here. Because I had already figured out what to do. And I didn't want her involved, in any way.

**Billy and Hap** were into it from the start. They were plainclothes burglary guys, this was their district. It was perfect.

Right after Michelle left, I tracked down Billy's cell phone number and called.

"You jokers working today?" I asked.

"Unfortunately."

"Can you meet me at 42nd and Reno?"

I'd known Billy and Hap for a long time. They were both in their late forties now, their temples getting gray, but they were still aggressive, still hungry for pinches. They'd been a burglary team in the 16th for years, and they knew every alley, every passageway. When someone called 911 about a prowler, they could usually tell by the address who was calling, and sometimes even who the prowler was.

"Sounds like Stanley's trying to get into Mrs. Jones's house again," they'd say.

When they got to Reno, we had a little powwow. I told them all about Victor and the furs, and my suspicion that he might be Roy Knopfler's killer.

They were very interested.

"Whatcha got in mind?" asked Billy.

I said that Victor seemed to have a habit of leaving his garage door open when he was gone for short periods. Such as right now.

"I like the sound of this," said Billy.

"There's probably reports of burglaries in the neighborhood, right?" I asked.

"Sure," said Billy. "There's always burglaries."

"And of course," I said, "when you get these reports, you check in on nearby businesses, just to make sure they're okay. Right?"

"Say no more," said Billy. "Say no more. Just leave it to us."

"Are you sure?" I asked.

"We knew Roy Knopfler," said Hap.

"Since he was a kid," said Billy. "His father used to be our sergeant. Don't worry, we'll get you that fuckin' warrant."

They got in their car and drove up 42nd to the garage. Ten minutes later, they were back.

"How'd it go?" I asked.

"Smooth as my ex-wife's ass," said Billy. "We just happened to
be passing by, and saw Victor Knight's garage door open."

"Naturally," said Hap, "we figured we'd stop in and let Mr.
Knight know about the recent burglaries in the area. We're very
responsible in that way."

"Yes, we are," said Billy. "But Mr. Knight didn't seem to be
around. 'Mr. Knight,' we called. Several times. But there was no
response."

"So now we got an open property," said Hap. "Ohmygosh,
maybe Mr. Knight's inside, hurt. Maybe a burglar's inside. So, of
course, we have to check it out."

"We didn't find anybody in the garage," said Billy, "so we walk
to the back, to the office. The door was wide open."

"Wide open," echoed Hap. "We're still calling for Mr. Knight.
Maybe something's happened to him. Now, behind the office is
another room, and this door was open, too."

"And the light was on," said Billy.

"Right," said Hap.

"Because otherwise," said Billy, "some idiot who was trying to
turn it on would have spent three years feeling around, tripping
over shit, because it would have turned out he was trying to find
the switch on the wrong side of the door."

"To be fair to him, though," said Hap, "switches can be on either
side."

"Maybe in Finland or someplace," said Billy. "But not in
America."

"Okay," I said, "so the light was on."

"Right," said Billy. "So we looked around for Mr. Knight or a burglar. And what we saw was two tables of furs matching the description of the furs taken from a burglary in the 20th on Monday."

"Along with other items that could possibly have been stolen," said Hap.

"So we immediately left the garage," said Billy, "and asked Police Radio to send a supervisor."

He held his radio to his mouth and clicked the mike.

"Sixteen-BD-four," he said.

*"Sixteen-BD-four,"* the dispatcher answered back.

"Could you have a supervisor meet us at 42nd and Parrish?"

Billy lowered the radio and smiled at me. "That's our story, and we're sticking to it."

## twenty-four

**illy and Hap's expedition was a success. I had to** put in a brief appearance at the 20th, but when I swung back by the garage an hour later, there were a half-dozen marked and unmarked police cars parked on the street. I pulled up behind the last one, and Billy and Hap spotted me and walked over.

Major Crimes was going before a judge to get a search warrant, they said. Some of their guys should be here with it soon. Meanwhile, everyone was hanging around outside the garage, waiting to go in.

"Victor Knight come back?" I asked.

"No," said Hap.

"Yes," said Billy. "And there the fuck he is."

He was looking down the street behind my car. I looked in my rearview mirror, a beat-up yellow van was chugging toward us.

Victor was smooth, I had to hand it to him. He didn't screech to a stop, then jam into reverse. The van came to a slow, tentative halt, as if the driver was just passing through and was thinking of trying to squeeze by all the police cars. Then, very slowly, the van began to back up. If we hadn't been looking, it probably wouldn't have caught our attention.

But we had been looking, and I shifted my car into reverse, put on the red and blue lights, and followed the van backwards. The faster he went, the faster I went, and pretty soon we had a reverse pursuit going, with cops on foot running behind. It had to be a rather odd sight to the locals on their porches.

I don't know that I could have backed up a van at thirty-five miles per hour, under pressure, for a block and a half, but Victor was so good at it, I wondered whether it was the way he usually drove. Except that at the end of the block and a half he ran a stop sign, and the back of his van broadsided a huge black SUV.

Victor didn't hesitate, he bailed out and took off down the street on foot, and I bailed, and now we had a foot pursuit going. He was moving faster than I was, but all I had to do was keep him in sight, relaying to Radio his location for the other cops streaming through the streets.

Unfortunately, I couldn't even do this. Victor was nice enough to take me on a tour of the charming vine-walled passageways that snaked between the houses in his neighborhood. In other circumstances, I might have paused to snap a photo here and there, but as it was, I was gasping for air and getting further and further behind my guide. It hadn't yet got dark, otherwise I would have lost him long before.

I did manage to round a corner from one passageway to another just as Victor was scaling a tall chain-link fence. He was good at this, too, flying up the fence, picking his way over the barbed wire, dropping down on the other side like a cat burglar.

I had my Glock out now.

"You keep running," I yelled, "I'll shoot."

"No, you won't," he said, and took off.

And he was right. You can't shoot someone simply because they're running from you, even if they just killed the Pope. My gun was worthless.

I looked at the fence. I could have made it over eventually. By the time I did, though, I'd have no hope of picking up Victor's trail. So I stood there and clicked my mike, and gave Radio one last update on Victor's location and direction. I was hoping the other cops would grab him, but somehow I knew they wouldn't. He was gone. And I was the one who had let him get away.

. . .

**I had also** revealed my presence in the 16th. When I returned to the garage, the district's captain, a short black female, came up to me and said, "What are you doing here?"

This was Vivian Raye, the one who had told Desmond's captain that I had been poking around up in the 16th.

"You're not supposed to be in my district," she said. "Do you have a reason?"

Meaning, a good reason.

"I've got a snitch up here, Captain," I said. "I was on my way to hook up with him, and came across this drama here."

"And you just happened to be on this street?" she asked, her voice full of both skepticism and disdain. "On the exact same street where you were a few weeks ago, doing an unauthorized investigation? Do I look stupid to you?"

I always hated when captains asked me that question.

"No, ma'am," I said.

"You know, you're under investigation by Internal Affairs."

As if this were news to me.

"First, you come here a few weeks ago, to the block where Sonny Knight's nephew happens to live. You also go into my operations room and mess around with the patrol logs. Now today you're back here again. And you're lying to me about why."

What could I say? She had pretty much covered all the bases.

A car pulled up. The detectives from Major Crimes, with their search warrant. There were three of them, and they got out of the car and approached the captain. She gave me a quick I'm-not-through-with-you-yet look, then turned to meet them.

She hadn't actually ordered me out of the district, no doubt because she figured I'd have to be an idiot not to leave. But I had to stay at least long enough to convince the detectives to collect samples of Victor's DNA.

I knew only one of the detectives, Lenny Funderburke, and I

didn't know him well. We'd been patrolmen in the same district years ago, but we never hung out together. I'd heard he'd made sergeant, and that he was in Major Crimes, but our paths hadn't crossed in a long time.

Lenny talked to the captain for a couple of minutes, and when they had finished and she walked away, I went up to him.

We shook hands, asked what each other had been doing.

"We should talk later," he said. "Right now I got to do a search of this garage."

"Yeah, listen, Lenny, I know this guy, the owner. I think he might have been the one that shot Roy Knopfler."

This startled him into silence for a moment. "We were just told about stolen merchandise."

"I know. But can you get the Crime Scene Unit here? If we can get some DNA, we could nail the guy."

"That's not in the warrant."

"I know. But get 'em here anyway."

"How am I going to do that?"

"Call 'em. You want to use my cell phone?"

"Yeah, but what am I going to say? We never check for DNA in cases like this. This is just stolen property."

I couldn't figure out whether he was stupider than I remembered, or whether he had become one of those sergeants who was more worried about covering his own ass than making any real decisions.

"I know you don't usually do it, Lenny," I said. "I'm talking about making an exception."

He looked around. "Does anybody else think he's the shooter?"

"No. This is something I've been checking out on my own."

"So, it's just speculation on your part."

"Yeah."

He shook his head. "Well, then I can't change the focus of the search. I mean, this isn't a murder investigation. I wouldn't be able to justify something like that."

I glanced over at the captain, who was near the entrance of the garage with another detective. She was looking right at me.

"Lenny, can you at least give the place a real thorough search? You know, upstairs, downstairs, the desk drawers, filing cabinets. There might be bloodstains somewhere, something."

He hesitated. Trying to figure out a way to cover his ass.

"How we going to justify looking for fur coats in a desk drawer?"

"You're also looking for electronics equipment, right?"

"Yeah."

"Well, some of that shit's real small. You know, portable CD players, they're real tiny these days."

He looked at me, pained at having to make an actual decision. Some people just should not become sergeants.

"Lenny. We can't let this fuck get away."

"That's not going to happen. We can get him for receiving stolen goods."

"And how long is he going to go to jail for that? A year? Eighteen months? It's a fuckin' property crime."

Another pained look.

"Let me think about it," he said. "I'll see what I can do."

"Lenny. He could be the one."

"I'll do what I can. But I'm not going to bring the crime lab here."

"Yeah, all right," I said. "I understand."

What I understood was that this search was going to be a waste of time.

**I spent the** next half hour across the street, under a tree, trying to stay out of the captain's range of vision. A couple of times she glanced in my direction, just to let me know I wasn't doing a good job of hiding. But she didn't seem to be interested in dealing with me, at least not for the moment.

While I was standing under that tree, Carl Knight pulled up in a
car, got out, and hurried toward the garage. He noticed me across
the street and gave me a strange look. I couldn't figure out what it
was. Not anger. Something else. Billy and Hap were with the captain, and Carl walked up to them. I could see he was asking questions.

A couple of minutes later, I motioned for Billy to come across
the street.

"What's Carl Knight want?" I asked.

"He got a call from the captain, she told him what was happening here."

"She called him?"

"I guess out of courtesy to the family."

"It pays to have connections."

Neither of us noticed Gene Desmond walking up from behind.

"Hello, Sergeant," he said.

I turned, and almost shit a brick.

"I got a tip I might find you here," he said.

"Did that tip by any chance come from a certain female captain?"

Desmond glanced over at her. "Captain Raye? Yeah, that's who
called me. She's concerned about you being up here in the Sixteenth."

She was bringing everybody to the scene. What was she doing,
selling tickets?

"The captain told me you were interfering with the detectives,"
said Desmond. "Getting in their way."

"Just talking to an old friend," I said.

I could see Billy didn't know who Desmond was. "You guys
met?" I asked him.

He shook his head no, so I introduced him to Lieutenant Gene
Desmond. From Internal Affairs.

In other words, Billy, watch what you fucking say.

They shook hands, then Billy said, "Gotta go," and took off
across the street.

"Do you always have that effect on people?" I asked Desmond.

He nodded, watching Billy go. "Quite often, actually." He turned to me. "What are you doing here?"

The same question the captain had, but Desmond didn't make it sound like an accusation. He seemed genuinely curious. I realized he didn't have to be here, there was no need for him to make the trip all the way from the Northeast just to give me a hard time. Which meant he came because he wanted to know what was going on with Victor Knight.

What was I going to tell him? Well, Lieutenant, I think he might be our shooter, and by the way, I found this out doing an illegal search of the garage. That's not the kind of information you want to give to Internal Affairs.

Or I could have told him that I had persuaded 16th District police officers to enter the garage under false pretenses. Those false pretenses now being the basis for the search currently under way.

Also not what you want to tell Internal Affairs.

And yet I felt that at last I had Desmond's ear, that I was finally getting through to him. There had to be some way I could tell him what I knew. Some way I could dance around the truth.

I still hadn't answered Desmond's question, as to what I was doing here. And it turned out I didn't have to, because Carl Knight was crossing the street, coming right toward us. He walked up and focused on Desmond, as if I wasn't even there.

"I understand you're a lieutenant with Internal Affairs."

"That's right," said Desmond.

"I'm Carl Knight."

"I know who you are. I'm sorry about your father."

"You know that Victor Knight's my cousin?"

"Yes. Yes, I do."

"Well, there were some things my father couldn't tell you. He wanted to, but he couldn't."

"What kinds of things?" Desmond asked.

"Things that would get my cousin in trouble. Serious trouble." He glanced back at the garage. "But it's too late for that now, isn't it?"

Desmond nodded. "Yeah."

"Then it's time you were told the truth."

Desmond waited. So did I, I wanted to see what the hell he was going to say.

"This sergeant was threatening my father."

I started to look around, then realized he was talking about me.

"This sergeant?" Desmond asked.

"Sergeant North," said Carl.

"What?" I said. "When did I threaten your father?"

He glanced at the garage again, then turned back to Desmond.

"They told me they found stolen merchandise in there. Well, guess what? It was stolen by police officers. Including this sergeant here."

"This sergeant?" Desmond asked. It seemed like that was all he could say.

"My father knew what Victor was doing, he knew Victor was buying stuff that cops had stole. He tried to stop it. Did everything he could. Including telling Sergeant North he was going to ruin his career."

"Carl," I said. "What the fuck are you talking about?"

Carl gave a little laugh. "Acting like he doesn't know."

Desmond glanced at me. I just shrugged.

"So what happened was," said Carl, "North threatened my father back. He told my father, stay out of this, or you're going to get hurt."

I was starting to understand.

"That's why they beat him up," said Carl. "My father came over here that night, and North got those two cops of his to follow him, and to do what they did."

"I assume, Carl," I said, "you got this story from your father."

"No, I got it from a homeless guy on the street."

"And when your father talked about this sergeant, did he mention my name?"

"He didn't have to."

"Did he mention anybody's name?"

"He didn't have to. It was your two cops that beat him up, and you were there. Trying to cover it up."

I started to say something, but Desmond held up his hand. He turned to Carl. "Do you mind if I talk to the sergeant in private?"

Carl couldn't resist a bitter smile. "Not at all," he said to Desmond. "Not at all." This was what he wanted—to get the revenge on me that his father hadn't been able to.

When he was back across the street, I said to Desmond, "If that story's true, then the sergeant he was talking about? That was George Laguerre."

Desmond nodded. "The possibility did occur to me."

"You know that Laguerre was here that night," I said. "Along with Sam Robbins and Lewis Portland. If any cops followed Sonny Knight, then it had to be those two. They followed him right into the Twentieth, right to Forty-third and Market. It was the perfect place to pull him over."

"Sonny Knight identified your two cops," said Desmond.

"Yeah, but he also said the cops tried to hide their faces at first. And he got knocked down to the ground. Hope and Knopfler said they found him on the ground, unconscious."

Desmond considered this.

"Sonny Knight woke up," I said, "saw Hope and Knopfler, and just assumed they were the ones that followed him and pulled him over. And then when I showed up, well, I was just working with Laguerre."

"That scenario would be a little hard to prove."

"Unless Robbins or Portland talks," I said. "But why would they, right?"

Lenny and another detective had come out of the garage with a cardboard box, and everyone was gathering around to see what they had found. Desmond and I crossed the street and joined them.

"What you got?" Desmond asked.

Lenny showed him. Inside the box were three handguns, each in its own plastic evidence bag, along with a black ski mask, also bagged.

"We found all these in a filing cabinet," Lenny said.

I let out a breath. We wouldn't need the DNA after all.

Carl was there, and he looked into the box, too. What he saw startled him. Lenny handed the box to one of the other detectives.

"Put this in the trunk, would you, Walt?" he said.

"Lenny," I said, "you should have those tested by Ballistics. See if any match the bullet that killed Roy Knopfler."

There was dead silence, everyone was staring at me. I wasn't surprised. You raid a place full of stolen merchandise, you're probably going to turn up a few weapons, it's no big deal. Even the ski mask wasn't that unusual.

"Carl Knight can tell you," I said. "Can't you, Carl?"

He had been standing there, uncomfortable. Now everyone turned to him with surprised eyes. He looked back at them, but said nothing.

"Carl," I said. "Tell them."

# twenty-five

**I**t couldn't have been easy for Carl to look at all those cop faces and decide to betray a family member. But he did. Check the guns, he said, and then he turned and walked down the street toward his car.

If it hadn't been for him, I doubt those guns would have been delivered to Ballistics the next morning. Or that one of them, a nine-millimeter SIG-Sauer, would be found to have been the gun that killed Roy.

That afternoon, an arrest warrant was issued for Victor Knight, charging him with first-degree murder. Carl probably heard about it before it made the evening news. Someone probably gave him a call. Out of courtesy to the family.

I wondered whether he had suspected his cousin from the beginning. Whether when he had heard first about Buster, then Paulie, then Roy, suspicion gave way to a growing certainty. Like his father, he had protected Victor, he had kept the dark family secrets. In the end, though, he had given his cousin up. He had made his choice.

And what about his father? Sonny Knight had been beaten for his trouble. Instead of letting it go, he'd gone after the cops he thought did it. Knowing they'd keep their mouths shut, for their own sakes, about their wider criminality. It was a gutsy move. Except that he had made a mistake, and never questioned it. Maybe that was a choice, too.

Our whole focus became trying to find Victor. Carl gave Homicide a list of addresses where family members lived, and detectives fanned out across the city. Throughout West Philly, Victor's home turf, Narcotics teams grabbed every drug dealer they could get their hands on and offered a deal. You tell us where Victor Knight is, the cops said, and maybe we won't try to send you away for ten years the next time we lock you up, which is right fucking now.

I gave it my best shot, too, and I got a break, or at least thought I did. I knew a small-time dealer on south 60th. He was a semireliable snitch, which meant that his information was good about half the time. He always insisted on cash, usually one or two twenties, but he never gave me a refund when he was wrong.

"It's an inexact science," he'd always say when I confronted him about it. I don't know where he got that phrase, probably TV, but he loved to use it.

When I tracked him down that afternoon, standing outside a bar, hands in his pockets, at first he said he didn't know where I might be able to find Victor Knight, then he changed his mind and said maybe he did.

"I'm gonna need some cash," he said, looking around.

I pulled out a twenty from my front pants pocket and showed it to him.

"This is all I got."

"For Victor Knight? Shit, I ain't working for free."

"I might be able to make it forty."

"That's still for free. How bad you want him?"

"You probably don't even fuckin' know where he is, do you?"

"Not for forty, that's for damn sure."

We settled on sixty, though I added the condition that I would beat his fucking brains in and take the money back if he tried to rip me off. This gave him pause.

"I can't give you no guarantees," he said. "I only know what I heard."

I told him I had to hit a MAC machine and would be back in ten minutes.

When I returned, he was gone. I realized that maybe I shouldn't have threatened him. Just give him the sixty and take my chances. But maybe it was all bullshit to begin with. I never found out.

**A day later,** Philadelphia learned that its police commissioner was about to be fired. At least that's what it said in the morning papers. According to City Hall sources, the mayor was finally making the move.

It was because of Roy Knopfler's death, the sources said. If he hadn't been on the street, he wouldn't have been killed. His death had to be placed at the police commissioner's feet.

I didn't know any cop who believed this explanation. The truth was, the mayor was finally caving in to the unrelenting pressure from the black community. In the churches, in the neighborhoods, there was a widespread belief that Ellsworth was selling the community out, betraying his own people. They were done with him.

Even many white politicians suggested that perhaps if the commissioner weren't so interested in protecting cops, he might be able to find out who had murdered Sonny Knight. The consensus was that Ellsworth had to go.

A lot of cops were outraged that the mayor would blame Ellsworth for Roy's death. Outraged, but not surprised. The mayor was, after all, just a politician.

During all this time, Elijah Ellsworth had acted more honorably than the mayor. More honorably than anyone. And now his career was over.

I got the news about him that morning from my lawyer. Who called my house, waking me up, saying, "Did you see the paper?"

I got a pit in my stomach. This is not what you want to hear when you open your eyes in the morning.

"You there?" he asked.

"Should I have a drink before you go any further?"

"So you didn't see the paper."

"Would you just tell me what it says?

So he did. Actually, he read me the stories. There was no hint of who would replace Ellsworth, but according to those same wonderful sources, the mayor wanted the new commissioner's first order of business to be me and Alan Hope.

"What does that mean?" I asked the lawyer. Which was a stupid question, because I knew the answer. He told me anyway. Mutt and I would both be fired. I'd get indicted, I'd go to trial . . .

"Okay, okay," I said. "I get the picture."

**That night, a** mini-drama unfolded in the Yard at district headquarters. I had been on the street for a couple of hours, and I'd stopped at the district to take a leak. When I came back outside, Buster was standing by the double doors, smoking a cigarette, and we started talking.

A minute or two later, Sam and Lewis came through the doors, heading for their car. George was right out the door behind them.

"Hold up, guys," he said.

They stopped and turned.

"Lewis, can't you fuckin' fill out a double-A forty-five?"

That was the book-length accident-report form they made us fill out whenever there was a crash with an injury. It usually took at least an hour to complete, and it wasn't uncommon for cops to do a half-assed job so they could get back on the street.

"From this afternoon?" Lewis asked. "What's wrong with it?"

"Maybe you should ask the captain. He's still here, and he just dumped this on me. He wants me to stand over you to make sure you do it right."

"I thought I filled everything out."

"Well, you fucked up. How come Sam didn't take the report—he can do it right."

"It was my turn," said Lewis.

A call was coming over the radio. There was a burglary alarm at the leather-jacket store near Penn. It was in Lewis and Sam's sector, and Radio assigned them to the job.

I could see George's ears perk up, he was like a dog that had just heard some distant barking.

"Shit, you guys got to go to that," he said.

I almost laughed. This was just George's cup of tea.

"What do we do?" asked Lewis.

"Sam, you go on ahead," he said. "We'll get this report done, and we'll catch up with you."

Sam looked doubtful. "Maybe we should get someone else to take the job."

"No, no, I want you to handle it. Hey, you got to have pride in your sector, right?"

George didn't give a shit about sectors. He just didn't want to lose the opportunity to snag a few leather jackets.

Sam was resisting, though, trying to come up with more reasons why he shouldn't go.

The dispatcher still hadn't heard back from them.

*"Twenty-eighteen, did you copy that assignment?"*

"Tell Radio you're taking it," said George.

Sam looked at him.

"Do it," said George.

Sam clicked the mike on his shoulder. "Twenty-eighteen, we got it."

George nodded, satisfied, but then Sam said, "I'll check the property. If it's okay, I'll come back for Lewis."

This was not what George wanted to hear. He grabbed Sam's arm and led him further into the Yard, well out of earshot. Buster had gone back inside, leaving me and Lewis alone.

"I'm not surprised Sam doesn't want to go," I said. "Not after what happened at that garage in the Sixteenth last night."

Lewis didn't say anything, he just watched George and Sam argue.

"By the way," I said, "anybody from Internal Affairs talk to you yet?"

Lewis almost sprained his neck turning to look at me.

"What do you mean?" he asked. "Are they going to?"

"Probably."

"Why would they do that?"

"Why do you think, Lewis? They know you three guys were up at that garage."

"What do you mean? When?"

"Oh, I don't know. Maybe when Sonny Knight got the shit kicked out of him."

"We weren't up there."

"Right. C'mon, Lewis, you're going to have to do better than that. These guys from Internal Affairs are very good at what they do. Take it from me."

"There's nothing I could say to them."

"Sure there is. You could tell them why the fuck you allowed the reputations of two good cops to be destroyed."

"I didn't do that."

"The fuck you didn't. You pound Sonny Knight into the ground, and then let Mutt and Roy get blamed for it."

"We didn't do that."

George was pointing his finger in Sam's face, half yelling something we couldn't hear.

"Nice, huh?" I said. "That's why you're keeping your mouth shut, isn't it? For your sergeant. Look at him, he's forcing one of his men to go out and steal. How low is that?

Lewis didn't answer.

"And you're going to be loyal to him?" I asked. "You think he has any loyalty to you?"

**Twenty minutes later,** as I was cruising through the streets, I got a call on my cell phone. It was Buster.

"You got to get over to Fortieth and Walnut," he said. "They're locking Sam up. They're putting him in fuckin' handcuffs."

When I got to the leather store, there were a couple of unmarked cars in front, but most of the activity was around back, in the alley.

Sam's car was parked near the store's rear entrance. The trunk was open, and inside were seven or eight leather jackets. A police photographer was snapping pictures.

Sam was in the back seat of an unmarked car nearby, his hands cuffed behind him. He looked terrified.

Gene Desmond was there, along with a half-dozen other cops I assumed were from Internal Affairs. They didn't just happen to catch Sam, I realized. This was a sting. If it hadn't been for Lewis's sloppiness in filling out accident reports, he and George would have been nailed as well.

A minute after I got there, George and Lewis pulled up in George's car. They must have gotten a call, too. And when Lewis saw Sam in the back seat, his face went white.

George was at the car, too, and he tried to talk to Sam through the rolled-up window.

"What happened?" he asked.

Desmond came over and put his hand up.

"You can't talk to him, Sergeant, I'm sorry."

"What do you mean, I can't talk to him? You're locking one of my cops up, I want to find out why."

George knew why, of course. He just wanted some contact with Sam, some assurance that Sam was going to keep his mouth shut. Desmond was no doubt aware of this. He didn't want them communicating.

George saw me looking. Was I going to rat him out, tell Desmond what I knew? Sam could probably be trusted, so could Lewis. They were his guys. But what about me?

Just about every cop in the squad had a cell phone, and word of Sam's arrest was spreading quickly. Guys were pulling up, getting out of their cars to take a look. They saw Sam, saw him looking back through the car window, and they stumbled. One moment he's next to them in roll call, the next he's cuffed in the backseat like a street thug.

George went up to Desmond. "Can you at least get him out of here?" he asked. "So they don't have to see him like this?"

Maybe it would have helped Desmond to humiliate Sam, maybe it would have made his prisoner a little more willing to cooperate. But he told one of his men to take Sam to their headquarters, and we watched as the car pulled off down the alley, the back of Sam's bobbing head looking no different from a thousand other suspects we'd all seen getting carted away.

Lewis turned, and my eyes met his. I didn't have to tell him what I was thinking, what I wanted to say to him. He knew.

George and Lewis didn't stick around much longer, which was smart. No sense encouraging people to start asking questions. When they were gone, I looked around for Desmond, and found him inside the store, picking up a couple of jackets Sam had dropped on his way out.

"You got a second?" I asked him.

He stood, and put the jackets over his arm.

"I guess you're going to be asking him about Sonny Knight?" I said.

"We're going to ask him about everything."

"Glad to hear it. Me and Mutt are kind of running out of time."

"I wouldn't throw a party just yet, Sergeant."

"What do you mean?"

He wouldn't tell me any more, except that I would find out soon enough.


**The next afternoon** George called for an assist, and for a long time afterwards I wondered whether he did it simply to see whether I would show up.

Sure, he needed help, but not at first, not when he could have handled the situation in a different way. He let the trouble unfold, and perhaps even helped it along.

It was about two in the afternoon. George was in his patrol car, cruising along Christian, when a man flagged him down.

There's a crazy guy with a knife, the man said. He's on his porch, down the block, he's threatening people. George found what looked like the right house—a man was on the porch, yelling at the top of his lungs.

"I'm gonna cut every motherfucker on this block!" the man screamed. He was a black guy in his late twenties, short but powerfully built, wearing a dirty, sleeveless white undershirt with holes, and old jeans. Nervous, wild-eyed.

"I got a knife!" the man yelled. But George saw his hands, they were empty.

Still, at this point, George should have called for a couple of sector cars. You have a man who's either drunk, on drugs, or mentally ill, and potentially dangerous. George didn't get on his radio, though. Maybe he felt he could handle the situation on his own. But maybe he just wanted the situation to escalate a little.

"Sir," George called to him, approaching the porch. "Sir, what's the problem?"

It took a while for the man to notice him, but when he did, he turned his wrath on George.

"You, motherfucker," he yelled, "I'm gonna cut you!"

"Sir, you want to calm down and tell me what the problem is?"

George said later he was pretty sure at that point that the man was a 302, probably off his medication. All the more reason to call for help. No one on the street is more unpredictable, more prone to sudden violence, than a lunatic.

George wasn't that stupid—he had his hand on his gun. But still, he moved closer to the porch, asking a rational question of an irrational man. You keep doing that, and sooner or later the guy's going to think you're invading his personal space. Which was apparently what happened, because the man reached down to a porch chair and came up with a long knife.

"I'm gonna cut your heart out!" he yelled.

It was at this point that George finally got on the radio. His voice was urgent but calm.

*"This is Twenty-Andy, I got a priority, six-five-six-two Christian. I got a violent three-oh-two with a knife."*

George hadn't specifically asked for help—he was simply informing Radio of his situation. This was a point of pride. But he knew very well that an assist would be called, and a moment later it was, and sirens arose simultaneously from two dozen locations across West Philadelphia.

I actually thought about not going. Fuck it, I'm halfway across the district, other cars will get there before me. And so what if George gets his ass sliced up? Fucker deserves it.

The only problem was, when these thoughts occurred to me, I had already turned my car toward Christian, and the speedometer was approaching 65 mph. It was like a primal impulse. Survival of the species. In this case, the species of Cop. It doesn't matter how slimy any individual is, you have to protect the entire gene pool. I cursed George for needing help and cursed myself for going, but I didn't slow down.

By the time I got there, the street was jammed with police cars. I ran toward the house and saw a half-dozen cops trying to pull a man to the ground. They were all over him, but he was moving, and moving them with him, like some wounded animal that somehow has found unexpected strength. Use your pepper spray, I thought, but then I caught a whiff of its acrid smell and realized they had already tried, and it hadn't brought him down.

The cops were on top of the man now, trying to immobilize his arms and legs, and I threw myself on the pile. There was someone next to me, throwing on his weight, too, and I looked over to see the smiling face of George Laguerre. His eyes were red from the pepper spray—cops always seem to get the worst of it—but George looked happy as a pig in shit.

"I love my job," he said to me.

A few minutes later, after the 302 was safely in a wagon, George caught up with me as I was heading back toward my car.

"I was a little surprised to see you here," he said.

I shrugged.

"You know what I mean," said George. "I figured that once you heard me say Twenty-Andy, you'd head in the other direction."

He was testing me. Watching for my reaction.

"It was an assist," I said.

"Yeah, I know. That's good. You support your local police."

We had reached my car, and I pulled open the door.

"I got to go," I said.

"Yeah, okay. I just wanted say thanks, North. It's good to know I can count on you."

"If I were you, Laguerre, I wouldn't push my luck."

He laughed. "Aw, you got that loyalty thing, I know. Hey, you got to, right? Can't let the bad guys win."

I climbed in the car and shut the door.

"Eddie."

I looked up at him.

"Thanks," he said.

"Fuck you, Laguerre."

He just smiled.

# twenty-six

ommissioner Elijah Ellsworth was able to hang on to his job for two more days, but on Friday afternoon, the word came down. He was gone, replaced by a deputy commissioner who was promising loyalty to the mayor. I had a feeling it would be a long time before the department got someone like Ellsworth again.

We were off that day, and all afternoon, my phone rang nonstop. Everyone was asking how I was doing, whether I had heard anything. About getting fired, they meant. I hadn't. I kept expecting one of the calls to be from Kirk. That's how you usually get the news you've been fired, from your captain.

I waited around my house with Michelle, into the evening, bracing myself every time the phone rang. C'mon, I thought, call. Let's get this over with.

Michelle spent half the time sitting on the couch with me, the other half cleaning up the place. She was as nervous as I was.

"You doing okay?" she asked me.

I was on the couch in front of the TV, flipping from channel to channel, watching nothing. She was straightening the magazines on my coffee table, trying not to get in my way.

"Sure," I said.

She came around and climbed on the couch, close to me.

"You're not going to lose me," she said, "if that's what you're worried about."

"It had crossed my mind. Christ, I've lost everyone else. You know, I think about Roy every day."

"I know you do."

"All the different decisions I could have made."

"Eddie . . ."

"And Mutt, too. Both of them. Everything I did."

"That's not true."

"You know, it's unbelievable—when this whole thing started, I was fine, I was okay, I hadn't done anything wrong. And since then, everything's gone out of control. It's like every decision I've made has been the wrong one. It's truly amazing. I should win some kind of prize or something."

"You know, Eddie, you think about decisions whether they're right or wrong. But that's after the fact. At the time, you're just trying to do the best you can."

"I haven't been too successful."

"But you've tried."

"What good is that?"

"It's all you can do, Eddie. You just have to try to find the best way through."

Kirk never called. Michelle and I went to bed around one. She went right to sleep, unaware of how tight I was holding her.


**My squad returned** to daywork the next morning, and I showed up for 8 A.M. roll call. What else could I do? I was still on the payroll. Mutt was there, too, just as puzzled and uncomfortable as I was.

Right after roll call, though, Kirk called me into his office. It was unusual for him to work on a Saturday, and I figured that's why he had come in, to give me the news. At least I'll get off work early for once, I thought.

"Close the door," Kirk said.

I pushed the door shut.

"Sit down."

"I'd rather you just told me," I said. "Don't draw it out."

"What, that you're fired? I don't know that. No one's told me that. This is about something else."

"Why am I not fired?"

"How the hell do I know? Maybe the new commissioner doesn't work weekends."

"So I'm still working."

"As far as I know. I mean, if I were you I wouldn't count on being here Monday, but no one's told me anything about today."

"How come you're in, then?"

"No big deal, just to make sure we're okay for Umoja."

That was the annual black pride festival in West Philly, along 52nd Street.

"Go ahead and sit down," Kirk said.

This time I sat.

"I wanted to ask you about something," Kirk said. "Gene Desmond was here yesterday afternoon. Turns out Mutt's missing a gun."

"What do you mean?"

"It means he's supposed to have one more than he does."

"I don't understand."

"You know how Ballistics tested Mutt's gun after Sonny Knight got shot?"

"Yeah, it came up negative. Just like mine and Roy's."

"Well, they found out Mutt has two guns. Or had two. Both Glocks. One is city-issued, the other's his own."

"Yeah, he likes his own better because it has rubber grips," I said. "That's the one he carries."

"Or used to carry. The one they tested was the city-issued one. When Homicide asked Mutt if they could look at his personal gun, he said he had lost it."

"What do you mean, lost it?"

"Remember that night when he and Roy chased that garbage truck hijacker down the alley?" Kirk asked.

"Sure."

"Mutt says it happened that night. You know, when the guy jumped out of the truck, and Mutt started wrestling with him."

"That's when Mutt says he lost it?" I asked.

"Yeah, Mutt told Desmond the guy grabbed his gun and took off. He said he was too embarrassed to report it, so he and Roy drove to his house and got his other gun, the city one, and got back before anyone realized they were gone."

"That's interesting."

"I think it's a bullshit story, Eddie. Desmond was in here yesterday, asking me whether I thought it was true."

"What'd you say?"

"I said I had no idea. But what about you? Do you know anything about it?"

There was a knock at the door and a corporal poked his head in and said, "Sorry to interrupt, Captain, but I have to ask you something." He and Kirk started talking, but I didn't hear anything they said.

Maybe Mutt's wrong about which night he lost his gun, I thought. Maybe it wasn't the night with the garbage truck, but some other night, a different foot pursuit, and Mutt's just getting them mixed up.

Because I remembered that night. Some asshole robbed a gas station, Mutt and Roy started chasing him, he crashed his car and bailed, they chased him on foot, and he actually carjacked a garbage truck. Guys were dumping trash into the back, he comes up and points his gun at the driver, and says get out. Driver jumps out, he jumps in, and takes off. The other workers don't realize what's happened, the truck pulls off, and suddenly they're emptying trash onto the street. So now Mutt and Roy are chasing, on foot, a garbage truck. The streets are pretty narrow, and the garbage truck drivers know what they're doing, but this guy didn't, and he was smashing into one parked car after another. Finally he jumped out, took off running again. Mutt did chase him into an alley and tackle him, and they did wrestle, and the guy did take off. But I pulled up right after that, and I saw Mutt come out of the alley, looking around, trying to figure out which direction the guy ran.

Mutt saw me in my car and yelled, "Which way?"

"I didn't see him," I yelled back.

Mutt shook his head and said, "Fuck." And then he took his gun, which was in his hand, and shoved it back into its holster.

I didn't wait until Kirk finished his conversation. I got up from the chair and headed out the door. Mutt was in the operations room, sorting through incident reports. He looked up when I walked in, and I nodded my head toward the door, meaning, follow me.

When he caught up with me, I said, "Take Twenty-seventeen. Meet me at the park."

"What's up?" Mutt asked, but I didn't answer.

Dogshit Park was empty. I got there before Mutt and waited in my car by the curb. Three minutes later, he pulled up behind me. Without a word, I got out and headed down the slope through the trees. Mutt was a few steps behind, trying to keep up with me. When we were far enough into the park, I wheeled around to face him. He stopped short, waiting.

"Heard you lost one of your guns," I said.

He nodded and gave me a very serious look.

"Yeah, I did lose one."

"That guy who stole the garbage truck. He took it off you."

"Yeah."

"You're sure it was the guy from the garbage truck."

"Yeah. What do you mean?"

"When you came out of the alley and called to me, you didn't have your gun. You didn't have it in your hand."

Mutt let out a slow breath.

"I was hoping . . ." he said. I waited for him to finish the sentence, but he just stood there, looking at me.

"What, that I was going to lie for you?"

He hesitated.

"Was that what you were hoping?"

"Eddie . . ."

"Did you kill Sonny Knight?"

He tried to speak, but nothing was coming out.

"Did you kill him?"

Still no words.

"You motherfucker," I said.

He almost, but not quite, dodged my punch. I sent my right arm and fist out toward his jaw, and he jerked his head back, but I was able to adjust for the movement and my knuckles cracked into his face. Somehow he kept his balance, and I shot out my left fist, a feint, and when he tried to block it I came around with my right again and caught his cheek, and he fell backwards onto the grass.

"Did you just wait around and then fucking assassinate him?" I asked.

Mutt didn't answer.

"No, that would have taken at least some intelligence. What'd you do, go there to threaten him? What'd you say, 'Stop fucking up our lives, or I'll fucking kill you?'"

Still no answer.

"He didn't back down, did he? No, he started threatening you back. And then, Bang, he's dead. And then you're standing there saying, Oh, boo-hoo, I didn't mean to do it."

Mutt slowly got to his feet.

"And now you assume that I'm going to protect you," I said. "You just fucking assume it. No question in your mind. It's like a fucking God-given right."

"Eddie, wait . . ."

"No, you wait, asshole. You fucking get your partner killed and you now expect me to protect you."

He took a half-step back. "I didn't get my partner killed."

"You know you did, Mutt."

"No."

"You betrayed your partner."

"I got shot, too, you know."

"Yeah. That kind of thing happens when people want revenge."

"You're just assuming I'm the one that shot Sonny Knight."

"I am kind of assuming that, aren't I? I'm also kind of assuming you're going to jail."

"Eddie. C'mon. Can't you help me?"

"Not anymore," I said. And I brushed past him and headed back up the hill, toward my car.

**As soon as** I left the park, I called Internal Affairs on my cell phone and asked for Gene Desmond. I always thought it would be tough to rat out a fellow cop. It wasn't. It was easy. Mutt no longer had any claim on me, and I had no compunction about cutting him loose. It's like when you're obsessed with a woman, and then suddenly the obsession simply ends. One day you'd give your life for her, the next, you wouldn't even hold open a door.

Desmond wasn't in. I left a message for him to call me as soon as he could.

Just before noon, Lewis called me on my cell and asked if we could meet. This caught me off guard—was he suddenly ready to talk?

"Where are you?" I asked.

"At the Shop-Now." That was a supermarket on the edge of University City.

"Give me five minutes."

Lewis's car was on the far end of the parking lot. Next to it was George's SUV. This can't be good, I thought. Whatever it is, it can't be good.

They were standing outside their vehicles, waiting for me. George was wearing a green polo shirt, jeans, and sneakers. Very casual.

"I think we can get Victor Knight," George said.

I just looked at him.

"This is no shit," he said. "Me and Lewis are going after him."

"What the fuck does that mean?"

"I know a way we can trap him. You want to do it with us?"

"You are so fucking full of shit, Laguerre, it's beyond description."

"I've already got in touch with him."

"Who?"

"Victor Knight."

"You've talked to Victor Knight."

"Twice. Last night, and this morning."

"And how the fuck did you do that?"

"I have his pager number. I paged him, he called me back."

"Why don't you page him again, so we can find out where the fuck he is?"

"He's not going to tell me that."

"I thought he was your pal."

"He's not my pal. I told him, if he needed some money to get out of the city, I could help him."

"Gee, that was nice of you."

"I told him maybe we could work something out. You know, something mutually beneficial for the both of us. He said he'd think about it."

"When was this?" I asked.

"Last night. Then this morning, he called me back. Said he had a plan."

Victor told George that supposedly a large amount of crack was being stashed at a house in Mill Creek, a neighborhood in the 16th District. If George went into the house and "confiscated" the crack, Victor would arrange for someone to buy it from him. Half the proceeds would go to George, up front. The other half to Victor, who'd get his share later, and use to cash to leave the city.

"What do you mean, later?" I said. "How the fuck are we supposed to grab him?"

"He's got to get the money somehow," said George. "All we have to do is keep an eye on our buyer, see what he does."

It was amazing to me that Victor would even turn to George for help. He had to know George was the one who sicced the two cops on his uncle. Sure, Victor may have thought those cops were Mutt and Roy—everybody did—but he certainly knew what the beating was all about.

And then I realized: Victor was using George, just as he always had. And George was still using him. These two guys were the same, they were two peas in a pod. They didn't care what the other did to them, they were like boxers trading punches. They didn't mind the blood. They didn't take it personally. They'd just keep going until they used each other up.

"Why are you coming to me about this?" I asked. "You two can do it."

George shook his head. "We need three people. It'd be too dangerous any other way."

"What about Mutt? Why don't you ask him?"

"I did. He's not interested. C'mon, Eddie, we can do it. He's going to leave the city soon, anyway. This is our one shot."

"I don't know."

"We can't wait, Eddie. We have to do it now."

And there it was. The chance to do something good for a change. If my career was over, if I was going to go to jail, I wanted to do at least one thing that I could say, Yeah, I'm proud of that. I finally did something right. Something for Roy.

But it would mean dealing with George, trusting him. And how was I going to do that?

If it hadn't been for George, his corruption, his desire to teach Sonny Knight a lesson, Roy would probably still be alive. It was George who had set everything in motion, everything that was destroying us all.

And what about stealing drugs from drug dealers? A victimless crime if there ever was one. But cops had gone to jail for it before. There wouldn't be much risk if we were smart, but the risk would be there. I thought about Michelle. Was it worth it?

George was waiting.

"It's easy," he said. "Just think of how you would feel if you let Victor Knight get away."

. . .

**Forty minutes later,** George, Lewis, and I were sitting in George's SUV, across the street and down the block from the stash house in Mill Creek. There was no activity at the house, no one coming or going. Not what you'd expect.

This was a very ragged neighborhood. The rowhouses all had porches, but they were mostly rotting, and the overhangs sagged. Three or four houses on each block were boarded up and covered with graffiti. Wherever there was a patch of dirt, it was filled with weeds, not grass. People didn't so much move into this neighborhood as wind up here. For many, this section of Philly was simply the end of the line. There were upstanding, law-abiding, hardworking families here, but fewer and fewer all the time.

The stash house seemed to be one of the more well-kept places on the block. It had been painted in recent years, and there didn't seem to be any loose pieces of wood falling off anywhere.

"You sure this is the right house?" I asked George. I was sitting in the front passenger seat, Lewis was in the back. Lewis and I had changed into our street clothes, like George.

George pulled a piece of paper from his shirt pocket.

"Fifty twenty-one Brighton," he said. "This is the place."

It was definitely 5021—the address was posted in large numbers, made of mirrors, next to the front door. In fact, it was one of the few houses on the street that displayed their numbers. Cops, firefighters, ambulance crews come onto a block like this, they look for any house with an address showing, then start counting over until they find the house they want.

"Everyone ready?" George asked.

I looked at him, disgusted. With him, with myself. It was like he had pulled me into the same hole that had swallowed up Sam and Lewis, and Mutt. What the hell was I doing here?

He eased the SUV out of its parking space and moved ahead a

hundred feet before pulling back over to the curb. We were still out of sight if someone in the house looked out the window.

We all stepped out of the truck. George opened the back, and he and Lewis pulled out the battering ram. George had taken it from the office at district headquarters where the Narcotics guys did their paperwork. It was a solid black metal cylinder, about six inches in diameter and four feet long, with handles on the sides and a thick square of metal on one end, to smash against a door.

George had one handle, Lewis the other, and together the three of us hurried across the street and up to 5021. We didn't hesitate, we just kept moving—onto the sidewalk, up onto the porch. George and Lewis steadied themselves, and gave the battering ram a few practice swings toward the wooden door, gathering momentum, like they were getting ready to throw someone in the pool.

"One . . ." George said, "two . . . three!"

The butt of the ram cracked against the wood, popping the locks. The door swung wide open. That threw us for a moment—the door wasn't reinforced, it wasn't even very strong. And that should have been our first tip-off, if you didn't count how nice looking the house was. But we had to keep moving, fast.

I had my gun ready, and I was first through the doorway and into the house. The living room was empty, but there were people in the dining room, through an archway, halfway back. In the three seconds it took me to sprint the distance, I caught unsettling glimpses of the living room—an expensive-looking sofa, covered with a clear plastic protective cover. A tidy mantelpiece, with framed photos of young people in graduation photos. A coffee table with neat stacks of magazines. If this was a drug house, it was like none I had ever seen before.

George and Lewis had dropped the battering ram and pulled their guns, and they were behind me now, all of us rushing toward the dining room. I had my gun out in front of me, ready to open fire if I had to. I came through the archway, pointing the gun, but at who?

There were two black women in the dining room. They had both been sitting, but had jumped up from the table. One was young, a teenager maybe, the other was older, nicely dressed. She was holding a baby. There was an open book on the table, I glanced down at it. A Bible.

George and Lewis were cascading through the archway behind me, pulling up short. All three of us stood there, mouths open, adrenaline lifting us off the floor.

The older woman gave us a pained look, like she was asking why in the world we were doing this. But if she was frightened, she wasn't showing it.

"You the police?" she asked.

"Yeah," I said. "Yes, ma'am." I lowered my gun, and then so did George and Lewis.

"We don't have drugs here, if that's what you're looking for."

She was angry, but calm, steady.

"No, ma'am," I said. I didn't know what else to be, other than polite.

"But you might want to try next door."

"Excuse me?"

She pointed to the wall on her left. "That's the big drug house on the block. There's others, but that's the big one."

I glanced over my shoulder at George. He gave a slight shrug. The three of us began backing into the living room.

"You're going to have to fix my door, you know," the woman said. "I can't have those locks broken like that."

"We'll take care of it," I said.

"I'm going to need your names."

We turned and headed for the front door.

"Officers," she called after us. "I'm going to need your names."

In a few moments, we were back on the front porch, the woman right behind us.

"Now what?" asked Lewis.

George and I looked at each other, deciding whether to go for the house next door. They had probably heard the commotion over here, though they wouldn't know exactly what it was. But if they had some inkling, and we lost the advantage of surprise, it could be very dangerous.

"What do you think?" George asked.

"Let's do it," I said.

We had to move fast. I climbed over the low wrought-iron rail onto the next porch, and George and Lewis followed, carrying the ram. They got in place. I stood to the side, gun ready.

The lady from next door had her hands on her hips.

"Don't you forget about me."

"Ma'am," I said, "can you just give us a minute? We'll be right with you."

George and Lewis were swinging the ram back.

"One . . ." said George.

"Hope there's no Bibles in here," I said.

". . . two . . . three!"

The ram crashed into the door, but the door just shook.

"Again!" yelled George.

They swung the ram back away from the door, high into the air, and then brought it back down with all their strength. The door opened three inches.

"Police!" George yelled through the gap, then nodded at Lewis. "Again!"

They smashed the ram into the door, and this time it slammed open, splintered, askew. George and Lewis let go of the ram, dropping it onto the porch, and we all stood back, waiting for gunfire. When none came, I jumped through the doorway, into the gloom.

The front room was empty, but just barely—two or three people were running through the back kitchen and out the rear door. I let them go. In a normal drug raid, we would have had guys stationed in the back to snag them. But this wasn't a normal raid, and as far as we were concerned, the fewer people who got in our way, the better.

We could also hear people stomping around on the second floor. We gathered at the foot of the stairs, our guns ready.

"How many?" George asked me.

I listened. "Two or three," I said. "Here they come."

But they didn't come. They seemed to be running in all directions. I had seen this kind of thing before—they were probably jumping into closets, changing their minds, jumping back out, crawling under beds, crawling back out. Not wanting to come down, but not knowing where to hide.

"Police!" I yelled up the stairs. I turned to George and Lewis. "Let's go."

I led the way, taking the stairs two at a time. Based on the size of the house, we figured there'd be three rooms on the second floor, one for each of us, and there were. I ran into a bedroom in the back, just in time to see a young guy jump halfway out of a window, then catch himself. There wasn't any fire escape, and he was staring down at the ground, trying to decide whether to jump. I didn't feel like waiting around for him to make up his mind, and I ran up and grabbed the back of his shirt with my free hand. I wrenched him down onto the floor, onto his stomach, and held my gun to his head.

"Hands behind your back," I said. He obeyed. I got the cuffs on him and quickly patted him down, then lifted him to his feet. I could hear George and Lewis wrestling with the others in the next bedroom. I pushed my guy in front of me and took a look. George was cuffing a teenager, and Lewis was on the floor, slithering around with a woman in a purple tank top and red shorts. She jumped up and away from him as I was coming in the door, and I pointed the gun at her face. She froze. Lewis was on his feet now, and pulled her arms behind her back and got out his cuffs.

We did a quick search—in the closets, under the beds—but these were the only three. Downstairs was empty. I put my guy in the room with the others. We had them lie on their stomachs, with their heads turned away from us.

"Where's the drugs?" yelled George.

He gave me a look that said, Hey, it never hurts to ask.

"Where's the drugs?" he yelled again. The guy I'd grabbed started to say something, but the woman hissed at him, "Shut up!"

We had Lewis stay with the three of them, and George and I started searching the house. This place was a different world from the one next door. There was furniture, but it was all broken down, and close to the floor. Everything looked like it had been picked up off the street—sagging and torn sofas and stuffed chairs, wooden dressers that were deeply scarred, even smashed. There were holes in the walls, and the floors were littered with clothes and magazines and CDs and even a few toys here and there, though there were no other signs of children.

It was not an easy search. We checked all the obvious places first—the refrigerator, the stove, the kitchen cabinets. Then we moved on to the dressers, the insides of the sofas and chairs, the dropped ceiling in the living room, the heating vents. We looked for hidden compartments under carpets, inside closets. We found nothing.

We knew all along it might be a losing cause. Victor had the address wrong, maybe he was off by more than one house. Maybe we were on the wrong block. But I had a feeling that drugs were here, if for no other reason than the way the three people upstairs were reacting. They weren't protesting their innocence, as you might expect if the place was clean. They expected us to find the drugs, sooner or later, and saw no point in getting us more pissed off than they assumed we were.

George was the one who noticed the light fixture, on the side wall in the living room. It was actually pretty nice, it had wavy glass, meant to look like a scallop shell, and a shiny brass backing. George called me over and pointed to long indentations on the wall along the sides of the backing.

"Somebody's been taking this on and off," he said. We found a screwdriver and carefully pried the fixture from the wall. Instead of a small hole for the cord, there was a neatly cut square opening in the drywall that was slightly smaller than the base of the fixture. Someone had built a couple of shelves inside the opening, and there, staring us right in the face, were dozens of sandwich bags, all filled with tiny clear-plastic packets of crack.

"Jackpot," said George.

He went back to his truck to get a small gym bag, and we started stuffing the sandwich bags inside, counting as we went. There were forty of them. We figured each contained about twenty-five of the smaller packets. Which meant we had a thousand in all. A thousand hits of crack.

I took a look at the rocks of crack inside the packets. They could have been little broken slivers of Ivory soap. Except they weren't.

"These are all ten-dollar bags," I said.

George was making his own evaluation, and came to the same conclusion.

"Yeah, the rocks are a pretty nice size," he said. "Probably got a street value here of ten grand."

"Though the dealer would have only paid five," I said. "That's all we'll get for this."

George smiled. "Not bad, though, huh? We're going to make a nice little bundle today."

I looked at him. "What, you think this is about the money? Is that what this is about to you?"

"Lighten up, would you, North? This is a side benefit—and I'm not going to turn it down."

He looked at me, knowing what I thought of him, not caring.

Upstairs, Lewis was where we had left him, standing in the door-way, watching the prisoners.

We uncuffed them and left them there, on their stomachs on the floor, arms at their sides, palms up, like little kids lying next to a pool, drying off in the sun. I knew that as soon as they heard us leave, they'd come downstairs and see the hole where the light fix-ture had been. And it wouldn't take them long to figure out why we had let them go.

When we came out onto the porch, the woman was still there, hands on hips, waiting.

"We'll take care of your door," George told her as we headed down the steps, onto the sidewalk. "We'll have somebody from the city come by today."

She watched us go, not believing George for one second.

## twenty-seven

**e left the neighborhood right away, we didn't** hang around. George headed south to Market Street and parked a couple of streets over from 52nd, where the Umoja festival was going strong. People were streaming along the sidewalks toward the festival, young couples, parents with kids, women in bright orange and red African clothing. We could hear music from one of the stages, a doo-wop a cappella group sending smooth sounds through the air.

George took out his cell phone and called a pager number. This was the guy Victor had said would take the drugs off our hands.

A couple of minutes later, George's phone rang.

"You beeped me?" I could hear a voice ask.

"This is Victor's friend," said George. "We took care of that thing we were going to do."

The caller gave George the address where we were supposed to go: 4915 Brighton. One block over from where we had just been. It was starting to fit together—we had probably just robbed this guy's competition. Everybody using everybody else.

We drove back into Mill Creek, and took a quick pass by 4915 Brighton to have a look. It was a typical crack house—abandoned by its owners, yet in regular use. Sometime in the past it had been boarded up, but nearly all the plywood had been torn away. The house's brick facing and the remains of the plywood were covered with graffiti. Whatever had been used to seal up the second-floor windows was gone—there were just three gaping holes that invited the wind, the rain, and whatever else to come right in.

"I know about this house," George said. "This is a shooting gallery, nobody sells drugs out of here."

George and I got out of the SUV and headed toward the house. Lewis stayed behind to watch our backs. All three of us had Narcotics radios—also "borrowed" by George—with encrypted transmissions. We'd be able to communicate with each other, but in private.

In a few moments, George and I were on the decaying porch.

You don't knock on a crack-house door. If there even is a door. You just walk in, and whatever is there, is there. This particular crack house, like the finest ones everywhere, boasted a plush carpet of empty crack vials, hypodermic needles, burnt matches, and used condoms. There was no furniture, other than the occasional milk crate, no toilets, if you didn't count the shit buckets and piss bottles, and nothing on the smashed-in walls but graffiti. There was no electricity, no water, no gas, nothing that might make the place even remotely habitable. Unlike the house where we had stolen the drugs, no one lived here. It was just a place where people got high, and where crackhead whores took their customers.

We stepped gingerly through the crack-house door. You have to do it gingerly, because you never know whether that first step is going to take you down through a rotted-out floor and into the basement. We both had our flashlights, but we didn't need them— the front room was getting plenty of sunlight, thanks to the empty window frames with their lovely southern exposure. This was our third house on the same street this afternoon, and I realized we'd gone the whole range, from fairly nice to barely standing.

We didn't see anyone, but the place didn't feel empty. Someone was around, somewhere.

"Yo!" I called.

"Yo," a voice came back from a darkened doorway, where there had once been a kitchen. "Who is it?"

"Federal Express," I said. "Someone here want to sign for a package?"

A figure emerged from the darkness. "Huh? We got Federal Express?"

"A rocket scientist," said George.

The guy was wearing a ratty camouflage T-shirt with the sleeves ripped off.

"No, man," I called to him. "We're Victor's friends."

"Oh, yeah. Okay." He ducked into the kitchen.

"Where's he going?" George asked.

A moment later someone new was coming through the doorway toward us, with the rocket scientist tagging along behind. This new guy was both thin and short, which are not highly prized attributes in a drug dealer, but he had the tough, predatory look of the street, which did seem to help. For good measure, he was wearing a blue T-shirt that advertised a muscle gym. He stepped into the sunlit room, and froze when he saw George.

"Oh, shit," whispered George. "It's Pee-Wee."

"Who?"

"I know this guy, I've locked him up before."

Pee-Wee half turned back toward the kitchen.

"He's going to bolt," I said.

"Pee-Wee," said George. He held up the gym bag. "We're just here for this."

The little drug dealer didn't seem reassured.

"I didn't fuckin' know it was going to be you," he said.

"Well, Pee-Wee, I didn't fuckin' know it was going to be *you*. We going to do this or not?"

Pee-Wee thought it over. "How many bags you got?"

"Forty."

"All right, that's worth four thousand. I'll give you two, Victor Knight gets the other two."

"Get the fuck out of here," said George. "Fuckin' two thousand. I want three. At least."

"Man, you cops are greedy," said Pee-Wee. "You even greedier than me."

"That's right," said George. "I'm very fucking greedy. And I'm also in a position to fuck you over, don't forget about that."

This stopped Pee-Wee, it gave him pause. A negotiation like this was nothing to him, he did it all the time—but only with other dealers, not corrupt cops. He was on unfamiliar ground now.

"I'll give you two," said Pee-Wee.

"Three," said George. "And I ain't gonna sit here and fucking haggle. This ain't a fucking yard sale."

I smiled at Pee-Wee, but this was just to keep him from noticing all the pissed-off vibes I was sending out toward George. This asshole would stop at nothing if it meant an extra dollar.

George's threat must have made an impression on Pee-Wee, because he reached into his pants pocket and pulled out a wad of hundreds. He counted them so we could see, there were twenty. Then he handed them to the rocket scientist to hold, and reached down and pulled up his pants leg, revealing a bulge in his white sock. He counted out ten hundreds from that bundle, put the rest back in his sock.

"Yo, Pee-Wee," said the rocket scientist. "How do we know they're not real cops?"

I looked at the guy. George looked at the guy. Pee-Wee, still bending down, slowly swiveled his head up, and looked at the guy.

**We left them** there, the deal done, and began staking out the house, waiting for Pee-Wee to leave, or Victor to arrive. I was at one end of the block, Lewis at the other. George was in his SUV on the street behind the house, in case they tried to come through that way.

I had a pretty good location, in front of a corner mom-and-pop store. Pee-Wee's house was closer to the other end of the block, but

I'd be able to spot him if he came in this direction, and with people coming and going from the store, I didn't stand out.

The only problem was that everyone thought I was a drug dealer. That's because when I got there, the regular dealers realized I was a cop and took off. So now I was in their spot, and the whole time I was there, people kept coming up to me asking what I had. It didn't matter that I was a white guy in a black neighborhood. I was on the dealers' corner, so I must be a dealer.

It was clear I was interrupting a very lucrative business. There was a steady stream of cars, half of them with white guys behind the wheel, from the city's working-class neighborhoods, from the suburbs, from across the river in Jersey. Hey, man, they'd say. Give me two. Give me a nickel. They were dying for it. If I would have kept one of those bags we found, I could have made enough in a half hour to take Michelle on a very nice Caribbean vacation.

My cell phone rang. It was Gene Desmond.

"I'm out in West Philly," he said. "You want to talk?"

This always happened to me. "Uh, not right now, Lieutenant. I'm tied up on a job."

"That's okay, I'm in no hurry."

"It could take a while."

"Why don't you page me when you're ready." He gave me the number.

Pee-Wee was coming down the sidewalk alone. I quickly stepped into the corner store.

"I'm going to have to get back to you, Lieutenant," I said, and hung up.

Pee-Wee reached the intersection and turned right, crossing the street. A black school backpack was slung over one shoulder. He'd brought the drugs with him, which wasn't surprising. He obviously didn't want to leave them at the shooting gallery, or trust them with the rocket scientist.

I pulled the radio from my back pocket.

"He's heading south on Forty-ninth," I said.

Now it was just a matter of staying with him. We had decided in advance that if we needed to follow Pee-Wee, we'd do it on three parallel streets, one of us behind him, the others on the streets to the right and left. That way, if he turned, we'd always have someone close enough to keep him in sight.

I waited until Pee-Wee was about a half block away, then stepped out of the store and followed. Lewis was on 50th, to my right, and George, in his SUV, was on 48th, to my left.

Pee-Wee moved at a steady, unhurried pace. Occasionally when he'd get to a corner, he'd glance around, and sometimes turn and look behind him. I'd have to jump behind a building or duck behind a car. But the best places to find cover were the groves of weeds that could be found on almost every street in Mill Creek.

Perhaps at some point in history, before West Philly was West Philly, there had actually been both a mill and a creek in Mill Creek. Now nothing remained but a quaint name for an inner-city neighborhood of crumbling streets and rotting rowhouses. And yet in a way, the forgotten rural landscape had begun to return. Over the years, abandoned houses had been pulled down on every block, sometimes five or even six in a row, so that there were sprawling vacant lots, many of them thick with wild green foliage. Not only high grass and canopies of ivy, but a rain forest of exotic weeds, some as thick and tall as small trees, some with huge round leaves like fronds. It was as if green nature was bubbling up from under the streets, pushing through every crack of the sidewalk, every random patch of bare earth. All this gave Mill Creek, with its sleepy poverty and broken-down buildings, the feel of a South American village being reclaimed by jungle. It also gave me plenty of places to stay hidden from Pee-Wee's view as I tracked him through the streets.

But then Pee-Wee cut over to 52nd Street. This was not good. He was heading right toward the Umoja festival, we could easily lose him there.

Five blocks of 52nd had been closed off for the festival, and the street was jammed with hundreds of people. Bands were playing at every other intersection, and on both sides of the street, vendors were selling food, African art, woven hats, jewelry. Everywhere there was color and music, and the air was thick with the smell of ribs and spicy Jamaican jerk chicken on the grill.

There was rarely any trouble at the Umoja festivals, and we generally had a light uniformed police presence. Yvonne and Marisol had volunteered for the detail, and I saw them up ahead, studying a table of African carvings. Their backs were to me, and I slipped past. I didn't feel like explaining, even to them, what I was doing there out of uniform.

Now and then Pee-Wee paused at a table or to look around. A couple of times he almost spotted me. And then, at Spruce, he abruptly took a right, leaving the festival. Spruce was a quiet street of rowhouses, and four blocks down, it dead-ended at Dogshit Park. Pee-Wee was probably going to cut through there as well. I let George and Lewis know.

George said he'd circle around the festival, swing by the park, and wait to hear from me. But a minute later, he got on the radio again.

"He's here," George said. "In the park."

At first I thought he meant Pee-Wee, but I could see Pee-Wee, and he was still more than three blocks from the park. George was talking about Victor.

"What's he doing?" I asked.

"Sitting on a picnic table, by himself. Like he's waiting for somebody. He's right out in the open."

I pictured George in his SUV, looking down in the park at Victor. And I felt something in my stomach. George was alone with Victor now. What was to stop him from simply killing Victor, right there in the park?

I should have realized this before, I thought. George knows that if Victor gets locked up, he's going to try to make a deal with the DA. Victor's going to look for any edge. Including ratting out a few cops.

My first thought was, Let George do it. Let him just go ahead and do it, if that's what he wants. What do I care?

But George got back on the radio.

*"Let's grab Pee-Wee now,"* he said.

Maybe I was wrong. George's suggestion to get Pee-Wee was a smart move. We didn't need him anymore. And if we took him out of the picture, that would just leave Victor waiting in the park, and it would give us time to regroup and figure out a plan.

I had Lewis cut over to Locust and meet me. We pulled our guns, and together started running towards Pee-Wee. George drove down the street from the opposite direction, from the park—we had Pee-Wee boxed in.

George jerked the wheel and popped the truck up onto the sidewalk, right at Pee-Wee.

"He's going too fast," I said. I was sure he was going to smack right into Pee-Wee, knock him into outer space.

Somehow, though, George skidded the SUV to a stop two feet from Pee-Wee. Pee-Wee just stood there, eyes wide, and then Lewis and I were on him, pushing him to the ground. I cuffed his arms behind him, and we pulled away his backpack and searched him. He had rolls of hundreds in his pockets, in his socks, and a pistol in his waistband. We checked the backpack, the drugs were there. We threw everything in George's truck. I knew he'd want to keep it all, but there was no time to argue about it now. We'd have to deal with it later.

We boosted Pee-Wee onto his feet.

"I knew you was gonna lock me up," he said. "I just knew it."

"Sure you did," said George.

"You guys are good, though," said Pee-Wee. "You outsmarted the fuck out of me." He seemed genuinely impressed. "I would of bet every dime I had that you two was bad cops."

If he only knew.

The only problem was, what were we going to do with him now? We couldn't take him to the park.

"How about this sign here?" Lewis asked.

It was an eight-foot-high pole, with a NO PARKING ANYTIME sign attached. We got Pee-Wee on his feet, and I unlocked one end of the cuffs and clipped it to the pole. Pee-Wee pulled, testing it. He wasn't going anywhere.

We were only a block and a half from the Umoja festival, and two young black couples walking toward it had stopped to watch the drama with Pee-Wee unfold.

"That's a man, not an animal," one of the guys said. "You can't just chain him to a pole." They were all nicely dressed, wearing the latest fashions. They didn't look like they lived in the neighborhood.

"You want to get locked up, too?" George asked him.

As the guy was trying to think up a comeback line, George added, "Then get the fuck out of here."

One of the girls stepped forward. "We have a right to be on the sidewalk. What's your name and badge number?"

"You ever been locked up before?" George asked her.

"No, I certainly have not."

"You want to find out what it's like?"

She was about to keep arguing, but something in George's face kept her quiet. I could tell she'd seen that look before, she knew it, understood it. This was not her first time in a tough neighborhood.

"C'mon," the other girl said. "Let's go."

They drifted away, toward the festival, stopping occasionally to turn back and stare at us like they were memorizing our faces.

George got back in his SUV, found a more conventional parking space, and then the three of us walked the rest of the way to the park. We stopped on the sidewalk across the street, ducking behind a row of parked cars.

And there, down in the center of the bowl, sitting on top of a picnic table, was Victor, staring off into space. He was facing to our right, so we had a side view of him, and he was alone. The whole park was empty, everyone was at the festival.

I took out my cell phone.

"What are you doing?" George asked.

"I'm calling Radio. I want to get some guys in here, seal off the park."

"Forget it. He sees the first police car, he'll take off. Let's just grab him."

"How are we going to do that?" I asked. "He'll see us, too, he'll start running. Or start shooting, if he's got a gun, which he probably does."

George shook his head. "We can do it. See those trees there?" He pointed to some oaks scattered on the left side of the park, to Victor's rear. "I'll come in that way, behind him. Just sneak right up."

"You're crazy," I said. "That last tree is a hundred feet away from him. You'd never get close enough, he'd hear you coming."

"Not if you guys distract him."

"And how would we do that?"

"Come in from the north side, where he can see you. If he turns and runs, he'll run right into my arms."

"What if he starts shooting?" asked Lewis.

"By then I'll be close enough to take him out. And I won't miss."

"That's what you want, isn't it?" I asked. "You want to take him out."

George didn't answer. He started walking away from the park, down the street, and motioned for us to follow.

"Now where you going?" I asked.

He pointed to an alley. "This cuts through to the next street. I can come around to that side of the park."

"Forget it," said Lewis. "I'm not going to do it."

George stopped. "What's the problem, Lewis?"

"You're going to kill him, aren't you?"

"If he pulls a gun, I'll kill him, sure."

"No, the sergeant's right. You're going to kill him no matter what. You've been planning this."

"Lewis, you don't know what the fuck you're talking about."

"Yeah, I do."

"He killed a cop," George said to both of us. "Whatever happens, happens."

"I'm not going to help you kill someone," said Lewis.

George raised his eyebrows, like he was surprised at this.

"So you're just going to let me walk into the park by myself?"

"I guess I am," said Lewis. "You want me to risk my life for you, Sarge. But you'd never do it for me."

"Sure, I would."

"No. No, you wouldn't."

George stared at Lewis hard, then finally said, "Do what you want, you fuckin' pussy. Me and Eddie can do it alone."

George turned and headed toward the alley, jogging now.

# twenty-eight

**ewis and I walked back to the row of cars over-**looking the park, and waited.

"What are you going to do, Sarge?" asked Lewis.

I didn't answer, because I didn't know. It was too late to call Radio now. By the time everyone got organized, and all the various supervisors and commanders got involved, George would be well into the park.

"There he is," said Lewis, pointing to our left, toward the south end of the park. George was emerging from between two parked cars, gliding into the trees. He stopped behind a large one, then stuck his head around and surveyed the park, planning his attack.

I had no doubt that if George didn't get help, he wasn't going to be able to pull this off. There was just too much distance between the last tree and the picnic table. He'd have to come out in the open to get a good shot at Victor, and once he was exposed, anything could go wrong. He'd be an easy target.

George must have known that, too. And yet he moved to the next tree, and took cover again, with a calm confidence, as he if he were absolutely certain what the outcome would be.

As if he were absolutely certain I would not let him down.

This was why he wanted me along from the beginning, I realized. Not to help him get the drugs—he didn't really need me for that—

but to help him to kill, to execute Victor. He may not have known exactly how he would do it, just that he would.

With each step that George took further into the park, he was asking me, What are you going to do, pal? You gonna let a cop get killed? Huh, are you? Are you? Who you gonna side with? Huh?

Each step pulling me, like there was a rope around my waist. George had seen me pulled before, seen me tested. He had watched as I stood by my men, at great cost. He had even tested me himself. More than once. And I hadn't let him down, had I? Just like I wasn't going to let him down now. Wasn't that right?

Not like Lewis, the way George saw it. Lewis wasn't a real cop. Wasn't up to the test. But then again no one ever expected he would be. That's why Eddie North had to be here.

I turned and walked back down the block, thinking, This fucking bastard, I hope he does get shot. I don't care if he's a fucking cop, he deserves whatever he fucking gets. Fuck the son of a bitch.

Lewis was following me, watching me head toward the alley that would take me around to the north side of the park.

"You're not going to help him, are you?" he asked.

"I don't know what the fuck I'm going to do."

He jogged until he caught up with me.

"Laguerre isn't worth it."

"You're fucking right about that, pal."

I was walking fast, but Lewis kept pace.

"I decided," he said. "I'm going to talk to that lieutenant, Desmond. Whatever happens here."

"Good."

"I'll keep you out of it. You know, about all this shit today."

"Good."

"You were right about what happened that night on Forty-third Street. What me and Sam did."

I stopped short. "That you beat Sonny Knight."

He nodded.

"For George."

"Yeah."

"And you're going to tell that to Desmond."

"Yeah."

"I'm glad to hear that, Lewis."

I started walking again.

"Wait," said Lewis, "let me tell you what happened."

I kept going. "Can we talk about this later?"

"No, I got to tell you now. So you don't help that asshole."

"Make it quick."

We were approaching the end of the alley.

"Sonny Knight was threatening him," said Lewis.

"Who? George?"

"Yeah. Sonny Knight and George were having this argument out-side the garage that night. They both showed up there at the same time."

"Looking for Victor?"

"I guess. Sonny Knight told George to leave Victor alone. You know, not to bring stolen stuff to him anymore. And Knight was threatening to do all kinds of shit to George if he ever came to the garage again."

This was pretty much the same story Carl had told Desmond outside Victor's garage. Sonny Knight hadn't been involved in any-thing illegal, he had just been trying to protect his family. Trying to do the right thing.

"And so," I said, "George had to teach him a lesson."

"Yeah. He called for us on the radio. Got us to do it. We were so stupid. He used us, just like he's trying to use you now."

We hit Locust and we turned left, back toward the park. A gold Saturn was parked at the corner, across the street, and we crouched behind it. I studied the trees behind Victor. There was no sign of George. Had he given up and gone back? Could I be so lucky?

Victor hopped off the picnic bench and walked in a little circle, stretching his legs. As he did, he scanned the four sides of the park, probably looking for Pee-Wee and his money. We could hear music from the festival, and Victor looked like he was listening to it, too.

He finally sat back down, not on top of the table as before, but on the bench, using the edge of the table as a seatback. He lifted his shirt in the front and pulled something out of his waistband. I was too far away to see it clearly, but I knew what it was. He put it on the bench next to him and leaned back against the table. Just making himself more comfortable.

There was a movement behind one of the trees, so slight I wondered whether I had imagined it. But then George's form appeared, he was moving slowly, carefully, through the trees, toward the last one. From that point, there would only be open space between him and Victor.

George disappeared from sight again. He had no way of knowing where I was. For all he knew, I might be at the Umoja festival, drinking a beer and laughing at the thought of him getting his brains blown out. Good, I thought. Let him sweat. Let him worry his fucking balls off. Because if that fucker thought I was going to save his sorry ass . . .

George stepped out from behind that last tree, his Glock in his right hand. It was done.

I stood up and looked down at Lewis.

"You coming?" I asked.

"What? What are you doing?"

"Are you coming?"

He shook his head. "No way."

I stepped around in front of the Saturn and crossed the street into the park. George was still on the move, but when he spotted me he stopped short, waiting to see what I had in mind.

At almost the same moment, Victor glanced up and saw me. Or saw someone coming into the park, I didn't think he recognized me yet. He reached for his gun, but in a casual way. Just wanted to be on the safe side.

George began moving again, slowly now, keeping directly behind Victor, staying to his back. Victor had his eyes on me. In a moment, he was going to realize who I was.

And now Lewis was walking quickly across the street, toward

me. Not for George, I knew. For me. He wasn't going to let me do this by myself.

Victor gave a start. He recognized me or Lewis or both of us, and he jumped wildly to his feet and brought his gun up. I doubt he could have hit me from that distance. I pulled my gun out, and held it in front of me and down, still moving toward him.

C'mon, George, I thought. If we're going to do this, then let's do it. George was closing in, he had a shot now. He lifted his gun. Just fucking do it, I thought.

I didn't know whether George stepped on a branch or what, but Victor heard something behind him and swung around. And that probably saved Victor's life right then, because as he turned, George fired, and instead of hitting Victor square in the back, the bullet caught his side.

He fell, and now George was running toward him, and I was running, too, with Lewis behind me. I could see Victor writhing in the grass. He still had his gun.

George reached Victor, and he didn't hesitate, he just aimed his gun at Victor's head. He was going to finish him off.

"Laguerre!" I yelled, still running. "Wait!"

It was a mistake for me to yell. In that kind of situation, you don't want to distract your partner. You don't want him to take his eyes off the man with the gun, even for a moment. I shouldn't have yelled. But we had Victor now. He wasn't going anywhere. We didn't need to kill him.

George glanced up at me, just for an instant. And that instant was all it took. Victor fired a shot that hammered into George's shoulder and spun him around, onto the ground.

I finally reached Victor. He was trying to sit up, trying to point his gun at George and squeeze off another shot. Victor's side was turning bright red, but he didn't seem to be in pain. He looked like he was just trying to get his gun aimed, and was having trouble, as if someone were holding him down, and he seemed more irritated than anything else.

My gun was pointed at Victor's chest and he noticed me now, saw what was going to happen, and I fired, and he slammed against the ground. He was still alive, though, and his eyes searched the sky until he saw my face. He tried to sit up again, and I fired once more, and this time he just leaned back, and the gun slid from his hand, and he was still.

George was lying on his side, watching. The upper right quarter of his green polo shirt had turned red. He had a slight smile, nothing more. Just the hint of a smile, as if this were all a joke, and he was the only one in on it.

**Everyone showed up,** of course. Patrol cars were still screaming up to the park with lights and sirens five minutes after Rescue had taken George away. Even Mutt was there. He had been doing paperwork when the district emptied out, and he grabbed a ride with another cop.

"You all right, Sarge?" he asked.

He knows I'm about to send him to jail, and he's worried about me.

"Yeah, Mutt, I'm fine."

He has seen Victor's body, lying next to the picnic table.

"I'm glad you got that asshole," he said.

"Me and Laguerre both did."

"Well, I'm sure Roy thanks you both."

I looked at Mutt. I wasn't sorry for believing in him when I did. He had fucked up, and he was going to have to pay for it, but at least he was a better man than George. He at least deserved some respect.

A few minutes later, I heard Michelle call my name. She came up and hugged me, and then looked me over to make sure I wasn't hurt in any way. And then she hugged me again.

She said she had heard the call on J Band, which ran citywide, and had gotten to the park as fast as she could.

"What happened?" she said. "You have to tell me everything."

"You want to know what we're going to say happened," I asked her, "or what really happened?"

"What do you mean?"

"I did what you said, Michelle. I tried to find the best way through."

An inspector came over and told us that George was going to be okay, the wound wasn't life-threatening. I found that I really didn't give a shit.

Crime-scene tape had been stretched from tree to tree around the shooting, circling Victor's body, which was still on the ground, though now covered with a yellow plastic sheet. Clusters of onlookers gathered on the edges of the park, and many people came closer, up to the tape. Some had angry voices.

"Cops shot that boy down," we heard a woman say. "Just shot him right down."

The woman saw Michelle and me glancing over at her, but didn't focus on us. We were just cops, no more worthy of notice than any other.

I spotted Gene Desmond talking to a couple of the bosses. This didn't surprise me—he had told me he was in West Philly. I watched as Lewis took him aside. That's right, Lewis, I thought. Tell Desmond all about Sergeant Laguerre.

They talked for a minute or two, then moved further away from the crowd of cops, toward the trees.

Mutt was still hanging around the park, coming over every once in a while to say something to me or to listen in on a conversation. He was like a condemned man trying to draw out the minutes, trying to keep whatever connection he still had with the world. And he was there when Michelle told me, almost in passing, about a strange sight she had seen on her way to the park.

"It was just a couple of blocks from here," she said. "Right up Spruce. You won't believe it, but some guy's cuffed to a pole. And he's drawing a pretty good crowd."

I turned in that direction, in a panic. I had forgotten all about Pee-Wee.

. . .

**There was some** kind of hammering, I could hear it as I ran. Metal on metal, bang, bang, bang. As I got closer, it looked like somebody was doing something to the top of the pole where Pee-Wee was handcuffed.

I really didn't need Michelle and Mutt, I was just going to let Pee-Wee go, but they were running alongside me. They figured I needed some kind of help, and they weren't going to just stand around.

There had to be at least fifty people in the street and on the sidewalk around Pee-Wee. Maybe it wasn't such a bright idea to cuff a black man to a pole right next to a black pride festival, and just leave him there.

Someone had pulled a car up next to the pole, and a guy was standing on the hood, trying to hammer off the No Parking sign. He was banging at it, bending it all to shit. Obviously, the plan was to slide the cuff—with Pee-Wee attached—up over the top of the pole. What were they going to do, put Pee-Wee on their shoulders?

People in the crowd saw us running up, and started shouting at us. They were hot, and now they had an outlet for their anger.

"Get him off of that pole!" someone yelled.

A woman in a powder blue sweatshirt with Tweety Bird on the front hissed, "Who do you people think you are? Chaining this man up like a slave?"

No problem, I thought. You want me to let him go, fine. I didn't particularly feel like explaining to my bosses what the hell he was doing here in the first place.

We elbowed our way through the crowd to get to Pee-Wee.

"Cops just shot a brother in the park," someone yelled. "Shot him dead."

I heard gasps, curses. The guy on the car hood had stopped bending and banging, and he stood there, hammer in hand, giving us a hard stare. Everyone in the crowd was staring at us.

We reached Pee-Wee. He seemed a little dazed by all the noise and attention, but when he saw me he stiffened.

"Who got killed in the park?" he asked me. "Did you shoot Victor Knight?"

I ignored him, and instead told Mutt and Michelle to push the crowd back to give me room.

"Who got killed in the park?" Pee-Wee called out, to anyone who might know.

"Here's the deal," I said to him in a low voice. "I'm going to let you go. And you're going to get the fuck out of here. And you and I are never going to see each other again. Got that?"

Pee-Wee shook his head. "I ain't doing it. You going to shoot me if I run."

"I'm not going to shoot you."

"You killed Victor Knight. Now you going to kill me. You fuckin' setting me up."

"Jesus Christ," I said. "You can't even turn people loose these days."

I put the key in the cuff that was connected to the pole, and it popped off. But when I reached for the cuff on Pee-Wee's wrist, both it and Pee-Wee were gone. He had panicked and was running through the crowd. And Mutt, who thought he was escaping, was running after him.

**Sometimes you make** mistakes that don't count for much. And sometimes your mistakes count for everything. They shift the world, crush it. I should have told Mutt that I was going to let Pee-Wee go. It would have been simple. I don't know why I didn't, except that I wasn't smart enough, or a good enough cop, to foresee what would happen.

Pee-Wee turned and saw Mutt chasing after him, and ran even harder. And as he turned, for a brief instant, he caught my eye. I had betrayed him, just as he had expected.

I yelled at Mutt to let him go, but the crowd was cheering now, cheering Pee-Wee's miraculous escape, and Mutt didn't hear. Then Pee-Wee was beyond the crowd, sprinting down the middle of the street toward the festival, loose cuff flailing through the air, with Mutt ten steps behind.

Pee-Wee was fast, but so was Mutt. He was one of those big guys who can fool you into thinking they could never get up much speed. But then they step on the gas, and they're racing along like a horse in full gallop, huffing and puffing, nostrils flaring.

I ran after them, still yelling at Mutt. Pee-Wee reached 52nd and veered to the right, into the festival, and Mutt followed, and they disappeared around the corner. When I got to 52nd, I could see them a half block ahead, weaving through clusters of people as they ran, dodging left and right.

Pee-Wee was obviously trying to lose Mutt in the throng, but heading into the festival was a tactical error, for it gave Mutt the advantage. Every time Pee-Wee hit a wall of people, he had to slow down. But they scattered for Mutt, seeing this big white cop bearing down on them. Pee-Wee gradually lost ground, until Mutt's hot breath was right on his neck. I was gaining, too, maybe a quarter block behind now, and I could see Mutt getting ready to strike, like in one of those wildlife shows where the predator is about to sink its teeth into its prey.

But then Pee-Wee lifted up his right arm, with the loose cuff, and jumped and spun around in midair, with the cuff leading the way, and he whipped it through the air and slammed it into the side of Mutt's head. Mutt's momentum carried him forward, and Pee-Wee stepped to the side as Mutt fell hard, facedown, and lay still.

If Pee-Wee had resumed his flight, he might have gotten away. But he saw me rushing toward him, and he reached down and ripped Mutt's Glock from its holster. I got my own gun out so fast I was barely aware of it, and stopped short, half kneeling, aiming at Pee-Wee.

Pee-Wee dropped down to one knee and put the gun barrel to Mutt's head.

"Stay back!" he yelled.

Mutt seemed to wake with a start, and began to get up, onto his knees. Pee-Wee grabbed him by the back of the shirt and twisted him around, so that Mutt was sitting on the ground, and Pee-Wee was crouched behind, using him as a shield. I could tell Mutt knew what was happening, he saw the gun, or felt it against his skull. He was bleeding from the side of the head, where the cuff had hit.

I would have loved to have nailed Pee-Wee right then, my trigger finger was begging for permission. But they were too close together, their heads were almost side by side. I was a good shot, but not that good. I could see in Mutt's face that he was trying to stay calm, trying not to be afraid.

Michelle was behind me now, on the radio, calling in the assist, giving our location. The festival crowd had scattered down side streets, into the protection of stores. A couple of brave people were watching, crouched behind booths.

"Let him go," I said to Pee-Wee. Which was a stupid thing to say, because he wasn't going to do that, not with me pointing my gun at him. Mutt was his protection. He wasn't going to give that up.

"You give up now, Pee-Wee," I said, "you'll be back on the street before I'm done with the paperwork."

"You gonna fucking kill me first. I ain't fucking giving up."

He was jumpy as hell, his hand was shaking, the gun was tap-tap-tapping against Mutt's head.

Marisol and Yvonne and other cops from the festival were already rushing in, drawing their guns, aiming at Pee-Wee. Sirens had arisen from all sides, and they were getting closer. Pee-Wee saw and heard all this, and he looked at me and shook his head slowly.

That's when I knew Mutt was going to die. Anyone else in Pee-Wee's shoes would have seen that the situation was hopeless, and surrendered. There was nowhere for him to run, and if he shot Mutt, there was no way he wouldn't be shot dead himself. Even Victor Knight probably would have given up.

But Pee-Wee wasn't thinking reasonably, and that made him far more dangerous than Victor Knight ever would have been. Fear was rushing through his veins with the adrenaline, clawing at him. He saw that there was no way out, and that just panicked him even more. Pee-Wee was going to kill Mutt simply because he had no idea what else to do.

Mutt couldn't see Pee-Wee's face, but he didn't need to. He looked at me.

"Sarge . . ." he said, but didn't go on. Saying nothing, saying everything.

I should just take a shot now, I thought. If Mutt's going to die anyway, maybe I can stop it. But what happens if I hit Mutt, and Pee-Wee wouldn't have shot him after all?

Do I fire? What do I do?

Roy died because I had failed him. And now, because I hadn't stopped Mutt from running after Pee-Wee, it was happening again. I was killing my own cops.

In the end, though, Mutt decided not to leave his fate to me or anyone else. He pulled his arm back so fast that I barely saw the motion. I just saw his elbow in Pee-Wee's chest and Pee-Wee popping backwards onto the street.

Mutt, still facing away from Pee-Wee, used his right hand as a brace and kicked his feet so that he spun around toward Pee-Wee, and then, in a fluid, almost graceful movement, he was up on one knee, then half rising to his feet.

He was going to dive onto Pee-Wee, he reached out his arms like he was going to give him a bear hug, but Pee-Wee still had his gun, and as Mutt fell on him, he fired.

Mutt came down on Pee-Wee hard, and reached with both hands to grab the gun, and he yanked the gun away and it skittered along the street. I was running toward him, remembering Roy in the car that night, remembering the blood. I tried to call Mutt's name, but I had no voice. No thought, except that another friend was dying.

Mutt flipped Pee-Wee over and put his knee in his back, pinning him with his weight, holding him down. I couldn't understand how this was possible. Sometimes when people are shot, they don't slow down, at least not at first. They seem to have even more energy than ever. But they had been only five feet apart, how could the bullet have had no effect? Mutt must have wondered the same thing, because he started patting himself on the chest, searching for the wound. I was looking, too, on his chest, his arms, his legs. There wasn't a wound, there was nothing. He hadn't been hit.

We eventually found the bullet in a storefront wall. Pee-Wee had simply missed. He had jerked the gun up, and panicked, and fired too soon. But for all of us, right then, there seemed more to it than that. It was as if we had just witnessed some kind of magic, as if the bullet, on its way to Mutt's chest, had somehow vanished, just disappeared into the air.

Pee-Wee never told detectives about me and George, which was probably smart. Some other cop had put him on that pole, he didn't know why. He served a few months in jail for assault on police, but that was all. In the end, it wasn't much more than paperwork.

**Gene Desmond showed** up on 52nd that afternoon, along with everyone else. As I talked with Mutt, I saw him hanging nearby, waiting for me.

Mutt followed my gaze, saw who I was looking at.

"It's all right, Sarge," he said, "do what you got to do."

I knew what that was. I didn't have to think about it, not anymore.

"Mutt," I said, "I want you to quit the department."

He gave a little laugh. "I don't think they're going to give me much choice about it."

"First thing tomorrow morning. I want you to go downtown, put in your papers. You don't have to tell 'em why."

"Yeah, but . . ." He stopped short.

It was slowly sinking in.

"You can't be a cop anymore," I said. "You understand that, right?"

"I guess I do, but . . . what about him?" He nodded his head toward Desmond.

I gave a little shrug. "The murder investigation's still open," I said. "Who knows, maybe someday they'll find some other evidence, nail you for it. I can't control what they do."

Mutt looked at me. I knew he wanted to ask why I was doing this. He waited, hoping I'd explain. I didn't, though, because there was no way I could.

I think Mutt knew that. "I'm sorry, Eddie," he finally said. "I'm sorry all this happened."

"Yeah," I said. "So am I."

"I just tried . . ." He didn't finish.

"To be a good cop? No, Mutt. You didn't."

There was pain in his eyes.

"See ya," I said.

"Wait, Eddie, wait a second."

"No," I said. "I got to go."

"Wait."

"See ya, Mutt," I said, and turned away.

Up and down 52nd, vendors were packing up, putting their African art and their woven hats back in boxes. The festival was over, people were drifting off. Michelle was around somewhere. I wanted to find her.